IN YOUR
DREAMS
A NOVEL BY GINGER SCOTT

For my fellow dreamers.

CHAPTER 1

Casey

I don't know why I thought wedging the full vase between two speakers in the back of my Nissan was a good idea. I was rushing. *Always rushing.*

I wish I could get places on time. It's one of my flaws. I'm habitually late. I cover it up with my devil-may-care attitude, but inside my gut is tying itself in knot after knot. The squeezing feeling gets tighter with every set of seconds that tick by *after* the time I was supposed to arrive somewhere. Like right now, at this stoplight, which is exactly forty-seven seconds long. I know this, because I've been late getting to my parents' house at least a thousand times, probably two thousand if I count the number of times I blew my curfew when I was in high school. I've counted the length of this stoplight since I was sixteen, and it always lands on forty-seven. I think the note I wrote to myself scribed with *47* is still stuffed in my center console somewhere.

That note must be three years old. I bet it's yellowed and the ink has disappeared. It's probably buried under piles of receipts and notes to remind myself of things I ultimately forgot. God, I'm a pig—I need to clean shit out of my car.

Another one of my flaws—I'm a pig.

I start to make mental notes about my messiness and lateness and other personal shortcomings I need to fix, knowing I won't really do jack about them, but it keeps me from bouncing my leg for the rest of the ride until I pull to the curb, to the familiar front lawn with the perfectly edged trim. The gutter between the concrete and the place where my parents' lawn begins is precisely one inch wide. It's perfect. It's always pristine. My dad does it himself. Spends his entire Sunday—his *one* day off—on that front lawn, making sure the green is just right, the weeds are nonexistent and the edge is an inch wide.

Asshole.

It's Saturday. So, he isn't home. Even though it's my mom's birthday, my father is at work. On a Saturday. Because he's the boss. She would have been at work too if she wasn't retired, because my father never really liked the idea of taking frivolous days off. Whenever she tried to take one, he made her feel bad about it.

Double asshole.

I guess I'm glad he's an asshole today, though. It means I get to wish her a happy birthday and step into this house I haven't been in for more than a year—since the day I told him I didn't want to be a mechanical engineer and work for the big fuel companies in the city just like he and Mom did. Apparently, he had plans—an internship lined up, a guaranteed job ready and waiting, a good salary that would set me up for a comfortable life. Something about bonuses and points and shares or taking limbs from my body. That last part may have only been in my head. He probably had a wife and house picked out for me too—all to his liking. I screwed it all up with my own goddamned dreams.

Look at me, being the *asshole*.

I cut the engine and step from my car, brushing the front legs of my black pants, trying to work out some of the wrinkles. I wanted to look good, but now that I see my clothing choice out in the light of day, I look like I just rolled out of the collection bin for the homeless on Broad Street. At least I have a vest on over my dress shirt. My roommate, Eli, is a serious preppy hipster. I make fun of him, but hell, his clothes are really nice.

I walk to the other side of the car, opening the door to the backseat so I can pull out the vase of flowers. About half of the water spilled out on the ride here, just as I figured. I push my hand into the fabric of my seat and it squishes. Awesome—it's going to mildew. I roll down the window crank slowly, but not slow enough. It broke last year, and sometimes the grip inside the door gives way and the pane of glass falls all the way in…like it did just now. I have to pull the inside door panel off just to push the glass back up. Looks like I have fun plans for the evening.

2

I sigh and shake my head, trying to forget about my shit car that's going to smell like old mop water in a few hours and turn my attention to the red front door at the end of the curved brick walkway. I recognize my sister Christina's BMW pulled in behind my mom's in the carport. I'm glad she's here. This way, I'll get credit for coming.

My sisters have been on my ass to visit my parents for months. For some reason, when I explain that I was kicked out and disowned, it doesn't register with them. Why would it—they're all engineers. Except for Christina, but she's married to one, so I guess that gets her a pass. Or maybe it's the fact that she's a lawyer and drives a car that's easily a billion times nicer than anything I own.

Before I make it to the door, Christina has it open.

"I'm shocked," she says, full smirk.

"Yeah, well, it's probably the Botox making you feel that way. Or…maybe it just makes you *look* that way?"

I get my dig in, but I do love my oldest sister. She's beautiful without the Botox that she thinks she needs. She isn't that old— thirty-two. But she also used to beat the crap out of me until the day she moved out for college, so I take my shots where I can. She bunches her face in disapproval, but pulls me in to hug me as I step through the door. I'm suffocated by her perfume, which oddly feels like home.

"Still trying out the asshole thing, I see," she laughs, motioning me inside and shutting the door behind us.

"Yeah, well, everybody's got one. Just putting mine to good use," I say.

My mom rushes in behind her at the sound of my voice.

"Casey? Case? Oh…uh…wow…" She's fidgety and nervous, and she's waving a spoon covered in batter in her hand. I bet she's making her own cake. I quirk a brow at my sister over my mom's shoulder as we embrace, the dripping spoon held far over my back. Christina invited me to join her and my other sisters for lunch today, so I'm not sure why me being here is a surprise.

"It's your birthday, and I figured…you know…since Dad won't be home for a while, I'd…come for this lunch that Christina arranged?" I hand her the flowers, and she pulls them against her chest, her eyes flitting to and away from me in one-second intervals.

"Oh, right. Yes, thank you," she says, glancing to my sister and then back down to the daisies.

What the hell?

Mom has always been okay with me sneaking in to see her without Dad. At least, that's how we've managed the last year. I see her when she stops in at my sisters' houses, or when she's out on lunch errands. Always alone or without him. She doesn't hold the grudge for me walking my own path; she just doesn't stick up for me when my dad gets involved in my life. And I get it—he doesn't make it easy to argue.

He doesn't listen.

I follow her and my sister down the hallway to the kitchen and pull out a stool to sit at the counter. I glance at my sister, who just shrugs and busies herself with texting or emailing on her phone. Christina's always working—clients, cases, opinions, making partner. That world—it's so full of status climbing and proving oneself to other people. I could see that in my parents' lives, too, even when I was little.

Sure, I have some fond memories from the late nights when it was one of my sisters putting a series of frozen dinners in the microwave, and we'd all climb in front of the television to eat. When I was seven or eight, those nights seemed like fun. But a thousand nights later—when I was eleven—the good vibes were replaced with a sort of abandoned kind of feeling. My sisters had their own lives, the oldest two—Christina and Myra—gone, and Marie and Annalissa wanted little to do with a pre-teen boy. I heated up my own dinners. And if I didn't understand my homework, I went to my best friend Houston's house, where his dad would sit at the table with the both of us and make sure we knew our fractions and understood decimals. Hell, any engineering skills I *might* have in my blood are really thanks to that man.

By the time I started high school, I hardly even remembered dinner with my sisters. Dinners with my parents were fictional— something I tried not to envy others for. I came home to an empty house, and I'd been trained not to even bother mentioning events in my life to my parents when we passed one another in the kitchen in the mornings—like shift changes. My senior year, I was crowned homecoming king. To this day, I don't think my mother knows. At some point, I just didn't want to tell her, because I could tell it would make her feel bad. Of the two of them, she was always the one who felt guilty for missing out on family time.

I didn't bother to walk for graduation, either. Nobody from my family could come; so I figured there wasn't much point to spending a hundred dollars on a polyester cap and gown not a single relative would see me in. I convinced my dad that it was a better investment to give me the cash he would have spent on my graduation package and put it toward my college books and fees. I used his practical logic against him, and he gave me the money that Saturday afternoon when I told him I was heading to the college book store to get a "jump on scouting out my textbooks for the next year." Instead, I bought a hundred dollars' worth of cheap beer and got wasted with my best friends in an alley behind the mini-mart to celebrate the end of our young-adult lives.

My dad would say that I never fully grew up. I just didn't grow up like him.

It's awkwardly quiet now, and I'm a little peeved I hurried over here since my other sisters haven't even arrived yet. Seems I'm not really late for anything.

"So," I start, gripping the front of the stool between my legs while I hunch my shoulders and lift myself slightly in the seat. I'm so uncomfortable here. I always am.

My mom rinses off the spoon, dropping it in a soaking bowl in the sink. I can smell chocolate cake baking.

"The flowers are lovely. Thank you so much. You're a good boy," my mom says, a little more like her normal self. She dries her hands on a towel and steps over to me, kissing my cheek as her hand cups the other side of my face.

"It's your birthday. You know I'd never miss it," I smile. Her gaze lingers on me for a minute along with her palm, and in that small space, she almost looks like she might cry.

"Mom, you know I would come more often. But he's made it clear—" I start to walk through my usual diatribe about how stubborn my father is and how much I refuse to give in, when all is interrupted by the man himself.

The sound of his throat clearing comes first, followed by the shutting of the front door. I'd sprint for the back door, but he's likely already taken in my piece-of-shit car out front. I rub my forehead and stand from my stool, pushing it back in place—exactly how I found it. I fish my keys from my pocket and have the car key poised between my thumb and finger by the time he enters the kitchen.

"He's home early. That's…that's what the weirdness was for," I say just loud enough that my mom and sister can hear, my head hung low as I try to figure out what face I need to make to keep my mom happy and my father calm. I glance at her with empty eyes, and her face falls and her head tilts to the side. That's her nonverbal: *I'm sorry.* She hates it when we fight; so for her, I'll try to avoid confrontation.

"What are you here for? Do you need money? Did you decide to get a real job? Or are you still living in fantasyland?" It's like he picked up right where he left off the last time we spoke. That conversation was more than twelve months ago, and it happened almost exactly the same way. I dropped by to see Mom, and he came home early.

"I was just wishing Mom a happy birthday. But I have to go now, so how about you spend your energy doing something nice for her, huh?" My words come out cruel and sharp—I don't mean to engage, but there's this trigger he hits, and I can't seem to stop it. I step into my mom and kiss her cheek, then turn away from him. I won't look at him.

"You mean like provide for her with a good job that guarantees her future and uses my brain and real talent?" he pipes in before I can get too far.

I slow down, but I keep moving forward until my hand lands on the doorknob.

"Yeah, I guess you're right. Math is a dream talent, pops. Way to follow your dreams. Now, I'm going to go back to following mine," I say, shaking my head as I pull the door open. I walk through and nudge it closed behind me with my fingertips.

I almost make it to the solace of my car, but I'm a step or two too late.

"You're wasting your life on that...what...music mixing? Jesus, you don't even play an instrument. It's not like you're a prodigy. You have a talent, Casey. Your gift is numbers, and you could do so many things..."

That's the thing with his lectures. They teeter on nice. But they're not *really* nice. It's like his words are disguised as kind and caring—with just enough bite to remind me he thinks I'm a loser. I fell for it most of my life. I'm done falling for it now.

"I play six instruments, Dad. Six," I say calmly as I open the car door and put one foot inside. My hand flattens on the roof and I swallow hard, giving in to look up at him. He's wearing his typical suit. The tie is off, but other than that, he's exactly the same. He doesn't change. "And that *mixing* thing, it makes me happy. Tell Mom I hope she likes her flowers."

I pat the roof once and climb inside the car; I turn over the engine the typical three times before it catches and I can drive away.

My car is silent for the first few blocks, and I don't pause at the stop signs long. I stay in this trance until I turn the corner and know I'm completely out of sight of him—not that he's still looking. When I reach the red light, I let myself have one solid tantrum as I pound my fists against the steering wheel over and over again.

"Fucking fuck!" I yell, pulling my hat from my head and throwing it hard on my dash. My hair falls down into my eyes; I hate that when I'm driving, so I pick the hat up again and twist it backward.

My AC is spotty, so the air pumping through the vents is doing little to cool me off. Or maybe I'm just on fire from being so pissed. It's summer, and I'm wrapped up in a vest and pants like I'm getting ready for the family Christmas card. I unclip the seatbelt—while the crosswalk sign flashes a countdown—tugging the knit vest over my head, my hat getting caught in it and my hair flopping in my eyes again. Fuck it—I'm leaving it off this time.

When the light changes, I buckle up again and move into the intersection with just enough push to get me to the middle before the engine cuts out and my car dies; it coasts to a stop in the mini-mart parking lot on the other side of the street.

This has been happening a lot lately. That's what I get when I buy my car for two hundred bucks on Craigslist. I start to laugh at my shitty day. All I wanted to do was wish my mom a happy birthday, maybe see her smile. Instead, I got the weirdness vibes of her anxiety, because she knew my dad was coming home, and I got another lecture, of sorts. And now, I'm pretty sure I'm going to need to call Houston for a ride, because I have all of my shit in the trunk, and I have a gig tonight.

I pull my phone from my pocket and step out of my car, kicking the door closed with my foot while I dial my best friend.

"Yo, I need a ride," I say the second I hear him answer. I tuck the phone against my shoulder and take out my wallet to see how much cash I have. There isn't enough for mini-mart lunch, so I grab a cup for a drink and fill it with Coke.

"And I need lunch. What time do you work?"

He hasn't spoken yet, but I hear the sigh.

"Hey, Houston. It's Casey. How are you today?" he says, putting on that voice he uses when he imitates me. It sounds nothing like me.

I pause and blink, looking at the small bubbles bursting from my soda.

"That's a ridiculous way to start a conversation. It totally wastes my time and yours. I just get right to the meat," I say, snapping the drink lid in place and ripping a straw from its paper packaging.

"Ha, you mean you get right to whatever it is you need from me," Houston laughs.

"Whatever, same thing—the point, needs. Blah blah, blah," I say. "Dude, I'm at the mini on Fourth and June. I'm starving. The car is dead. Like…*deeeeaaaad.* And I have a gig, so can I borrow yours for the night? I'll bring it to you in the morning."

I keep talking, because I've learned if I don't give him a chance to say *no* right away, then my odds are drastically higher for him saying *yes* to whatever I need. I've been using this technique on Houston since we were kids. It worked on ice cream pops at the Little League field when they were down to only one flavor of each; it worked on girls in junior high when we both liked the same one, and it works with rides when my shitty-ass car breaks down. I talk until he's overwhelmed, and eventually he just agrees to get me to stop.

I hear the sigh. It's coming.

"I'm working *now,* so you're going to need to sit tight for about twenty minutes until I can take a break. And you're going to need to hang out with me at the store until I'm off so you can take me home. *And* I want the car back tomorrow morning," he says with that parental tone.

I'm older than he is—by a month, but older still. He's really a parent, though, so I guess that gives him the right to be the more responsible adult between the two of us. Houston had a kid in high school, and now he's a single dad. I'm not sure how he does it. On top of everything, he's still a solid friend. My best, really. He's probably the most family-like person I have in my life.

"Deal. I'll be kickin' it on the curb," I say, tossing my change on the counter for my drink and tucking my phone in my back pocket.

I wait while the cashier digs through the drawer to give me back my seven cents. She makes a face when she drops the coins into my palm like I'm a douchebag for actually waiting for my change. Whatever, I'm not in the business of rounding up my mini-mart purchases to the nearest dollar just so whatever corporation owns this joint can have a fatter bottom line. I want my seven cents.

When I get to my car, I reach in through the broken window and drop my change in the center console. I squat down until I'm sitting on the curb, my feet facing the road so I can see Houston pull up. My phone *dings* as soon I get comfortable, so I lean to the side and pull it out again, hoping it's not a text from Houston about how he can't leave, or how I can't use his car. I hate that I have to depend on him so much. It isn't fair to him; I know it isn't. But I call him every time I'm in trouble anyway.

Best friend code.

I slide my phone *on* and open my messages to find one from my roommate, Eli. I'd ask him to pick me up, but he rides a bike everywhere he goes—a bike with a banana seat. Hipster with a Schwinn.

ELI: *Dude, check this link out.*

He follows up his text with another, and it's only a link. It's a short link; I bet it's spam.

ME: *Do you get money if I click this? Or like…points in some app where you're building a world?*

ELI: *Am I really that lame to you?*

I pause for a breath and mentally run through the things I know about Eli.

ME: *You might be. Yes.*

ELI: *Click it, fuckhole.*

After shaking my head, I give in, because I have time to kill, and maybe this will be a good source of entertainment. A video pops up, but it's dark and grainy. It looks like someone filmed this from a bar or something. I can see tables with drinks on them, and the viewpoint keeps moving around. The motion is making me a little sick, but eventually, I can make out just enough of a form to tell there's someone sitting on a stool on a backlit stage.

"This one's called 'In Your Dreams, Casey Coffield,'" a chick's voice says suddenly over the uneven background noise.

What the fucking hell?

I hit the pause button out of panic and pull my feet in closer to my body while my fingers push into the volume tab on the side, turning it up as high as it goes. I look around, and nobody's near me, so I slide the video back to the beginning and hit PLAY again.

The same background sounds of laughter, talking, and clanking glass; then, there she is again. "This one's called 'In Your Dreams, Casey Coffield,'" she says again. I don't know why I thought it would be different. Though, I do have vivid fantasies. But still…

A few people applaud, and the lights go even dimmer. I can't see her face, only a vague form. I think she's in a dress, but I'm not even sure of that much. She could be just about anyone, but I swear I don't know this girl.

The strumming of the guitar starts soft, and then her voice comes in.

"Shadow of a girl, lurking in other people's shadows…let her go by, let her dance all alone…"

I hit pause, and play that first part back a few times, trying to get a hint of familiarity in her tone—some clue with the lyrics, anything. The info under the link just says: WEDNESDAY SINGER SONGWRITER NIGHT AT PAUL'S. *Where the fuck is Paul's?* I need to be on a computer, because now I'm opening more windows—Google searching for "Paul's" and sifting through a list of seventy-some-odd options of places in Oklahoma, one a feed store, so I eliminate that right away. Shit…this might not even be in Oklahoma.

I go back to the video and play from where I stopped.

"Wonder what she sounds like, wonder if anyone's ever seen her...would they watch her in a spotlight, or bother casting stone."

Goddamn she can sing. It's like that quirky kind of style—her voice a little soft and jazzy, but with these raspy breaks that sound like crying, even though she's not. She isn't crying, but damn does this song feel sad. And it shares my name.

Who is this girl?

I text Eli: *Where'd you get this?*

Thank god he writes back immediately, because I have a lot going on with the phone now, and I can't juggle this much. *Just Google searched your name and this came up. Weird, huh?*

Weird.

Yes, weird. I'm not even going to touch the fact that my roommate is Google searching me now, but this is what comes up?

I hit PLAY again and for several seconds listen to the guitar break. There's nothing but she and some guy playing a snare with brushes. It's soft and understated. Almost jazz, but not quite. Almost country, but not quite that either. These are real musicians. I'm a hack. I learned the shit I learned because I want to make riffs to fill in mixes. This girl—whoever the hell she is—she's an artist.

I lean forward and cup my hands around the phone wanting to get a better view, trying to block out some of the light. Everything is still too dark though. All I can see is the rapid movement of her arm moving along the body of the guitar balanced on one leg. I can also tell when she's about to sing again, because her form leans in toward the mic.

"In your dreams…Casey Coffield."

Pause.

I play that last line again just to make sure I heard it correctly. I play it four more times. Then a fifth. And then, I turn it down and press the phone to my ear to play it once more, but quietly, because now there are people pulling into the mini mart and that line doesn't sound like this girl likes me very much. Not that anyone knows my name, but it feels like they should with the bite in her verse.

After about the seventh play through, I let the music keep going and listen to the rest of the song. It sways back and forth…from sad lines about being invisible and liking life that way…to more defiant tones where her voice almost speaks the words. Those spoken things, I *really* pay attention to. It's like the entire song is about how much better her life was before some guy showed up—before *I* showed up. Only…I didn't. I have no idea who the hell this chick is!

"Are you watching porn in the mini-mart parking lot?" Houston kicks my feet.

"Dude, you *have* to see this," I say, standing up and dragging the PLAY button back.

He quirks a brow at me, and I halt my stare on him, waiting.

"It's not porn," I sigh, shaking the phone. I guess I do show him a lot of porn.

Houston purses his lips, but takes my phone in his hands.

"Start it from the beginning," I say, but he's already waving a hand at me like he's got it and understands.

I stand to look over his shoulder, and just when my friend is about to lose interest it comes—my name.

"Holy shit, who is this?" he chuckles.

"No fucking clue!" I respond, my eyebrows almost in my hairline.

He plays it through the rest of the verse as I watch his expression shift from wincing to awe, just like mine did the first time I listened. He hands the phone back to me finally, and I rewind and pause when the lighting is at its brightest—still unable to make out the singer's features.

"Dude, that is absolutely some chick you've screwed over. No way it isn't," he laughs.

I roll my eyes in his direction, but I keep my mouth shut, because I'm thinking the same damn thing. I follow Houston to his trunk and help him load my things from my car to his, then get in the passenger seat next to him. I prop my feet up on his dashboard and push the seat way back, but he smacks my legs to the floor just before he turns the motor over.

"Not your living room," he says, looking over his shoulder and pulling out of the mini-mart lot.

I shake my head and mimic him, but pull my attention right back to the video on my phone. I text Eli and ask him what he searched, since somehow he found this video looking for my name. He says it was just the first thing that came up with my name and Oklahoma. Awesome—hundreds in advertising for my sound mixing and deejaying, and this comes up first. I check out the video stats and quickly learn why—more than sixty thousand views. Not bad for a poor-quality video from a dive bar in…shit…I don't know where.

It doesn't take long to get to the grocery store where Houston works, and rather than harass him for once, I turn to investigating the source of this video, sitting quietly in the back of the store with the laptop I usually use for gigs. I log into the store Wi-Fi. It would probably send Chuck—the store's owner—into a fit if he knew I had the password, so I position myself to see his office door just in case.

My sister Christina calls in the middle of my search, so I let it go to voicemail. She probably wants to scold me for bolting from our parents' house. This mystery is more enticing than rehashing a rerun of my family's favorite argument. I put in the same search, get to the video, and open up the keywords—making a note of anything that might help. After about an hour of hunting online, I narrow it down to two possible "Paul's" locations. I call the first one and ask about open-mic nights. The woman tells me they don't host those, so I move on to my last option. I'm actually nervous when I call—I've made this into something important.

An older man answers, and his gruffness throws me off my game a little.

"Uh yeah, I was wondering…do you have open-mic nights or something called Singer Songwriter—" I start, but he cuts into me quickly.

"We're all full. If you want in, see Cherry at the door before tonight's performance, and she'll let you know if anyone cancels," he says, hanging up as soon as he's done.

Rude.

But…informative.

If that's Paul, I think maybe he and I could be mates.

"Houston!" I shout, leaning just enough that he can see me several aisles away through the open door of the back room. Chuck leans out of his office and furrows his brow at me. "Good afternoon, Chuck. Pleasure seeing you," I say, saluting the grumpy old man. His heavy gray brows lower as his glasses fall down the slope of his nose, and he grumbles something as he walks back into his office.

"This is not your home, Case. You can't just yell out for me like I'm in the backyard and you're calling me in for lemonade or

14

whatever. Jesus, you're lucky Chuck tolerates letting you hang out here."

"Uhm, he doesn't tolerate me. But I don't care. And...lemonade?" I chuckle, pulling my hands behind my head while I laugh at my friend.

"It was a bad analogy. What do you want?" he huffs.

"First, it was a terrible analogy. Maybe your worst," I say, and he starts to leave, so I move right into the real reason I called out for him. "What are you doing tonight?"

He pauses and turns around, squinting.

"Depends," he says.

"I have a gig. But this thing," I say, twisting my computer and tapping a pencil end at the screen where the video is still paused. "I guess there's open-mic or something like that tonight, and maybe, I was thinking, if you weren't busy, you could..."

"You want me to ask my mom to babysit Leah, so I can go spy on some mystery girl who hates you so much she wrote a song about you?"

Yes, he gets it!

I nod.

He sighs.

"Please?" I say, leaning forward with my head in my hands, my lips pouty. His brow lowers more and he makes a sick face. This method isn't working.

"I'll pay you," I say. His brow raises a tick. "I'll give you half of tonight's paycheck. It'll be like when you have to come assist me with my equipment, only instead..."

"Instead, I'll be stalking some Internet obsession," he fills in.

"Exactly," I say.

He leans back on the doorframe, and I know that means he's considering it.

"I'll have to borrow my mom's car, because well...you're borrowing mine, remember?" I didn't think about that.

"Yeah, you'll need to do that," I agree. Better to just agree with his plan rather than open room for argument. He opens his mouth for a second then shuts his lips tight in a line. His eyes are closing. He's on the fence.

"Five hundred bucks," I lie, feeling my gut burn a little because I'm getting fifteen hundred tonight, and I promised him half. I hold it in, and eventually he agrees. I'm an asshole, but I need the cash.

"What do you want me to do when I'm there? You want me to talk to her or…I don't know, get her number?" he laughs.

I don't.

"Just listen, maybe record more of her set. And if there's a contact card or something, or she's selling CDs? I don't know…pick something up. I just need to get more info, and if I don't know her—she's talented, and maybe she's the first artist I could help or maybe…" I trail off, twisting my computer back around and slamming it closed.

Houston watches me for a few seconds, but eventually nods and laughs out an "a'right" before going back to his work. There's something alluring about this chick, but I know it's probably just the fact that she somehow knows me or there's a really fucked up coincidence happening. But she is talented. And I do want to get into recording and producing. I didn't get a chance to break the news to my mom today, because of my father, but starting Monday, I won't be a student at McConnell any more. I've officially withdrawn. I know the fact that I'm walking away with only a semester left on my degree for some pipe dream will disappoint both of my parents, but it feels right. And maybe there's some small part of me that sees the fantasy playing out to an end where I get to show my family how successful I am—and they're proud.

John Maxwell heard me at one of my shows a few weeks ago and liked what I was mixing with some of his artists, so I'm taking an internship with his label. He said he was looking for ways to bring more of his indie folk vibe into the clubs, to reach the younger crowd with some of his *quieter* artists, and he thought I might be up for the challenge.

16

Quiet isn't exactly what I do, but there was no way in hell I was passing up on a job with John Maxwell. Plus, it pays a little, too. And I can learn how to deal with quiet.

Mystery girl—she's quiet. Yeah.

I pull my phone out to watch the video one more time and notice the message notification from my sister's call earlier. I stare at it for a few seconds and consider putting it off, but she'll just call back, so I press PLAY and settle into the metal chair, ready for my reprimand.

"Case...hey. It's Chrissy. You're probably in the car, or work or...whatever. Listen, you need to call me. Case, it's Dad. He...he has cancer. And he doesn't have long."

Her message just ends.

Like a boot to my chest.

I wait to feel it.

For the next thirty minutes, I sit in the back room while my friend finishes his shift, my phone balanced between my thumbs and forefingers in the same spot it was when I played the message. I don't play it again. I don't need to. It was short. There isn't much left to be said—no questions unanswered. Nothing more I need to know.

My father is dying.

It doesn't change a thing.

It probably should, but it just...doesn't.

CHAPTER 2

Murphy

I guess it was just a matter of time before someone I recognized turned up at one of my shows.

Shows—I say that like I put on shows. I sign up—for space at open-mic nights—on legal notepads with beer rings on them. I get to *show* off my talent. It's good enough though. At least for now, until I grow my confidence and I figure out how to perform somewhere where people can see me while I sing.

That's the other reason I picked Paul's. It's busy here, and the people are more interested in having date nights and enjoying a few drinks after the busy week. It's kind of cosmopolitan for the type of music I play, but they keep letting me write my name on the sheet of paper every week, so they must not completely hate what I do on the stage. As long as it's dim in here, and I can afford to keep this up, I'll keep taking that open slot the second they put the paper down on the bar after the weekend show.

There's that word again—*show*.

I wonder if Houston still hangs out with Casey? I'm sure that's why he's here. I was pretty freaked out when my brother posted that video on YouTube last week. I'm not ready for that much...*public*, I guess? I want to get better first. One more year.

That's what I said last year.

Lane's been dying to come see me perform though, and I made sure he had a decent seat last week. Sam sat with him, and he was excited to impress her with the new tricks he learned with his video app on his phone. And of course, she indulged him, probably encouraged him a little, too. My best friend thinks I'm ready. She has for years.

Maybe I am.

Perhaps Houston showing up tonight is a good way to test things—to see if I fall apart with someone I *know* watching. I go on second; I won't have to wait long. Of course, I've been pacing in the back like a wolf waiting for my prey to weaken so I can go

18

in for the attack. I should probably just go talk to him now, get it over with.

My feet betray me—in cahoots with my streaming thoughts, it seems—because I'm steps away from him when he leans forward, resting his folded hands on the table in front of him and leaning in to hear something from the waitress.

"Water's fine," he says.

"And your date?" The waitress gives me away, and Houston twists in his seat to make eye contact, his brow bunched in confusion.

"Oh, no…I'm not. I was just saying hi," my words already unsure and jumbled. I'm failing this test. Yep, not ready yet.

"But…I'd love a water," I say quickly, raising my hand before she fully turns away. She nods and heads back to the kitchen, leaving me alone with my high school years…and an unsure feeling I'm really going to get that water my mouth now desperately needs.

Houston's head tilts and his eyes squint with his smirk. I always liked him. Not in *that* way, but just in a he's-a-decent-person kinda way. He's scanning my face, digging in the depths to see if he can pull my name out of that old, dusty hat from adolescence. I don't look very different. Maybe…older. And my hair is purple. But I'm still very much the same.

"Murphy," I say, my mouth twisted into a pathetic half smile. I feel awkward for a few seconds until recognition hits him and his mouth curves into a full-on grin as he stands.

"No way!" he says, stepping into me. He's going to hug me, which…oh god, I can't avoid. I don't hug. Ever. But, yeah…here we go. I'm hugging him in return. I pat the center of his back twice and step away—thankful he breaks his hold too.

"Wow, this is crazy. I haven't seen you since…what? Graduation?" Houston says, returning to his seat and sliding the one out next to him. I glance down at it, and then back to the line of performers all pacing near the back. I should probably get back in line, but I don't want to be rude, and maybe talking to him longer will make me more comfortable singing in front of him. I sit on the edge of the chair, nervously, and my eyes dart to the wall in the very back where my guitar still rests.

"Yeah, probably. How's..." I pause, because I don't think I ever really knew his child's name. I just knew he had one. Everyone in our school knew his story. It was tragic. His girlfriend, Beth, got pregnant and died in a horrible car crash when their baby was an infant. Houston finished school as a single dad, and last I heard he was studying at McConnell. I don't see many people from our high school any more, not since my parents moved to Archfield on the other side of the city. I live with them to help take care of my brother and teach music part time at the elementary school, at least until I find something more permanent.

"Leah," Houston says, filling in the unknown for me. His expression shifts to something proud and warm. "She's great. She's starting kindergarten, which is..." He finishes that statement with a puff of air and high eyebrows. It makes me smile.

"I bet," I say, glancing over his shoulder again at my guitar. Someone is standing near it, which makes me uneasy.

"So how are you? Do you still do that theater thing? Weren't you into that stuff?" I smile through tight lips. I'm not sure why I'm hiding it, because he's going to see me in about five minutes.

"I...did that in high school, yeah. I studied music in college, though. That's what I was really into. Theater was just the only place it fit in our high school," I chuckle. My gaze falls to my lap and twisting fingers.

"Yeah, I guess so," Houston says, leaning forward again, staring at his own hands folded together on the tabletop. He pats his thumbs together, but freezes after a few seconds, and his head tilts up toward me. "So you're...singing here tonight?"

I nod *yes*, and my stomach flips, rumbling inside with the threat of a volcano.

"You...play here often?" he asks, leaning in his seat, stretching out one arm over the back.

"Lately, yeah," I say.

He's heard the song. There's no way he hasn't heard the song. Which means...

20

"Actually, I'm on soon, so I'm gonna…" I nod my head to the side, toward my guitar, as I stand and push my chair back under the table.

Houston stands with me, and I make an internal wish on repeat that he doesn't hug me again—or ask me about the song. I won't be playing it tonight. And maybe, with a little luck, he'll just assume it's all a coincidence and go back to wherever it is he lives and not breathe a word of this to Casey Coffield.

"Yeah, I can't wait to see you perform. Good luck, or…break a leg? I don't know, is that a thing with music?" he says, pushing his hands in his pockets. Thank god he's trapping his hands. I step back more and laugh nervously, shrugging.

"I think it works here. I appreciate it. Hope you enjoy the show," I say.

Show—there's that word again.

Casey

Murphy Sullivan.

The club is loud, so I can't hear the video Houston just texted me. It's her—the mystery girl. I recognize the way she sits in that stool. I don't, however, recognize the name. Murphy Sullivan.

I write him back a series of question marks and wait for a response, but one doesn't come, so I give up my investigation for the next hour while I blend pop songs with seventies disco for high college kids to grind to under the neon lights.

It's a good gig. The club is called Ramp 33, and it's built under the Exit 33 underpass outside the airport. I played here a month ago, and was out of my mind happy when they called me again for this weekend. The pay is ridiculous, and I'm hoping they like me enough to keep me for a while so I can replace my car. I might be able to get something decent with the money I make here, so I can start saving what I get from John Maxwell. I found an old Volkswagen Rabbit on Craigslist this morning, and I may be able to swing it with tonight's paycheck if it's still available.

It's almost two in the morning when I finally pack up. There isn't anything more from Houston, so when I get everything tucked into the back of his car, I lean on the trunk and play the video again.

The song is different. It's a cover of Cyndi Lauper's "Girls Just Wanna Have Fun." I've heard this before—a lot of people cover it. She nails it, even though it isn't original. That break in her voice, and the cool way she hits the guitar for rhythm—it's all there.

"Murphy Sullivan," I whisper her name. It's literally meaningless to me.

I dial Houston as I pull out of the parking lot, and when it goes right to voicemail, I hang up and dial again. He picks up on the fifth ring.

"You're such a prick," he growls.

"Yeah, I know. But I needed to talk," I say, glancing both ways at the red light and pulling through the intersection anyhow. It's two in the morning; feels pointless to sit here for nobody.

"Case, we can talk in, like…four hours. When my alarm goes off. And I'm up for work," he sighs.

"Dude, I won't be up then. I'm up now," I say.

"I hate you," he says.

"Nah…you don't," I chuckle.

He doesn't. If he hated me, he wouldn't pick up the phone all the time. I know I'm an asshole for waking him up, but I've literally got nobody else. Houston—he's my family, and my chest is all tight from spending the last six hours trying *not* to think about the phone call from my sister. When I think about that, I think about how little it hurts, and that scares the shit out of me, because I think maybe I'm broken. Or, maybe I really hate the man who gave me life—or maybe I really don't have a home or a family, because I'm supposed to love those things above all, right?

"So did she play it? The song?" I ask, blinking to clear away other thoughts.

"I sent you what she played," he yawns.

"Oh," I respond. "So that was it? Just the one song?"

"I sent you the whole thing. But I talked to her. Crazy it's Murphy, right? So...what'd you do to piss her off?" he says through a half laugh and cough.

"Huh, I have no idea," I say, not finishing the statement that I also have no idea who the hell Murphy is. Houston catches on to my silence though.

"You know we went to school with her, right?" he says, his tone rising at the end. He's going to give me shit.

"Oh yeah, yeah. Murph. Totally—she looks...a little different..." I swallow, not knowing if she's different at all. Houston breaks into laughter in an instant.

I guessed wrong.

"She looks exactly the same, except for her hair might be a little longer, and it's purple. You have no idea who I'm talking about, do you?" he chuckles.

"Dude, I don't know. I knew a lot of people back in high school. I can't remember everybody," I say, pulling up slowly to another pointless stoplight. I give both sides a quick glance and then move on to the freeway ramp.

"Whatever, man. Our school graduated like...a hundred people. You just didn't pay attention to girls unless they were interested in you," he says.

"Uhm, that's not true. I paid attention to Beth, and Logan Sheffield," I say, throwing out the only chicks from our high school that I honestly really remember. Beth was Houston's girl, and Logan had enormous tits and put out like crazy, so yeah...I remember her.

"No wonder Murphy wrote a song about you being an asshole," he says, punctuating his words with a laugh. It's a joke, but it kinda hurts.

"Fuck off," I say. "It's not that kind of song. Or...whatever, even if. Point is, she's good. Did you get her number?"

"Shit," he says. "No, I was too caught up in the fact that I knew her. We only talked for a few minutes. I bet her parents still live in that house though..."

"And that house would be…" I fill in, waiting for more direction.

"Well if you *remembered* her, then I guess you'd know," he teases.

"Houston, come on. Where does she live?" I ask.

"I'll show you tomorrow," he chuckles. "You crashing here so I can have my car in the morning?"

"Yeah, I'll be there in half an hour. I'll try not to wake you," I say.

"Gee, thanks," Houston says, laughing once more before hanging up.

Murphy Sullivan.

I hit PLAY on my phone in my lap and listen to her voice a few more times during my drive to Houston's. It isn't familiar. Nothing about her is familiar. But hell if she isn't gifted. And fuck if I'm not obsessed.

CHAPTER 3

Casey

Houston's alarm sounds at five on the nose. It's loud, and it plays country—old-fashioned, unhappy, dog-died country. He hates country, so I have no clue why he would torture himself at the crack of dawn with that noise, but what I really care about right now is why he would make that thing so loud that it wakes me up too.

"Mornin'," he says with a smirk, coffee in one hand and newspaper spread open in the other. Who the fuck still reads a newspaper?

I slide in my socks the rest of the way down the stairs and flip him off, which only makes him chuckle. I spent the night in his spare room on that bed made of rocks. Houston and his daughter live with his mom, so the house is quiet. It's also kept at eighty degrees, and every time I spend the night here, I sweat my balls off. The last person who slept in this room was Houston's new girlfriend, Paige. She went home to California for the summer, but I swear she left a gallon of her strong-ass perfume behind on this bed. Add being hot—and smelling like lilacs—to the fact that my friend woke my ass up before the sun, and I'm pretty much a ticking bomb right now.

"Why?" I ask, rubbing my face and climbing into the chair on the opposite side of the table from him. I pull the hoodie I'm wearing up over my head, trying to shade myself from the glaring lights of his kitchen.

"Why what, Case?" he answers, not really looking at me. Goddamn smile is hovering over his coffee cup, though.

"Since when are you a country fan?" I ask, letting my forehead fall to a complete rest on the table.

"Oh, I'm not," he says. I roll my head to the side and quirk a brow as he bends the newspaper down to do the same and meet my gaze. "But I know *you're* not, and that made a rough wake-up call worth it."

He stares at me for a few seconds, and I let my eyes fall to slits.

"You're a real dick," I say, rolling my head back toward the table, hiding my eyes again.

"Sure I am, Casey. You keep telling yourself that," he laughs.

"I need your car again," I say.

"No," he answers quickly.

"I'll drop you off at work and have it back to you in time for you to be done with your shift. I'm buying one on Craigslist today," I say, talking over him and ignoring his first response.

"I'm pretty sure I said *no*," he says.

"Yeah, but you always do. Anyhow," I say while he sighs at the other end of the table. "Where does this Murphy live? Show me on the way to the store."

"Case, it's…" he twists in his chair to look at the clock over his shoulder, "…not even five thirty in the morning. You can't go to her parents' house right now."

"Uhm, believe me. I'm well aware of how butt-crack early it is right now. I'll go later. Just show me where it is so I can," I lie. I'm going to that house the second I drop his ass off at work. I won't wake anyone up, but I'm sure as shit sitting in the driveway until I see some sign of life inside.

"Fine, but just…I don't know…be a gentleman? Murphy's always been sorta shy, so maybe just try not to be so…so…*you*," he says. I turn my head to look up at him again, keeping my eyes on his until he breaks away, shaking his head.

Less me. Less selfish. Less…unable to feel. My mind flashes back on the voicemail I haven't played again, but can't seem to delete.

"Fine. I'll be less…me," I say, rolling my eyes, playing the part of Casey, the asshole. Being this guy is easier. I give in to the broken parts. I push away from the table and grab a mug from Houston's cupboard, emptying the rest of the coffee pot, and dropping in two ice cubes so I can drink it fast. I hate coffee. I just like what it does.

Houston finishes his cup and clears off the table, shutting out the lights and locking the back door behind us as we head to his car. It's a warm summer morning, but my shaggy hair looks like I spent the night in an alley, so I keep my hoodie pulled tight around my body.

We hit the main turnpike and drive about six or seven miles out of our way, taking the exit for Cloud Road. I've lived in this town since birth, and I don't think I've driven down this street once. We pass seven or eight houses when we get to one on a corner. It's small, but nice, and there's one of those wagon wheels buried halfway in the front yard for decoration.

"That's it?" I ask, taking in the sight. The house is plain, and the only car in the driveway is some hybrid electric car that probably gets a hundred miles to the gallon.

"I think so," Houston says, taking in a deep breath and spinning around at the small intersection where the neighborhood streets meet.

He glances at the house one more time as we pass a second time on our way to his store. I crane my neck to memorize everything about the way it looks, the numbers, the streets, the exit. I'll backtrack this entire trip the second he gets out of the car.

"So, if I don't know this Murphy chick, how do you know her so well?" I ask, unzipping my hoodie and turning the air vents toward me to cool off.

"Why are you wearing a sweatshirt?" Houston asks, jerking to the side as I pull and tug at my sleeves, trying to get the damn heat blanket off.

"My hair's all whacked. I didn't shower," I say, finally freeing myself and throwing the sweatshirt in the back. I twist in the seat and search the floor of his car, grateful to find one of his hats there. I push it on my head, stretching the tight fit a little. It will have to do.

"I hate it when you do that," he says, eying me from the side.

"I know," I say. No real excuse, and it ruins his hats. But I'm a mess, and I haven't seen him in this one in months. I'll get him a new one if he throws a major fit.

"Murphy's mom was going to watch Leah. She ran an in-home daycare," he says, his attention now focused intently on the road.

He doesn't talk about the past often. I get it. He had just married Beth, and an accident took her away from him. His dad died in that crash too.

"Oh," I say, not adding an apology or anything more. Houston's had years of apologies. He always told me they get old. *I wonder if people will apologize to me about my dad?*

"My dad's sick," I confess, the out-loud admission stunning me a little. It felt good to say, though. Maybe it just feels good to say it to Houston, because he's my real family. Maybe that's how grieving works—perhaps this step, sharing, is important. "Real sick," I add, and for the first time since my sister called, my tongue sours, and my mouth feels the burn of acid. My breath hitches, but I hide it by letting my forehead fall to his passenger window.

Maybe not completely broken.

Houston doesn't respond for almost a minute, and when he does, it's with the same understanding that comes with being lifelong best friends.

"Oh," he says.

I watch his expression for a second or two as he swallows and his eyes dart about the roadway. We pull into the lot on the side of his store, and he pushes the car into park, stepping out while I walk around the front to take the driver's side. He takes out his backpack from the back seat for his summer class in the afternoon.

"I'll pick you up outside the student commons. What time?" I ask.

"Four," he says, backing away a pace or two before swinging forward again and leaning down to look at me through the window. "It's harder than you think it's going to be. Just…I know you and your dad aren't close. And you're angry at him. And I'm on your side with that. Don't think I'm not. But I just…I don't know. As your friend, I need to tell you what you don't know, and even if you think you hate him, it's still going to be hard; harder than you think."

Houston looks up at me with his last word, and our eyes meet for a second—long enough that I get it. I'm just not sure I believe it—at least, not for me. Houston had a dad he worshipped, a man

28

who didn't miss a single game, who came to birthday parties and who hoisted him up on his shoulders. I had a set of instructions—a life plan to follow, that he checked in on periodically. I don't think he attended a single birthday party. My mom planned them, but even when she held them on Sundays, my dad was missing. Work always came first.

Whatever. I'm sure there's a mother load of emotional problems brewing in the background—shit I'll probably come full tilt against when I'm thirty or when I have kids of my own—if that ever happens. But right now, all I care about is this Murphy girl.

"Good talk," I say, lifting a brow. I reach to the back seat and pull my sunglasses from the pocket of my hoodie and slide them in place, looking at Houston one last time as I drive away. He gives me that older, wiser, big brother stare, and I do my best to ignore it. I have it mostly out of my mind by the time I make my way back to the house on the corner with the environmentally-friendly car. I turn into the driveway and kill the engine, then lower the seat a few notches for comfort so I can begin my wait.

After twenty minutes, I begin to see some activity inside, a head moving past the open window that overlooks the front of the house. It looks like it must be the kitchen window. A few minutes later, a couple walks through the front door, locking it behind them. They're dressed for work; he's in a suit, and she's in a long skirt and red shirt. They're young, too. Way too young to be the parents of someone my age, which means…

"Can I help you?" the man asks, opening his passenger door and dumping a briefcase in the back behind the seat.

"I think I might have the wrong house. I was looking for the Sullivan family? They used to live here?" I ask, hoping I'll get some clue, or maybe I'm just one house off the mark.

"They moved four or five years ago," he says.

Awesome.

"I see. Thank you. I'm sorry for being all creepy in your driveway," I wince and chuckle uncomfortably. The man doesn't laugh in return, which makes me feel like a total douche.

I turn the engine over and push the seat back into a good driving position before reaching for my belt. I'm about to leave when the woman speaks up, shoving her hand in front of me with a card pinched between her long, red fingernails.

"We rent from them, though. Here's their business card," she says.

A card. With a phone number.

"Thanks," I grin, taking the card from her and rolling it in my fingers once or twice before sliding it into the cup holder.

I wave in acknowledgement and back out of their driveway. I pull over on the side of the road before the turnpike and wave once more when they pass me on their way to work. The sun is up now and practically blinding me; I head to Sally's near campus to grab a breakfast burrito and some much-needed coffee before stopping at my apartment to take a shower and figure out my next move.

There's no address on the card, and the only hint at the website is some clever email address about rental gods. I give up and finally dial the number, and am just about to end the call, and scrap this plan completely, when a woman answers.

"Hi, this is Jeanie," she says in the most cheerful voice I think I've ever encountered. I smile at her first word, and I don't even realize I'm doing it until I pass by the mirror in my bathroom. I try to scowl quickly, but it's no use. She injected pep right through the phone, and I'm full on it now.

"Hi, Jeanie. My name's…Eli," I barely recover. "A friend gave me your card and said you might be able to help me find a new place. I'm…moving. For work."

I'm the shittiest liar ever. I throw my hat from my head and run my fingers through my still damp hair. I'm sweating from this conversation.

"Oh, wonderful. Who recommended us?" she asks, same fairy godmother voice.

Shit.

"Uh…" I pause for a breath. I've got one shot at this. "Tom."

In the millisecond it took to think of a name, about a dozen, completely typical names flew through my head. I almost went with Michael, but I had a feeling in my gut. Everyone knows a Tom. She *has* to know a Tom.

"How nice," she practically sings. I collapse on the bed. Thank you, sweet baby Jesus.

"Yeah, so I'm in a bit of a pinch. My lease is up here, and I need to find something ASAP, so…"

"I've got time this afternoon. I have three properties that are all near downtown. I'm not sure what area you need, but they're great deals. How about we meet near the State campus?" Her business side is kicking in, which is good. But campus won't get me close to Murphy.

"I'm getting dropped off, and my friend has to work early. Is there a restaurant or something near you I can meet you at and then just ride with you?" I bluff, pinching the bridge of my nose while I silently whisper *please.*

"That sounds fine. How about the bagel shop on Ninth and Wood on the north side? I'm in Archfield," she says.

Archfield.

"Perfect. I'll be waiting there," I say, grabbing my keys and heading to the car before she has a chance to hang up.

I pass my roommate on my way out down the main walkway and wink at him, doing my best to embody his personality for the next hour. He looks at me like I've been taken over by an alien. Maybe I have. Or perhaps it's the jolliness in Jeanie Sullivan's voice infecting me. I hope her daughter's just as nice as *she* seems to be on the phone.

It takes me almost an hour to get to Archfield. I spot the bagel shop on my first pass, pulling around the corner and parking in a far spot, then walking around the building once more to make it look like I was dropped off. When I enter the restaurant, I scan for anyone watching people walk through the front door. My eyes meet a woman's with bright yellow-blond hair that falls down to her waist in loose curls, and she quickly offers me a short wave.

I approach her table and smile with the same enthusiasm I had on the phone an hour ago. I'm not sure what her deal is, but I'm starting to think she might be a witch.

"Jeanie?" I ask.

She stretches out her hand and about a dozen metal bracelets slide forward on her wrist as our fingers meet for a firm grip and shake.

"Eli, glad you made it," she says. "Hope it wasn't hard to find."

"Not at all," I say, silently repeating *Eli* in my head to remind myself to answer to it for the rest of the day.

"So, what exactly are you looking for?" she asks, folding up the few notepads she had out on the table and tucking them into the bright orange canvas bag slung over the back of her chair.

"Nothing much. An apartment or studio or something simple like that. I could do a house, but I would need to find a roommate…" I trail off as I realize how far I'm taking this lie.

"That's not what I meant, dear," she says, sliding a pair of black-rimmed glasses down from her head to the tip of her nose.

"Oh, I guess…you need my price range? Or…" I begin to answer, but stop when the right side of her lip curls.

"Honey, you're too young to need a realtor. And I saw you drive by the first time. You weren't dropped off, and you can't keep this lie going, so how about you tell me what this is really about?"

Witch. That's it. She's a witch.

I suck in my bottom lip and nod with a small laugh.

"Okay, my name's Casey Coffield…"

I don't need to say anything more, because Jeanie is full-on belly laughing at me now. She lets her laughter go for several seconds, stopping only for a drink of her coffee with her other palm flat on the table, finally regaining her composure after nearly a minute.

"And there he is," she says, leaning back in her seat, her tongue pressed in the side of her cheek. Her eyes twinkle like a gypsy, and taking her in now completely—her long skirt and silky shirt with sleeves that flow around her arms like she's a fortuneteller—I'm starting to think my witch theory might hold up. "You know, she said she made you up," she interrupts my thoughts. "But I knew better. I looked in her old yearbook."

Her eyes linger on me in a way different from before. I think this expression might just be suspicion.

"Not made up," I say, eyebrows rising as I adjust myself in my chair. I miss the Jeanie from the phone. This Jeanie, she makes me nervous.

"Not made up indeed," she chuckles, the sound deep. She stops laughing only to sip her drink again, pulling the lid off when she's done to add another packet of sugar. I notice all of the empty packets on the table. That must be the sweetest drink on earth.

"I was hoping I could maybe talk…with Murphy?" Even saying her name feels weird. Foreign. I don't know her. But it seems I'm a very popular topic in the Sullivan house.

"Wouldn't that be a hoot," Jeanie laughs, her voice raspy.

"I…guess?" I respond, my hand coming to the back of my neck. I feel like there's a joke happening, and I'm the victim. I really wish the cameras would come out or someone would yell *surprise*.

"You know, she won't tell anyone the truth about that song, but damn if that's not the one that's a hit," she says, reaching forward, her fingers grazing my chest with a gentle punch. "I think it pisses her off, that that's the song people like? What's your story, Casey? Are you really just *nobody* like she says?"

Fuck…nobody? I mean, yeah…I'm nobody. But the way she says it sounds less like Murphy and I are strangers and more like I'm an asshole.

"I guess that's something Murphy would have to answer," I say.

My response makes her hesitate, and she leans forward, letting her glasses slide halfway down her nose, her eyes taking me in above the rims again with a quirk in her brow. Her lip ticks up with a single short laugh.

"You're just as cagey as she is," she winks, taking one final swig of her coffee. "So what brings you here then, if it isn't to solve the mystery of why you're starring in my moonbeam's lyrics?"

Moonbeam?

Witch. That's it. Witch.

"I'm working with a record label," I start, regretting that beginning and wishing I had a redo. It's too late, though, because Jeanie has already seized the key words and is standing, her eyes lit up with hopes and dreams for her daughter.

"Oh my god; you're kidding me? You want to…what? Like…sign her?"

Jeanie's hands are fumbling in her giant orange bag, searching for her phone, which finally lands in her grasp, one swipe away from a phone call that would probably only make this misunderstanding even more impossible to explain away.

"No," I say, holding my hand out toward hers. She stops. My heart drops from the shot of adrenaline. Talking to this woman is going to kill me. "I just want to talk with her. Maybe work with her. I do mixing, and sound. Recording and whatnot, and I thought maybe I could help."

I thought maybe your moonbeam could be my big ticket, actually.

Jeanie nods, then looks at her phone in her palm, I presume to check the time.

"She's at the school, where she teaches. It's summer session," she says.

I nod in response, as if I know all of this information. Thankfully, she keeps talking.

"She'll be home a little after one. I'm sure she'd love to see you," she says, that sly grin showing again for a brief second. I'm not sure what it means. I'm afraid of what it means. It makes me swallow and second-guess this half-hatched plan I'm on.

Jeanie leans toward the table, propping her bag up on the seat she just vacated, and pulling a pen from deep inside. She tugs a napkin loose from the holder on our table and scribbles down an address, folding it in half and handing it to me when she's done.

"Get there around one thirty, just to make sure she's there," she says, closing her hands around mine and the napkin. Our eyes meet and a gentleness paints her face. "So glad to meet you, Casey."

I thank her and follow her out to the parking lot where she waves me off as she steps into an old pickup truck, the metal

34

bracelets on her arm jangling with her motion. I wave back, and as she pulls from the lot, I realize she's done it—I'm smiling again, ear-to-ear, and I have no idea why I'm so happy.

Witch.

Murphy

"Miss Sullivan? I have to pee!"

Sasha, the very loud and very hyper seven-year-old, is bouncing in front of me with her fist stuffed between her legs. She's gone to the bathroom twice already, but lord help me if I think I can call her bluff. The last time I tried, they had to close down my classroom for two days to disinfect.

"Sasha, there are three minutes left in class. Do you think you can make it?" I ask.

As predicted, she shakes her head *no* emphatically. I hand over the pink pass and she darts out the door. She'll be back just in time to grab her bag and run to the curb to go home. It doesn't matter, though, because Sasha will never go anywhere in music. I know I shouldn't label my students, or limit their dreams, but that girl— she's completely tone deaf. I thought once that if I could just hold her head still for long enough that maybe she'd be able to pick up on something in the class, but even at her calmest, the sounds she makes are just...well...they're awful.

"Can I try one more time, Miss S?"

Now Bronwyn, on the other hand, is a musical genius. She is always here when I open early in the morning, and she's asked to borrow so many instruments over the weekends. She always brings them back, and so far, the only one she hasn't been able to sort of figure out is the trombone. I think that's only because her arms are short and her lips are small. In a few more years, I predict she'll be mastering that one as well.

I nod *yes* to her and let her play the selection from our Mozart for Beginners book on her small keyboard, which she glides through easily, her fingers effortless on the electric keys. I praise her and consider giving the next bar as an assignment to the dozen or so other kids in the summer class before the bell rings; I'm left holding the music book in the air with nobody in the room to talk to. Sasha breezes in quickly, grabbing her bag, and the door slams closed behind her.

I chuckle to myself as I clean up the aftermath of today's set of classes. The summer school music program doesn't pay as well as the regular classes taught during the school year. I quickly realized that my role over the summer was more about babysitting and filling in between activities until parents could come pick up their kids. But if working the summer classes keeps my foot in the door for the regular ones in the fall, I'll manage to endure them.

Teaching isn't my passion. I love the kids, well…at least the ones who love music, like I do. I get a kick out of seeing them succeed, and even the ones who aren't dedicated to practicing make strides. It's inspiring. But it's not writing my own music and performing on stage. That's where my heart is. Unfortunately, my confidence has yet to catch up to my heart.

My parents didn't want me to teach over the summer. They wanted me to head to Nashville instead, to spend the summer with my cousin Corrine, maybe get a taste of what a real music town is like. I thought about it for almost a week, and worked myself into having panic attacks. As soon as I signed the contract to teach over the summer, I could breathe again.

Nope. Not ready.

It seems in the race to personal success, the order goes: heart, parents' required belief in me, and then my own nerve.

The entire episode did open up my creative side, though. That's how the song happened. Actually, *the* song is really only one of maybe a dozen that I wrote over two weeks. It was a very Taylor Swift time in my life, minus any real actual breakup. That one song, though, just happened to hit a certain nerve with people. I know it's the one that gets me added to the list at Paul's every week. It's the one people have started shouting when I don't play it, and, except for last night when I ran into Houston, it's the one I usually give in and play.

I love that song. I wrote it as a way to clean out a lot of crap left over in my head, old feelings and frustrations from high school. It's been four years, and really—I'm over most of it. But there are still those days where a thought penetrates my daily routine, and I think about how I never quite fit in. It's partly my fault; I didn't want to fit in. That was my thing, being...*different.* But then I realized I'd put up this strange caution tape around me by being that way, and breaking out of it was impossible.

Or maybe, just maybe, I've stepped through some weird time-travel portal because what the fuck is Casey Coffield doing standing next to my car? And why is he kneeling next to it, running a finger along the driver's side door? And motherfucking hell...

"Did you...seriously just hit my car?" I ask, stopped at the front driver's tire, my hand slung forward, my fingers pointing at the deep gash that runs about four feet along my car. My guitar strap slides from my other shoulder, and I manage to catch it before my guitar case gets cracked too.

"Ah...uh, no. No, I didn't," he says, standing and folding his arms around his body, his feet shuffling as he tucks his chin into his chest. He's either nervous with guilt, or he's a tweaker. I glance to the side, to the matching scrape tinted with the red paint of my car on the front passenger side of his. I point to it.

"Uh, there's a matching mark on your car," I say, my eyebrows in my hairline as my sight shifts slowly from the evidence to his shaking head.

"Yeah, I mean so weird right? I wonder if there's someone who hit both of us? We should check other cars," he says, releasing his arms from his body so he can run his hands nervously through his hair and lift his hat from his head.

He seriously just said that. Out loud.

"That's the kind of lie one of my second graders tells. No...actually...even they wouldn't lie so blatantly and poorly," I say, stepping closer to touch the damage he left behind. I hear his feet move backward as I come closer. Good. He should be afraid. I kind of want to punch him right now. "Dude. You wrecked my car!"

My blood pressure rises with my voice, and I start to think about everything wrong with this scene: Casey Coffield is here—at the place I work—and he's dented my freaking car! How the fuck did that happen?

"It was really only a tap. I don't think all of this was me…" he starts.

"Are you serious? Oh my god, you're serious," I laugh. I start to pace a little, because this is a nightmare.

I bend down and reach into my purse to pull out my phone and begin taking pictures of both cars. I get about four snaps in before Casey completely folds.

"Shit, yeah. Okay, all right? I hit your car. There was a guy parked next to me, and he was all jacked in his spot, on the line and shit. It's Houston's car, and his car is tiny, so I thought maybe I could fit in the space and…"

"And you couldn't fit in the space!" I shout, pointing once again at the evidence.

He stops fidgeting and lets his body slump, pulling his hat from his head and running his hand through his hair, pausing at the top of his head, the strands all pulled from his face and poking through his fingers.

"I might have misjudged it a little," he winces, letting go of his hair and holding up his thumb and forefinger, pinching the air.

And with one look, he's seventeen and angling to get out of every ounce of trouble he'd ever buried himself in. He hasn't changed one single bit. Only that act, it doesn't work with me. It never has, and it's the reason I was maybe the only girl in our town who was actually disgusted by Casey Coffield.

I step back and hold my head in my hand, my phone pressed against the bridge of my nose. Think…

"That's Houston's car?" I ask, working through this unbelievable scenario.

"Yep," he says. His mouth is tight, and he looks like a kid holding his breath, praying to get out of trouble. I'm so pissed I could throat-punch him. At least the asshole looks scared.

I stand still, and so does he. I'm pretty sure he's staring at the top of my head while I shut my eyes to think, but I don't care. I might stand like this long enough for him to count every stupid hair. And if he's holding his breath still…he'll turn blue. And pass out. God, what I wouldn't give for a rewind button for life. I would park somewhere else. Or…maybe I'd walk today.

"It's fine," I say, holding a hand up and moving to the back door. He steps slightly out of my way, and I hear him breathe out in relief. That's right, Casey—you're off the hook, because I like Houston. I slide my guitar into the seat, shutting the door behind it. "I have to go. I'm late."

I work the keys in my hand and open the driver's door, cringing at the scraping sound it makes where the metal is bent at the hinge. I could throw a bigger fit until he paid to fix the car, but then I'd have to deal with him. The dent—I can live with it if it means he'll go away.

"Well, now you're lying," he says.

My eyes fly wide, and I toss my purse into the passenger seat before standing with one foot in the car, my fingers wrapped tightly around the keys, squeezing.

"I'm sorry?" I say, my gaze finally meeting his squarely for the first time maybe ever. He has nice eyes, and I notice. Brown, big and kind of…well…perfect. But that's it. Do those eyes really get him out of shit? Is that how Casey Coffield gets his way? They aren't so nice that I can overlook all of the other flaws in his personality.

"You just lied," he says, growing more assertive. He folds his arms over his chest again, and my gaze moves to the wrinkle he makes in the center of his chest in the gray T-shirt that is tight…so…so tight everywhere else. And wait—I just lied?

"Did not," I say, with an actual *pshaw* sound at the end. I'm so mad at how he's affecting me. I breathe deeply through my nose in an attempt to relax, but it's hard because he's smirking and looking at me like he has the upper hand. It pisses me off, and now I'm going to make him pay for my car ding. I might even sue him! I open my mouth to lay into him, but he cuts me off.

"You did, too," he says. I glance around looking for schoolyard swings and kick balls because he and I have gone *way* back. We have just regressed. "You aren't busy or late. You're going home."

I'm a fairly passive person, but I'm fairly certain my entire head is beet red right now. I want to punch him. My heart is also racing because what he said is catching up with me—he knows where I'm going. Oh my god, he's following me! He's *been* following me!

"Okay, now you're creeping me out, and I'm about, oh, six seconds away from calling the police," I say through gritted teeth.

"Who says six seconds?" he asks right away, flustering me. I open my mouth in response, to argue, but shake my head because what? "That's such an arbitrary number," he continues. "I mean, okay, then give me a seventeen-second head start, because I have to go put eleven dollars of gas in the car."

My lips purse tightly, and I work to narrow my eyes, but a small laugh breaks through and betrays me. Damn reflex—that was funny. Fucker. I give in to chuckle once, hard, and I try to make it sound mean. I shake his charm off quickly, because it's still strange that he's here, and knows that I'm going home. *Oh god—does he know where I live?*

"Why are you here, Casey?" I ask, hoping this is all going to be explained away with some niece, nephew, cousin, or relative that goes to or teaches at the school, too.

"I called your mom," he says.

Damn. There goes that theory. And the fact that he knows where I am and my schedule is becoming way more clear. Jeanie Sullivan wants to play matchmaker. And now, she knows Casey is real, so she has a pawn. Only he's the worst possible game piece in my life. There were so many better options. Hell, the guy at the coffee shop on the corner, the one with the comb-over and affection for short-sleeved button-down shirts. Why couldn't she have picked him to give my itinerary to?

"Why did you call my mom?" I ask, my hand instinctively pinching the bridge of my nose. Something else hits me, though, and I shake my head and hold my hand to the side, incredulous again. "And how do you know where to find my mom? You don't know my mom."

"I looked her up. I heard your song," he says. I nod, because deep down I knew that was why he was here. I knew the second I saw him.

"It's not about you. So just…I mean, I'll change the name or the lyric if that's what's bugging you," I say, rolling my eyes.

"No, that's not why I wanted to find you. But…wow, I've never met an artist so ready to butcher a hit to get someone to go away," he says, leaning against Houston's car and stretching one arm out to the side.

I squint as I look up at him, the sun bright behind his form. He looks like a movie poster, except that the car in the poster probably wouldn't be such a piece of crap, and it would probably be dent-free.

"You think it's a hit?" I ask, my lips purse with skepticism. I hate that I'm engaging him.

He chuckles and moves his thumbs to his pockets, nodding as he crosses his ankles. He looks like fucking Jake Ryan.

"I'll make you a deal," he says, and my stomach gets all tight at the mere threat of a deal with Casey Coffield.

"Ah no, it's okay. Never mind," I say, shutting my door and turning the key quickly. Forget suing him. I'm getting a restraining order.

I back out of my space and pull out of the parking lot as quickly as possible, but every time I catch the reflection in the rearview mirror, I see the front of Houston's car. I consider taking a long route home, but I know that won't matter—*thank you, mom!*—so I stick with my leisurely pace and pull into my driveway, getting out and waiting for him to exit Houston's car behind me.

"I know where you live. Your mom sent me here first," he says the moment he steps from the car.

"Unbelievable," I say, moving to the back seat to get out my guitar. "She gave you my work address, too? Just in case you were early?"

He shakes his head *no*, and I pull in my brow.

"It's a small town. So I just Googled the school. She said you worked at one," he says.

"Wow, what a crack detective you are," I say, snarkier than I normally am. Snarkier than I *ever* am. He's making me snarky!

My head is starting to hurt from the tight bun my hair is twisted in, so I pull the two pins out and hold them in my teeth, running my fingers along my scalp to massage my head and comb through my hair.

"Your hair…was it always so long and…purple?" he asks.

I freeze, catching just enough of what he said to realize.

"You don't remember me?" I ask, my head cocked to one side, my eyes zeroing in on his. He may be charming as hell, but damn if he's bad at poker faces. "Oh. My. God. You don't remember me!"

I laugh harder, slamming the car door to a close and pulling my purse and guitar strap up over my shoulder.

"I sort of remember you," he stammers, walking behind me to the front door.

I ignore him, pushing my key in and stepping up into the foyer of our small house. Lane will be home in a few minutes, and I want Casey gone.

"You are such a…" I start, but his hand holds the doorknob as I try to shut the door from the inside, and he cuts me off. Restraining order happening ASAP!

"I'm a lot of things. I know, trust me. I've been told," he says. I laugh at first, but his eyes meet mine in our small struggle with the door, and there's a certain unfiltered honesty in them that I must give him credit for. The quiet that accompanies them makes me listen, but I keep my muscles poised to push and punch, my vocal cords ready to scream.

"Look," he swallows, glancing down, then up at me again, a slender smirk to his lips. It's charming. It's goddamned charming. I shake my head because I think of all the times he's probably gotten his way with this single expression. Well, it's not working with me. Nope…

"I'm working with John Maxwell," he starts, and that little bit...well that's different. John Maxwell is famous, and he makes records. *My* kind of records. I take a short breath and let him finish.

"I do a lot of recording, mixing and studio stuff. I think I can help you. The YouTube hits—I can turn that into a million, two million—more. I know I can. I've heard you. You're...you're special, Murphy. Just...here, take my card."

He fishes into his back pocket and pulls out a bent business card that looks like he ran it off of a home computer. I glance at it and run my thumb over his name and number, looking up again at the sound of his voice.

"I'm just like you. I'm trying to find my place in this business, and I just think we can help each other," he says, his head falling against the frame of my doorway. I laugh out of reflex.

"You are hardly like me, Casey," I say through the laughter. His mouth twitches at the sound of his name, and his eyes snap to mine. I don't think I ever really looked at them when we were younger, and I wonder if they're different now, or if they were always so perfectly symmetrical and dark. I still don't trust them, but I concede—they have a certain something.

He sighs slowly, his mouth tugging up on the corner in an acknowledging smile.

"Yeah, in most ways...we're probably different," he says, his gaze drifting to the side before coming to me again with a little more softness.

"But in this way," he gestures toward my guitar—his fingertips landing on the case I'm holding between me, the door, and him—and tapping. It's almost as if he touched me, the tender way his finger runs along the side of the case then falls away. And damn, the eyes come to me again. I'm being seduced. I flex my legs and arms again and straighten my posture, digging in. I'm stronger than this. "Musically, we're the same. And I can help you. Please, just...just think about it."

I search his face for several seconds until the relentless pounding of my heart begins to take over, so I nod once and hold his card in front of my face so I have something sterile to look at.

Right now, all I want is for him to get off my porch so I can think and feel rational.

"I'll think about it," I say, closing the door as he nods with a smile, taking a step back. I hold my breath, and for the briefest second, my arms tingle from that one single glance he gives me.

I lean my forehead against the door and peer through the peephole to watch him leave, and he does, maybe even a slight skip to his step. He's hopeful, and I have a feeling he might also be persistent.

This visit. Him finding me. His interest. It's all selfish. It's all exactly what I expect from Casey Coffield. But, and I hate to admit it, it also felt really nice to hear him say I'm special.

CHAPTER 4

Casey

"So, let me get this right. You didn't get *your* car today, and instead, you wrecked mine," Houston says, his hand doing that rubbing thing it does on his forehead.

"I'd hardly call it *wrecked*," I say, kneeling in his driveway, pointing toward the deep scratch. I squint because the scratch looks less awful when I do that. I suppose I can't ask him to squint when he looks at it. "Don't worry, though. I'll pay for it."

"Oh, I know you will," Houston says.

I'm going to find a way to fix both of the dents—Murphy's and Houston's. I just don't want to talk about it, because I'm not sure when I'll be able to afford it, and I don't want to have a looming deadline. I hate blowing expectations. I do it a hell of a lot. My debt to Houston is probably un-repayable. Sometimes, I lie awake at night and think about all the things I owe him, only to get up the next morning and take so I can owe him more. I'm like an addict for his kindness.

I follow him inside, where his mom and daughter are busy at the kitchen counter baking cookies. Leah's a sweet kid. She calls me Uncle; sometimes I wonder if I'll like my real nieces and nephews as well as my pretend one—when my sisters finally have kids.

"What are we making in here?" I say, startling Leah where she stands on the chair next to Joyce, Houston's mom.

"Uncle Casey!" Her arms ring me, and I lift her from the chair to swing her around before putting her right back in place. My heart melts every time. This...this unconditional love that comes from every direction of this house—it's why I come here.

"We're making homemade cinnamon rolls for the church, but I imagine there may just be a few extra left behind," Joyce says with a wink.

"You spoil me, Joyce Orr," I say, kissing her on the cheek and dipping my finger in the frosting as I leave. She swats my knuckles. Damn...she's fast.

"Everyone spoils you," Houston says, sliding his school bag into the small nook by their front door. I make a mocking face to him, whispering his words in the voice I put on when I imitate him, which doesn't faze him. Probably because he's right—everyone spoils me.

Except for the people who made me.

I move to the living room, and Houston follows. His mom brings us each a bottle of water and an Oreo cookie, which makes me chuckle silently as she walks away.

"Dude, I love that your mom still brings us snacks after school," I say, twisting the cookie in half to lick the cream.

Houston smiles in return.

"Not gonna lie—I do too," he says, eating his cookie whole and twisting his water bottle open. "So," he mumbles through chewing. "What came up today that put the whole new-car mission on hold?"

I choke a little on my cookie. He's been so focused on the dent in his car that he hasn't asked about my talk with Murphy.

"They don't live there anymore...the Sullivans?" I say. His brow cocks for a second, but he quickly shuts his eyes when realization creeps in.

"How early did you go? You went right away, didn't you?" he asks.

"Well, if you're just going to know the answer, why bother asking me?" I respond.

Houston leans forward to set his water on the coffee table, his hand on his head again. He's going to get a wrinkle in his forehead from all of that rubbing.

I sigh and lean back into the sofa.

"Yes, I went there...*early*," I say, a little shrug to avoid the judgment on his face. Patience is not my thing. "They rent that house out now. But..."

His head falls to the side and his eyes grow wide.

"You tracked them down..." he fills in, his mouth a straight line.

"Dude, I had to find her. And so yeah, I did. I got her mom's business card from the renters, and she told me where to find Murphy, and we had a nice chat," I say, glossing over most of the embarrassing details while I pop the last bite of Oreo in my mouth.

"You...chatted," he says.

Okay, I don't use the word *chat*...ever. That's probably a tell that I'm feeding him a lot of bullshit.

"We did. We *chatted,*" I say, folding my arms over my chest. He mimics me and glares in my direction. I can play this game though. I'll just stare back. "It was a very nice *chat* if you must know. I complimented her music, and we reminisced about the old days, and then I left her with my business card so she could call me to get some recording time set up."

"You reminisced? And...you have business cards?" he says, one eye all screwy.

"I'm professional, yo. If I'm going to intern with John Maxwell, then I need to have something I can give people," I say, pulling my wallet out and handing a card to Houston.

"You haven't even started yet. You start next week," he says, taking my card in his hand and flipping it over a few times between his fingers. "These look terrible."

I reach forward and snatch it from him as he laughs.

"That was mean," I huff, poking the card back in my wallet. He's right, though. They didn't come out like I wanted them to. Houston's girlfriend is good at design stuff, and she comes back in a few weeks. I'd planned to ask her for help. Paige gets me. Or she tolerates me. She doesn't hate me, at least, and I'm never anything but full, selfish, pig-headed Casey with her.

"Forget about the cards. So this...*chat*...," he says, making finger quotes, "it went positively? You think you might actually get her to record something with you?"

"I think...I think there's a lot of positive that came out of it, yeah," I stammer, letting the fact that I smashed her car with Houston's sneak into my stream of thoughts while speaking. He notices my facial tick. I need to get better at lying.

"Case?" He tilts his head and looks at me hard.

I shirk my shoulders up and lean my head from side-to-side. "I may have…sort of…not lead with my best…self?" I half admit. *I fucking smashed her car with yours.*

"I said less YOU!" he says, but his tone is joking, which is the reason it only hurts my feelings a little. If only he knew how much of me *I'm* not fond of. My mental list of defects is so long that I forget the old ones to make room for recent ones.

"Well, there's a whole lot of me, so it turns out that even less me is still, like, a shitload of *me!*" I say, falling back into the couch, this time tossing my hat to the side in frustration. "And I might have hit her car."

I throw the last part in quickly, mumbling and pulling the cap from my water bottle fast to drink. I don't like lying to Houston. I had to tell him. I feel like a kid who broke a lamp.

"You…that dent…my car…" he stutters chopped up sentences. I only nod. "Damn it, Casey."

That single phrase has been uttered by my best friend so many times.

"I know," I say, an apologetic half smile. It's all I got. I smile my way out of messes. "I really will fix your car."

He stares at me for a few long seconds.

"I know," he blinks. My stomach rushes with relief—not because he isn't yelling at me, but because he knows I'm good for my word—that I at least have some integrity. It makes me feel less like a bum.

After a minute of silence, my head falls to the side, and I nod to regain his attention.

"She's probably not going to call me," I say, my face scrunched up.

"Probably not," he agrees.

I'm really disappointed that I screwed this up. She's talented, and something about her voice motivates me to think big. And, oddly enough, it's not just because I think she could help me get ahead, but I really think I can help her, and the thought of helping her makes my chest squeeze the way it's supposed to.

"I really think she's good though, man," I sigh.

48

"She is," he approves again.

I look into my friend's forgiving eyes and build up the courage to test him again, to add to my ever-growing list of IOUs.

"I'm gonna want to go to her next open mic," I say.

"I know," he says, holding up his hand to stop me from saying more. "And yeah, I'll go with you."

I breathe out a soft laugh and smile at him, even though he's standing and not looking at me. He's frustrated with me. I do that to him a lot. If I could afford it, I'd buy him an entirely new car. Hell, I'd buy him a new house. Maybe one day I'll get to.

Murphy

I threw that ugly card away a dozen times over the last week. Two dozen! I threw it away again on my way into Paul's. I thought if I threw it away somewhere public, where I didn't have the safety net of knowing it was my own fairly-sterile trashcan, that I wouldn't go diving back in after it.

Chalk this one up to a fail. I got mustard—or at least I *hope* that's mustard—on the sleeve of my blouse as I reached in to pull his card back out.

It's that whole *special* thing he said. I'm pretty hung up on it. It wasn't a line or some cheesy hook to push me into something. In fact, the entire time we talked, that one sentence about me having a real talent was the singular time it felt like Casey Coffield was truly being real.

I know it's weird to have a dream, but to also be terrified of it. But that's where I'm at. I have a dream—and living that dream scares the ever-loving crap out of me. I want to write songs and sing them and have people download them into their iTunes accounts. Then, I want to be so popular, people will bother to buy my music in record format, to play on vintage turntables, because I love that retro sound with the small pops and cracks that accent the crisp magic that comes from a needle on vinyl.

But…I also don't want them to *boo*. I don't want them to say my lyrics are weak, or that my voice doesn't evoke enough emotion, or—like on those reality singing shows, when the judges tell the contestant they're *pitchy*. Sometimes, I am pitchy. I just don't think I can handle someone saying it to my face, or in print, or on Twitter. This is why I freaked out when my brother put the video on YouTube—that place is a gateway to criticism, and my hard shell, it's still soft. And mushy. I have a mushy shell.

"Murph, hey!" says Steph from across the room.

She's another regular here on open-mic night. She and I have a similar vibe, and we hit it off instantly. I like it when we're both performing on the same lineup. She's quiet in crowds, like me. A friend. I step through the small gathering forming at the tables near the back of the club, and grasp her hand when we reach one another. She knows I don't hug—one more thing I love about her.

"Congratulations!" she says through a bright smile. My hands freeze and fall from hers as my head tilts to the left. My eyes catch hers and I know I look puzzled.

"Your deal?" she continues. There's something I'm supposed to know. But I don't know it. That makes my stomach feel a little sick.

"My deal...uhm..." I say, my head turning to the side just enough to lock my eyes on the explanation.

Casey stands and Houston shakes his head behind him in apology as they both approach me.

"Murphy, we're really looking forward to the show tonight," Casey says, that fucking smile that had me confused all week simply pissing me the hell off right now.

"I'm sure you are." My eyes narrow on him. Houston chuckles.

"I knew you'd be the first one plucked outta here," Steph says next to me.

"More like conned," I add in a hushed tone.

"Huh?" she asks, her lip bunched and one eye squinting.

"She said she's excited," Casey fills in quickly.

Steph does a double take because that sounds nothing like what she thought she heard. Probably because it's nothing like what I actually said.

"Sorry to surprise you like this, Murph," Houston says, stepping beyond his friend and hugging me quickly.

"Wow—y'all must really go way back, or she must trust you, because Murphy don't hug anyone," Steph says, her hands on her hips. I swallow under the heat of everyone's instant attention.

"I just...it makes me feel trapped," I explain.

My family is a huggy family. They all hug. Unfortunately, even the uncles who get a little too touchy feely when they drink. Nothing ever worth throwing a punch over, but enough to put me at odds with hugs for the rest of my life. My brother Lane is the only one who I can take affection from without red flags flying up all around me, and that's because he's the brightest sunshine in my life.

"Sorry," Houston mouths. I shrug him off and tell him not to worry about it, but I doubt he'll hug me again, and I'm okay with that.

"I'm up soon, so I'm going to head toward the front," she whispers, shaking Casey and Houston's hands again, and telling them how happy she was to meet them. God, I wish they were here for her instead of me.

As soon as Steph is out of earshot, I turn to Casey, happy that Houston walked back to their table to give us privacy.

"You are out of line!" I whisper as sternly as I can. I pull out the teacher voice, but all it does is make him dimple one cheek and laugh at me.

"She misunderstood me," he begins, but I raise a hand.

"Your Jedi powers are no good on me, Casey Coffield. Don't you dare start spinning. It's a waste of your breath and my time. You thought you'd get my friend all excited and then I'd just cave in because of her happy dance and all of the merriment and shit, but listen here, buddy," I pause, my chest heaving with my breath. His dimple is gone. Good. It's a Jedi dimple. And it might work if he throws it out there enough.

"I...am impervious to Casey Coffield. And you can have your ugly-ass card back," I say, pulling his hand up in my own and stuffing the card in it. I fold his fingers into a fist and walk away, my feet stomping a little to the beat Steph just started on her guitar.

What I did not count on was him following me.

"I'm sorry, all right?" he says, his mouth a little too close to my ear. Shivers happen quickly, and I shrug them off before they turn into tingles. He's close, so I smell his cologne, which is...not strong and overpowering like I'd assume. It's masculine and little bit like a good cocktail. He catches me off guard—drunk on his pheromones—and manages to walk me backward into the small nook at the far end of the bar.

"Oh...oh no you don't," I start, my heart beating hard as I put my palm flat on his chest, which is...hot. It's warm, I mean. But it's also hot. And hard. And really big and immovable. My eyebrows narrow, and I push harder as his arms fall to his sides and his thumbs find his pockets. "What are you, like a bouncer on the side? Were you always this...big?"

I look up realizing what I said and the right side of his mouth ticks up. *Jedi dimple.* I roll my eyes in response.

"Stocky," I say, my lips pursed. "I meant stocky. And...pushy. I definitely mean pushy."

"Just hear me out," he says, stepping closer to me. My eyes dart erratically from side to side. I'm willing to scream for help if I have to. He senses my panic and holds his palms up on either side of his face, a small flash drive between his right thumb and forefinger. My eyes zoom in on it. "I meant every word I said on your porch, Murphy. I can't change what you think of me, or shit...anything I may or may not have done to earn that reputation with you. But the fact remains that you have a talent, and whether you like it or not, so do I. And mine—it complements yours. In the best possible way. You're special, Murphy Sullivan. I can make you believe it."

Goddamn it; that was some speech. My eyes leave his just enough to take in the flash drive he's now holding out for me to take. I'm skeptical. But I'm also curious, so I pull it into my fingers carefully. As Casey lets go, a heavy breath escapes him.

"What is this? Is this...a bribe?" I say, one eye smaller than the other.

"No, it's proof," he says quickly.

I twist my lips and squeeze the drive in my palm, sliding it into the front pocket of my dress. It's my navy blue fifties dress, and I wore my hair up in twists tonight. I wanted to feel like a pinup, I guess, but somehow now I only feel vulnerable. I think it's the cologne's fault.

"Proof, huh?" I say, pressing my shoulder blades as flat to the wall as I can, trying to buy space. Casey notices and takes another small stride back, pushing his hands into the pockets of his dark blue jeans. I notice his shoes when I look down—PF Flyers, green ones. He taps his right toe out and back, and I chuckle.

"I've had them since high school," he says, his grin lopsided.

I nod in response, but the thing is—I remember. I've watched those shoes take center stage every chance they got. I've watched them get the laugh, watched them get the girl, and watched them break her heart. I've also watched them walk right by without stopping. I never really cared, though I always thought they were kind of awesome shoes. They're still awesome. And now, the toes are pointed right at my Mary Janes.

"It's a demo. Of you. But...in a way that will make people—the *right* people—take notice," he says, tapping his toe again and bringing my eyes to his.

"Demo," I repeat, flipping the small square drive around in my palm, which is buried in the pocket at my side.

"One listen. When you get home. That's all I'm asking," he says, using that same tone—the one that I swear to god is honest and real. If not, then I'm a fool. Please don't let me be a fool.

"One listen," I say in agreement. His mouth curves the moment I nod. I've made him happy, which makes me feel nervous and sick.

"You won't regret it," he says, kicking his foot forward just enough to nudge the tip of my shoe. It startles me and my heart skips, but I hide it from him.

He walks over to his seat and settles in next to Houston, and I watch them talk for a few minutes while Steph finishes her set. I'm up next, and my mouth is completely dry. I feel my hand in my pocket for the small plastic device that I'm terrified to listen to, yet dying to race home to play.

"Can I get a water?" I ask at the bar, guzzling it down the second the waitress rests the glass on the napkin, my other hand never leaving my pocket and *the proof.*

I give Steph a nod as she walks down from the stage, and I step up to the stool for my set for the night. I adjust the mic and fix the strap of my guitar around my neck. I close my eyes briefly with my back to the crowd—to Casey—and draw in a deep breath through my nose.

You're special. Damn it if he doesn't make me believe it just a little.

I smile as I turn around, even though it's fake and plastered on. I'm hiding my nerves with extra work tonight. Sometimes, the act is harder.

"Thanks for coming out tonight," I say, the sound of my own voice in the mic just as startling to my ears as it always is. My eyes settle on my muse—though I swore he wasn't, he barged his way into the role, just like he does with everything. Green PF Flyers on a boy who demands my attention.

The crowd grows quieter, and I clear my throat lightly. Let's see how brave I can be.

"This one's called 'In Your Dreams, Casey Coffield.' "

CHAPTER 5

Casey

"Dude, I think maybe you need to quit stalking her at this point," Houston says. I have the phone tucked between my cheek and shoulder, and it's giving me a cramp, but I need to lock my car.

I finally claimed my new Craigslist chariot—a 1989 Volkswagen Rabbit. It's hideous; the locks are old-school push buttons that require keys in holes and shit. It smells like a lawnmower when I drive. I fucking love it.

"This is the last time I show up on her unannounced; I swear," I lie. If she turns me down after hearing the sample I made her, there's no way I'm quitting. In the few days that have passed since I gave her that thumb drive, I've mixed two more versions of the song about me.

Houston thinks I have a God complex because I like that I'm the hook in the song, but that's not it. Her voice is meant to be the center of everything. She's like one of those singers where you hear them on some awards show one day acoustically and your mind is blown. I like the mix I made last the best, and I want her to hear it. I raced over here the second it was done rendering, and I dumped it on my phone. Houston just happened to catch me leaving my apartment on my way.

"Good luck, man. I have a feeling you're going to need it," he chuckles just as I knock twice on her front door.

"You're supposed to believe in me, asshole," I grimace to myself.

"Oh, I believe in your talent. It's the dumb shit you do in your free time I'm not on board with," he laughs.

"Ha ha," I say, crudely before hanging up in time for a guy—*maybe he's a boy?*—with messy blond hair and glasses to swing the door wide open.

"Who are you? Are you selling something? We don't take sol…solis…we don't want it." He fires questions right out of the gate. I can tell by the slight lisp and trouble with his speech that he has some kind of disability.

"I'm Casey. I'm friends with Murphy?" I say tentatively. His face lights up the second I speak my name, though.

"Casey Coffield?" he asks.

Shit, she's really made me famous. At least, in her circle.

"That's me," I smile.

He begins laughing, clapping his hands a few times and pushing the door the remaining few inches so it's opened completely.

"Murphy is working on her face in her room. Come with me. I'll take you to her," he says.

I quirk a brow, but my new friend is letting me in, so I don't question him out loud. I shut the door behind me and think about how he might have let just about anybody in if they said the right name, and it makes me worry a little about Murphy's safety.

"Murphy!" I think this is her brother. I recognize the way he's yelling; it's how I used to call out my sisters' names.

There's no answer, so he pushes a door down the hallway open and steps into what must be her room, judging by sheets of music scattered on the floor, an open guitar case and stench of nail polish. I'm a few steps behind him when he starts swaying back and forth and giggling. I understand why when I step through the doorway, too.

Her purple hair is twisted in knots on either side of her head, and there's a small white bandage across her nose. But that's not what has me rapt. She's literally bouncing where she sits, her head bobbing like a drum to whatever beat is pumping loudly in the headphones she has looped under her chin and pressed to her ears with both palms. She's in a musical nirvana, and it's both sweet and familiar. Every now and then, she mouths a sound, but never a lyric. She's into the music of whatever this is—not the words.

We both watch her for a solid twenty seconds before her eyes flutter open at the floor. Her head moves just enough to catch our shadows, though, and she jumps to the center of her bed, bringing her knees in and tossing the heavy headphones at us.

56

"Lane! Oh my god. Casey! What is he doing here?" Her eyes widen in a flash, dashing between the two of us, and then she freezes, her eyes crossing as they take in whatever the hell is on her nose. She slaps her hand over her face, cupping it.

"Get out!" she shouts, standing, and shooing at us both.

"I'm sorry, Murphy," Lane says, sounding worried and sad.

"He was just helping me find you," I say, holding a hand up and glancing from Lane, who's leaving her room. He looks upset.

"Yeah, well, you did. Imagine that; you found me in my own house," she says, her voice super pissed off and irritated.

"Hey," I say, leaning with one arm over her doorway, blocking her escape. She still has her hand over her nose, but I can see her mouth. It's a straight line. I look into her eyes, and they are definitely on fire, but I glance over my shoulder again—to where Lane has now rounded the corner—and look back at her to find a hint of sympathy creeping in.

She steps on her tippy toes and looks over my arm, sighing at the empty hallway.

"I'm sorry, Lane!" she shouts. "You just scared me. I'm not mad."

Her eyes come back to me, and she deflates a little more.

"What are you doing here?" she asks, bending her pinky finger up so she can speak under her hand.

"I came to find out if you've listened yet. To the demo? I haven't heard from you, and I'm kind of anxious. Plus, I made a few more…" She cuts me off.

"You made more?" she sighs.

"Wow, so…you must have really hated the first one?" I question, frankly a little surprised. Even if the dance vibe isn't her taste, that cut was good. There was something in there for everyone to like.

"I haven't heard it," she finally responds with a shrug before switching the hand that covers her nose.

"Are you kidding me? That's it; you're listening now. And instead, I want you to hear this one," I start, pulling my phone from my pocket. "Headphones?"

I hold my hand out, but she only crosses her arms over her chest.

"I guess I could just play it, but it sounds better right in your ears. The sound is richer," I say, thumbing to the file on my recording app.

"Casey, I'm not interested. This thing I do, it's not like you think. It's a hobby, and really…I don't want anything more from it," she says.

Her words stop me. Not because she's rejecting me or my help, but because of the tone in her voice. She's lying. I recognize it—I spent a lifetime pretending I was all right with my path, and my voice sounded the same way when I told people I was going to be an engineer. Music was my hobby too. Because I was afraid to say I wished it was more out loud. Her words sound just as painful and rehearsed. I bite the tip of my tongue and engage her in a stare off, and eventually she nods her head slightly and blinks her gaze away from mine.

"What's up with your nose?" I ask, changing topics. I'm going to try Houston's advice and be a little *less me.*

"I was cleaning my pores," she sighs, taking a few steps back into her room, away from the door. She's wearing this old-fashioned dress that looks like something from a barn dance in the fifties, and as she falls back to sit on the edge of her bed, she reaches with one hand and tucks the plaid ruffles of the skirt under one knee. She's like this jazzy little Dolly Parton mixed with Adele. God, I want to make her famous.

Keeping my eyes on hers, I tilt my head to one side and smirk. I stare at her until she grows suspicious of me; I look at her until she feels me looking at her and has to turn away again.

"I use soap and water," I say. It makes her laugh once, quietly. This laugh sounds almost as nice as the notes she sings. Probably because for once, she isn't laughing at me.

"It's a Bioré strip," she says, finally pulling her hand away from her face to tap on her nose. The surface sounds solid, so I hold my hand up cautiously and raise my chin, asking permission to touch her face. She scrunches her brow, but eventually shrugs.

"Sure, go ahead," she says. I take my finger and touch the very tip of her nose, running it up the bridge and then down one side. The band is hard like plastic.

"Those things actually work?" I ask, quirking a brow.

"You'd be shocked," she says, her lips curved in a tight and timid smile. She's so damned cautious around me. That's why she won't listen to the recordings—because they came from *me.*

"So that's like…what? A sticker?" I ask, moving closer in small, planned steps until I'm able to sit on the floor next to her bed.

"It's more like a cast, but yeah—sticker works too. It yanks all the crap out of your pores," she says, tugging on the corner of the one stuck to her nose lightly, peeling slowly until her skin is free, leaving only the pink outline of where the strip had been on her face. "See?" she says, holding it toward me in her palm.

I lean forward and glance at it. It doesn't look like much to me, so I shrug.

"Believe me, there's a ton of dirt on there," she says, holding it up to her eyes and glancing at it from the side. "Come look."

I do as she says, sitting up on my knees, and I look out over the surface of the small strip and see a few raised bumps of dirt, but it doesn't take long for my eyes to meet her gray ones across from me. Her pupils flare, and she glances away, dropping her hand.

"No way my nose is that dirty," I say, trying to hook her and make her forget how uncomfortable she is all at once.

"I bet it's worse," she laughs, standing and moving toward her small trashcan where she drops the strip inside.

"Okay," I say. "Let's bet."

She turns to me, her lip quirked on the side, her eyes narrowed. Her feet are bare, and they're tiny and cute. Her toes are painted pink. I need her to listen to this demo before I forget why I'm here and start hitting on her.

"You put one of those thingies on my face, and if I have less pore junk on it than you did, you have to listen to the demo I made," I say.

This is a stupid bet. I sound desperate, but I don't think I care how I sound. I may very well be desperate. She holds my sightline for a beat, her mouth twisting, and her tongue pushing into the inside of her cheek.

"And if *I* win?" she asks.

"Then I'll head out of here and quit popping in for surprise visits like this," I say, knowing full well that I won't stop, but also secretly hoping that my morning shower cleaned my face good enough to win this really weird bet.

"Lane!" she yells, her eyes still locked on mine. I start to smirk, because she's going to take my wager, which means I've got at least five more minutes to talk her into trusting me.

A few seconds pass and soon I hear footsteps coming down the hallway along with a slight pant. "I was watching my show. What do you want?" Lane says, sniffling into his sleeve.

"Casey and I have a bet, and I need you to be the judge," she smirks. I nod, because it's fair. I also know there's no way I'm leaving without getting my way.

"I can do that," he says, moving into the room and sitting on the floor between us.

"We'll be right back then," she says, standing and nudging over her shoulder for me to follow.

I start to, but stop at the inside of her door when she's just out of earshot, and lean down toward Lane. "We got this one, right buddy?" I say, holding out knuckles for Lane to pound. He does and laughs, but my plan falls flat instantly.

"You're on your own. I'm the judge, and we have to remain impartial," he says.

Shit.

"Right...right," I smile, tongue in cheek while nodding.

I turn back to the hallway where Murphy is waiting for me, a hand on her hip, at the bathroom door.

"My brother is not a cheater," she says flatly.

"So I've learned," I admit.

Her eyes narrow on me, and she puts her small hand on my back, pushing me into the bathroom. Her fingers are cold through my T-shirt, enough so that when she pulls her hand away, I can remember where every single finger touched me.

"Sit," she says, pointing to the edge of the tub.

She turns on the sink, running hot water for several minutes over a small washcloth as she pulls out a new strip from the box. She lines everything up, then shuts the water off, stepping in front of me with the cloth in her hand.

"I need to steam open your pores," she says, moving toward my face.

"How hot is that...ah...oww...never mind," I wince as she holds the cloth over my nose, pressing into the skin as her other hand cradles the back of my neck. The smile on her face is slightly sinister, and I think she might enjoy torturing me.

This process is deeply clinical, but I'm also enjoying her hands firmly on me. I tell myself it's because she seems comfortable, which is ultimately good for me getting her to listen to my demo. But that's not it at all. I just like her hands on my neck, and her eyes on me. And I like her pink toes and twisty hair. I think maybe I'm smitten.

She releases her hold briefly, and I watch every movement of her hands as they pick up the strip and press it against my skin, her fingertips massaging it around my nose. I don't care how ridiculous I must look. I hope it's crooked and she has to do it again because I like the way her touch feels—which goes completely against my mission.

I stand quickly when she gets the strip in place and move out from the front of her, toward the mirror, toward fresh air. My head feels weird, and I'm definitely not in control. She is. That much is probably evident by the piece of plaster I let her slap on my face. I've gone from *less* Casey to pussy Casey.

"So how long does it take?" I ask, glancing at her reflection. We stare at each other like this for a breath, and I'm the first to have to look away.

Yep. Not in control.

"Five, maybe ten minutes," she says, busying herself with cleaning up after our facial experiment. She pauses in front of me, the small box in her hands, and I reach for it on instinct, my fingers tangling with hers.

"I can put it away," she says, shaking her head quickly and blinking again. That's her nervous trait, and she's done it twice since I've been here.

We both walk back to her room, neither of us dominant. Lane is now holding the headphones to his ears and bouncing on the bed just as Murphy was when we walked in on her. She moves to take the spot next to him and leans her head against his, just enough to hear the beat in the earpiece, and she begins to sing.

"Hey, hey, trolley, come on pick my brother up. Hey, hey dolly, how'd you like a buttercup?"

Lane laughs, and it's deep and lengthy, and just the sound of it makes me smile, too. Murphy laughs with him, running one of her hands along the side of his face and cupping his cheek, her eyes raking over him with the most beautiful adoration. Something stabs me internally—I'm pretty sure it's envy.

"I love your songs, Murphy," he says, pulling the headphones loose from his ears.

"That's not my song, Laney. It's yours," she says.

"Noooo," he says, shy and bashful. Her hand still on his cheek, she tilts his head to look at her and nods *yes.*

"Did you just make that up?" I ask.

She shrugs, and eventually her hands fall away from her brother. He pulls the headphones back on and goes back to bouncing on her bed.

"It's part of a song I wrote for him when I was in high school. He had bad dreams," she says, her eyes flitting to me briefly, then back to the carpet at her toes, which are circling in the threads, pushing them flat into shapes. I sit back down where I had before, on her floor, and try not to stare at her toes.

"What's wrong with him?" I ask, scrunching one side of my face hearing how my question sounds. "I mean…I don't mean that in the wrong way, I was just curious."

"It's okay," she smiles quickly, her mouth falling into a soft line—a sweet one. Her lips are pink to match her toes. I swallow and look down at the carpet and begin pressing my hands into the fibers, to make shapes, too. I need to stay away from her lips and toes.

"Lane has Down's," she says, and I nod, because that's what I had assumed. I just didn't want to be wrong. "That's why I stuck around the house after graduation. Well that, and I don't really have a career path."

I glance up at her just as she looks my direction with nervous laughter, and our eyes lock in a way that makes me feel it in my gut, for just a second. I look back down to the carpet.

"He's only two years younger than me, but he's still just a sophomore in high school, and there are just some things that are going to take him a while to get through," she says, looking up at him with nothing but love in her eyes.

"He seems like a good brother," I say.

"He is," she breathes, relaxing her weight into where she sits and turning her eyes back toward me, more certain this time. "You have sisters?"

"Four," I say, eyes wide. I roll up the right sleeve of the flannel I'm wearing and turn my arm over to the series of marks and scars on that arm. "They're responsible for most of these," I laugh, running a finger over the proof of stitches, glass cuts and a burn from the time my oldest sister, Christina, tried to convince me that letting hot oil dry on my skin proved I was a man. All it proves is that yeah, hot shit burns.

"Wow, they seem mean," she says with one short laugh.

"Nah, I deserved almost everything I got," I say, rolling my sleeve back down.

"Almost, huh?" she says, her head resting to the side.

"Yeah...almost," I say, stopping short of unleashing the mountain of shit that is my family life and the disappointment duckling role that's all mine.

Silence settles in quickly, and soon we're both poking at the strands of her carpet again. I glance at her toes in my periphery, and it makes me laugh lightly that we're both nervous now. I pat out the design I've been pressing into her floor and lean back on my hands, watching her brother live in bliss.

"What's he listening to?" I ask.

"Oh, uhm…" she pulls her iPod into her hands and waves at him that it's okay to keep listening. "Ratatat."

She sets the device back down and smiles at me.

"*You* like Ratatat?" I ask, quirking a brow in disbelief. I was expecting maybe Ellie Goulding or Ingrid Michaelson—something more girly, I guess.

"I like everything," she says, a freeing shake of her head. Her hands move to the twists on either side of her head, and she pulls out the pins holding them in place, her long hair falling in slow motion into glossy purple twists that she rustles out with her fingers. I am mesmerized, and when her gray eyes hit mine again, it feels like someone's taken the paddles to my chest.

She's in charge now.

"I'll remember that," I say, catching my bottom lip between my teeth. Her eyes flicker in question. "That you like everything."

Her chest expands with a slow draw of air, and she holds it. I don't look away before her this time. I work extra hard not to, because I suck at losing, and for a while here, I was. This may have just become about more than music. I might be all right with that. I'm sure it's a bad idea, but I'm also sure I don't care.

"I think it's time," she says, tapping her brother on the shoulder, eyes fluttering in fast blinks. Nerves—that's her nerves.

"So what, I just…" I reach to pull the strip away, but she leaps forward, placing her slender hand on mine, stopping me—stopping everything in me. She's touching me, and I've just ceased breathing.

"No, you'll mess it up if you do it too fast…just…" she pauses with her eyes on mine. I work to be the last to look away again, to win the battle twice in a row. Her tongue makes a small pass along her bottom lip, and I watch it. Paddles to the chest. I lose.

"Let me do it," she says.

"Okay," I whisper.

I crawl up on my knees, and she does the same in front of me, placing cool hands along my face. I close my eyes, because I'm pretty sure I have to. When I open them, I catch her looking at my shut lids, moving her attention quickly to the strip on my nose and her other hand.

"Is it going to hurt?" I ask.

She breathes in slowly through her nose, eyes coming to mine once more before glancing away.

"Most certainly," she whispers, her mouth serious, and her eyes lost somewhere between worried and maybe a little sad.

"Ready?" she asks. I shake my head *no* lightly against the touch of her hand, and our eyes meet. For a small second, I think we might be talking about something else—I think we might both be talking about the same thing.

Without warning, she begins to pull the strip away, and the tug burns a little. It also wakes me up and helps me focus—my sample, her music, the point of coming here. I need to remember that, but then, she's done with the strip, and her hands have left my face feeling cold. Her touch is gone and I miss it.

I shake my head, rattled by feeling something other than ambition and drive. It's not that I'm attracted to her. Of course, I'm attracted to her. I'm attracted to lots of girls. It's that I'm *more* than attracted to her.

"Well? What's the verdict?" I ask.

She steps over to her trashcan and pulls her original strip out and lays them both on the small desk near her window and calls her brother over.

"What do you think, Lane? Is his worse than mine?" she asks. I step up behind them, my heart beating hard, because now I'm not so sure I can lie my way into bending the rules, into sticking around longer than she'd like. Even though now I want to more, for even greedier reasons.

"His is gross," Lane laughs. I laugh, too, but it's fake. I'm gross…okay, fine…whatever. Does that mean I lose? Does that mean I don't get time to feel that hand on my face again?

Music. I'm here for music. I close my eyes as I stand behind them both and try to clear my head.

"Yeah, it is," she agrees with her brother, sweeping the evidence into her palm before I can see. She throws them both away in the trashcan and thanks Lane, opening the door for him to leave. I'm panicked, because I now have to leave, and I haven't accomplished a damn thing I set out to by coming here. If anything, I've only dug a bigger hole in my chest and made my craving for her that much larger. My hands stuff into my pockets, and I grip my phone.

"Mine was still worse, though," she says, her voice light and unsteady.

"I swear you'll like it. Please, just listen…wait…" I stop my begging. "I win?"

I'm all awkward and flustered, and I hate feeling this way. This chick is like my antidote, only the opposite of an antidote. I guess that makes her my poison. Shit.

"Give me the damn song, Casey," she says, her mouth a hard line. I don't question her, and I slap my phone into her palm, my eyes on her while she pushes her headphones into the jack on the bottom, pulling them around her ears. Her lip ticks up, and I catch her working to hide it under a different expression. But I catch it— it's there. She wants to hear this song, and she's playing me, too.

Let her play. I know she'll love what she hears.

She holds my phone out for direction, and I swipe to the app and open the file—the one I love best. I can tell by the small flickers in her eyelids that it's playing, and I can tell she's reached the best part when her gaze moves up in short ticks to meet mine. The volume is loud—I did that on purpose. She can't hear me, and she can't hear the sounds she's making. Her breathing changes, and it hitches when she gets to the best parts—my favorite a tiny break in her voice where I cut out everything in the background completely, just to leave her sound out there bare and vulnerable. If I hadn't heard it a thousand times in editing, it would give me chills right now.

Damn, it still does.

Her bottom lip pulls loose from her teeth with a tiny puff of air, and her eyes sweep shut. I'm standing in front of her and I feel like I should touch her, hold her hand or dance or…I don't know. I also feel a little voyeuristic—like I shouldn't be watching. She's listening to herself, but she's also hearing me—the *real* me. She's hearing what I'm capable of. The reason I found courage to tell my father *no*, the reason I let my family down to choose my own path, the reason I don't care how much it disappoints them. This girl is the key to everything I want to do. She's barely swaying in front of me, her eyes closed and my phone clutched in her palm, my dreams held right along with them.

"I know you like the song, Murphy. Please just trust me," I whisper. I know she can't hear me, but her eyes fly open and match mine. My fingers twitch, and I press my thumbs against each fingertip one at a time trying to work out the sensation.

A full minute passes, and I know the song is almost over as she moves her hand up to the cans of her headphones, cupping them and sliding them down against her neck. Her eyes blink slowly, her gaze off to the side, and her lips not giving away a damn thing. She's an enigma.

She's beautiful.

If my music had a physical form, I think it might just be her.

"This label, or studio, or whatever it is," she says, eyes flashing to mine. She knows what it is. She's pretending to be aloof. I'm going to let her.

"It's both. John Maxwell—he's both. He's…he's big," I answer fast.

"And you work there?" she asks, her expression still unchanged.

"Yes, Murphy. I work there," I answer, suppressing the inner voice adding that I've been there for three days, and so far have sat in on one very intimidating meeting and have pulled tapes and samples from old hard drives in a dirty basement.

"Okay," she says.

I nod, not really sure what *okay* means. Okay, you can pitch my song, play my demo, make her famous? Or, okay, good for you for getting a job Casey, now get the fuck out of my house?

"When will you know?" she asks, her mouth moving slightly upward. It's almost a smile. It's enough of a smile.

"I'll pitch it this week. And then we'll just see," I say, my heart beginning to pound on adrenaline.

"Alright," she says, her voice breaking with a small giggle. That sound—it's her getting excited. That's her giving me a shot, her own hope on the line.

"Alright," I repeat, my right side of my mouth leading my left one into a full cheek-aching grin.

"Oh my god," she breathes out, bringing her hands to cup her mouth, my phone still held in them.

"You can call me Casey," I say, causing her to roll her eyes. It also makes her relax, her shoulders falling back into place. I reach to her hand, and she gets stiff before realizing I'm reaching for my phone.

"Oh, yeah. Sorry," she says, handing it to me.

"Don't be. You've made my day, Murphy Sullivan," I smile. Our eyes lock briefly, the awkward pause making her cheeks turn red. I can't see myself, but I think I might be red, too.

"No pressure," she giggles again, stepping closer to her door. I know I should leave. I've gotten what I came for, but now that I have it…

"Dinner," I blurt as I reach her door. "I…I was planning on grabbing a bite when I left your house, if you'd like to come. We could talk about the song, oh…and I should probably get a better recording of the original to mix. We should meet in the studio, maybe tomorrow. Or at my place—I have equipment. That might be faster—"

"I'm not interested in you, Casey," she cuts in, her rejection swift and harsh. I'm at a loss for words. The paddles are back on my chest, but this time it's not for explosions and fireworks. This time, I think I just died. I've never really felt foolish before. My dad—he's made me feel small; he's made me feel scared, or like a screw-up. But right now—I feel like an idiot. "We're just partnering on this song. That's…that's it," she stammers out.

Her eyes flit from me and dance around the room. She swallows away about a thousand pounds of tension as she takes a nervous step back.

"Right," I say, a slight shake to my head. The heat around my face is intense. "Uhm…I only meant business. I want to pitch the best quality recording, and I ripped that one from the YouTube video, so…"

"Right," she blinks and laughs nervously. A minute ago, I thought her nervous laughter was cute, but right now—my chest still heavy with the brakes she put on me—I kinda resent it. "Recording is probably smart. Tomorrow is okay, after I'm done with class. Just tell me where," she says.

I think she might feel bad. I'm pretty sure I feel worse, though. Maybe I was just taken with the song and her dream. Maybe that's it. Maybe I didn't really feel butterflies at all.

"What's your number?" I ask, back to all business. I can't look her in her eyes anymore. And I can't really smile. I'm shit at faking it.

She hesitates, and the battle she's having with herself in front of me over giving me her number is making my palms sweat. You'd think I was some goddamn creeper praying on teens at the roller rink.

"Murphy, this is business for me too. Frankly, you're not my type. So quit thinking I'm out to get you in bed and just give me your damn number," I say, regretting it the second I see her eyes tear up and widen in a flash. I open my mouth to fix it, but then my brain kicks in, knowing it's better leaving that line in place—despite how tactlessly I drew it. I shut my mouth and keep the million *I'm sorrys* begging to spill out tucked deep inside. I say one in my head, though, to the sad gray eyes that now look like they regret ever saying *yes* to me at all.

"Right," she swallows. "Here," she says, taking my phone back into her now trembling hands. She types her number nervously and sends herself a text.

"Good, now you have mine, too," I say. She nods, but won't fully look at me. This is what Houston was talking about when he said *too much Casey*. Though, the voice that came out of me…it kind of sounded like my father's.

"I'll call you when I'm done with class, and you can give me directions, or whatever," she says, turning from me, flitting her hand over her shoulder as if our meeting again is no big deal. A voice in the back of my head tells me to rush over to her and grab her hand before she can take it away. My feet stay put.

In a matter of seconds, I've given this girl all the confidence in the world and stripped her of it just as fast. What a fucking asshole. I'm not even sure how to write this one down on my personal list of flaws. But I know it's at the top.

"I'm looking forward to it," I say, trying to sound softer. As if that can some how make up for my bad reaction to what was probably just her being nervous.

She nods, her lips tight. She's gone back to giving me nothing. But she hasn't changed her mind. This dream is bigger for her too, whether or not she wants to admit it. Our dreams are bigger than butterflies, so whatever it is that just happened—it's probably for the best.

"Great, I'll see you tomorrow then," I say, backing out through her door, patting the frame once. I pause waiting to see if she looks my way one last time. She doesn't. My chest burns a little.

I can hear the television on some travel show in the living room as I pass, her brother repeating things, almost as if he's making a mental list of the many places he'd like to go. I wonder what life is like in this house when it's full; when her parents are home, too? I bet there's even more of this feeling—of family. I wonder if it's always felt so beautiful, and full of simple joys. I wonder if that feeling will come back for Murphy the second I leave.

I hope so. I hope I'm not stealing it from her by taking her voice. I'll give it back when I'm done. I swear it; I'll give it all back.

I'm not sure how much of me I'm going to lose in the meantime, though. That's the thing—if she were my type, I'd know exactly how this all plays out. Instead, I haven't got a clue.

70

But I have a song. And I'm going to get it in John Maxwell's ears if it kills me.

CHAPTER 6

Murphy

"You should bring coffee. Stop somewhere and pick up one of those drink carriers and bring in two black, one caramel, and one light," Sam's voice echoes from the phone in my lap. I don't have Bluetooth, but I hate holding the phone when I drive—even for my best friend.

"How are you the expert on this? Why would I bring coffee? And what's with that list of flavors? What if there are five people there?" I ask my barrage of questions with my forehead wrinkled. I glance at the directions on the Post-it that is stuck—scratch that— has just fallen from my dashboard to the passenger side floor.

"Uhm, I'm a secretary? Hello! I do this for the ad execs here at the paper every Wednesday before the big meeting, and I always only get four. My boss says they are for the four most important people in the room."

Sam has been working as an assistant at the Oklahoman since graduation. Her degree is in finance, but she really doesn't know what to do with it. I feel like coffee delivery might be selling her skills short, but she's happy, so I keep my mouth shut.

"Right, well…I'm not so sure I want to set the precedent that I'm here to bring them coffee—no offense," I throw in.

"Whatevs," she says. "But you're going to wish you had coffee."

I drive in between the iron gates in the back of a two-story building made of tinted glass, the undercarriage of my car scraping the curb as I roll in. Always making an entrance.

"Sam, I'm here. I gotta go," I say, hanging up after her short "Kay" and tossing my phone into my open purse in the passenger seat.

I have a feeling Casey is the only one who knows I'm coming here. It's after five, and I bet when Grammy winners have an appointment at John Maxwell's studio, they get a late morning timeslot—and reserved parking in the front. I pull up to a bunch of guys in blue overalls, smoking. I think it's probably the cleaning staff.

"This is nuts," I whisper to myself.

For a second, I consider backing out—a three-point turn, as if I came in here just to flip around—but Casey swings open the back door and heads right to my car. Pulling away will look really strange now. And he'd probably just chase me on foot.

Deep breath.

"Hey," I say, opening my door. He takes over, swinging it wide and reaching for my hand. I look at his palm and let out a small laugh.

"What? I can actually be a gentleman, you know," he says.

I glare at his lips, the way they purse and smile only on one side. He gets a dimple when I tease him. I have to admit...I like it.

"Fair enough," I shrug, taking his help. His hand is warm and it covers mine completely. The full touch startles me a little, and I stumble as I climb boot over awkward boot out of my car. Casey catches me by my elbow, and my face slams into his chest. That's warm too.

"Sorry," I say. "I...I'm a little nervous."

I shake my head and squeeze my eyes shut.

"It's fine. Everyone's gone," he says.

I knew it!

"Oh, are we...allowed to be here?" I ask, my stomach thumping with the beat of my heart. I'm not good at breaking rules. I play by the book. I'm a book player.

"Relax, I got permission," he sighs. "That's why it had to be late. They have someone coming into the other studio all night, and they're booked tomorrow completely, so this was our only shot."

"Oh, good," I say through a whoosh of air.

I move to the trunk and pull out my guitar, looping the case over my shoulder, then grab my purse from the passenger side and follow Casey to the door. He holds up a badge against a small metal plate that beeps to let us in; then he holds the door wide for me.

"Here, let me take that," he says, reaching for my guitar. Nervously, I grip it fast to my side and shake my head.

"I'm good. It…it makes me less nervous to carry it. Makes me look legit, like I have a reason to be here…that's all," I say, my cheeks burning a little.

"All right," he chuckles, a slight shake of his head.

The door shuts behind us and he slides by me in the narrow hallway, his body brushing against mine one more time. I need to quit noticing that. But then again, Casey Coffield was always good looking. He's built like a bouncer, and I don't think he owns a single shirt that doesn't cut perfectly against his chest and abs. He always has a hat or a beanie hanging out of his back pocket, too— when it's not on his head. That hair is in a constant state of tousled, and well hell, that's appealing too.

But *this* is a business relationship. He made that perfectly clear. I suppose…so did I. Which is perfect, since the very thought of Casey—and his personality and most of his circle of friends, Houston excluded—has always annoyed the shit out of me. I need to remember all of those things. The grating character traits. The way he uses his brash humor and forced charm to get his way. That's right—he needs me. I'm in charge here. I call the shots!

"So, let's get started," I say, my voice loud and confident as I step into the soundproof door of a small studio room at the end of the hallway. My guitar case scratches against the nearby console. As I turn, it knocks over a rack of headphones. I reach to catch them, snagging my purse on the arm of a rolling chair, which both opens my purse wide, spilling my things all over the floor, and has the equal effect of slingshotting the chair into the glass wall of the sound booth. It all ends with a thunderous *crack*—that somehow doesn't leave behind any permanent damage.

That's right. I'm in charge.

My eyes are wide and frozen on Casey, waiting for him to react. His are just as wide as he runs both hands along his stubble-covered cheeks and looks around the room that I've now knocked to bits and pieces.

"I'm so sorry," I blurt out quickly, dropping my last hold on my purse strap and moving to my knees to gather back my lipstick, hair pins, roll of Tums and…motherfuck there's a tampon.

"It's okay," he says, bending down and picking up a few stray pens and my notebook. I can't find my keys, and I start to panic, pacing around the very small space, my eyes on the floor and my hands at my forehead.

Casey chuckles.

"Murphy, really. It's fine. Stuff in here is meant to withstand rock stars and metal bands. Look, it's all cleaned up," he says.

"Yeah, but my keys. Shit…I don't know where my keys went," I say, walking in fast circles and looking in nooks and crannies as if my keys somehow took flight, grew legs and walked into a crevice somewhere.

"Uh…Murph?"

Casey tugs at my thumb, which is pressed against my forehead, along with my…keys.

"Oh my god," I roll my eyes, flickering them shut momentarily. *I am not in charge.*

"Relax," he says, his hand resting on my shoulder. His hand is still warm. He's made of heat. That's his superpower. Fire. He makes fire.

Breathe, Murphy.

I let a gradual pass of air drag out through my lips and nose, then inhale again slowly. I'm using the laws of biology, and my heart finally slows enough that I can hear my own thoughts again.

"Look, I'm allowed to be here. People know you're here. I reserved time to work on a personal project. I haven't even mentioned your song to John yet. I wanted the recording to be ready first. So, this afternoon…it's just me and you hanging out. It's no big deal," he says, punctuating it with a crooked smile. I swear his tooth just gleamed out a flare.

Just me and him hanging out. No big deal.

"Okay," I say, nodding with a tight smile. It still feels like a big deal.

"How about we set you up and get something on digital?" he asks, eyebrow ticked upward. I nod again and pick up my guitar case, resting it on the arms of the chair I just made into a weapon. I pull my guitar out and step through the glass door he's holding open, then sit on the small stool in front of a mic, and the visual of exactly where I am makes my body flush.

"I don't know, Casey…" I slouch and let the strap weigh on my shoulder again.

"There's nobody watching. Look…I won't even watch you while you sing. I'll be too busy moving those dials up and down. I'm like a man possessed when I start working," he says, his head cocked to one side and his eyes promising. This might all be charm, but I'm buying it. He crosses his heart with one finger, making a crease in the tight black shirt, and my eyes take in every line.

Man possessed. That's what I hear out of all of that.

I gulp, but nod again—the kind of nod where my head never quite stops moving. Casey breathes out a small laugh and puts my headphones in place against my ears as I keep twisting my head like I'm psyching myself up to enter an MMA ring. I might as well be. Intimate performances like this actually make me *more* nervous.

When he's done adjusting the fit on my headset, he looks up at me and holds up a thumb. I mimic him, even though I'm nowhere near ready.

The door closes gently, and the second I hear it *click* secure, I exhale. The room smells like whatever it is Casey wears. This is going to be the single hardest thing I've ever done. My lips feel tingly, and I'm worried they won't work. My hands—I can usually trust them. I look down and strum a few chords, tuning as I go, playing small bits and pieces. For a spilt second, I lose myself and forget that I'm here, in a glass booth on display for a really hot guy…a guy who's not my type.

Not my type.

I say that phrase again in my head. I say it a few times, and my lips move with it, but I don't even whisper a sound. I'm here because what Casey did to my song was perfect. It's like I gave him a blueprint and he understood how to make it a skyscraper—this little blend of coffeehouse and pop. The electronic touches were so freakin' cool. And if there's a chance that he can make more of that—that he can build me a city of those skyscrapers—then I can manage to get through a two-minute song without falling into old habits.

"You ready?" he says. His voice fills my ears. I like having him in headphones. It's safer. His voice is calming.

I don't look up, because I know that will just shoot me back to square one. Instead, I hold up a thumb and nod my head to get my beat.

"Whenever you're ready."

One two three. Two two three. One two three. One more time. Here I go. Hands are live. Touch the strings. Sound is good. Smile.

I run through the opening pass three times on my guitar, just to get a feel—to get a little more lost. But I keep smiling. I grin because this guitar—it has never sounded so good. Everything about it is smooth and crisp and I swear somehow it sounds like it's playing from an old forty-five on my dad's turntable. I love this room.

"Shadow of a girl…" I begin, but stop quickly, my tongue feeling fat out of nowhere.

"I'm sorry," I say, my eyes still closed. I shake my head, but keep playing.

"It's fine, just pick up from there and start again. I can edit in," Casey says.

I like having him in my ears. He's like my confidence—if I *had* confidence.

I strum again. The rhythm is there. One two three, two two three.

"Shadow of…of…of," I say, my lip quivering when I realize what's happening.

I stop playing this time, but I leave the headphones in place. I don't want Casey to come in. I want him to stay in my headphones—*out there.*

"I'm sorry," I say again, opening my eyes, but looking down where my hands are stilled on the base of my guitar. They're shaking now too.

"I'm coming in," he says.

"No…" I say, but not quickly enough. Stupid small room. I don't like it any more. He's standing in front of me in a breath, leaning on the ledge of the glass window that I was happy to have separating us. My heart is beating more wildly now. That's the nerves. It's the nerves, which feed the problem, and I can feel it all pulling me out of line. I'm a squiggle. I'm not going to be able to get back to normal—I'm not going to be able to make it through this if he stands there. It's too much.

"What's wrong?" he asks.

I let out a sharp laugh-slash-cry, and the sound surprises me enough to make my eyes sting. I'm literally going to lose it.

No. I lost it.

"I'm so sorry, Casey…I…I…" I begin, and my mouth is so heavy. My lips refuse to round to form the right letters, and my brain is in a fight with my muscles—my mind throwing punches and swearing and my fucking nerves!

"Let me see your guitar," he says, his hand suddenly next to mine along the strings. I glance up at him, blinking away the evidence of the tears that just shot out of my ducts without warning. "Just for a second," he smiles.

I nod, pulling my strap from over my body. He pulls it around his and sits on a small stool in the corner of this closet of a room.

"I always wanted to be really good at guitar," he says, his fingers slowly picking out a melody. It's faintly familiar at first, and I soon realize it's Van Halen. "My dad thought music lessons were a waste of time, so I had to teach myself. I had a buddy down the road—Brandon Morales? You remember him?"

I nod. I remember them all—that's what happens when you spend four years of high school with your mouth shut, only whispering in the chorus for school musicals. Four years of hiding in the back gives you plenty of time to watch the people out in the front.

78

"Brandon's dad owns that music store in Stillwater—Low Notes? Anyhow, he'd let me come over and mess around, and I could hang out in his dad's store and play whatever I wanted. I didn't have money for lessons or whatever, so I taught myself what I could," he says, sucking his top lip in and focusing on his fingers. He isn't smooth, but he's not bad. He plays a run and then holds a note, swaying the guitar like he's Eddie Van Halen. "Anyhow…what you do? I wasn't bullshitting you, Murphy. It's amazing. You're special. Trust that."

He plays a few more lines, messing up once or twice and restarting, laughing at his fumbles along the way. When he hands the guitar back to me, my heart rate has calmed some. It's still not to the level of alone in my bedroom. But it's at least close to a usual Saturday night at Paul's with strangers.

"Let's take it from the top," he smiles, handing me the headphones. I smile back, sliding them in place, and this time when he points at me to begin—through that ever-so-wonderful piece of glass between us—I begin singing on time, and the words come out just as they're supposed to.

I played the song no less than a dozen times in the hour I sat in the recording booth. Casey kept his promise and never looked up at me once, except for between takes when he circled his finger in the air and mouthed "again." Each time, it was better. And the last one actually left me feeling proud.

I collapse in the rolling chair next to him—the match to my nemesis chair—and let out a puff. My shoulders hurt from scrunching, but I did it.

"Wanna listen?" he says, his right lip tugged up as his eyes sway to me. I nod, and he tugs my chair closer, plugging in a second set of headphones, handing them to me. I put them on and try not to notice the fact that my knee bumped into his—and just like the rest of him, it's warm.

"I'm still going to do more layering, but here's the general idea," he says, his voice still loud from the music playing in his ears. "Sorry," he laughs.

"It's okay," I smile.

Our headsets go silent as he drags the song back to the beginning, then I count out just as I do in the booth and wait to hear my own voice begin. I can't look at him just yet. It feels oddly personal—both of us listening to me sing about him. Not that it's about him, but it's a little about him. It sounds so unreal. I don't sound like this. This girl, the one playing back to me, is a professional. If I weren't here to witness everything, I'd swear sleight-of-hand occurred. But it didn't. This is just the me that Casey brings out.

He's right about one thing. He's good at what he does.

We get to the part with the pause—the dramatic break before the chorus—and then something amazing happens. There's my breath. It's so real and beautiful and raw. He left that in there…from the last take. I can't help it and my eyes fly to his, and I'm startled when I find they're waiting for me.

"You like that," he smiles.

"I do!" I say, realizing I'm yelling too. We're alone in here, though. And we both have the music playing loud in our ears.

"I was so excited when you did that. I pulled it out and was like *oh yeah*," he says, lifting his feet from the floor and pushing himself to spin around once in his chair. The cord wraps around his body, so he shimmies his feet against the floor in the opposite direction to unwind it.

I giggle, and cover my mouth when I realize. He narrows his eyes on me, smirking, then pushes the arm of my chair around so I loop in a circle too, then he stands and begins wrapping more of the cord around my arms and head, crossing over my nose and eyes.

"Untangle me," I laugh, fighting to free myself.

"Not until you admit it," he says, spinning my chair one last time, hard enough that my headphones unplug and the sound of me singing breaks into the air of the studio. I look up and my mouth falls open, but slowly works into a smile.

"Admit what?" I ask, my hands outstretched, but only the few inches they can reach being pinned to my sides with cable cord.

80

He's teasing me. I'm teasing back. I've left the back row and stepped into the spotlight just now and it's not scary. It's nice.

"That you're special. Listen to that…and tell me you're not," he says, resting against the small desk by the console and folding his arms over his chest.

"I'm…" I begin, a small shake of my head. My own voice hits the final notes of the song, and the beat slows. I'm the blueprint. Casey is the artist. "I'm grateful."

His head sags to the left and his eyes blink once slowly before coming to rest on me again. Being tied up—though I know I can easily escape—and under his scrutiny, does something to me, and the longer his eyes stay set on mine, the hotter I become.

"What?" I finally ask, looking down, my neck what is I'm sure the color of a beet.

"You're something," he says, reaching out a leg and nudging my chair an inch or two away from him. I shrug.

"Can you untangle me?" I plead.

He lets out a heavy, exaggerated sigh.

"Oh, I suppose," he says, unwinding me and draping the cord lightly around my body until I'm free.

When his phone buzzes on the console, I take the opportunity to stand and work out some of the nervous energy in my legs and arms. With my back to him, I shake my head one more time in disbelief.

"So, what happens now?" I ask.

"Uhhhh," Casey begins. I turn to see him squinting at his phone, reading something. He puts it down where it was and begins shutting off controls, clearly affected by whatever he read. "I need to get time with John. Which…don't worry. I will."

"Okay," I say.

He's moved into a rather manic mode, cleaning up the studio and making sure things are shut off and put back in place, so I turn my attention to my guitar, opening my case and putting it away.

"Does he listen to things right away?" I ask, my eyes noting how agitated he's become. He's nervous about something. Shit…I bet we really aren't supposed to be here.

Casey's stepped into the sound booth now and is looking over things in there, moving the mic back in place and scanning the floor and the outlets. He rubs his chin as he stands in the center of the room, his eyes down and looking at nothing. He's rattled. He pulls his hat off and scratches at his head before glancing up and realizing I'm watching. Only then does he force a smile back in place.

"I'm sorry, what?" he asks, but his smile isn't a solid one.

"Nothing, was just wondering how long he takes to listen. I'm patient though…" I say as he locks up the small sound booth.

"I'm hoping right away, but I guess I'll have to wait and see," he says through a deep breath. His chest seems heavier all of a sudden.

He swings the key ring around his thumb a few times, his eyes once again lost, looking toward the door to the hallway. After a few seconds, he holds them up and looks at me. "I need to make sure these are back at the front desk. Be right back?" he says, almost asking permission to leave me alone.

I nod and lean against the table, the handle of my guitar case in my hand because I have a weird sensation that I might need to make a break for it now. The door swings shut behind him, but doesn't latch completely. I tip it open slightly and catch the sight of him walking down the hall, his arms swinging, his steps normal—he isn't running. I can still hear the other group faintly down the hall. We aren't totally alone, which gives me some relief that maybe I'm wrong.

His phone buzzes again. And again. At the third buzz, I grow dangerously curious, so I slide from my position toward the console, glancing through the small glass window in the door before flipping the phone over on the table.

I can only see the beginning of messages.

Christina: You can't keep ignoring this…
Myra: Christina said you haven't called…
Myra: It's so bad, Casey. We need you…

82

I flip the phone back over. It's personal. Whatever that is—Myra and Christina. Whoever they are. Something's bad. They need him. And…what if it's an emergency?

I glance at the door again and step closer, to gain a better view through the small window. I don't see him, and the hallways are quiet, so I'll probably hear him coming.

My thumb moves back to the phone, and I hover over it for a second, pretty sure I'm invading his privacy, but something is definitely weird. The phone buzzes again, making my decision for me, and I flip it over again.

Christina: He's going to die, Case. We're meeting with…

I swipe the phone awake and touch the message icon.

…Hospice.

I swallow.

Casey walks in.

His eyes move right to the spot mine were—to the phone pinned under my finger—to the open message. We both freeze in our positions—me because I'm not sure if there's a way to delicately extricate myself out of this, and because of what I just read; him because he clearly knows I've just read his messages.

"It was buzzing…a lot…and I…" I say, a tear threatening my composure.

I hear Casey swallow. He steps closer to me, dragging the phone out of my hold with his forefinger. He twists it so it's facing him. I hold my breath, careful not to make any sound. I don't want his eyes to come to me. I don't want him not to read everything there waiting for him. Something is wrong.

He sniffles finally, a slight sound—a manly kind of sniffle that indicates he's pretending and whatever he does next is going to be bullshit.

"You know your way home?" he asks, his eyes shifting to mine, his mouth flat.

What?

"I'm sure I can figure it out, but…" I say, but he turns from me when he's heard what he wanted.

"Okay, good. I'll call you when I have the final ready, and when I've had a chance to meet with John," he says.

He's moving toward the door, and without warning, he flicks the light off, and I'm standing in the cascade of florescent hallway illumination coming through the half-open door propped by his forearm.

Okay. So, we're going to just leave. And whatever that was is…it's none of my business. He's right. It's none of my business.

I step under his arm out the door, and I follow him down the same corridor I did on the way in. As quiet as it was then, it's even more so now—and not just because the sun has gone down. This silence—it's almost palpable. I taste it.

We walk through the back door, through the group of guys still hanging around smoking, and one of them nudges Casey, asking him for a lighter. He shakes his head that he doesn't have one, then adjusts the hat on his head, smoothing his hair underneath and rolling his shoulders as if he's trying to lose something—a burden perhaps. He walks me to my car, and takes my guitar from my arm without even asking. I let him, and move to my trunk, opening it and watching him quietly lay it back inside.

"I hope you enjoyed that," he says, only half of him smiling. His eyes are warring against the smile though—they want to go back to being lost in thought, so I don't keep him.

"I did. Very much," I say, laughing lightly and swinging my arm toward the handle of my car door. I pause with my fingers on the latch. "I know it didn't look like it, but…but I did. I enjoyed that very much."

I glance up at him and his eyes are waiting. His hands deep in his pockets, he merely lets out a small breath and smiles tightly. So much locked behind that façade. He can't hide that he's shaken, but he's stubborn enough not to share any of whatever it is with me. Or maybe I'm just too afraid to ask.

"Drive safe," he says, pulling one hand from his pocket and swinging it toward me. It grazes against my side, and I shudder from the touch. At least he's too distracted to notice.

I watch him spin on one leg and walk away, his shoulders high and his hands both tucked away again in his pockets. His head is slung low, his eyes on his feet, careful not to look too far ahead. Casey's future is like that, I'm guessing.

As he rounds the building, I slip into my car and start my engine, letting the tear finally fall, but only halfway down my cheek before I swipe it away. I'm not even sure why I'm crying, only that…I felt something. I felt something for him, because of him, or maybe it was that I felt *him*—his pain. Whatever. It's private, and I shouldn't have looked.

Just like I shouldn't have driven around the building as I left and paused at the exit long enough to catch his reflection in my mirror. The sound my blinker makes is assaulting—*clicker-clonker, clicker-clonker, clicker*... That sound drowns out everything else. I can't hear him. But I see him pounding on the roof of his car with two angry fists, his hat wadded in the right one. I see him kick at the door until I think he may have dented it, or broken his foot. I watch as he throws his hat against the metal side and grasps the edge of his car with both hands, hanging his head forward until his body shakes.

I see him completely fall apart for a full minute and a half. And then I watch him wash it all away, picking up his hat, smoothing out his hair before placing it on his head, climbing into his car, and driving to the opposite end of the parking lot.

CHAPTER 7

Casey

Sometime around three in the morning, I quit punishing myself with guilt for not going to see my family and replaced it with obsessing over Murphy. That's also around the time I sobered up after having three shots of whiskey the second I came in the door.

Okay…four shots of whiskey.

And a beer.

And three beers.

And by sober, I mean…I mean lucid.

It's a miracle I didn't drunk dial her.

My yearbooks are all at my parents' house, which is just putting myself back into the cycle of thinking about that thing that I'm not going to let myself think about. I spent the last two hours searching online for plan *B*. Plan *B*, of course, in my *lucid* state, was to find some land of all yearbooks online where I would be able to type in Murphy Sullivan and get a magic play-by-play of all of her high school greatest hits.

What clubs she was in.

What dances she went to.

Who she dated.

Who her friends were.

And…most importantly…what she looked like.

Of course, now the *truly* sober, and slightly hung-over, me knows that the magic yearbook-land is a crazy figment of my imagination, and I wasted a shitload of time on Google a few hours ago. My fuzzy mind is also in this weird place—like I'm on the verge of making a connection. I remember her, and I can even sorta, kinda, almost, make out what she looked like at seventeen. But I know if I could just get my hands on a photo, see a picture, it would clear it up.

Which is why I'm joining Houston and Leah for breakfast this morning.

"Juice me," I say, opening the back door to the sound of frying bacon and the sweet scent of Joyce Orr's cooking.

"Do you ever knock?" Houston says, flipping over a notebook on the table next to his breakfast, only glancing up for a second before scribbling more notes. He shoves a piece of toast in his mouth and mumbles to himself.

"Are we grouchy because we forgot to study and have a test today?" I tease.

Houston looks over to his mother, confirming her back is turned, and then flips me off.

"Mrs. Orr, your son just gave me the finger," I whine.

"Houston, your daughter's at the breakfast table. Show some class," she says, never once turning away from the bacon in front of her.

Houston leans back and rolls his eyes, landing them squarely on me.

"Seriously," he breathes.

"You started it," I say.

"Uhm…okay. Whatever," he shakes his head and returns to his notepad. "I did stay up late studying, for one test…but not the other. I had to practice my Spanish over the phone with Paige. I'm passing that class this summer if it kills me. The other test, this one," he lifts the pad and lets it fall back to the table, "is just programming. I'll be ready in five more minutes."

I nod and slide out a seat at the table just in time for Joyce to put a plate of bacon and eggs in front of me and hand me a fork. She pats the top of my head like I'm seven. I love it. I love coming here. This house—it's always been more of a home than any other place on earth. My mom's half Italian, and her parents—my grandparents—were very loud and proud people, big on hugs and family. When I was really little, maybe five or six, I remember holidays with a full house and the smell of food. But when her parents passed, all of that sort of stopped.

My dad comes from a different world. His parents were hard workers, nose-to-the-grindstone people, and he was their only kid. Their house was always in perfect order, and I hated going there; I wasn't allowed to touch anything. I'm pretty sure my parents had a big family because kids made my mom happy. If Dad had his way, I think they would have stopped at my sister, Christina. Because there were so many of us, I still got to experience being the runt of the litter with four big, loud, embrace-your-Italian roots sisters to beat my ass at every turn. Things only got quiet when Dad came home.

Home.

Hospice.

I shake away the thoughts creeping in, and dig into my breakfast, massive forkfuls of egg all at once. My plate is clean in less than a minute, and I prop my elbows on either side and run the napkin over my mouth.

"Daddy? Can I wear a robe to pre-school like Unco Casey?" Leah asks. She's now standing next to me, tugging on the red, velvet sleeve on my arm.

"No, sweetie," Houston says, standing from the table and reaching for her. He slings her up on his hip and touches her nose. "Uncle Casey is dressed like a bum, and I just don't think that's a good way to go to school."

"All right," Leah says, her voice disappointed. I'm rooting for the puppy eyes, because what's wrong with going to school looking like a bum? *Get your way, Leah!*

Houston sets her down and pats her butt once as she sprints up the stairs to finish getting dressed.

"So what's the deal? Why are you wearing your hangover robe?" Houston asks, sliding his notebook and laptop into his backpack.

"Uhm, probably because I'm hungover," I say, not thinking that Joyce is standing nearby. She smacks the back of my head and points at me. It hurts. "I'm sorry," I say to her.

She points at me once more with gritted teeth, just for emphasis. Over the years, Joyce has pointed at me like that a lot.

"Recording with Murph not go quite as planned?" Houston asks after his mom walks away.

88

"It was good," I say, splaying my hands flat on the now-empty tabletop in front of me. I rap my fingers against the wood a few times, playing out Murphy's melody in rhythm—only I can really hear it. "Hey, you still have your yearbooks?"

My transition into the real reason I'm here is neither suave nor subtle, and Houston chuckles.

"You still don't really remember her, do you?" he asks.

"I do, I do," I say, pulling my hat off and resting it on the table. Joyce walks by quickly and snags it, placing it on a hook by the door. I smile at it and run my fingers through my messy hair. "It just...I have this hazy picture, and now that we're hanging out..."

I don't know how to finish that sentence, so I shrug and roll my neck a few times.

"You want to know more about her," Houston finally fills in.

"I don't know..." I say, not able to look him in the eye. My lips purse.

He doesn't prod. He also doesn't say anything for about fifteen seconds, and it makes me really uncomfortable. For fifteen long seconds, my stomach squeezes and I picture her hands strumming her guitar, grazing over the small butterfly painted on the wood. I think about how one of the wings is larger than the other, and how her brother—Lane—probably painted it there for her. I think about that time in her house. I think about the stupid Bioré strip I let her put on my nose. And how cute hers was.

"You do," Houston finally says through a light chuckle, breaking me from my thoughts. I nod just enough for him to notice and let my eyes meet his to admit my guilt.

He jerks his head toward the stairs, and I follow him into the hallway closet. He pulls a few boxes from a top shelf, finally sliding one out labeled HIGH SCHOOL STUFF, and then hands it to me.

"They're probably in here, but I've gotta get Leah to pre-school and head to campus for my test. Just throw them in the box and leave it in the hallway when you're done," he says.

"Right on," I say, bumping his fist.

He laughs under his breath, but I ignore him and step into his room, dropping the heavy box on his bed and discarding the various certificates and photo collages his mom made. I dive into our senior one first, because that one's probably the closest to her looking like the version of her I know now. Our classes weren't very big, so I get to the page of *S* students quickly and scan until I see her name.

Murphy Lynn Sullivan: Theater, Chorus, Future Business Leaders of America. I smirk at how that third one doesn't match the other two—or her. I run my thumb toward the center of the book and then I land on a very plain, quiet-looking blonde. Her hair is wavy, like it is now, and it's long enough to cut off at the bottom of the picture. It isn't purple, and other than a large flower pin on the side of her head, tucking back a small braid, there isn't much that's flashy or memorable. All this picture does is confirm my hazy memory. This is how I pictured her, and I'm starting to think that maybe that's what she was in high school—a haze.

I flip through the pages until I get to the section for group photos, stopping at the chorus one and running my finger over every penny-sized head until I find one in the middle that looks like it *might* be her. This photo doesn't help, so I flip through more pages to the theater section, repeating my process on the group shot until I get to her. She's standing in the front on this one, wearing a dress that looks a little more like the kind I see her in now. It's red with large black polka dots, and she's wearing black tights and Doc Martins. The image still isn't familiar, but it makes me smile.

Hoping for more, I flip the page and am greeted with a spread of photos from the various plays performed at the school. I'm about to give up that she's in here when one on the bottom right catches my eye. Her hair is darker in this photo—I think maybe dyed—and she's wearing a dress that looks like its made of rags. She's clutching another girl around the waist and looking out into nothing. Her eyes—the gray—*my god.*

My god.

She's somehow appearing to cry without tears. I think about how if she hits it big in music, I'd put her eyes on her first cover. I should tell her that. Right after I tell her that I'm crazy, and that I apparently stalk her and stole my best friend's yearbook so I could bring it home and look at this photo when I can't sleep at night.

I toss the rest of the photos and papers back into the box and leave it by the closet as Houston asked, then head down the stairs and give a short goodbye to Joyce as I grab my hat from the hook and leave, the yearbook tucked inside my robe. I don't reveal it until I'm in the safety of my car, and I laugh at myself, because I'm behaving absurdly. Joyce would tell me to just take it, and Houston hasn't looked at it in years. There aren't even many signatures in it, other than mine.

Before I pull out from the driveway, I flip the book open against my steering wheel and land on that picture wishing I could black out everything but her. I read the caption—which says the play was *Helen Keller* starring Murphy Sullivan—and smile. Of course, she starred in the play where the lead never speaks. I linger on her eyes for another minute before forcing myself to slide the book to the passenger seat to drive home. I leave it open, though, because I want to look at it a few more times.

I want to remember her more.

I want to go back in time and get to know this girl. Of course, then maybe she'd never write an anthem about me, and then she'd never have this shot that she has right now—this shot to make it, to have a hit that people play on the radio and download on iTunes. And she's got one. I couldn't trade her dream for my own gain. And that's a first for me.

That's an *only*.

Murphy

It didn't take much.

Lane asked if he could see Casey again sometime, and suddenly I found myself in the car on the highway headed south toward his apartment with Lane in tow—at least, toward what I *hope* is his apartment. I Googled him and this is what came up.

I probably should have called and asked if he was home, or at least called to confirm his address. That would have been smart. But then he would have had the opportunity to tell me he was fine, and I wouldn't have known for sure, because I feel like a person kind of needs to *see* someone to really get a read on how fine they are.

"Do you think Casey will let me play music on his stuff? Does he have stuff like that at home…like at the studio? Like you described? Can I record a song, too?"

Lane has been super curious about how the whole recording thing works ever since I got home last night. Frankly, it was nice having his questions there to distract me. It kept me excited and thinking about the song and what might happen to it. It kept my thoughts on how it sounded when Casey put the headset on my ears. It reminded me of the smile on his face when I listened.

I didn't dive into the other visual—the one of him falling to pieces—until Lane went to bed. And then, I thought about nothing else. When sleep came, I dreamt his pain.

The irony that this one guy I wanted to never—not ever—notice me, is now not only consuming my thoughts and dreams, but he's spurred me to action. I filled up the tank and drove the forty-five miles or so to the other side of the city suburbs just to make sure he's okay. All under the pretense that my brother wanted to see if they could hang out.

I laugh once out loud as I wait at the light before the last right turn that leads to his apartment, a light rain beginning to fall and dust my windshield. I'm being ridiculous. I have no plan beyond knocking on the door. He's going to think I'm nuts.

"You should turn on the wipers," Lane says, swaying his fingers back and forth in front of his face.

I smile and thank him, pushing the button to clear the window. I leave them on low, and by the time we park in the only free space along the road near Casey's apartment, the rain is pouring down. I should leave. This is a really stupid idea.

"You ready? We should run," Lane says.

I'm letting him call the shots. Coming was his idea. I keep lying to myself.

"Right," I smile, pulling my purse from the floor in the back and clutching it to my front as I pull the keys from the ignition. "On the count of three, okay?"

"Okay," Lane agrees.

"One," I begin, pausing for several seconds as my eyes watch the rain blur everything on the other side of the window. I shouldn't say *two*. I should leave, go home and wait—wait for him to call about the song and forget everything else. Quit worrying about things that don't concern me.

"Two," Lane finally says, clearly ready to run, his hand poised on the door handle.

My breath hitches with fear, but he doesn't turn to look at me. He doesn't catch subtleties, and he's locked in on this visit. He wants to see his new friend. I nod and bat my lashes slowly. These next five minutes—they're going to hurt.

"Three!" I shout, and we both fling our doors open, slamming them in our wakes as we spring up the slick walkway toward the door marked one twenty-nine.

There's a small eave above the door, and it shields most of us from the rain, but with every gust of wind, our backs are pelted with freezing cold water. Summer storms in Oklahoma are not to be reckoned with.

"Casey! It's us!" My brother is yelling and pounding a fist on the door, and my eyes are lit up like stadium lights. Oh my god!

"Dude, Casey's…" starts a man wearing an outfit that looks like it came right off of Mr. Rogers. He twists his head to one side as his eyes bounce between me and my brother. "He's not home…yet?"

He says it like a question. Am I supposed to know where Casey is?

"I'm sorry. We should have called first," I say, putting my arm around Lane, whose shoulders are about as sloped as an anthill now.

"He'll be home soon. It's…it's fine; come on in," the guy says as we're turning to leave.

I'm about to argue that it's all right when Lane shrugs off my hold and steps around me, into the dark apartment. I have no choice but to follow.

"Okay, thank you," I say, my lips tingly with the awkward smile I'm forcing on my face.

"I'm Eli," the man says, rubbing his right hand dry from the soda he was holding, but has now switched to his left hand. He holds his palm out to shake, and I do.

"I'm Murphy," I smile.

His eyes squint and a smirk begins on his lips as he points a finger at me.

"Yeah, you're the chick with the song, right?" he asks, stumbling ahead of me toward the couch. He quickly grabs a few open gaming magazines and closes them, setting them on the coffee table before picking up no less than six empty beer cans. He shakes out a blanket that's wadded in the middle of the sofa and spreads it out.

"Have a seat," he smiles, gesturing to the couch.

Lane leaps into the far corner of the sofa, and I slide to sit close to him, a little self-conscious that we're soaking his couch and the knit throw he put down to protect it.

"So, the song?" Eli asks again.

"Yeah, that's me," I smile.

"Casey's going to make my sister famous," Lane says, his cheeks like cherries and his smile beaming. I glance from him to Eli and shrug, hoping he understands that my brother is sort of an optimist. He sees the world in bright colors, full of possibilities. I wish I were more like him. I'm working on it.

"I bet he is," Eli says softly. He isn't making a joke or mocking us; he's being kind.

"Can I get you anything to drink?" Eli asks, and before I can answer, Casey's voice booms from behind me.

"No more shots, man. I can't drink any more of that shit in the bottle today…" he trails off as he steps into the living room, a

94

plastic bag looped around one arm. His eyes land on me with surprise.

"I'm sorry. We should have called," I say, tucking the folds of my skirt under my legs nervously. "We can go...if you have plans."

"No!" he cuts in quickly. Eli chuckles and walks into the kitchen, and I catch Casey glaring at him briefly before looking back at me. "No, I'm glad you're here. I uh...I got some sandwiches from the store. Houston...he works there, and he makes them at the deli. I didn't get enough, but they're big, so..."

I stand and start to open my mouth to protest, feeling awkward about him offering Lane and me part of his dinner, but the words fail me at first. I'm tired, and it's hard to articulate when I'm tired sometimes, so I stutter. The *i* sound of *it's okay* all that I can repeat while my mouth stretches awkwardly. Casey's eyes flinch when it happens, and I stop speaking immediately.

"You know what? They can have mine. It's cool. I was actually about to head out," Eli says.

His gesture is sweet, but it only makes me feel worse, because I can tell he really wasn't planning on going out. Before I can stop it, though, Lane is already thanking them both and taking the bag from Casey to take into the kitchen.

"Your brother's pretty comfortable around me," he chuckles.

"Yeah," I nod, a tight smile holding in the overwhelming need to vomit my nerves all over the living room.

Silence settles in again, and Eli, Casey, and I are standing around the small coffee table in their living room—them with hands in their pockets and me with my skirt bunched in my fists at my side. At one point, Eli actually whistles and sways forward, which makes Casey and me laugh.

"All right, kids. This looks like a fun night, so...you three have a good time, and I'll see you in the morning, Case," Eli says, patting his friend on the shoulder as he moves over to the wall behind their front door. He pulls a bike from a metal rack mounted on the wall and walks it outside, closing the door behind him.

"He's going for a bike ride?" I ask, my eyes fixated on the now shut door.

"Yep," Casey says.

"In the rain?" I ask.

"It appears so," he says.

It takes me a few seconds to flit my eyes in his direction, and when I catch his looking over me, he turns away quickly.

"What's in these?" Lane yells from the kitchen.

"Turkey and ham. Pick your favorite, and Murphy and I will split the other," Casey answers, one side of his mouth raised in a smile at me. "I hate ham, so I hope he picks that one," Casey whispers.

"I'll take turkey. Thanks, Casey," Lane responds, and Casey laughs silently along with me.

"Sounds great, buddy," he says loudly through stifled laughter.

Eventually, the funny fades and his expression shifts into something more understated. There's a hint of smile there and his eyes are sort of dancing. They can't seem to leave mine, and the scrutiny makes me hot and fidgety until I finally have to look away and join my brother in the kitchen.

"Sorry for the surprise visit. Lane wanted to see some of your equipment, and…" I start, but Casey interrupts.

"It's fine," he smiles, pulling two plates from a cabinet and setting the sandwich on one to cut in half. He slices it unevenly, giving me the bigger piece, then glances up when he's done, sliding the plate in my direction, the slight smirk back again. "You can come here any time."

I nod, then turn my focus to the sandwich on my plate, taking a bite that is probably far too big for me and definitely way unfeminine. I have to chew with my mouth open for the first few seconds, but it's better than locking gazes with him. He's looking at me like he knows a secret. Or maybe…

"Are you drunk?" I ask.

He chokes on his bite and pounds at his chest with a fist through his laughter.

"Right now? No. About twelve hours ago? Definitely," he laughs.

"Oh," I say, looking back to my sandwich. I bring it to my mouth and take another ridiculous-sized bite, my eyes busy reading the ingredients on the back of a bottle of soy sauce sitting out on the counter.

We all chew in silence for a few minutes, and I memorize the first sentence on the soy sauce label: ALL PURPOSE, NATURALLY BREWED AND OVER 300 YEARS OF EXCELLENCE. That feels like a really long time to be excellent at soy. I'm working on the second line when my brother pipes in, folding the paper around half of his sandwich.

"I'm full," he says, pushing the paper toward the sink. Casey grabs it before it falls in.

"That's okay; I'll eat the rest," he says, winking at me. He's hardly touched the ham.

"Can I see your recording equipment?" Lane asks.

"Lane, let him finish his dinner," I say, mouthing an apology at Casey. He shrugs it off.

"Sure…yeah, let me set you up with something in my room. Come with me," he says, fingering over his shoulder. My brother practically skips after him, and I follow them a few steps behind.

I wait at the entry to his room, watching while he twists my brother toward his desk and shows him his headphones. He pulls a mic forward next, unwinding the cord and plugging it into a jack on the side of his laptop.

"You can sing or talk or make whatever sound in here, then this…" he pauses, dragging his finger over the touchscreen to open up a set of files, "is where you can mix it with other sounds. If you find something you like, hold it like this…and drag it down here. When you think you're done, hit the play button and put these on to see how it sounds."

"Awesome," my brother breathes out, his feet kicking nervously under the chair he's sitting in.

It doesn't take Lane long to begin, and Casey eyes back toward the kitchen with a smile. "I have a turkey sandwich with my name on it," he grins. I giggle and follow him out of the room, leaving my brother's heartfelt but off-key vocals in the room with the door mostly closed.

"Thanks for doing that," I say, picking at the edge of my bread. I'm not really that hungry, but I don't want to waste the sandwich Eli gave up. I'm picking at it to make it look like I gave it hell.

"Of course," he says. "If he wants, I can take him to a gig sometime and show him how I mix for a club."

"He'd like that," I smile at him. His eyes linger on me again, like they have since we've arrived. It's arresting.

"Are you...okay?" I ask, partly to turn the focus away from him looking at me.

It works, and his gaze falls to his plate, where he's now picking at the edge of his bread too. He tears away a piece of cheese and pokes it in his mouth, nodding slowly. Eventually, he pushes the sandwich away, and I feel double amounts of guilt. Two sandwiches wasted.

"My dad's sick," he says, his eyes narrowed and his attention on the smooth counter before him. He runs his hand along it, pushing a few small crumbs into the sink.

"Casey, I'm so very sorry," I say, remembering everything I saw on his phone.

"Don't be. It's...it just is what it is, I guess," he says, looking up. His eyes hit mine like stones through glass. There's the hint of tears in them, but he laughs them away quickly with a sharp guttural sound. "It's...cancer, I guess. I don't really know much. I...we don't...talk."

He leaves that thought in the air and closes his lips tight, keeping his gaze on me. My head falls to one side as I imagine how that's even possible. My father travels between here and Dallas a lot for the few rental properties they have. He's the handyman for them. But he always comes home. I can't imagine life if one day he just...didn't. I can't imagine what it would be like for my mom.

"Casey—" I begin, but he starts to talk again.

98

"I never really wanted to beat to his drum," he says, his gaze falling back to the counter, where his hands push together, his fingers forming a diamond. "My dad's an engineer. So's my mom. My sisters are all successful, all...you guessed it...engineers," he chuckles once, but his mouth remains a flat line. "Except for my oldest sister, but that's because she's a lawyer. And her path was...I don't know...acceptable?"

He glances up for a moment and shrugs.

"I'm sure it sounds petty and stupid. I mean, every parent wants their child to be successful. It's not cruel; it's wanting something good for your kid. But..."

He stops mid-sentence and purses his lips, taking in a long deep breath as he drags his fingertips along the counter, rounding it as he walks a path toward the couch. I follow him, sitting on a chair opposite him. His eyes lock on mine, and it feels sort of like he's waiting for me to give him the answer to some riddle.

"My grandparents were serious people, and my dad's never really said anything, but I know his dad was always pretty strict—like a drill sergeant. This part I only know because my mom told me once. My dad wanted to be an artist," he says, his eyes moving from the floor to my face, his mouth open and aghast as if he's hearing this himself for the first time. "Fucker was apparently this brilliant painter. When he met my mom, he painted her portrait and gave it to her as a gift. I've seen the painting. It's wrapped up in sheets in their attic. I'm pretty sure he has no clue my mom still has it."

"Why would he hide it? I don't understand," I say.

"Because it makes him weak," he laughs, stopping quickly, his face falling into a serious expression. "He got into this really great art school in Rhode Island, and he was going to go there, study, and maybe try painting in Paris or London for a semester. And then he told his father the plan."

"He didn't approve?" I ask.

His eyes find mine again, and they grow dark.

"He beat the shit out of my dad. Hit him so hard he lost sight in one of his eyes. He ruined him. My dad tells everyone that he was born that way—even us kids. But my mom knows the truth," he says.

"And she told you..." I fill in.

"She told me," he repeats. "She was trying to explain why he is the way he is, why he's so set on me becoming an engineer, why he basically kicked me out of his life when I wouldn't bend to his rules."

"Why would he do all that? Wouldn't he be just the opposite? Wouldn't he *want* you to follow your dream since he wasn't allowed to?" I ask.

Casey breathes a short laugh and leans forward, folding his hands in front of him with his elbows on his knees.

"I guess there are a lot of ways broken people heal. For my dad, he twisted everything around in his head—probably focused on some of the shit my grandfather had said when he was hitting him. You know what he said when I told him I was going into deejaying and sound mixing?" Casey pauses, his eyes sweeping toward me slowly.

"What?" I whisper.

"He said 'dreams are excuses for not doing what *needs* to be done in life,'" he says, chewing at his bottom lip as his eyes trail away from me again.

I don't have an answer for him. I wish I did, but that kind of dynamic, that style of parenting—my family is as opposite as it could possibly be from the Coffield house. Dreams in the Sullivan house are fluid—growing, and changing, and always reachable. Limits are hurdles you just jump over. Unless, of course, you're me and your fears loom larger than life. But even my fears are things my parents have always believed could be overcome. I guess I *am* overcoming them. I guess they were right.

"You want to see something?" Casey asks, bringing my attention back to him. He's leaning forward and looking at me from the side, his head tilted and his smile crooked. There's a light in his eyes, and it's the first time I've ever seen it.

"Yes," I smile.

100

He nods and sucks in his bottom lip, looking back down at his folded hands, his thumbs tapping together nervously, almost as if he's working up nerve.

"Okay. Come with me," he says, directing me back to his room.

Lane looks at us when we walk in, the music playing loudly in his headphones. He gives us both a thumbs up, and Casey reaches his knuckles forward for Lane to tap with his own fist. My brother does and laughs loudly, louder than normal, thanks to the volume in his ears. He turns his attention back to the computer and begins moving more sounds into the timeline to play. I glance over his shoulder and realize he's moved about fifty of them in there, and my eyes grow wide. Casey places a hand on my shoulder and looks over with me, stunning me and quickly turning my attention to the feel of his breath so close to my neck.

"Wow, he's really into farm sounds, huh?" he laughs.

"Ha ha, yeah...I guess," I say, the words coming out robotic.

Casey's hand drops from my shoulder quickly, and slowly I unfreeze and become human again. I spin and see him reaching into his closet for a small box on the top shelf. He pulls it down and sets it on his bed, nodding for me to come sit next to him. On his bed. Which is poorly made and has sheets that look so very masculine along with this fuzzy blanket with tiger print and...yeah...just as I figured, the bed is soft.

"You okay?" he asks.

I shake off my teenage jitters and clear my throat before scooting back and folding my dress under my leg so I can tuck one under the other. "Uhm, yeah...just getting comfortable," I lie.

Casey leaves his gaze on me for a second, his eyebrows dipped just enough that I can tell he's not completely believing my bullshit.

"What's in the box?" I ask, changing the subject.

It works. He raises the lid, setting it to the side, and pulls out a few brochures and design schematics along with a stack of business cards that read LEAP RECORDS. I hold one up and turn it to face him.

"What's Leap Records?" I ask.

"That's my studio," he says, his lip raised on one side.

I stare at him for a few seconds—waiting for him to say he's kidding—then turn my focus back to the card in my hand. There's a logo, a phone number, his name. I set the cards down and flip through some of the other things, stopping when I get to a photo of an old gas station with boarded-up windows and busted red pumps out front. I turn it toward him, and he grins, taking it from my hand and laying it flat on the bed between us. He pulls out the roll of blue prints and opens one up, lying it down next to the photo.

"This is the building I want. It's been vacant for years—since I was a kid," he says. "I'm going to earn enough to buy it, then I'm going to gut the insides and build out a recording studio. I had the blueprints done a year ago. A guy I know from school, he was studying architecture—he did them. And Houston's girlfriend, her name's Paige—she made me a logo and designed these cards for me. She's got an eye for things like that," he says, his smile pushing dimples into both of his cheeks.

I watch as he pulls out a few more things, telling me his plans, where he wants to put things, why he loves this building. When he was little, they had to pull over into the parking lot once to look up directions to some office building in the city where his oldest sister had an interview for a scholarship. Casey started wandering around the vacant parking lot, peeking his head through small cracks in the boards to see inside. At the time, he thought the building was just the perfect place to play ditch 'em with his friends. But when he was in high school, and started to get into house music, the studio idea hit him.

"Casey, this is amazing," I say, picking up each drawing, each scribble of an idea. I continue to look for a full minute before glancing up at him, his happy eyes waiting. His prideful expression turns into bashful, and his cheeks actually begin to redden, which strikes me even more. It makes him human. It makes me like him. It makes me *really* like him.

"Anyway," he says, rolling his head to the side and looking down at the things all on display. He rubs his hand on his neck, and some of his happiness begins to disappear, his smile fading fast. "It's just this stupid dream."

All traces of the youthful dreamer from seconds before are gone. He begins to roll up the plans and tuck the photos and cards back into the box. The only thing left is a hat with the logo Paige designed on the front. I grab it in my hands before he has a chance to put it away, and when he looks up at me, I stuff it on my head.

He blinks a few times, but slowly, the smile starts to reappear. It's not as big as before, but there's a hint of it on his lips.

"That looks good on you," he says.

I giggle.

"Thanks," I say, pulling it off and pushing my stray hairs back behind my ears.

I fold the back of the hat into the front and hand it to him, but he keeps it out of the box. After a few seconds, he looks at my brother, a kind of calmness shading his face while he watches Lane build the world's most complex farm-animal anthem and layer it with old-school Tupac.

"They're setting him up with hospice," he says. I can tell he's still watching Lane, so as badly as I want to look at him, to engage him while he shares this with me, I don't. I think he needs to focus on anything else in order to keep talking. "That's what the texting was about. My mom—she wants to have us all over, to have a semi-normal dinner like a family or something…while we can."

"That…that makes sense," I say, knowing he doesn't want to hear *sorry.*

We both watch Lane, and the few times my brother turns around, we give him encouraging gestures—raising thumbs, clapping and waving. We watch him in silence while my brother's ears are filled with his own soundtrack. All we hear is his clicking and the occasional overflow from his headset. The quiet doesn't seem to bother either of us, and it isn't uncomfortable. It just *is.*

"Will you come with me?" Casey asks finally.

Part of me knew he wanted to. I have a feeling he's been thinking about asking me since he walked in and saw me in his apartment. We've only spent a few hours together over a handful of days, but already I see how codependent he can be. My mind has been working in the background this whole time to find a way to tell him *no* when he asked. I can't take this on for him. We're friends, maybe. Business partners for sure, but now…maybe friends. And it's all still new. I shouldn't be at their table for something so personal when I don't even have a splinter of understanding. It wouldn't be fair to any of them.

I don't answer right away, instead letting my brother turn to me one more time, pull his headphones free and unplug them so we can hear his masterpiece. We both praise him, Casey even going so far as to clap along with the surprisingly spot-on beat my brother managed to build into his strange little song. When the music finishes, he turns back to his computer and replaces the headphones, going in to add more.

Casey's attention is still on Lane, but I can feel him grow more tense at my side. He's anxious, and he's scared. I can't be that crutch though.

I suck in my bottom lip, breathing courage in through my nose while I form the right words that will let him down easy—words that will give him the strength to get through this on his own, words that are sensitive and full of sympathy, but that aren't self sacrificing, because I…I'm not that person to him. There must be someone better. Anyone would be better, wouldn't they?

"Casey, I—"

"Please," he whispers before I finish. I shift to look at him, but he doesn't break his concentration on my brother. His eyes are terrified, glassy, and red. He swallows hard to keep the pain at bay just as his eyes close and his breath comes in ragged. This is the man I saw in the parking lot—the one wearing his pain.

"Yes, Casey," I say, feeling his eyes move to look at me. I should say *no*, even with his plea. Going with him to this—it won't be good for me. It's only going to make me feel sorry for him, and I can't do that, because that clouds my judgment. Those lines of trust have already been blurred though. And maybe…maybe they should be. I never really knew him well. Perhaps this is the real Casey Coffield, and the picture I had in my head four years ago was all wrong. Maybe he isn't as selfish as everybody thinks—as *I* think. Maybe he just needs someone who's willing to walk through the fire with him and hold him through the ugly parts.

Maybe I'm stronger than I think.

I keep my focus on Lane even though I feel Casey's eyes on me. I look at my brother because he's brave, and I'm scared. I'm scared because I like this Casey Coffield. I *really* like him.

"I'll go with you."

CHAPTER 8

Casey

"You look nice," Joyce says as I trickle down the last few steps into the Orr's living room.

"Thank you. Tell Houston I'll get this back to him," I say as she leans in and straightens the collar on the gray suit jacket.

"Casey, Houston hasn't worn that thing since high school. I doubt he'll miss it," she says, tugging the front lapels one last time to make sure everything's straight. I smile and she pats my cheek.

I called my sister Christina after Murphy and Lane left my apartment. She didn't tear into me as I expected. She cried. I let her.

She told me that Mom wanted us to dress nice for dinner, like we would for the holidays. I missed the last round of holiday meals at my parents' house, so I was at a loss for what to wear. I called Houston, of course. We've always been the same size. He called his mom, since he wouldn't be home. I can tell she knows the full story—about my dad—but she hasn't brought the reason I need a suit up once.

I didn't mention to Houston that Murphy was coming with me. Not that it's a secret, but it's also not something I want to dissect. Houston wouldn't necessarily say anything, but he would sigh, and there would be that look. I'd like to get through this dinner first. And then I can move on to looks and questions.

Murphy's meeting me at my apartment, and as I glance at my watch, I realize she's probably going to beat me there. Because I'm always late.

I kiss Joyce on the cheek and thank her again, then step out through the back door toward my car in the driveway. Joyce calls after me, and when I turn, she has a small bouquet of flowers wrapped in plastic.

"Here, I almost forgot. Bring these. You don't have to say they're from me. Make them from you…for your mom," she says.

106

I smirk at them, recalling the last time I tried to bring my mom flowers.

"Thanks," I say, taking them in my hand and nodding goodbye one last time.

I get a lucky break on the small distance between Houston's house and my apartment, and somehow manage not to catch a single light. Murphy's still waiting for me in her car along the curb, though. I pull up behind her, and neither of us gets out right away. I know the minute I do, she'll step out of her car and walk toward mine, and then this dinner thing will really happen.

With a deep breath, my eyes set on the face reflecting in the review mirror in front of me, I kill the engine and open my car. I walk to Murphy's car and open her door for her, catching her hand in an awkward moment as she slips sideways on one of her heels and falls into me. Selfishly, I love that's she's so unsteady. Her hand squeezes mine for balance, and the grip draws my focus. She lets go quickly as she rights herself, but my fingers flex wanting her hand back.

"Sorry. I'm...I'm not good in shoes like these," she says, sweeping her uneven skirt to the side and kicking one foot forward to show me her brown shoes that wrap up her leg to her knee. "My friend Sam got them for me a year ago, and I've never worn them."

My eyes stick to her leg because the shoes make them look unbelievably sexy.

"Well, if ever you're going to try out something new, I'd say tonight's the night to try it," I say, my mouth falling into a tight smile.

"Well, that new thing might be walking around barefoot before the night's over," she giggles. "These things hurt like hell."

I glance from her feet to mine, which are in a pair of black Converse. I don't really own dress shoes, and Eli and Houston's feet are nowhere near my size. Murphy notices my feet and kicks her toes forward, catching my attention.

"I should have done that, too," she says.

"Huh?" I shake my head, finally looking up at her, and losing my awareness again the minute I do.

"Worn shoes like that," she explains.

"Oh…yeah," I smile, moving my gaze toward my apartment, pinching my brow and acting as if I'm thinking about something else rather than the way she looks right now. Her dress is this plaid country-style thing that's shorter in the front and long in the back, and it fits her like a corset—hugging every curve and ending at her bare arms. She has a small tattoo on her right shoulder that I've never noticed, and between flits of my eyes from her bare skin to anything else I can think of to look at, I take in the form to see a small music staff with a few notes. Eventually, I give in and look long and hard, and she twists to the side, her chin tucked in to look at it with me.

"I brought a sweater. It's in the car, in case your parents don't like tattoos…" she begins.

"Don't worry about your sweater," I cut in.

I tilt my head and do my best to hum the melody in my head.

"It's the first few bars of 'The Scientist.' You know, by Coldplay?"

I look again, humming along, and I smirk when the recognition hits.

"Why that song?" I say, my eyes moving away from the small line of notes to the rest of her, her arm, the faint pink on her fingernails, her neck, her collarbone, the way the thin gold bracelet clings to her forearm…I feel dizzy and have to look away again.

"Promise you won't laugh?" she asks.

I want to, merely at her question. How could I possibly laugh at her?

I swallow while my head is turned away, then squint as I turn back to look at her, as if this is something I need to think about. I tilt my head to the side and cross my chest with my finger. "Swear," I say.

She sucks in her bottom lip briefly, then lets go of it. The entire scene plays out in slow motion—the way it slides loose from her teeth and quivers with a tiny breath. It's like one of those National Geographic videos I watched when I was a kid—where the flower

108

blooms in an instant with stop-motion photography. Her lips—a flower.

"It's my power song." The words stumble out of her mouth, and her hands fly up to cover the lip I'm staring at. Her cheeks are a shade or two pinker than they were a moment before. I smile, but I don't laugh. I wouldn't at what she said, only at how absolutely captivating every single gesture she makes is.

"Most people go with something like Metallica, or AC/DC or…"

"Van Halen," she says, winking and remembering the small little phrase I picked out on the guitar for her the other day.

"Yeah," I smile. "Van Halen."

She takes in a deep breath, and glances at my car behind me, her mouth poised to speak for a beat before words finally come.

"I guess I just felt like that's what love is supposed to feel like, and it seemed…I don't know…kind of beautiful. Poetic maybe?" Her eyes trail back to mine, and her lips quirk up on one side in an embarrassed smile. "It sounds stupid out loud, but I don't care. It's worth waiting for is all."

"What is?" I ask, my heart beating a little more than I'm used to. I step to the side so she'll follow and begin walking toward my car.

"Anything," she says, pausing right in front of me and looking up—the gray, honest eyes I've become obsessed with catching me in every lie I've ever told. "Everything. If it's worth it, it's worth waiting for."

I suck in my top lip and hold her stare as long as I can.

"Can't laugh at that," I say quietly. Her eyes stay on mine, and my heart squeezes a little. "I like your dress, Murphy. I like it a lot."

She blushes. I breathe.

"Thanks, Casey," she says, looking down as she takes careful steps up the curb to the passenger door. "That means a lot."

Yes, Murphy. I do believe it does.

My parents house isn't far, but far enough that I'm late—again. My sisters don't lecture me, but I think that's only because I walked in with Murphy. She's changed her hair a little—her purple more of a grayish tone now. It looks like silver in winter. I noticed my youngest sister, Annalissa—still older than me—seemed to be quite taken with it. She was the only one, though. The others gave it the same unprofessional stamp of disapproval.

My mom barely looked at us when we walked in. Even her hug felt stilted and unsure. I'm beginning to think that despite my sisters begging me to be here, perhaps I should have stuck to the plan of ignoring everyone. I'm the match in the house filled with kerosene.

"It's pancreatic cancer," Christina says to me, pulling me by the arm to a corner in the kitchen so she can whisper/not whisper. My other sisters are helping set the table, dressing it in the full linens and candles while my mom runs manically around the table, setting out pots of beans and potatoes, bowls of salad and a platter with sliced beef.

"Is he…in his room?" I ask, my eyes darting from every moving person in front of me. The only other person standing still is Murphy, a foot away from me. It's like that game I played when I was a kid—freeze tag—and Murphy and I have been frozen while mania swishes around us.

"He is," Christina says. "He doesn't look bad, but he's already losing weight. I can tell."

"Are they doing…" I swallow and lean into her so my mom doesn't hear me speak. "Is he doing chemo or…radiation or something?"

My sister's eyes meet mine quickly, and she shakes her head in a small motion before looking to our mom to make sure she's still in her blissful state of denial.

"Why?" I mouth.

"There's too much," she whispers. "It's too far along."

I look away from her, back to the quiet chaos and the sounds of cabinets opening and closing.

"You should go up and see him…before he comes down. Go up alone, and talk with him. It would be…I think it'd be good," she says. I think about her suggestion. My sister has always pushed for some sort of reconciliation between us. They all have. But none of them were here to hear the words spoken the first time he disowned me. He called me an embarrassment. No. He called me an abnormality.

He called me a *cancer*. What irony.

"Maybe after dinner," I lie.

Murphy's knuckles graze against mine at my side, and I flex my fingers in hope as she cups her hand in mine. The second her palm is flush with mine, I squeeze it—and that same feeling when she stumbled out of the car less than thirty minutes ago fills my chest. It's like I can breathe.

I clutch her tightly and pray she doesn't give me a sign that she wants me to let go as we both walk to the far end of the table. As we sit, her palm remains in mine, and I leave them linked on top of my thigh out of view. I'm sweating—my palm is sweating, and I know she can feel it. I run my thumb over the top of her hand in small circles to clear more nerves. It doesn't help, but it doesn't hurt. It's peaceful, as opposed to the quiet storm brewing above the table.

She has no idea how grateful I am for her, how much I need her to survive this. I've made it this far and it's only because she's by my side. I lean on her, my hand clenching more tightly as my heart speeds up. With every squeeze I give, she gives one back—silent courage.

"How nice," my father says, stepping through the small hallway into the dining area. He's dressed as if he's ready for a day at the office, but I can see the small change my sister warned me about. It's only been a few weeks, but his shirt collar is loose around his neck, the bones and tendons more pronounced.

"This was a nice idea, Gina," he says to my mom.

She pulls out a chair next to the one she just rose from, and he smiles and slides it out farther, almost as if to prove he can still do it on his own.

"Casey," he says, his eyes landing on me for a brief second before he sits. He looks down at the plate in front of him as he slides his chair forward. "I see you brought a friend."

"Hi, sir," Murphy says, standing and circling around the table. I rub my hand on my leg to dry it, then panic that she won't hold it again when she sits back down.

I glance around the table to see half of my sisters looking down into their own laps, the other two staring nervously as this stranger I've brought home tries to win over the unwinnable.

"My name's Murphy. Thank you so much for inviting me for dinner," she says.

My father pauses a second, finishing a sip of his water, then finally bothers to reach for her hand, shaking it. He smirks and glances to me then to my mom. "Did we? Invite you, I mean?" he says, that familiar pompous smirk making it's first appearance of the day.

I see everything in Murphy freeze up—and sick or not—I want to punch him for treating her like an extension of me.

"Luke, don't joke with her," my mother says through a nervous giggle. Nobody thinks he's joking. Nobody thinks it, because we all know he's not. But maybe Murphy doesn't know, and that's why my mom says it—to smooth the waters and dial back the storm.

My father chuckles and his eyes wrinkle with his smile as he looks at me again, his eyes telling me the truth before he glances back to my now-speechless friend. "Right, I'm sorry, Murphy. My humor…it isn't for everyone," he says.

She laughs in response nervously and lightly before letting go and slipping back into her seat. Her hand finds mine quickly, and I stroke her wrist with my thumb this time, hoping I can soothe her.

My mother glosses over everything and begins passing dishes around. My father asks Christina about some real-estate contract she's been negotiating for a new high-rise downtown, and then the rest of my sisters and he begin talking about some new chip being manufactured, and how the process has an "anomaly," but nobody can figure out where there's a misstep. My eyes glaze over for

112

their fifteen-minute conversation, but as I silently count how many green beans are left on my plate, I'm brought out of my trance when my father says my name.

"Casey was always good at that, finding the hiccups in projects? Seeing what's broken in the process," he says while chewing. He runs a napkin over his mouth and looks at me, and I breathe in slowly through my nose to fill my chest. If I'm going to be held under water, I may as well prepare.

"Weren't you, Case," he says, putting the napkin next to his plate and laying one hand flat on the table next to his setting.

"I guess," I say, not quite audible enough for his liking as he tilts his head to the side and cups his ear. My mother stops eating and places her napkin and hands in her lap, looking down.

"I said, I guess," I say, now overcompensating as if he's deaf. I copy his posture and look right at him.

My father grunts out a small laugh, his tongue pushed in his cheek.

My mom and two youngest sisters all stand and begin clearing the table, asking if anyone would like coffee. My father holds up a finger indicating he'd like a cup. We continue to stare at each other.

"So what do you do, Murphy?" he asks, his eyes still on me. The smirk is there. He's treating this dinner as a process problem, weeding out the error. I should save him the trouble and just leave.

"I teach music," she says.

"And how does that pay?" There's almost a low grumble of a laugh in his chest. It's barely audible, but I hear it. It's that satisfying checkmate laugh he does so well.

Murphy stumbles in her answer, not really sure how to reply, so my father saves her. "Not well then, hmmm?"

"No, but it's not what I ultimately want to do, so it's okay," she says. I squeeze her hand tighter for a second to let her know I'm proud.

"If that's not your goal, then why are you wasting time on it?" he asks.

I open my mouth, ready to end his interrogation, but Murphy straightens up next to me and begins before I have a chance to speak.

"That's a really good point, actually," she says, glancing at me and wiggling our locked hands in reassurance along with her smile. "Your son has kind of helped me with that, you know."

"Really?" my father chuckles.

"Yes," she says without missing a beat. "I want to make a record, and Casey made my demo for me."

I hear the short breaths she's taking, and I feel badly, because I know my father isn't going to be impressed. I run my hand over my face and prepare myself for the laughable response that comes the moment my fingers touch my skin.

"A…demo. That's…what…like, a recording of your song?" He's being patronizing.

Murphy nods and smiles. She's proud of it, and I love that she is. He's going to pick it apart now. I wish he'd listen. I could never get him to do that, though.

"And this demo, it means that you'll have a job then? Do you get paid for it?" Here it comes.

"Well, no…" she says, her brow bunched and a small giggle mixed with her words. She thinks he's not understanding. He is, though. He is making a point, working through the process, flagging the faults.

"So you made a recording with my son, and that's your life goal. You've peaked, then, huh? And be damned paying bills," he says, leaning back and letting out one huge belly laugh. "Boy, Casey. I don't know how, but somehow you've found someone who is more lost than you."

My mother walks in just as I'm about to stand and flip my father off. I grip the edge of the table instead and look over at my oldest two sisters, getting an ounce of satisfaction in the expression on their faces. For once, at least, they hear the judgment I get.

"Two months," my father says, and everyone freezes. My mom falls to her seat and turns ghost white.

"I'm sorry," I shake my head, looking from person to person, until it hits me. I look my father in the eyes, his hand rubbing along the stubble on his chin.

"First, my weight will drop. Then, my motor skills will fail. Soon after that will come the cognitive things, and the basic biological functions until there's nothing left but a heartbeat waiting to fade into the sunset," he says, floating his fist out over the table then opening it as if it's turned to dust. His mouth is a hard line and his eyes stay on mine. "You can have all the time in the world. Or…"

He stands and pushes his chair in, his hands resting on the wood back.

"Or you could have two months," he says. "If that happened to you, would you be at peace? Or would you think about your friend here, about how the only thing you've left behind to take care of her is some…some…recording on a computer that nobody really gives a damn about? Can she live off that? What if she was your wife? What if you had a child?"

"I give a damn about it," Murphy says, her voice surprising us all. My father's eyebrows lift as he turns his attention to her.

"Well, isn't that wonderful," he says.

The silence in the room is more than suffocating, it's toxic. My mom's shoulders quiver while her muscles try not to give in to the cry fighting to escape her chest. All the money saved in the world isn't going to soothe this woman when he's gone. What's going to make her feel better is the goddamned painting she has to keep hidden in the attic. And that legacy dies there. The other legacy— the one of Coffield engineers—isn't anything anyone cares about. It's all just files and shredded pay stubs.

"Don't you ever miss it?" I ask as I look at the top of my mother's head. She works to steady her breathing before looking up at me, her eyes nervous. I chew at my bottom lip while nobody answers. The man the question was for won't—he's spent a lifetime refusing to answer that question of himself. No way will he bend from my asking of it. But I'm angry, and I want to storm out of here, never to come back, to make a scene.

115

Two months, though. And then that's all that would be left—the last taste on the tongue.

I stand, and Murphy turns to sit sideways, her legs are facing me.

"Have you ever been to the museum at McConnell? Anyone?" I ask, looking around the room. Two of my sisters studied there, and the campus is close to our home. Nobody nods *yes*, though. But my mother knows where I'm going with this. She takes a sharp breath, probably an attempt to stop me. "It's a shame. You really should make time to go there. The art…" I bend my head toward my father, my eyes narrowing. "It's an impressive collection. The works span maybe a hundred years."

"Wasted resources," my father says, his gaze lowered and his jaw hard.

I lock onto his face and search his eyes, but nothing behind the pale green looking back at me says he believes otherwise. Whatever passion ever existed inside Luke Coffield was struck down and murdered by his father. I'll be damned if that legacy continues with me.

I nod and bow my head, my eyes drifting to Murphy's as she looks up at me with pity. I don't want her to feel sorry. I'm not. And I'm not angry, either. I don't feel anything anymore. I'm letting go of it—right here, right now. Because there was never any convincing that could be done. This wasn't an argument to win. It was a diverging of paths—the place in the family tree where a branch simply falls to the ground.

I'm the black sheep. When I walk into the McConnell museum, I see stories in the strokes and colors hung on the walls. And when I plug into my music and manipulate voices and words and rhythm to make it tell a story, I feel alive.

Two months.

Sixty-seven years.

What's the difference?

"We have to go," I say, my response surprising everyone but my father. Murphy stands quickly next to me, her hand curling around my arm. I lead her around the table, and we stop in front of my

116

mother. I bend down so she doesn't have to stand, my hand cupping her face as I kiss her opposite cheek. "Thank you for having us. I'm okay, and I love you," I say in her ear. She nods, a short jerky motion.

I embrace each of my sisters as well, but I don't give them the explanation. That's for a later time, and I can tell there's an understanding among us by the way they don't berate me. My sisters have never been quick to take my side, and they may not now. But they are okay with my quiet and respectful exit.

For once, I'm being a little *less Casey.*

I stop finally at my father, his hands now in his pockets. I take him in, knowing that this will probably be my last memory. I reach out my hand and hold my breath, not sure if he'll reciprocate or not. After a few seconds, he brings his right hand to mine, and I grasp it, covering the other side and embracing him with two hands. We stopped hugging years ago, he and I.

There are a dozen things I could say now, all thoughts that I've whispered in the car during rides home from their house, things I've muttered to myself after phone calls from him or after long talks at this very table about my future. None of it means anything, though. And none of it will magically snap him back to the man he was at eighteen. Enlightenment to the things that really matter when facing death is all relative, and to Luke Coffield, those things are the same as they always were. No grand speech from his son wearing a borrowed suit is going to change that.

So I say nothing.

I look into his eyes and do my best to make him let go too. I won't bend. He won't bend. And it's fine. This parting is of no fault of our own. It's cancer's fault. It's my long-dead grandfather's fault. It's brain chemistry and abuse swept under a rug.

I suck in a full breath, and my father does the same.

Okay.

"Ready?" I ask, releasing my hold of his hand and turning to Murphy, whose eyes are glossy and red. She nods lightly, and I hold out my hand for her to take.

I pass through the kitchen and front room to the main door, knowing nobody will follow. I close the heavy door behind us and walk with Murphy to my car parked in front of the neighbor's house, and then I unlock her door and pull it open. She steps in front of me to get inside, her eyes meeting mine by chance, the gray like lightning, like a sign that for once, I did something right, and my heart surges.

My hands act fast, catching her face in my palms as her body turns and I step in so I'm flush against her. My hands slide quickly into her hair, her lip quivers as I stare at it, and my gaze flits to her eyes and back to her waiting mouth. The soft pink like fruit. I hunger to taste it, and my tongue passes over my lips as my eyes roam over her delicate features, so fragile in my hands. My eyelids grow heavy, and my chest seizes—breathing becoming harder by the millisecond, and finally I close my eyes and rest my forehead on hers, our lips almost touching, but not quite.

Not like this.

I feel the gentle tickle of her lashes against my cheek as I roll my head to the side and search for my will not to ruin this, too.

"I'm sorry," I whisper. "I…"

I release her and back away a full step, no longer able to look at her, but unable not to hear the rapid breath escaping her lips.

"I'll take you to your car," I say, turning away and forcing one foot in front of the other.

She falls into her seat and closes her own door, and we drive home in silence. When she leaves, I finish the whiskey and beg Eli to pick up more. Like a good friend, he does.

CHAPTER 9

Murphy

I'm not a prude. I've been kissed before. I've had sex. I've had boyfriends. What I've never been is *almost* kissed. I think maybe I like the almost kiss even better. Or maybe I hate the almost kiss. It's ruined my week, because I can't stop thinking about it. I even pulled out my notebook at one point and started to write a song about it. I haven't written anything new in months, and suddenly I'm inspired.

I'd call the song *I hate you, Casey Coffield.*

But I don't hate him.

I don't hate him at all.

It's Friday night, and my parents just called out for the pizza. This marks the sixteenth straight Friday night I've spent at home with my parents and Lane. I enjoy spending time with my family. But I'm also twenty-two, and this is supposed to be the time of my life. Instead, I've seen every classic hit from the eighties that my father can find on Netflix.

"Murph? We have a request in for *Ghostbusters*," my dad says, scratching at his graying beard and looking at me over the top of wire-rimmed glasses. One day, my father is going to look just like Santa. He's giving me a signal, because we just watched that movie last Friday...and the Friday before that. It's quickly become Lane's favorite, and because of that, we will probably be watching it a lot. My brother takes disappointment all right, but it makes all of us so happy to make him happy; we usually cave to the easy things, because why not?

"What's one more," I say, raising my shoulders in sync with my eyebrows.

"What's one more, she says," my dad smiles, raising his finger in the air and leaning in to kiss my cheek. "You're a good sport."

My smile grows a minute later when I hear my dad tell my brother that his movie choice wins and that we're watching his favorite again. What we watch doesn't really matter to me, because if this week is any indication, I'm going to be spending the next two hours dissecting every frame of my *almost* kiss along with the five days of complete silence from Casey that followed.

I suppose I didn't call him either, but I kinda feel like that ball's in his court now. The last thing he said when he dropped me off after the most-uncomfortable-family-dinner ever was that he'd call me as soon as he got time with John Maxwell. My inner voice was screaming "or when I'm ready to talk about whatever the hell that...*almost* was." My outer voice simply said, "okay."

He didn't even wait for me to walk all the way up to my car. My foot hit the pavement, and his right one hit the gas.

"Murphy, I get the recliner!" Lane yells.

"I call beanbag!" I scream from the inside of the fridge where my head is stuffed looking for a caffeine-free soda. My dad buys them for me, because nobody else really likes them, but somehow everyone else drinks them and I can never find one when I want it.

"Dad's already in the beanbag!" Lane yells.

Damn, you mean I can't even win the beanbag battle? "Some Friday night," I chuckle to myself. I spot a gold can in the far corner and clutch it in my hand. The doorbell buzzes loudly around the corner, and as I back out, I smack the top of my head on the freezer door.

"Shit!" I hum.

"Murphy! Language," my mother scolds, breezing by me toward the front room.

She swears worse than I do, but she says a parent always wants better for their kids, and when it comes to me, she's focusing on the potty mouth.

I rub my head with one hand and pull the tab on my golden soda with the other. I'm bringing the can to my lips when my mom rounds the corner, her eyebrows waggling and her lips full smirk. I know instantly, thanks to that face, and am grateful for at least this small half-second warning to run my fingers through my hair one time before Casey follows her into the kitchen.

"Hey," he says, all cool and suave. It's a cool-guy word...*hey*. He's wearing an old baseball T-shirt, black jeans, and one of those snap-front hats my father wears out on the golf course. If I saw that outfit in a clothing bin and a thrift shop, I wouldn't even glance twice. On Casey, I'm making mental snapshots.

"Hey," I say back, leaning my hand on the counter next to me, but missing by about half an inch. I stumble to the side and lose my balance, smacking my right temple on the Formica on my way down. I'm determined to give myself a concussion.

"Oh dang! Are you all right?" he says, rounding the kitchen island quickly and coming to my rescue. He grabs a hold of my arm and rights me. I wish I was seeing stars, anything to make what just happened seem anything other than god-awful embarrassing.

"I'm good, yeah. Thanks," I say, tugging my over-sized *I'm a Camper* T-shirt straight again. Cool guy…meet loser girl.

"You're downright clumsy," he teases.

I smile and turn my cheeks into cherries as I shrug.

"Strange, she's never been clumsy before," my mom adds behind him. He doesn't see the eyebrow waggle, but I do. And I die. Well, no…I don't die—I squeeze my eyes closed tightly and wish that when I open them everybody is gone.

"Still here," Casey whispers, apparently knowing this move.

I crack an eyelid open and am relieved that at least my mother has moved on. There's no way my cheeks aren't red, but I know there's also no way to cover it up, so I purse my lips in a guilty half smile and breathe in slow and deep to try to stave off an anxiety attack.

A full breath clears my head, and I start to realize that Casey's here—which means he's either ready to deal with the WTF moment we shared, or he has news. I'm almost equally anxious for either reason.

"Did my brother invite you to film night at the Sullivans?" I ask, quirking a brow. It's easier to be clever than honest after you bop your head on a counter in front of the cute guy who almost kissed you and whom you used to kinda loathe.

Casey's forehead crinkles as his mouth curves into one of his dimple smiles, glancing over my shoulder to the living room where Lane is still king of the recliner.

"No, I'm sorta bummed that I didn't get the invite," he chuckles, scratching at his chin with one hand. It makes the best sound—like rough sandpaper.

"Well, maybe next time," I shake my head.

"Yeah, maybe…" Casey says, pausing when our eyes meet. It's awkward for a second—a second too long—and he takes a step back, putting the kitchen island between us again.

"So, why the Friday-night visit?" I ask. Mental high-fives are happening in my head for having the balls to just come out and ask.

"I've gotta gig in the city, and just got off from work so I thought maybe I'd see if you wanted to…I don't know…come see what I do?" His hand comes back to his chin, and I wait to hear the scratching sound before I answer. Really cheesy eighties music drowns it out though, because my dad's started the movie in the other room. It catches both of our attention, and we can't help but look into the living room.

"*Ghostbusters*…nice!" Casey says. I snap my eyes to him as he's watching the screen in the distance. He's smiling, looking on at my family, and the sight of that makes me smile. It also makes me a little sad, because after last weekend's dinner, I understand the difference between Friday nights in my house growing up and Friday nights in his.

"You want me to watch you work?" I ask, not sure what I would do hanging out at a club in some corner, probably sipping on sodas and water for six hours.

"Yeah," he says, his eyes finally coming back to me. "The club I'm at is this new joint on top of the bank building downtown. It's a pretty big gig, and I don't know…I thought maybe if you didn't have anything to do. But you've got family plans…I probably should have called…"

"No, it's okay. I can go. I mean…I'd like to go. It's just movie night, and we do this…well, we do this a lot," I say, leaning

122

forward and cupping my mouth to whisper "we watched this movie last Friday."

"And the one before that," my dad adds in a monotone voice as he rounds the corner, a golden soda in his hand. I eye it and he swings it behind his back. I scowl at him as he shrugs. "I buy them, so I figure that means I can drink them when I want."

My scowl is fake, and I laugh and lean into his arm.

"So this is the famous Casey Coffield," my father says. The red creeps back into its familiar place on my skin.

"In the flesh, I guess," Casey says. There's the charm. I recognize it. He reaches out a hand and my father takes it, shaking firmly.

"I hear you two are working on a recording project together with some big studio?" My dad doesn't really follow today's music, but he has a decent business mind, so I caught him up on the plan before I met Casey to record. He's playing coy, but he's fully aware of my arrangement with Casey. He may not know John Maxwell, but he knows contracts. He worked as a district attorney before he and my mom both decided to get their real-estate licenses when my grandmother left them three properties. They wanted a way to spend more time at home for Lane. Their business grew quickly, and my father ends up traveling around the state a lot. My mom's usually near home, though. And I help when I can.

"We are. In fact," Casey says, glancing at me and raising his brow. My tummy grows excited. "I was able to get in with John today. He's the guy who runs the company." He says that part to my father, but this next part is just for me. "He had me transfer the file to his iPod so he could spend some time with it this weekend. He said he'd get me his feedback Monday."

I'm frozen for a second, but the knowledge that this is really happening starts to hit me, and my mouth curves slowly at first, until it has nowhere to go but up. My fingertips find my lips, and I'm stuck between wanting to chew away my nails and cover my mouth in amazement. "Really?" I ask, opting instead to lay my palm flat against my cheek.

"Really," Casey repeats, brown eyes and dimple there to top it off like warm fudge and whipped cream.

"I have a good feeling," he says, and his eyes stick on mine while I remain in my pose. I don't know what to say. My father gets me going again.

"You should. Murphy is gifted. Always has been. She's overcome so much, too. Makes for one hell of an inspiring story. I mean, I'm inspired by her." My dad delivers what is known in some circles as diarrhea of the mouth, and I lean to the side and slowly—but firmly—push my elbow into his ribs. He gets the hint, and stops before he makes me wish I could just fall and hit my head on something again.

Casey's confused look means I didn't stop him quickly enough, so I make a rash decision to change the subject.

"Dad, if you guys don't mind, I'd like to spend the night at the club watching Casey work, so I can see what goes into everything he does—maybe learn something," I say, making excuses. They're thin, and both my father and Casey see right through them. My dad's assuming I'm going because I want to spend the night with the guy who inspired this song they've teased me about endlessly…since finding out the guy in the lyrics was real. Casey is assuming I'm going to change the subject from all of my *overcoming*.

They're both right.

"You're an adult, Murph. You can go out with a cute boy on a Friday night if you want to; you don't need to ask permission," my dad says, getting one last tease in. The red flares up, and my eyes close.

"Excellent," I say, feeling my way around the counter with my eyes still shut. "Casey, I'll be out in a few minutes. Just let me change. And die."

I whisper that last part.

Maybe he said *okay*. Maybe he said *fine*. It doesn't matter what his response was, because I made my way into my room without having to crack an eyelid until I flung myself face first into my mattress and screamed into my pillow with a mixture of frustration, humiliation, and call-your-best-friend euphoria.

Appears my song was slightly prophetic, only I had a few things wrong. We're not in his dreams. My dreams, however, and Casey Coffield, seem to have collided.

Casey

If she only knew how many times I drove by her house this week. Monday's excuse was that I had a dinner meeting in Archfield and was just stopping by. There was no dinner, and my car never stopped, because I'm a chicken shit.

On Tuesday, I drove by earlier in the day, because I didn't have work at the studio. I was up late at the coffee house with Eli playing chess the night before, and that always makes me feel mature and quixotic. I thought I'd just drive right to her house and talk about what happened, like grown adults. I never made it past the stop sign on her corner.

Wednesday was another concocted excuse, something about needing to rerecord that night to fix something on her demo. I only made it halfway to her town from the city before talking myself out of that bad idea; it would have plagued her self-esteem.

I was ready to try again yesterday, but then John told me he'd take my samples home Friday, so instead, I rushed home and spent all night making sure everything was perfect on her song.

I really have a gig tonight. And the thought of having her see me in my element gives me this mental edge that, for some reason, I need around her. I didn't hesitate once on my way to her house, and ringing the doorbell even came easy. Her mom seems to like me, so I felt like a rock star all the way to the point when Murphy's piercing grays hit my system. If she hadn't fallen first, I'm pretty sure I would have found a way to make a fool of myself. Instead, she was just as rattled by me as I had feared I'd be by her.

None of that means I have the advantage though. I don't, and I know it the second she walks out of the hallway bathroom wearing this dark gray, skin-tight dress and flat sandals with ribbons that wrap up her legs; I'm not quite sure where the ribbon ends. Normally, her look is a little bohemian. And there's still some of that right now, her hair loose and draped over one shoulder—a *bare* shoulder. This look is sexy though—and it's taken everything about tonight out of my hands. Hell, I might even just hand my board over to her and sit back and watch. She could play complete crap and the dance floor would devour her just because of those legs.

"Should I drive separate? That way you don't have to come ba—"

"No," I cut her off. No, you do not need to drive separate. No, you are not leaving early. No, you are not dancing with some shark-fiend-asshole while I play sexy tunes for him to grind against you to. There are a million *no's* that roll through my brain right now. I cover them all with that two-letter word.

She blinks at me, and all I do is grin.

"All right then," she rolls her eyes.

Good. Settled. All of the *no's* agreed to. I know that's not *really* the case, but I'm not going to let any of those other things happen either, so she may as well just give in.

She steps into the living room, and I follow her, waving to Lane who sits up on his knees to say hi to me. She kisses her parents while Lane and I chat about our favorite part of the movie, and then she brushes my arm to let me know she's ready to leave. I look down convinced she's turned my arm to ice. I'm magically fine, though I haven't a clue how—because I swear she froze my arm with that touch.

We get to my car, and I remember to open the door for her—the *only* tip Houston would give me for tonight. He said if I could just get through that, it would be a miracle.

Asshole with little faith.

I get in, and my eyes go right to her legs. She catches me, and I grin sheepishly.

"Yep, you caught me staring at your legs," I say, looking back to the steering wheel as I shift into drive. I know she's blushing, but at least I'm not now.

126

I blush. Dudes blush. It isn't cool on a guy, though, because we also sweat when we blush. And unless we're swinging an ax or doing pull-ups on Instagram, sweat on a guy isn't hot. It's disgusting.

"You said *club*, so I thought I should wear something a little more contemporary," she says, the corner of her lip tucked in her teeth when I glance toward her. I will myself not to look at her legs again before I turn back, but I'm weak—I look. And I'm sweating up a shit storm.

"You look nice in anything," I say, looking at her one more time with a tight-lipped smile. She's blushing again, too, so at least we're even.

"Thanks," she whispers.

"So this club," I start, giving over my focus to the road. "Let me give you the rundown of what to expect. I'll be working in the middle, and the entire space is floor-to-ceiling windows with dance space and a bar on one end. It's part of John's brand, actually—it's called Max's. He hired me to host his opening first, before I got on with the studio. He had heard good things about me, and came out to one of my gigs at Ramp 33. I didn't know he was there, which…shoot, good thing!"

"Why's that?" she says, her body turned a little to face me. She's genuinely interested, which is something I'm not used to when I talk about this stuff. Even Houston's mom sort of glazes over and responds with "uh huh" and "how nice."

"I killed it that night—tried some *way* out-of-the-box things and had this vibe going that just made everyone feel kinda high I guess," I say, and I catch her stiffen and tuck her hands under her thighs. I reach over and touch her arm without looking. "No, don't worry. I said *feel* kinda high. They weren't high—it's not that kind of scene. Well, no…that's not true. I'm not going to lie; there are a lot of people who are on shit at these places, but that's not the point. I'm not into that. I meant that the music sort of took over."

"Oh," she relaxes, turning again to face me just enough.

We drive for a few minutes while listening to my stereo. I buy piece of crap cars so I can put my money into making the sound system worthy of my ears. I'm playing through some deadmau5 right now, just to get in the mood. I can tell she likes it by the way her right knee is pulsing with the beat, but I also wish she would sit still—because I can't help but notice the movement, and I'm compelled to look, and her dress isn't very long.

This is so not the girl dressed in rags and playing Helen Keller in that yearbook photo. I bring a hand up to my neck, blocking my view from her for just a beat—I need a breath.

"So, in high school, you…you did a lot of theater stuff, yeah?" I ask. I've been dying to ask.

"Kind of," she says, turning her head away from me, her eyes out on the city whizzing by as we get on the freeway. Her hair is down and wavy from the tie she had it in before we left, and she lets it fall over the opposite shoulder to block my view of her face.

"You were in *Helen Keller*, if I remember…" I say, wincing through the lie since she can't see me.

She takes in a deep breath.

"I was," she says through a light giggle. Her hands grab a hold of her hair, shifting it back to the opposite shoulder, and she lets her head turn to face me. I glance over to find her smirking. I cock my neck and raise an eyebrow. "You're such a bad liar, Casey. You didn't see the show."

I blink and suck in my lip, bringing my eyes back to the road.

"You're right on two counts," I chuckle.

"Two?" she asks.

"Yep," I say, filling my guilty lungs and glancing at her one more time. "I'm a horrible liar and no, I did not *see* the show."

"I know," she says.

I squint in question.

"Our auditorium was small, and I…I would have known you were there," she says.

I nod, but can't help but think of the next question that begs. She would have known because…she wished I was there? And as if she can read my mind, she continues.

"You had a pretty big personality, Casey. There weren't many rooms you could walk in unannounced," she says. It isn't flattering, and it twists my insides a little.

"I see," I answer, moving my hand forward to tap the volume button and make the music louder.

We ride for the next few miles with the music so loud it rattles the dashboard. But before we get to the exit for downtown, Murphy leans forward and turns the volume low again.

"I didn't mean that how it sounded," she says. I know the face she's making before I look at her to confirm it. I chuckle when our eyes meet, and her eyebrows dimple.

"You're a pretty bad liar, too, Murphy. You meant it *exactly* how it sounds," I say, shaking my head and rubbing my neck. I've been dished harsh criticism before, and I've built up a pretty thick skin, but for some reason her pin-point accuracy on these little things stings. "I was…am…a little arrogant. It's a flaw. I'm working on it." I tap my fingertip to my temple and glance at her. "I've got a running list."

I can feel her eyes on me as I drive through the tall buildings to the center of town. The music is just loud enough to fill the void, and the sights outside provide a good temporary distraction until I drive us into the garage; the lights dim as I continue several floors below the thirty-story building we're going to the top of in a few minutes.

I pull into a spot and force a smile at her, feeling about half the size I did when she first said she'd come with me tonight. Exiting my door and walking around the back to her side, I catch her door just as she opens it so I can hold it the rest of the way. I look away as one foot hits the garage floor, knowing that her skirt will get shorter, and that her tempting legs will bring out my worst. But then she stops moving.

"You have a running list of your…flaws?" she says. I don't look, but I sigh and nod slowly.

"It's a long list," I laugh, but a full smile never quite hits my lips, because it isn't really funny.

A few seconds pass before she steps from the car completely, and my eyes flit to the ground to let her move without my gawking. I'll have plenty of time to take her in tonight, and right now, I don't feel very worthy. She pauses right in front of me, though, bringing her hands up to the collar of my shirt and reaching her cool fingertips inside, running one finger around the edge to the back. I look up at her then; she's so close—so close I could kiss her if I wanted to. I could make that mistake all over again; I could go through with it this time.

Her eyes follow her hand, her neck tipped to the right, accentuating that long line that's so bitable and delicate. She dips her thumb inside my shirt and then presses her palm flat against the back of my neck and I see stars—for just a second, things are bright. Her eyes pop to mine, and her tongue barely edges out of her mouth, wetting her bottom lip, and I'm so close to caving.

"Your tag was out," she says.

I nod, and my head hardly moves. Her hand falls from my neck, and milliseconds go by—but feel as if they drag on for minutes—while I watch every opportunity to make a mistake slip through my fingers. I hold my breath and let it go, exhaling the moment she steps away from me, but not without giving into the craving and watching her ass set a new tempo inside my chest in my very favorite dress ever made.

The elevator ride is short and crowded—thank god. When we reach the top floor, I guide her to the right through a small hallway while the others in our car turn left to go to the restaurant attached to the club.

The lights are on and the only people on the floor are wait staff and bartenders who work there. It looks like a vacant loft space, except for the occasional round, white-leather seat placed sporadically throughout the room. The mood is coming soon, but first, I need to get set up.

"You must be Casey?" says a tall blonde walking toward me with an earpiece and a clipboard. Her legs are the second best set in the room, but I can tell Murphy disagrees. She hangs back a few steps, stopping at one of the leather seats to sit and tug her dress lower. I catch her insecurities out of the corner of my eye.

"That's me. Are you Kendra?" I reach my hand out and take her palm when she nods *yes* and smiles. Kendra is John Maxwell's daughter. She's off limits. And she's intimidating as hell. I could tell Murphy all of this, but making girls jealous is about number seventeen on my list of flaws, so I keep her in the dark for now.

"You should have everything here you said you needed. I think the guys brought over your board and equipment this afternoon?" She's all business, but still Murphy watches with pressed lips. I bet she doesn't even know the face she's making.

"It looks right," I say, stepping over to the booth and walking around, my finger touching the key pieces and seeing how everything connects.

"Great, well, do your thing—whatever you need to get ready. Doors open in an hour," she says.

I nod and watch her walk away, not even really looking at her, but knowing Murphy is looking at me. I glance back at her to see her eyes dart away from me toward Kendra. She's still making the same face, though, so I pull my phone from my pocket and take her picture. The flash gets her attention, and she jerks her head toward me again.

"Did you?" she points at me with question.

I wave my finger and gesture for her to come. She smooths out her skirt when she stands and walks, with a little extra sway, over to me. Her eyebrows raised, I hold my phone out for her to see.

"Casey!" she says, glaring at the picture of her pouting on the sofa. "I wasn't ready for that picture," she protests.

"I know," I smirk, taking it from her and zooming in on her face. "I wanted to catch this face…right here," I say, tilting it back toward her to see. Her eyes narrow and her mouth tightens. She glances up at me and shakes her head, her eyes squinting even more, like an angry bully.

"Come on, let me show you the board," I say, tilting my head to the right and urging her to follow. I slide my phone back in my pocket and turn to take her hand to help her up the few small steps.

Once her fingers hit my palm, my thumb falls over the top, and when the time comes to let go, I don't. I feel her fingers become still, and without thinking, I run my thumb slowly over each knuckle. Her eyes flash up to mine the second I do.

"That's Kendra Maxwell," I say, no longer wanting to torture her. "She's the boss's daughter. She writes my check."

Murphy nods a response, as if what I said is just new and interesting information, but she also sucks in her lip, and I notice how the corners of her mouth rise with the grin she's trying to hide. I won't tease her. But I sure as shit won't forget seeing her get jealous.

I slide out one of the stools for her to sit on while I test out everything and correct a few connections. I don't really like letting others set up for me, but when they're willing to pay five grand just so I can do what I probably would have done for free, I let them set up whatever shit they want.

I play through a few beats, looking for the right ones, then line up my lists on my laptop, getting every drop and sound bite ready to go. I get so lost in my work for a while, I can tell Murphy is growing bored, her phone in her hand as she concentrates on one of those mindless games dropping boxes and jewels in a line on her screen. I wave a hand to get her attention, and she startles.

"Sorry, I'm good. I was just waiting, staying out of your hair," she smiles.

I give in to temptation and stare at her small, perfect mouth. Her top lip curls just enough to show her teeth, and there are these small freckles that line her cheeks and nose. Her eyes catch a few of the lights being tested, and reflect the purples and blues. If I could paint like my father, I'd need a canvas right now. Her head leans to the side to break my trance. I notice, but I don't care—I keep staring. I smile and eventually call her over to me, pleased to see the pink on her cheeks.

"I wanted to show you how it all works," I say.

"All right," she says, her eyes scanning over the equipment. I watch her take it all in, and she catches me staring again. I don't care. I grin like a fool.

"I have all of my songs and clips here," I say, clicking through layers upon layers of sound. "This is called the DAW."

"Like, the stock market?" she questions.

I laugh.

"Close. One letter off. *D-A-W*…it's for digital audio workstation," I say. "It's kind of like what we used in the studio—when I laid down the tracks for your recording?"

She nods.

"I have a lot more going on here, though. It's sort of a hybrid of a bunch of programs. Houston helped me get it together into something that works for me," I say, clicking through and opening everything up. "Want to hear a cut?"

She folds her hands around her body and nods, her eyes bright. I pull out the Ratatat song she was listening to with her brother and let it start rolling, setting the intro to loop. Then I break up the beat with some new layers, so the song is recognizable, but unique.

"That's so unbelievably cool," she says, her body moving to the rhythm.

I'm about to blow her mind. I've had this planned since late last night, and the effect is better than I could have dreamed. I want to see her dance. I wait just long enough, smiling at her and moving my head along with the vibe until I feel it in my gut. There's always a moment—it's what makes me good. I've had it since the first time I touched a soundboard. I can sense when the craving is at it's peak, when the room wants more. It's like a slow-building orgasm, and I bring everyone to the brink, feeling their bodies fall in line with the count, giving their minds over to the melody. This is the high I was talking about, and Murphy—she's there. Her eyes are shut and her body is moving more than I think she realizes, and it's the hottest thing I've ever seen.

I'm about to be her undoing without even laying a hand on her.

My finger poised over the button, I wait until it's just right to let the first drop go. I picked Nina Simone, because she's jazzy—just like Murphy. She's full of fire; there's a swagger in her song—the moment her voice breaks through the beat, Murphy knows. Her eyes drag open and her body keeps swaying. Baby grays are looking at me and smiling. Her chest is rising and falling off rhythm even though her body keeps tempo. It's because I'm in her head now—my song is in her head, and she's feeling something different, something more.

The break I built is coming up, and I know it—she'll shiver. I step toward her, letting my headphones slip around my neck. I come closer and watch her for a sign that I shouldn't move more. She doesn't stray—she's drunk in seconds, and she wants me near. The break happens, and her head tilts back as she closes her eyes, and that goddamned perfect neck is exposed and my lips beg to touch it. I don't, but I linger, letting her feel my breath on her skin, small bumps rising in reaction. Chemistry and biology—beautiful. My nose grazes just below her ear as my hands carefully slide on her body, touching in just the right place above her waist. She doesn't flinch, because she's given over to the feeling—the performance of it all. That's all this ever is. I fill rooms with pheromones and bodies become mine.

Right now, Murphy is completely in my control. My hands urge her to turn, and her body spins slowly, every curve brushing against me until her back is flush with my chest. I drag one hand around her waist and up her spine, my palm flat as it follows the line of her zipper, my thumb feeling the jagged metal and my mind imagining dragging it the opposite way. I shut my own eyes as my hand pushes against her neck and my fingers find her hair, sweeping it up in my hold so my mouth can play against her ear. I bring my fingers down gently, both of us moving together to the sexy beat I built just for her, and I hold my breath as my hand opens wide and splays under her breasts, holding her tight against me.

My thumb close to god, I feel her lungs grow inside her, her breathing deep and desperate. I could take her now, but that…that would be a mistake. I only wanted to get this close—to feel this much. I wanted to see if my powers worked on her as well. They do, but hers have the equal effect on me. My mouth watering and my cock growing hard, my eyelids grow heavy as my self-made rules fight against my desire.

134

Leaning into her, my lips press against the inside of her neck, marking her with a cool kiss as my tongue takes one, tiny taste of her skin before my mouth finds her ear.

"This is what I do, Murphy. I...can make people...do...whatever...I...want," I whisper, and her breath falls away entirely, her head dropping back against me, her hands moving to my wrists and holding me with a tight desperation that begs for more.

My eyes close, and I indulge for a few seconds, dragging my hand up her body again, careful not to touch her too intimately, despite how badly my hand wants to go there. I trace her bare shoulder and move to her neck, my thumb running over the zipper that it now considers the enemy. I push her slowly in front of me, giving us just enough space for me to let my head fall against the back of hers so my eyes can rake over the perfect line of her neck one last time. My mouth moves forward, wanting to taste more, but I puff out a breath instead, and let go of her completely, knowing a second longer is the difference between being able to stop.

I kill the sound. An abrupt edge. And Murphy takes a step forward, as if I've just released her from a trance. I have. But I can put her back under it any time I want. And I intend to.

CHAPTER 10

Murphy

I'm stunned.

That's the only word that works for this state I'm in. Stunned. Casey. Has. Stunned me.

When he let go of my body, it was like a hold on me dropped me back to earth. I could hardly look at him, because I knew if I did, I'd want him to go back to *that.* His hand was so hot on my ribs. His breath…*ahhhh.* There were tingles—definitely tingles. But it was also this sexy song, and I've never really been held quite like that, so it might be that it was just the circumstances. It might not have anything to do with Casey at all.

The music stopped and so did the fantasy. He went right back to showing me things, and always no less than three feet apart from me. And my head went into blender mode. It got worse as the night went on.

"Watch me make them all fall in love," he said at one point. And I watched—I watched as Casey manipulated the hundreds of beautiful people all pressed together on a dance floor. He filled their ears with lust, and their bodies followed. Just like mine had.

That's all it was. It was a lesson.

Lesson learned.

I woke up this morning and had to write. It was early, even though I didn't get back to my house until two in the morning, I woke up at seven. There was something nagging me, something calling. I haven't felt the itch in so long, I had to do something about it. I can't quite get it right, but it's these words:

Pinprick
Burn
Ice cold
Sweat
Drugged and sweet and wet

I've been hunched in my car with my legs slung over the center console for three hours while I try every combination with every melody my fingers can find on my guitar. Nothing feels right—it's all jumbled and lost. Like my head. Because of Casey.

Just when I think I might have something, it disappears.

"Murphy! Murphy! What are you doing?"

Lane is knocking on the opposite window, pressing his face against the glass and blowing. My brother is light and air, and there isn't a single thing about him that isn't golden and happy. I lay my guitar against my chest, the neck between my knees, and I watch him make goofy faces for a moment before pressing the lock button so he can crawl inside.

"Move your legs," he says the second I let him in.

"Bossy," I tease, moving for him.

"I want to go to the mall. I need new pants. I grew…an inch," he says, lifting his leg awkwardly and showing me his sock.

My brother hasn't grown. He's twenty. He just wants new pants. But I love that he wants to get new pants with me. Being near him slows down the churn in my head. Lane is good for me—he's medicine.

I rub my face and smile before nodding.

"Pants it is. Let me put my guitar away and tell Mom," I say.

"She knows. She told me to come get you. She gave me money," Lane smiles, holding up what looks like sixty bucks.

I give him a thumbs up as I carry my guitar back inside. My mom's waiting at the door, and takes it from me.

"Thanks," I say.

"Some boys at summer school were making fun of him," she says quickly before I can get away. I slump and lean against the wall. Lane's been lucky, for the most part, and hasn't had to deal with a lot of bullying. He's sensitive and understands more than people think. And every now and then, some asshole preys on him.

"Because he likes khakis? They made fun of khakis?" I sigh, my forehead pinched in disappointment.

"Honey, teenage boys are idiots," my mom adds with a laugh. "Just help him pick out some jeans."

I nod and turn back to the door for my mission, my feet stumbling when I see the maroon-rusted Volkswagen pulled up next to me. Casey is in my driver's seat with the engine on, and he and Lane are leaning forward, patting their hands on the dashboard. Casey doesn't judge khakis, though I bet he used to.

I don't interrupt them until Casey's head swings forward and his mouth curves up on one side. He holds up a finger as I approach the door, signaling for me to hold on for a second. I can kind of hear the music playing inside—it's "Wipe Out," a classic, and my brother loves that song. The second it's over, Casey rolls down the window.

"Hey," he says. *Cool-boy word.* It makes me smirk as I bend my head down to talk to them.

"Hey, yourself," I say. "You're in my seat."

He looks forward at the steering wheel, running his hands along the curve of it and stretching out his fingers, slowly letting them wrap back around the width.

"It's a nice seat," he grins, giving me a sideways glance that I feel in my knees. I cross my legs to forget it.

"It is," I smile back, lowering my lashes in a challenge. I'm not in his league when it comes to this…whatever this is. And I know it. My relationships have all been with nerdy librarian types, researchers, the occasional fellow singer-songwriter kind of guy who wants to hug trees and play free music for the masses. Maybe that's why none of them ever made me feel the pinprick or the burn. I know that's what those words mean. I know that's why they flew from my pen onto the notebook that is…oh my god, *right fucking there!*

Casey's eyes flinch, and I know he saw me tick. With one glance at me, his eyes narrowed, he then looks to what I saw and sees it. He looks at me again, this time with a devil's chuckle as his hand reaches to the dashboard against the window and slides out my beat-up, bent and very-well-used spiral notebook.

"We're going to the mall," I say, changing the subject, my brain remembering everything in the book. There are words in there that he will turn into something—he'll make them about him.

Maybe they are.

138

I scratch at my ear and plaster a smile on my face and ignore the drums in my chest.

"That's what Lane says," he smirks, his eyes wide and moving from me to the book, looking for confirmation. I give away nothing.

"I'm gonna kind of need my seat though. So…" I say, my body motioning for him to vacate the car—*and hand over my book.*

He drops the paper in his lap, and my eyes follow, noting the way his thumb flirts with opening a page. A songbook is so much like a diary. Things are written in code, but my code—it probably isn't very hard to decipher. In fact, it's probably blatant and obvious. Oh god!

I reach in desperately, hoping this one shot will catch him off guard, but it doesn't, and his grip comes fast around my wrist, his laughter deep and brewing inside his chest just for me. He knows there's something good in there.

"Get in the back. I'll drive. Lane and me are having fun up front," he says, getting immediate approval from my brother. I feel betrayed, and kind of pissed that he's using Lane as a ploy to get his way, but more pissed that it's working.

"You don't need to spend your day shopping for pants," I say, my voice completely not bluffing at all. I *am* a shitty liar!

Casey laughs louder and picks up my book, tucking it under his leg—*damn it!* He pulls the seatbelt over his body and points with his thumb to the back seat.

"Get in, woman," he says through a snicker.

I let out a fast and heavy sigh in defeat, but reach in to grab the beanie from his head before backing away fast and climbing into the back seat. His hair is still damp and floppy, probably from the shower he took this morning, and I realize all I've done is give myself something to want to touch for the entire ride to the mall. I haven't phased him at all. He runs his fingers through the tousled mess once and glances at me in the mirror just to let me know that he's in control. Those words—all of them—I'm feeling them again.

After about the fifth time, I quit looking up to catch his eyes in the mirror. They're always on me, always smiling, often laughing. I'm a caught mouse, and I don't like feeling trapped. When we pull into the parking spot at the mall, I get out first; when Casey steps out of the car, my notebook clutched to his side, I smack him in the arm with his own beanie.

"Give me my notebook," I plead.

He smirks and shakes his head *no*, mouthing the word slowly just to taunt me. I fold my arms over my chest, his hat clutched in my fist, and start walking toward the entrance. He laughs at my fit.

"So, what are we shopping for today, Lane?" I hear him ask behind me. I look over my shoulder to see his arm around my brother.

"I need jeans. Khakis are for losers," my brother says, and my mouth grows rigid while I want to spit. I hate those boys.

"Who told you that?" Casey chuckles.

"The guys at school," my brother answers quickly. He doesn't have the same kind of walls the rest of us do—the ones that make people hold feelings inside and pretend they're okay when they're really not. It doesn't mean it doesn't hurt any less, though.

It's quiet behind me for a few seconds, until we get to the door and I hold it open watching my brother and *that* boy walk inside, still connected.

"Those guys are dumb-asses," Casey says, his eyes meeting mine for a flash, showing me he's just as angry about it as I am. "I wear khakis sometimes. They're comfortable, and they look very professional."

I fall in step behind them and smile, knowing full well that Casey wouldn't be caught dead in a pair of khakis. He's a better liar than he thinks, though.

We both help Lane pick out about a dozen different types of jeans to try out in the first store we come to. Casey helps my brother carry them into a fitting room, then tells him we'll be waiting nearby if he wants to show us any of them. I pull my legs up, glad to be wearing jeans myself, so I can sit on the giant ottoman in the corner of the store; a second later, Casey joins me.

My eyes glare at my book, but he tucks it under his thigh on the opposite side, leaving his hand on it for protection.

"Is Lane being bullied?" he asks, looking over at the dressing room where we can see my brother's socked feet shuffling and struggling to work on jeans under the door.

"I think it was just this once. People usually leave him alone, and he has a lot of friends at his school. It's just hard for him to fit in, because he's older, but then he's also…not," I say, meeting Casey's gaze between breaths. I turn back to Lane's feet. "They were just being stupid boys," I sigh.

"That doesn't make it okay," Casey responds, and I laugh lightly, my nostrils flexing at how amusing his statement is.

"No…" I say, shaking my head. "No, it doesn't."

It's quiet for a few minutes as we both keep our eyes forward, my mind trying to match up the immature asshat I avoided in high school with this older, oddly-sensitive guy sitting next to me, and eventually, I notice that he's brought my notebook into his lap. My chest squeezes, and I close my eyes, considering having what I know would be a childish tug of war over it. Instead, I stand and move to the dressing room door.

"I'm going to see if he needs help," I say, not looking back.

I get to Lane's door, which is across the store, and lean against the mirrored front, gently knocking.

"How's it going in there?" I ask.

"I don't like these. They're not soft like my other pants," he says. I can hear the frustration—trying to fit in is like that. We don't all go in the same box.

"Do you want me to see if I can find some softer ones? They have those skate pants that bunch at the bottom," I say.

"No, those are stupid, too," he protests.

"I like them," I say, my finger tracing a tic-tac-toe sticker pressed on the mirror.

"Okay, I guess," Lane says, as I hear a pair of pants get tossed on the ground.

I grin and catch my own reflection, not liking how sad my eyes are. I look on for a few seconds, and soon, my attention moves to

Casey's reflection, to the fact that my book is open on his lap, and he's reading with both hands on either side of the page. His head is slung forward.

He's reading.

He's not laughing.

I close my eyes and turn, opening up intent not to look at him again. I gather four or five other styles of pants and bring them to my brother, then take a seat on the wooden bench across from him. Every few minutes, I look over to see if he's still reading. Every time—he is.

After nearly twenty minutes, Lane finally comes out of the room in one of the last pairs I give him to try. He looks unsure, but as he spins slowly, I *ooooh* and *ahhhh.*

"Do they look okay?" he asks, pushing his hands in the pockets and pulling out the inside lining. "There's a lot of room in here for my wallet and my phone. I think I like these."

Lane looks up at me and smiles, his empty pockets inside out and his white socks glowing against the dark blue denim on his legs.

"They're no khakis, but they're pretty swag," Casey says behind me. I suck in air and keep my eyes on my brother.

"I think I'd like these, then, Murph," he says.

I nod and tell him to pass them to me under the door so I can pay.

As I wait at the register, Casey taps me on my arm with the weight of my notebook. My eyes flick up to his face, but he's looking at the notebook instead of me.

"I like this one," he says, his face sort of serious.

I take it in my hand, relieved to have it back while also nervous at which one he's opened it to. I swallow and say, "Okay."

I pay and hand Lane his bag, then fall behind him and Casey as we walk through the mall back out to my car. I'm expecting to find the page opened to the sexy lyrics I was scribbling this morning— about wanting to be touched and feeling excited…about boys with stubble on their face and music at their fingertips. But that's not the page he has opened. It's on one of the first things I wrote.

142

I don't even ask, getting into the backseat and leaving Casey with no choice but to drive us home. I haven't looked at this song in years. I wrote it as an exercise when people were pushing me to sing. I was fifteen, and angry and depressed. He doesn't even know what these words mean; they mean so much.

Boxes, locks, unspoken wishes
Traps, choking, candle burning dissonance
Inside, tangled, open mouthed pettiness
Coughing, breathing, whistles at a girl...he's a boy

Shouting, screaming, no mistaking
Pounding, breaking, overtaking
Staring, holding, touching, molding
Candy-coated kisses on the strings of my guitar

This is my song
You'll never hear it

I mouth the words until I look up and notice him watching. His eyes aren't the same as they were during the drive here. I'm relieved that he isn't teasing me anymore, but I also can't tell what his eyes are saying. I think they pity me. I wonder if he knows they should.

We get to the driveway, and Casey lingers at the door of my car, his eyes down and my keys in his hand, stuffed in his pocket. Lane rushes toward the house to put on his new jeans to show our mom, and when the door slams shut behind him, we're left in my parents' driveway all alone. This is that scene from high school that never happened—me and *that* boy kicking our feet awkwardly, not sure what to say, outside my house.

"Thanks for driving," I say, rolling my eyes, because that's such a stupid thing to say.

Casey breathes a short laugh and nods.

"No problem. Hey, let me know…how the pants go over at school? Or…just…if he has any more problems?" Casey looks up, one eye squinting.

I shrug.

"You can't fix his problems for him, Casey. But it's sweet that you want to try," I say.

He smiles, but it's short-lived, his mouth stretching to a straight line, his gaze falling to his feet. He pulls my keys out to hand them to me, then reaches into his back pocket, pulling out an envelope.

"What's this?" I ask, shaking my head and taking both the keys and envelope as he hands them to me.

"Last night was a good payday, and I promised I'd get your car fixed, so…" he stops short of finishing.

I turn the envelope in my fingers and peel open the flap to see several twenties.

"I had the bank give me cash because I didn't want you to have to deal with a check or whatever, and I wasn't sure where you wanted to take it or how much…"

"Thanks," I say, blinking rapidly in disbelief. I'd actually forgotten about the scratch on my door, and I figured he was thrilled I hadn't brought it up. My eyes look at it now, behind him, and it seems so small.

"Sure," he smiles. "Speaking of…I have to head over to Houston's. I want to get his dent fixed, too."

"Don't leave," I interrupt.

My eyes go wide, and I scramble because, what? *Don't leave?* That was out loud!

"Yet," I add to his confused face. "Don't leave until you see Lane in his new jeans."

"I saw them at the mall," he says, brow bunched.

"I…I know, but he'll want to show you again. In front of my parents. He'll be proud, and you represent the cool-guy opinion. So just come in…just for a minute." I somehow piece together a really flimsy excuse. My palms are sweating through the envelope.

Casey is staring at me, his head leaning slightly to one side and his lip curled just enough. I overlap this visual with the memory of his hand on my body and I quiver, having to take a step or two back just to mask it.

"All right," he says, the word a little tentative, but his smile more anxious now.

"All right," I repeat, walking backward and begging him to follow in my head.

I lead him through the door, and we stop at the hallway where my brother stands with one hand on either wall, kicking his legs out one at a time to show our mom how long his new pants are.

"They look very nice," she says, complimenting him.

My father is making a sandwich at the counter, but stops to look over the rim of his glasses, nodding to agree.

"Yep, they're pants," my dad affirms. My mom shoots him a look and he raises his shoulders at her, mouthing "What?" She juts her chin forward and wrinkles her nose, gritting her teeth, and my dad rolls his eyes. "They're *great* pants. *Amazing* pants. The best pants I've ever seen," he says, turning to my mom again and mouthing "happy?"

She smiles and mouths, "Yes!"

"I like them *almost* as much as the khakis," Casey says. My father stops making his sandwich, my mother freezes, and I hold my breath. We all look to Lane, who is still looking down at his own legs.

"Me, too. They're not as comfortable. The khakis are better. But it's nice to have something different," he says, turning to move back to his room. "Thanks, Casey!" he shouts over his shoulder before shutting his door.

"Anytime, buddy," Casey calls out after him.

I'm facing my dad, watching him look on at Casey with curious eyes. His hands finish building his lunch, but his gaze remains on the boy he doesn't know much about. Casey slides closer to the counter, and my mother joins us.

"Why'd you have to bring up the khakis. Didn't you tell him, Murph? The khakis were the problem," she explains, a gentle worry line on her forehead.

"No," Casey says. "The khakis weren't the problem."

My mom opens her mouth to respond, but shuts it quickly, taking in his words before walking away.

"You're right," she says as she moves down the hall to my parents' room.

My father's eyes have never left him; they're still scrutinizing the details. He's dusting crumbs from his hands over the sink, all the while looking, until I see his mouth begin to curve up in approval. My father's head leans forward so he can peer over his glasses, and Casey meets his gaze. No words are exchanged, but my father nods once, then walks past us, patting Casey on the shoulder with a heavy hand twice.

We both hear the television click *on*.

"Your dad…he's…" Casey says, looking out into the room, to the back of my father's head. "Kind of intimidating. Like…like a professor who knows you don't have the answer."

I chew at my cheek, but eventually smile and look Casey in the eyes. I wait for several seconds, then I step closer and pat him in the same spot on his shoulder before turning to walk toward my room.

"That shit isn't funny, Murphy. Not funny at all," he chuckles.

"It's kinda funny," I say, my chest thumping, because he's following me. He stayed. He saw Lane. He's still here.

I'm stunned.

Casey

I think the only person left in this house who I'm not afraid of is Lane. But I don't think it would take much for him to put me on edge, too. It's because I want him to like me. I want them *all* to like me. The way I want Houston's family to like me, only I've been *family* to Houston for so long that it's easy to be around them now. Murphy's family—they're all new.

And I like them—the way they laugh and tease, the way they talk. I love how they look at each other, and how nobody yells or lectures. Her house always smells like cookies.

146

Nobody here is dying with an iron heart like they are in my family's home.

I want Murphy to like me most.

I like Murphy.

It is most definitely, without doubt, not about just the music any more. It's about making her happy. It's about making her shine. And not because I want to ride her coattails, but I just want it for her.

Her room is still so young. It makes me smile as I follow her inside. I stop at the door and hold it, waiting for her to turn around.

"I don't know the protocol here, do I close this? Or…will your dad knock me out with a bat if I do?" I chuckle.

Her eyes grow wide for a second and she starts wringing her hands, then swallows.

"Oh, uh…well…I guess you can close it? I mean…yeah, just close it," she says, straightening her posture mid-speech and shaking out her nerves with a flit of her hand.

I smirk and look at the door handle, then back to her. Her eyes are wide on it again. She's nervous about being alone with me, which is either really good, or really bad.

"You know what? It's your parents' house, and out of respect…" I say, letting go with the door about six inches from closed. I see her exhale.

"Thanks for coming with us, and for what you said to Lane," she says.

My eyes find hers like magnets, and I hold them as long as she'll let me, eventually blinking, her long lashes sweeping over her freckle-dusted cheeks as her gaze falls to her lap and her teeth pin her lip in this perfect grin. Her smile is like her songs.

"Your brother is a really neat guy," I say.

She giggles. "Ha…neat. That's…that's just a really strange word to see come out of your mouth," she says.

My mouth twists as I raise my eyebrows once.

"I just meant…you're like…cooler than the word *neat*," she says, her tongue all nervous, the words having a hard time flowing.

I glance up and run my hand through my hair, holding it out of my eyes, and she remembers that she has my hat.

"Oh, yeah…" she says, standing and pulling it from her pocket. She hands it to me. "Sorry, I forgot."

"Thanks," I say, sliding it on and moving to the opposite wall of her room, sliding down with my legs out in front of me.

There's a short period of silence, and at one point, we're both chewing at the inside of our mouths and staring at each other.

"It's a neat hat," she finally says, giggling lightly and blushing at her joke.

I kick my foot forward into her toe and she glances up.

"You're neat," I say, which only makes her blush worse.

Satisfied, I lean forward and run my thumb along the spine of a few of her music books. I stop when I reach a thin booklet labeled THEATER PHOTOS. I pull it out halfway and look to her for approval. I already stepped over the line stealing her songbook, which I'm glad I did. I saw the one about last night at the club with me. But I didn't want to embarrass her. I meant what I said, too—the last song I flipped to, the one at the beginning, hit a nerve. She should put music to it.

Murphy shrugs, so I pull the book out, flipping through scrapbook pages of her in many of our high school productions. I recognize some of them from the yearbook, but there are others that are just of her with friends behind the scene. In a few of them, she's being held by a guy I faintly recognize. I bet he was a nice guy. I hate him.

"Boyfriend?" I ask, quirking a brow and touching the photo in question.

"Hookup," she says, holding my gaze. I wait for her to say she's fucking with me. She doesn't, so I widen my eyes and mouth *okay*. She laughs once as I gaze down.

"Like you can judge," she says once my eyes are no longer on her.

Her response stings, but I keep my eyes on the pictures in front of me and give her that one, because she's right—like I can judge. Though, since I heard her song, I haven't done any hooking up.

Nobody seems to be able live up to the temptation Murphy already is.

I flip to another page and she lets out a heavy breath, so I look up.

"Yes, boyfriend," she says. "I don't know why I said hookup. I just wanted to seem cooler than I really was, and now I feel stupid," she says, hooding her eyes and lifting her fingers one at a time to peek at me.

I give in with a half smile.

"It's okay. And…" I look down again, flipping through more pages, "I liked it better when he was just a hookup. Not really crazy about *boyfriend.*"

When I glance up again, her eyes are waiting, and her mouth is shut. She isn't blushing, but she's understanding a little more. *Yeah, Murphy…this is about more than music. You aren't just neat.*

Her book is in my lap, and her body is in front of me, and all I want to do is toss it to the side and sit up on my knees to touch the real thing, but then there are those little digs she takes. I'm pretty positive that Murphy wouldn't trust me if I did.

I don't really blame her.

"I stuttered," she says, breaking the silence. Our eyes are still locked as she speaks, her pupils dilating with her honesty. I can see the panic coursing through her veins, and I can tell her heart is beating harder. "You asked about *Helen Keller.* Earlier. I…I stuttered. I loved theater, and I wanted to be on stage, but I couldn't…I still can't…get the sentences out."

My eyes fall to her hands, which are twisting again.

"It was really bad when I was younger. My mom homeschooled me until high school, but I wanted to have friends and to have that *high school experience.* Totally overrated, by the way," she chuckles.

I smirk, because I understand. I lived the life of the party, and I said *yes* to everything and everyone in my circle of friends. I did it because I had nowhere else to be. If I went home, it was suffocating, unless nobody was there, which was most of the time.

When my father was home, the questions came fast and my answers were pointless. *Make sure you test high in AP. Did you ask for college credit? See if your counselor has scholarship packets. Did you say you wanted to take music? That's a waste of time. Don't waste time. Frivolous. Pointless. Useless.*

"And *Helen Keller…*" I say, looking up at her with that page open in her scrapbook.

"Yeah, she didn't talk. Kinda perfect role for me!" she grins.

I laugh lightly, my eyes falling back down to the photo—it's the same one in the yearbook, the same one I stole from Houston and look at almost every night. It's her eyes. Those unbelievable eyes.

"I bet you were great in it," I say, glancing up again.

She tilts her head to the side and takes in the picture, leaning forward and twisting the book in my lap so she can get a better view. She falls back to her bed, sitting on the edge, and lets a full smile stretch her lips.

"I was fucking phenomenal," she says.

I laugh without sound and shut my eyes, shaking my head.

"You seem to have found your voice just fine…and your modesty," I say.

"It just about kills me every day," she says, her smile falling into a more serious expression. She leans back on her hands and takes in a deep breath before letting her head tilt back, her hair fall down her arms and her eyes close at the coolness of her ceiling fan.

I don't ask her, instead waiting patiently for her to tell me. Whatever it is, it's personal—one of those deep scars. And for the first time since knowing *this* Murphy, since wishing I knew the one in the photo, I see the exhaustion on her body and face.

"It's like acting," she says, her head falling forward and her eyes meeting mine.

"What is?" I ask.

"When I sing. When I talk. When I…when I *anything* really. I'm constantly acting. It's a performance," she says.

I tilt my head, not understanding.

"That's how the music started," she says, leaning back again, this time falling flat against her bed and pulling her knees up, turning and lying on her side to face me. She's beautiful this way.

"Before my freshman year, I went to see a specialist who suggested I try singing as a form of therapy," she says. "I'd already played the guitar since I was nine, so he thought it might come easier that way."

"And did it?" I ask.

"Not at first," she says, pulling the familiar black notebook from her night table where she had set it and flipping through a few pages before stopping and tossing the open booklet to me. It's the song I heard her sing to her brother the other day. It's quirky and sweet, nothing but rhymes—almost like something my sisters used to sing in the street playing jump rope.

"This is Lane's song," I say, giving her a half smile. She reflects my expression and closes her eyes in fondness.

"It is," she says. "That one came so easy. I think because it's about him, and it made me think of him and these silly words he and I like to say. I wrote it to help him with bad dreams, stringing together all of our favorite things. And then I played it with my guitar, and for the first time ever—for as long I can remember speaking words—everything came out fluid. It was like water. So easy."

"That's amazing," I say, the nagging feeling triggering thoughts…memories.

Murphy lays flat against her hand, her other arm falling over the edge of the bed, tickling the strands of carpet below, her fingers delicate just as she is with her guitar.

"My therapist said it's common—for stutterers. When you're trying to just say what's in your head, it's too much. It's like the intersections in your brain that work on forming sentences and actually speaking them get overloaded, a kind of traffic jam. It causes all of these misfires in your brain and your mouth just mimics it," she says.

"You said it's exhausting. And sometimes…" I don't finish, because I don't want her to think I notice. It isn't noticeable, really. It's only that now that I know…I see it.

"When I get nervous. Like…really nervous. Which…being on stage makes me, like, *way* nervous," she says, closing her eyes and tucking her chin. I watch her lashes open slowly, blinking, before the grays open fully on me. "*You* make me nervous."

I don't react. I work hard not to react. After a second or two, I offer a crooked smile and lean my head.

"I shouldn't make you nervous," I say.

She shrugs.

"You do," she says, her eyes piercing me. She makes me nervous, too.

I swallow, and I know she sees it.

"So, what's exhausting?" I ask, wanting to get us both off the hook. She's not so anxious though. She seems comfortable with the silence. This is one of those moments where she's in charge. I pull my knees up and prop her book against my legs, flipping through more pages because *I'm* the one folding.

"The performance of it all," she says. "It's not like you can sing all the time. I mean…I guess you could. But then you'd be like one of those people in musicals that gets dropped into the real world and only knows how to function while singing, but everyone looks at you weird because…*duh!* There really isn't singing in the real world."

I laugh at her, closing her book and sliding it in front of me on the floor.

"You're amazing, you know that?" Her smile while lying down is better than the one she gives while standing. I lock the vision of it away and pray to see it closer one day.

"Are you *trying* to make me stutter?" she giggles.

"Maybe," I smirk.

She breathes in slowly, rolling on her back and stretching her arms over her head. The black T-shirt she's wearing rides up enough that I see her sides and bare stomach above her low-slung jeans, and I think to myself how far I've come. Any other girl,

152

some other place and time, and I would be switching gears right now, capitalizing, because I always get the girl. I just don't always *keep* the girl. They learn things, grow tired of me, or, more often, I am bored and done before anything has a chance. It's never been the right girl, really. But Murphy...she's a *keep* kind of girl. And this whole thing started because she hates me, so patience is necessary. But I have had my hand on that stomach. I've felt how warm her skin is through layers of fabric. I bet her skin is searing bare.

Patience isn't a virtue. Patience is a murderer of six-foot-one fools desperate to kiss girls who sing like angels and look like my dreams.

"I pretend it's all a performance," she says finally.

"What's a performance?" I ask.

"Life," she says, falling to the side again.

Her eyes—they're tired. I see it now.

"I think that's true for all of us," I say, exhaling and sliding down enough that only my head is propped against her wall. She throws a pillow to me, and I tuck it behind my neck. "Thanks."

Every fiber of my body wants to crawl up next to her. But I can't. Because she would think it's all about the seduction. For once...it's not. So, instead, I'm content staring at her, imagining how her lashes feel on my cheek, how her lips feel when my teeth tug on them, how her body reacts when I drag my hand from her bellybutton to her neck.

"I slip sometimes," she says. I wait for her to explain. "Like in the studio, when we were recording. That's why it was so hard. My nerves. And it's why I only play at Paul's. It took me forever to be able to play there. It still happens, though. I know you've heard it."

"It's not bad," I say, and I mean it. It isn't. If she hadn't told me, I probably would have just always thought it was part of her quirkiness, cute nerves that get the best of her sometimes. Stage fright, maybe.

"It's bad enough. Who wants to hear a girl sing and sound like a skipping record," she says, and I hate that she's frowning.

"I don't know," I say, lifting myself up on my elbows again. "But that's not what people hear when they listen to you."

"What do they hear?" she asks, her mouth crooked in question.

"God. Faith. Soul. It's spiritual," I say.

She laughs my words off instantly.

"You're corny," she says.

I laugh with her, because yeah...I get how that sounds. "I know, but seriously," I say, "you're a gift."

Her laughter fades. She sits up again, her legs dangling from the side of her bed. Gray finds me fast and holds me hostage. I submit with nothing but the truth.

"And you're beautiful," I say. No smile, no pursed lips. All I do is look at her, because she is.

"Casey," she breaths.

"You are."

Silence falls over us again, more comfortable than before. I could sit like this for hours, just looking, and it's so strange how content I am.

"Murphy? Murphy!"

Lane's voice echoes from a few doors down, breaking up what might have been my favorite full minute of breathing ever. It was definitely my most honest minute ever. And I didn't have to say a word.

"Sorry, I'll be right back," Murphy sighs, flashing a bashful smile as she gets up from her bed and steps around me. I pull my legs in and crane my neck to watch her walk down the hall, doubly pleased when she shakes her fingers loose at her sides. I look at my own hands and see that I'm clenching my fists too.

With a silent laugh, I pick up her photo book and move to my knees, gliding over to her small bookcase and sliding the book back into it's spot. She has a few songbooks in here, and I wonder if each is full, or if there are more gems waiting for someone to read them and declare them as worthy of her voice. As beautiful as her singing is, her writing is even more. Hell, there are artists I hear working all day at the studio that don't hold a candle to her writing ability. But they have swagger—and it gets them anything

154

they want, even million-dollar contracts and the attention of all the right people in the industry. This business is ninety-nine percent confidence, and that's what's killing Murphy.

I let my finger trace along a few more spines, stopping at the final four set of books, which I recognize immediately, because I just looked at the yearbooks in Houston's house a week ago. I tip the first one out and flip through a few pages until I find her freshman picture. It's young and barely recognizable, her cheeks rounder and her hair pulled back tightly in a ponytail. I skip through a few more pages without seeing her, and put her yearbook back, taking out the senior one I'd looked at before.

My hand knows right where to go, because I look at the picture so often, and I push down on the crease, exposing all of the image so I can take in her eyes. There are a few notes scribbled on the page with arrows pointing to other people in the drama club picture with her.

"You were great!" one reads.

"You're going to be a star," another says.

I smirk because, yeah…if I have anything to do with it, she is.

I flip through a few more pages, noticing the one of me at the talent show, rapping and pointing to people in the crowd. Looking back on it, I wasn't very good. But it didn't matter, because…well…swagger.

After flipping a few more, I get to the blank pages in the back, and there are only a few signatures left. Some people just signed names. One guy drew a picture that she's semi-scribbled out. I can tell what it is, though—I'm pretty sure I was friends with Mr. Cock and Balls. I flip a few more, and then there's a rush that hits me like morphine in the spine.

In your dreams!

~ Casey Coffield

My heart isn't beating. I think if I don't move soon, I won't be able to, because blood is no longer circulating in my body.

I'm a dick.

I'm a massive, unbelievably self-centered, insensitive dick.

The stutterer.

The girl in the freshman picture.

She wanted to sing in the talent show.

I repeated every word she said as she tried to sing it during her audition.

When she pulled out, I took her spot.

I was amazing.

Everyone loved me.

I'm a fucking dick.

I hear her laughing with her brother less than twenty feet away, and my eyes are red and my veins are full of adrenaline. I have to leave. I can't fix this. And those gray eyes are going to haunt me.

My mouth is watering as I shove the book back onto the shelf, aligning it so nothing looks out of place. I grab my hat from the ground and slide it over my head, holding my palms to my eyes and stretching out my mouth that wants to scream obscenities.

With a deep breath, I step through her door and move toward her brother's room, my keys dangling from my thumb as if this is all nonchalant, as if I'm leaving because something came up or I have somewhere better to go. I force the idea in my head that I am not running away when in fact that is *all* that is happening now. I'm running away, because I'm a dick.

Life is performing.

I'm on stage in five, four, three…

"Hey," I say, leaning into Lane's room. He smiles and waves, and I feel like a fraud.

She turns her head toward me, her fingers working on a knot in a pair of rollerblades. I can't look at her eyes, so I focus on that knot and her fingers and the color of the wheels. Orange. They're orange.

"Sorry, I promised him I'd fix these earlier and I forgot. He's meeting a friend, so it will just be a minute…"

"Actually," I interrupt, cheating and finding her innocent eyes waiting. I look away the second our gazes touch, and I know she notices. I see enough to see her smile fall. I swallow, holding my phone up.

"It's Houston. He needs some help with Leah, so I've gotta go. But...I'll call you," I lie. I'm a horrible liar, so I keep it simple. I say the words I've said to every other girl I've ever wanted to run from. Only this is different. This one—it burns.

"Oh." She knows.

"Thanks, though...for...just thanks," I stammer. My eyes fall to my feet and I pat the frame of the door, quickly putting one foot in front of the other and leaving without even acknowledging the goodbyes her mom and dad give as I head through the door.

I run away.

Because that's exactly what assholes like me do when they're caught.

Fuck.

CHAPTER 11

Murphy

I'm clearly not built for boys and drama. One minute, my tummy was full of butterflies, and I wanted to freeze time and take back all of the eye rolls and sighs I'd given Casey Coffield over the years. Then he left just as quickly as he came, with an incredibly fake reason—and I wanted to choke him for being ridiculous and wasting my time.

And for making my heart flutter.

And for getting my hopes up.

For having hope that I was anything more than a project in the first place.

This is not how things progressed with the nerdy librarian and the guy who was way more into his bass guitar than me while we were dating last year. I thought those relationships were weird, because…well, the guys were weird. But now, I'm thinking *that* is normal, because *this*…it's weird.

Of course, this is also not a relationship.

This is Casey Coffield, and honestly, this could all just be a convenient stop along the way taking over my songs and making them his and getting the credit for them. I don't really think that's what he's doing, but that's where my mind keeps going.

Thank god for Paul's tonight. I need it to clear my head. I also think I might try something new.

When Casey blew out of my house all twitchy and neurotic, I locked myself in my room and finished writing. The music came fast. This tune that's been stuck in my head for months was perfect. That song I was so embarrassed about—it isn't sexy at all. It's angry! And it's snubbed and maybe a little bit of a women's anthem.

I called it *Tease*, but I wrote a little note to myself underneath the title that says *Fuck you, Casey Coffield.*

I talked my friend Sam into coming tonight. She works Saturdays because she's the lowest on the totem pole at the paper, and she takes all of the classified ad calls that come in. But the paper isn't far from Paul's. I've already requested to go on last, which is good, because I've been practicing the new song out here in the alley, and it's only getting better.

My phone buzzes with a call, so I stash my pen in my mouth and tuck my notebook under my guitar strings, sitting on a crate and resting my instrument on my leg so I can talk.

"Hey girl. I'm bringing some of the office people. I hope that's okay. They're dying to see my famous friend," Sam giggles. I pause, taking note of the male voices in the car with her.

"How many?" I ask.

"Just Cam," she says, her voice trailing up on the end, which signals that it is *not* just Cam. He's the guy she's been flirting with at work. He's kind of her boss, and it's wholly inappropriate, but when I tell her she just giggles. Sam and Cam—that alone should be a deterrent for her. "And then his best friends work a few buildings over and they usually commute together, so I invited them."

"How many friends?" I shouldn't be nervous. They aren't anyone to me, and Paul's is familiar. But they're *unfamiliar.* And I'm not sure what that will do to the vibe here—my shelter.

"Four?"

She says it like a question.

"That doesn't sound like a very big number, Sam. Surely you can count that high," I say, and I'm being a bitch. But Sam knows my issues. She's known me since high school. She's the other half of the Helen Keller picture—she was my fucking Annie!

I hear the phone rustling, and I can tell that she's covering it with her hand and trying to move to a more private place. I thought they were in a car, though, so I don't know what that place could be.

"They're good guys, Murph. And they're excited to see you. I talk about you all the time when we go out to lunch. When they found out Cam and I were coming tonight they just sort of tagged along," she whispers. I hear a whistling sound in the background and that all-encompassing round of masculine laughter that comes along with a frat party.

"Are they drunk?" I ask. I can already feel my pulse racing.

"No...not...not really," she giggles.

"What the hell, Sam! Are you drunk?"

"No," she says, and her effort to hold in her chortle loses and she snort laughs. "Okay, okay. We got a party bus."

"What? A fucking bus?" I've set my guitar on the ground in my case and am now hunched over, rubbing my head and thinking of a good place to throw up.

"It's not *really* a bus. That's just what they call it. It's more of a limo, actually. It's fully stocked. Cam paid for it. It's fun; you should come out with us after you're done. Oh...hey, we're almost there. I've gotta go!"

My mouth is held open when she hangs up before I have a chance to tell her not to bother coming. It wouldn't matter. This disaster snowball is already rolling.

My arms are sweating. And I can feel the saliva overtaking my tongue. I lean forward more and spit, which is gross and totally ungirly, but it's better than retching.

My phone buzzes against my leg, and I consider tossing it into the garbage bin across the alley. I pinch the bridge of my nose instead, feeling a migraine threatening to break through and turn this evening into the most awesome nightmare ever when I focus on the text message that kicks off a whole new conflict of emotions in my belly.

It's Casey.

I need to talk to you.

That's it.

I need to talk to him too. I'm not going to. I just *need* to. I need to tell him to quit fucking with my head, and to not leave me hanging after saying things like I'm beautiful and special and...he called me beautiful, goddamn it!

"Murph? You out here?" I hear the smack of the door around the corner and soon my friend Steph is standing under the lights of the neighboring restaurant back entrance.

160

"I'm here," I say, raising a hand and palming my phone. "I was just working out a few new things."

"You look like you're getting sick," she says. Steph has seen my not-so-great performances. She just thinks its stage fright. If that were my only demon.

"Yeah, that too. I'll be all right, though. I'll be in in a few minutes."

Her feet shuffle in the gravel and I plaster a huge smile on my lips to look at her, because if she comes over to check on me, I'm not so sure that the fake grin will do the trick close up.

"All right. Well, your friends are here," she says.

My stomach rolls.

"Awesome," I say, holding up a thumb.

She chuckles and turns toward the door, her guitar hung around her back all Johnny-Cash style. Steph is hip like that. She looks like Joan Jett, but sings country. Maybe I can convince Sam to lie and tell her crew of boyfriends that Steph is really *me* on stage. Knowing that won't work, I bend forward and spit one more time, saying a quiet prayer that the contents in my stomach stay put, then close up my guitar case and head inside to Paul's. At this point, my performance is going to be whatever it's going to be. I shove my phone into my back pocket and pretend I never saw Casey's message in the first place, because really? I can only handle one hot mess at a time.

Almost an hour passes between Steph's session and the one right before mine. I've been hanging out in the back, pacing between Sam's table of misfits and the line of performers for the night at the bar.

I've never met Cam before, but he hugged me. So did his cousin Ted—I think that was his cousin. They look nothing alike, so they may have been messing with me. I'm pretty sure Ted isn't even his name. It doesn't matter really, because I don't care who any of these guys are. I'm *hopefully* never going to see them again. I'm most certainly never going to hug them again.

I'm next, so I haven't been back to their table for the last ten minutes. I shouldn't have ever visited them at all, but I wanted to

161

see Sam, and I knew she wanted me to meet Cam—who is still a horrible idea. At least he's nice. They were all nice, in that very drunk kind of way. They were really excited about hearing me sing, and they promised shouts and cheering, which I begged against. They didn't hear my begging, so I've been spending the last ten minutes contemplating faking the flu so I can get out of going on and being stared at and cheered for by the drunk table of five.

"Everyone take two to get another drink and then get settled for our girl Murphy Sullivan. She's sort of a crowd favorite here at Paul's, so if this is your first time, you're in for a treat," says Eddie, the Paul's announcer. He's the manager, and I think he might be in his seventies. He wears a three-piece suit every Saturday, because he says anything less would be an insult to "these fine paying patrons."

I love Eddie. He's a little gruff at first. He doesn't like to mince words, and he's always right to the point. But he's also fiercely loyal, and because he likes me, I know I'll always have one man in my corner.

"You're the big finale tonight, sugar," he says, stepping off the stage and resting a palm on my shoulder with a small squeeze. I smile and nod, but internally I feel every trigger that happens when I faint. If only I could *actually* pass out. That might get me out of this.

Eddie passes and I stand, swapping places with my guitar case, pulling the strap around my body and adjusting while I hold the pick between my teeth. And because I haven't been tested enough in life, my nightmare gets exponentially worse the second I turn around.

"Don't swallow that," Casey says.

He's wearing the same thing he was in when he walked out of my house this afternoon. Even the damn beanie that I tried to steal away is in its place, on his head. His smile is stupid and lopsided, and I want to spit the pick out of my mouth at his face, but I know I can't spit hard enough. With my luck, it would probably just get stuck on my lower lip.

162

"You didn't have to come watch me tonight," I say, turning my attention to the stage. It's so empty and inviting—nothing but a stool and a mic under dim lighting. This is why I like it here.

"You didn't write back, and I need to talk to you," he says, before both of us are distracted by the countdown happening a few tables away. And my fan base has just upped their blood alcohol content again.

"Hey, I know her, right?" My eyes dart to his, and the stupid smirk on his mouth.

"Oh sure, *her* you remember," I say with a roll of the eyes.

Sam was like a bridge in high school—she was a cheerleader because she loved gymnastics, but she also loved theater, so we hung out a lot. She and I always clicked, and when we found out we were going to the same college, we signed up to room together. We've never talked about Casey, because there was never anything to talk about. Even now, she just knows him as that guy from high school who it turns out works for a record label now and might hook me up. I don't tell her about the butterflies. I don't tell her, because they aren't supposed to be there, and clearly Casey would prefer them to go away, too.

I can feel him looking at me as I straighten my flowing blouse and tank top over my jeans, pulling the wrinkles free from my guitar strap. I pledge to keep my eyes focused on the stool, on my next mission—the next fifteen minutes that will be over soon. But then the son of a bitch talks and gets in my head again.

"I just meant from that picture. That's the girl in the picture with you, from Helen Keller," he says.

I give in and look at him, and his eyes are squinted and his mouth slightly askew. That's his pondering face—he's pondering if I'm jealous.

Well, I am. Good for you, Casey Coffield—I'm a mess of a jealous girl with a crippling disorder that I literally have to punch in the face every time I want to touch my dream. Thanks for the distraction, though.

"I'm on," I say, shaking my head and stepping up the side stairs opposite Eddie.

My senior citizen friend points a finger at me with raised brows, asking if I'm ready. No, I'm not—but I give him a thumbs-up anyhow, because nothing is going to get magically better in the next few seconds.

Eddie announces me as the last open-mic performer for the night, and I walk to my tiny island of a stool while my drunken best friend and her fraternity chant my name and pound their fists on the table. The scene is comical. It must be, because other people are laughing.

I search the front row tables for familiar faces, but there aren't any. Only laughing faces. And my ears quiet with the hum of stress that's now taking over my nerve endings.

"H...H...Hi," I say, feeling the pull.

I stall by pretending I need to adjust the mic, siting on the stool with my legs crossed and pulling the slender stand close to my body. I twist the coupling in the middle and lower it too far on purpose so I have to adjust it back to where it was. It's a ruse, and I'm pretty sure everyone knows it.

My hearing clears, but only long enough to hear one of Sam's friends whistle and call out my name. I chuckle, but it's pretend.

"Thank you," I say, my voice soft in the mic.

Why did I pick a new song to do? I should stick with my tried-and-true set. My guitar is tuned for something entirely different though. I spend long seconds staring at the strings, debating changing, and searching for something clever to say—a story to tell—to amuse the small crowd here while I fix my guitar for a different song.

"I just need..." I start, looking out, but only seeing lights. That's why I love Paul's—because I can't see people—the lights blind. Only tonight, I hear people I can't see. It's worse. There's a whistle again, and my eyes fall to my trembling hands, and my guitar slips, knocking the mic stand forward. I grab it in time, but the large wailing sound of a typical sound check deafens.

My heart hurts.

I've battled this so many times—even in recent years. I always keep my shit together. I can defeat it. I don't cry. I won't cry.

164

"I'm…" Nothing comes next. *I'm sorry.* That's what I'm supposed to say. My voice is supposed to come out charming. I'm supposed to be approachable and friendly. I should smile, but I can't even feel my face. The words are locked away.

"Murphy," someone says, louder than a whisper. "Murphy," my name is called again.

I lean forward and cradle my guitar, giving myself this one second to decide to bolt or keep fighting.

"Murphy," he says it again.

Casey. He's standing at the edge of the stage, holding my guitar pick. I tilt my head up, hiding from most of the world behind my hair. He's smiling. Not laughing. He's smiling, barely and his eyes are looking for me, to pull me back.

"You dropped it," he says, the silver pick nothing compared to the size of his hand. He holds it up between two fingers, and I take it, whispering "Thank you."

"You're all right," he says before I can look away. "Just jump. You're all right."

My heart is pounding, so I hold onto his gaze for a few extra seconds, my hands searching for the right hold on my guitar, the muttering of people in the audience growing louder.

"Jump," he says.

I never stop looking at him. I convince myself we're in the studio—and he's just played Van Halen for me, poorly. It's a joke that happens only in my head, but it makes me smile. I find the mic and tilt it into place, and I talk to him…and nobody else.

"Sorry about that," I chuckle. "I uh…I…"

No.

My eyes close and open for a reset. I smile, the outline of Casey's face all I see under the hot lights above.

"I dropped my pick," I laugh.

I will myself to charm the crowd I've lost, and I block out the catcalls from my friend and her friends. I focus on Casey's smile— and the fact that he is somehow here. Even though he makes a mess out of my heart and head. He's still here. And I lean on him.

"This is something new," I smirk.

His head tilts.

And as much as I wanted to make this song a hate anthem about boys like him, when faced with one that's rooting for me, I just can't.

"It's called 'Tease,' and I'll let y'all sort out what it's about," I say, a playful smile making my lips twitch as I lean forward and feel the energy of the mic calling me close.

Casey

"Tease"—there could not be a better title for that song.

I'm not sure if she realizes how sexy it is, but wow! I hit record on my phone the second she said she would be playing something new. I was expecting the song I told her I liked. This surprise is welcomed, though.

The staccato lyrics spill from her troubled mouth like poetry. She's putting men in their places—calling us all on our ways. She's putting *me* in my place. And I'm going willingly. This song is her dominating me.

By the second verse, she loses herself, and I know she's going to be all right. I lean back in my chair and just listen, my head internalizing and working out the rhythm. I can't wait to layer this with something soulful. This song—it's the kind of song people make love to.

My eyes open on her at that thought. My hand flexes at the memory of being splayed over her stomach, and I imagine more. By the final verse, she's so close to the mic that I watch her love it—her tongue slow across her lips in carefully timed swipes. I am mentally begging her to lick it. This is her performing, and she is a master.

I'm her slave.

I shut off the recording when her final note ends and the applause erupts. Her table of friends is obnoxious, and I can see it threaten her peace, so I lean forward again to catch her sightline.

"So good," I mouth slowly.

166

I don't smile, but only because I can't. The feelings she's stirred—they aren't the smile kind. They're primal.

They're probably the exact kind of feelings an asshole like me gives into, which is why I'm going to give her the news I came here to share, and then leave.

I suppose the news could have waited. When I think about it, it's selfish that I'm here at all. Of course it's selfish—that's what I do, isn't it? I want to tell her because she'll be happy, and that will make me happy. So if I reduce the formula, I'm here to make myself happy. I swear it's not that I want credit, though. It's only that I want to give her a taste of success, because she's worked hard, and she needs something to believe in.

And since I've ruined so much...

She finishes three more songs, then escapes to the edge of the stage. I wait patiently at my table near the front, nursing the small Pepsi I ordered instead of the double shots of whiskey I wanted. The loud table that's been cheering for her—*obnoxiously*—stands and meets her at the bottom of the steps. Her friend, the one I recognize, is tipsy, but is genuinely proud of our girl. The guys are clueless losers—especially the one that wraps his bear-claw arms around her and lifts her from the bottom step, spinning her once before setting her on the ground. At least, I *presume* he set her on the ground. I had to look away.

When I search for her again, a minute later, Murphy has moved to the tight area behind the bar where she's filling out something on a clipboard. It's probably the list to perform next week. Bear-claw is overly interested, leaning over the bar and watching her write, and before my self-discipline kicks in, I walk over there with the intent of pressing my palm against his forehead to shove his face away.

"Well, I'll be damned," her theater friend slurs. "In the flesh!"

I grin at her, tight-lipped, and pull my beanie from my head, tucking it in my back pocket before running my hand through my hair and stretching my palm out to shake hers. She stumbles into me and her hand grabs at my chest in that familiar way I've come to know at the end of the night in a club or bar. Only this time, I wish it were the hand of the girl watching me with disgusted eyes. And I wish it weren't a bar at all, but rather her bedroom, while on her floor, listening to her favorite records.

"Good to see you," I say, because while I recognize her, I don't remember her name either.

"That's Sam," Murphy says, her eyes set on the notepad she's still writing on. "You recognized her tits, remember?"

Her eyes shut instantly and she sets down the pen, her fingers flexing for a brief second before turning away. I think even she's surprised she said that. Good on her, though, because there's really no response for me to give. *No, I didn't recognize her tits* comes to mind, but only for an amusing second.

"Yeah, Sam. I remember," I lie. That was the wrong thing to say, because Murphy spins and gives me a sharp glare the second I do.

"I mean, from the theater photos…I saw your picture." I try to repair the damage, but it doesn't matter—Murphy's moved on, working to pack up her guitar and fend off the banal conversation from the bear-claw lips hovering over her.

"Murphy says you're helping her get a record deal?" Sam asks, her hands flirty, touching my collar and arm. I take a step away so she's closer to the guy she came with and begins touching him instead.

"Well, that's what he says, but…we'll see," Murphy hums, her tone doubtful as she snaps the clasps shut on her case and pulls the strap along with her bag over her shoulder. "Sam…*and friends,*" she grimaces, "thanks for coming. I've got an early morning, so…"

"Awwww, I thought you were coming out with us. Party bus!" Sam says, hopping on her toes. It's amazing to me how this behavior is so appealing when I'm lit.

"Sam," Murphy says, squaring her shoulders with her liquid-happy friend. "It's not a bus, dear. It's a limo—and it's a gross one at that. And you know I am not the party girl."

"I know, but…" her friend whines.

"I love you. I'll see you for lunch this week," Murphy says, tilting her head forward. The exchange is sweet, and I'm envious as she glances at me and furrows her brow before turning and marching right through the back door to her car.

"Murph, hey…wait," I call after her. She isn't running, but she's not wasting any time, either. "Murph…"

She turns and offers a tight-lipped, very fake smile. It catches me off guard so I stare at her for a second, my lips parted and my heart surprised at the way it feels. My eyes fall closed and my head tips forward with a breath of a smile.

"I'm sorry. You're just…you're kind of all fired up, and it caught me off guard," I say, cocking an eyebrow as I glance up to her.

She doesn't look at me—instead only fidgeting with her keys and chewing at her lip. The longer it takes for her to find her words, to look up at me and answer, the more I realize just how much damage I've done. I forced her to play pretend, and she has been trapped in that role ever since. I need to leave this girl alone, but I need to make it right first.

"Lane really liked your com…your company today," she says, her gaze still at her own feet.

A legit smile hits my lips at the memory of earlier, before pieces started falling into place. I swallow while I think of what to say, a way to answer that conveys exactly what today was for me, a way that say's *I'm sorry,* and means it for everything—*all* of the things.

"I heard from John…" I say instead, because that's what I can give her.

I can give her her dream.

Her expression changes, and her hands stop twisting as she pulls her lips into her mouth, sucking and holding her breath. She brings her eyes to mine, ready for disappointment.

No, Murphy. I wouldn't come out here tonight to disappoint you. I'm never going to disappoint you again.

"Think you can get a sub for your class tomorrow? He likes to sign contracts in the morning…when his lawyer is in…and…"

"Shut up," she interrupts, her bottom lip jutted out, her eyebrows rising slowly, realization sinking in. I can't help but smile at her happiness.

"He loved it," I say.

"Shut up," she says again, this time a small tickle of a laugh squeezing through. Her lips begin to curve and the light in her grays comes alive as her hand cups her mouth.

"I will…in a minute," I laugh. She steps forward and pushes the center of my chest, shoving me off balance. I laugh and catch her hand, but let her fingers slide through mine quickly because that's not what this moment is about.

"He loved it, Murphy. I knew he would. And he wants to get you in to the studio fast. He was going to call himself, but I…" I pause, thinking the truth. *But I'm a selfish prick, and I wanted to be the one who got to make you happy—just once.*

"Thank you, Casey," she says, taking a step toward me and throwing her arms around me.

The girl who doesn't like to hug pulls me close and buries her face in my chest, and I memorize the soft feel of her hair on my neck and chin. My hands grip for a second, holding the fabric of her shirt as my eyes fall shut and I breathe her in. I let go and step back after only that second, though—that's more than I deserve—and I push my hands in my pockets.

Murphy brings both hands up to cover her mouth again, but she can't hide the smile in her eyes.

"So you'll let me know? If you'll make it in tomorrow?" I say, taking a step or two in the opposite direction, my keys in my hand.

She nods *yes*.

"I'll be there," she says. "I'll get someone to cover, and I'll…I'll be there."

"Eight…if you can," I say.

"I can," she responds.

With tight lips, I smile and nod before holding up a thumb. I spin and move toward my car, looking over my shoulder to give her one more congratulations, but she's already moved into her driver's seat and shut the door. She's already pulling out and rushing home—to her beautiful family, who will embrace her and fill her head with positive thoughts about how this is only her beginning.

170

I stop at my car door and watch her pull away, satisfied that she has this new start, as my phone buzzes in my pocket. I pull it out, naïve to think it's her.

It's Christina.

It's my nightmare.

He's asking for you. You have to come.

I sit in the parking lot behind Paul's for three hours and try to think of a way to tell her *no*.

Because I'm a selfish prick, and I don't want to give him the satisfaction.

CHAPTER 12

Casey

She texted me that she'd be at the studio by eight, so I arrived at seven. She showed up at seven-thirty. Somehow, I knew she would.

"So the paperwork...is it...I don't know...a lot?"

She's polished off an entire pitcher of water in the conference room. I refilled it, and she's pouring her second glass from this round. When she finishes that one, I slide the pitcher away from her, moving it to the far end of the table, and her eyes flash up to me.

"You're going to drown," I smirk.

She smiles with tight lips and pushes her glass away, falling back in her seat.

"I'm nervous," she admits.

"I know. Don't be," I smile.

I've purposely remained two seats away from her, careful not to be too close. I don't want her to have a reason not to trust me, or for her to get some crazy notion that I'm going to swoop in and take this from her, too. I don't want to mess this up, but I also know she doesn't want to be left to do it alone.

I'm not naïve enough to think that John will involve me to a large extent in any projects with her. But when I spoke with him yesterday, he mentioned several times how much he liked the mix and what I'd done. A few weeks ago I would have seized that opportunity and come in guns blazing with ideas for other things I can do. But now I don't want to make this so much about me as much as I want to make it about her.

"All right, let's get this deal done. Murphy Sullivan, yeah?" John says, stepping in and looking at the papers that his assistant just placed in front of him rather than the girl the papers are about.

Murphy stands and moves her hand toward him to shake, but I hold my hand up and wave her off. As much as she doesn't like to be hugged, John Maxwell does not like to be touched. He's a

172

brilliant producer and an enormous name in the business—but it's not because of warm fuzzies. He's cutthroat when it comes to getting his artists the airtime they deserve. Murphy—she needs cutthroat in her corner, but I'm not sure she'll realize that.

She looks at me confused, but I shake my head and smile, winking, my signal for her not to worry.

"I really like your sound, Murphy," John says, flipping through the standard boilerplate contract, checking with a pen next to the places that already have his name signed. I'm sure he has a person that does that.

"Thank you," she says, her voice soft. I can hear her struggle.

John isn't easy. Most of his artists are men—the kind in the news for hopping through celebrity girlfriends they swoon with their guitars. So, assholes. *Yeah, I fit right in.*

"Murphy…look…" he says, finally dropping his pen and leaning back in his chair, his hands folded behind his head with his winning smile atop his perfect, crisp, white shirt collar. The man is success in a suit, and this is the move he makes when he wants something. I've seen it. It's how he got me. He wants her on his label. He wants her bad.

"I'm not going to kid you or waste your time. You have something…" he stops, leaning forward with an arm on the table as his mouth ticks up. "Unique. You're unique. And I…" his eyes squint, "don't come across unique very often in this business."

"Okay," she says, barely audible. Her eyes are terrified, and her hands are now tucked under her legs. She wore the gray dress from the night at the club, but she also wore tall black boots and a black business jacket that slims at the waist. Somehow, she's made that fucking dress even hotter, and I think John likes that too. Sex sells—it sells records.

"If we can agree on this," he says, waving his hand over the contract spread out in front of her, "I'd like to get you in the studio today."

Her eyes grow wide, and I see the anxiety coloring her skin. I jump in.

"Is this just for the song we demo'd? Or is this for the full contract?" I ask, and John's jaw flexes. I move my eyes to her, gesturing that I'm only trying to put her at ease, not act as her agent, though I know that's her fear—she'd prefer her dad get a shot at looking these papers over.

"For now, yes. We're looking at a single," John says, his mouth a hard line, and my shot at working on her mix down the toilet. "What you gave me—it's a hit, Murphy. If we give it the right push, the right touch. But I'm a businessman, so I'd really like to test the waters with it."

Disappointment crawls into her expression.

"But I have a feeling," John pipes in quickly. He saw it too. Disappointed artists don't sing with passion, they sing with reservation, and he can't have that. "I think we'll be sitting down here and talking about some bigger plans very soon."

He pushes the papers forward, turning them to her view and sliding the pen next to them. You can take as long as you need. My secretary, Cara, can take your signed copy and make sure everything is squared up. And if you're able, just head to the main studio on the end; I'd like to hook you up with Gomez.

Her frightened eyes find mine. I shake my head lightly, so she swallows her question down and thanks John again as he stands to leave the room. Her hand out again, John smirks at it and takes it into his own. Only I notice him wipe his fingers with a towelette on his way out of the room. I'm glad Murphy didn't see it. It isn't personal—he does it constantly.

"What do you think?" she says the moment the door closes and we're alone.

I remain two seats away, but turn my chair to face her, scratching at my chin and dragging the paperwork closer to me to review. I recognize the language instantly—it's the same exact thing I signed. It gives John control over her song—the one about me—but it's open ended after that, giving them both an out. It's the biggest shot she's ever going to get. And if John wants it now, it means there's a slim opening somewhere that he thinks it fits. Waiting a day—I don't think she can wait a day.

174

"I think…" I pause, returning the contract to her and letting go before our fingers have a chance to graze. "I think it's an amazing opportunity that *you* deserve," I say.

"Who's Gomez?" she asks, knowing, but not wanting to say it out loud.

"He'll do great things with you," I say through a soft smile, my heart breaking at the thought of someone else being trusted with her voice. This isn't about me; it's about someone else knowing what to do. I meet her gaze and try to force down the lump in my throat.

"But if I'm working with him…" She knows.

I nod.

"I'm new here. I'm…I'm not even fulltime yet. Gomez—he's…well…here, let me show you something," I say, urging her to stand and walk to the far wall with me, where gold records hang along with dozens of plaques and Billboard Awards. I point to the first one, and say his name. I point to the next and do the same. I credit him with at least sixty percent of the hardware hung on the studio wall.

"So that all…that means he's good?" she asks.

Does it?

I don't answer, instead letting out a long breath tainted with indecision. But I know the drill here—I know how easy this kind of deal is to blow.

"Murph, John isn't going to gamble on both of us. He already owns what he wants out of me, and he sees something special in you," I say.

Her eyes fall to the table—to the duplicate copies and legal jargon that always encases the best of hopes and desires. She steps closer, pulling the pen into her hand as she sits down and begins to read.

"But what if…what if I like the song the way you made it?" she asks, not looking at me, breaking me, and making my chest expand with pride and my heart rip with regret.

"I didn't make that song, Murph," I say, as her eyes flit to mine. "You did."

She chews at her lip, her eyes eventually falling back to the decision on the glossed maple planks in front of her. I wait for more questions that never come. I stand in the room, perfectly still and silent while she reads. I wait just in case her belief in herself wavers and I need to tell her she's good enough without me.

I will be her swagger.

When her pen begins to scratch along the paper, I step out of the room and let her revel in the strength she's found on her own.

I busied myself with tapes and phones for the rest of the day—mostly phones. I've been at the studio for just under two weeks, and I'm starting to realize that my role here is not necessary…or really wanted. No, that's not true—it's wanted, it just isn't very glamorous. I feel kind of foolish for going in with my big expectations.

My father's voice is in my head.

John's team and I have different ideas of what my scope is. John wanted me for his club; that much is clear. He wants my local buzz to put Max's on the map. He wants my allure to bring in local talent. In the few years I've been working this circuit, I've cultivated a nice little list of friends. They give me beats, make riffs for me to use in my mixes. I heard him throw my name around with a few other guys he was trying to work on this morning, something about building the Maxwell brand to include more than just folk bands and reformed-country-stars turned pop stars. I've been tasked with scouting YouTube and putting my signature on things to show artists how their sound can transform, be relevant.

Relevant. That's John's favorite word. It's how he hooked me. He said I was relevant and my eyes bugged out like Tweety Bird caught in a trap. An exciting trap—laced with sexy women and expensive cars and dollar signs. So far, all I've gotten in return is a key to use the studio equipment after hours and a used vehicle that loses about a can of oil every two days.

Murphy is relevant—John said it when he called me after hearing her demo, and I know she really is. It kills me that I wasn't in that room with her today, that Gomez is going to get to mold her sound. But that's my ego thinking that I'm the only ear that understands, that my hands are the only ones capable of building the right levels—that my taste rules. This isn't about me, so I block all things Murphy and *her record deal* out of my head as I pull up outside Houston's house, my belly hungry and my heart craving that feeling of home.

Christina hasn't messaged me again; our siblings have taken over the dirty work. Hourly updates laced with just enough guilt to repeatedly make me feel like shit. My father is getting thinner. He's refusing to work with the nurses. He doesn't want to take pain meds. He's questioning what's covered by insurance. He hid this from us all for months. Now it's too late. Mom is crying. Mom is constantly crying. And all she wants is me to come to the house.

It's that last one that stabs. This rift has never been between my mom and me. It was never meant to be, but I can't fathom how my presence in that house can possibly be good for anyone. I would be like shredded paper thrown on a candle. The flames would come fast and indiscriminant.

"Well, if it isn't my boyfriend's *other* child," says a familiar voice. I smile hearing it, but I hide it from her because fuck if she knew I actually liked her. Paige leans halfway out the backdoor, her arms crossed over her chest and her hip slung against the frame. I forgot that she would be here tonight—one more piece of evidence of how self-absorbed I am. I think the date has been circled on the calendar hung in Houston's kitchen for weeks. This date was important to him.

"Well, it's nice to see that your little stint in California hasn't made you go all soft," I say, stepping up toe to toe with her. "You know there's still time…"

"Time for what?" she asks, her mouth tugged up in that irritated face she makes—that *I* get out of her. Maybe I should send *her* in to deal with my sisters—she can handle herself.

"Time to tell Houston the truth—that you were just using him to get to me. Come on Paige, I mean…*all this?* You know you want a taste of Mighty Casey," I smirk.

Paige doesn't hate me…anymore. She doesn't necessarily like me, either. She tolerates me because she's in love with my best friend. That fact makes her all right with me. And picking on her is a wonderful distraction. She couldn't have come back to Oklahoma at a better time.

"You think you'd spend less time walking around in your boxers in front of me," she says, and I narrow my gaze, waiting for the zing. It's coming. "Because now we both know there is *nothing* mighty going on…well…"

My frenemy waves her hand about an inch away from my crotch, not intimidated or offended in the least. I look down and let out a chuckle as I step up and past her on my way into the house.

"Oh, I've missed you Paige," I say. I mean it. I honestly think I have.

"That makes one of us." She doesn't miss a beat.

"Uncle Casey!" Leah shouts, running to me from the sofa where she's playing with what looks like a pair of Paige's shoes. Her feet fall out of the purple heels quickly and she scurries into my arms so I can lift her against my side.

"Hey, princess," I say, twirling her once and walking her with her feet propped atop mine until we're back to her spot on the sofa.

"Paige brought me a new pair of shoes. She said she doesn't want these any more," she says, putting her feet into them and scooting toward the coffee table and television. I chuckle and part my lips, but Paige puts her hands on my shoulders behind me, pinching with enough force to get my attention.

"Don't you dare make a streetwalker joke about those shoes. She loves them," she says.

I shake my head and smile, because she knows exactly where I was going.

"I think you have a little more growing to do, but they look nice," I say instead, making both Paige and Leah's faces glow.

"Are you joining us for dinner, Case?" Joyce asks, busy in the kitchen.

178

"I will never say no to you, Joyce. Not ever," I smile, settling into the deep cushion and lying my head back with the weight of the day.

"Hey," Houston says, taking the final steps down the stairs into the living room. The house is full, and everything here just smells different—like the way a home is supposed to smell. Murphy's house smells like this. I'm thinking about her. I wasn't supposed to do that, but I am.

"So, Houston says someone important actually hired you to come work for them," Paige says, nestling next to Leah. Houston sits on the edge of the coffee table between us both not even phased by our banter.

"Yeah," I say, and I know I don't sound as cocky as Paige expects me to or as defensive and ready to spar as Houston anticipates. Paige quirks a brow, and Houston looks between us both.

His eyes settle on me, and before I can open my mouth to fill him in, my phone buzzes with a call. I pull it out to see my sister Annalissa's name. I watch each ring until the fourth one falls short and she goes into voicemail. I push my phone into my pocket and look at my friend.

"Murphy came in to record," I shrug.

Houston doesn't react, instead lowering his brow and resting back on his hands, studying me.

"We have chairs, Houston. Get your rear end off my table," his mom shouts from the kitchen.

"Yeah, don't be such a Neanderthal," I tease, not really wanting to talk about Murphy.

Houston frowns at me, but moves to the couch next to Leah and Paige.

"Murphy came in," he gets back to it right away.

I nod.

"And you're not boasting about the big score, beaming with your amazing greatness, bragging…"

I cut him off before his choice of verbs continues to disintegrate.

"She's not working with me. John wanted her with Gomez. He's…he's probably the smart choice," I say, careful not to sound as bitter and sad as I feel. I'm happy that my phone is ringing again so at least I don't have to see the expression on Houston's face. He knows landing Murphy was important to me, but I'm pretty sure he also has some semblance of an idea that I'm also a little into her.

A lot into her.

And more than scoring professionally, I wanted to be there to see her fly.

I'm out of my comfort zone. I like a girl, and I don't deserve her, and I'm going to end it at that. The buzz in my pocket comes again, interrupting. This time it's my other sister calling, and I'm hit with that familiar clenching feeling in my stomach that I get when my sisters aren't going to stop. This is how they wear me down. It's effective—or at least it was, when I was a teenager, or when I was ten and I didn't want to clean my room. This thing is much bigger, which means their attempts are probably going to be even more relentless. I push the power button to turn my phone off and step into the kitchen, grabbing a Coke from my surrogate family's fridge.

"Who's Murphy?" Paige asks, and my mind works fast to have a witty answer that will send her in the wrong direction. But I'm not on my game it seems, and Houston beats me to it.

"She's this girl that dear Casey seems to be quite smitten with," he says.

"Dude… seriously…smitten?" I say, pulling the tab on my Coke and moving it to my lips fast to catch the fizz bubbling along the top. "Why do you have to choose pussy words?"

Joyce's hand finds the back of my head fast. I swear, that woman is a ninja.

"Sorry, Mrs. Orr," I say, rubbing where she swatted me. I have a permanent bruise there from her church-loving violence.

"Ugh, is she some new conquest of yours?" Paige says, making all of the assumptions I figured she would.

"Yep," I answer, just hoping to leave it at that.

180

Houston's eyes narrow as he cocks his head and smirks, parting his lips about to blow my secret wide open for his vulture girlfriend to pick apart and make me feel like a sad, smitten, pathetic pussy when his phone rings out loud. He points at me with one hand while pulling his phone out with the other.

Lucky bastard. That's what he's saying with that grin.

"This is Houston," he answers, and I mock him while he cups his ear, trying to listen to the other line.

Paige steps up in front of me, prepared to take her boyfriend's place in grilling me over the new girl, when Houston commands my attention.

"Case," he says, phone now at his side.

His expression is dour.

I know without asking.

My sisters have called him.

The time to run has come to an end.

Murphy

"So this is it? You're legit now?" my best friend says while honking at someone who apparently cut her off.

Sam is the size of a Polly Pocket doll—wafer thin and reaching to my nose if she stands on her tippy toes. Her personality, however, makes her simply *feel* bigger. Her voice is loud; she's brimming with confidence; her blue eyes even turn me on, and her blond hair has always been on my wish list of wants.

Well, no, actually. Not always. When I started dyeing my hair colors other than the dirty dishwater one that naturally sprouts from my head, I fell in love with my trusses. My hair is the one thing that I have absolute faith in, and it comes out of a bottle I buy with a coupon at the drug store.

"This isn't anything, Sam. This is a song deal. Which makes it even more stressful, because what if it isn't good enough? What if…"

She cuts me off.

"You're good enough," she says. I slump down on my bed, letting gravity pull me completely down, my eyes blinking slowly as I watch my ceiling fan whirl in slow-moving circles above me as I wonder if that's true.

"What does Casey think?" she asks.

I don't like the tone in her question. There's a hint of assumption that Casey is more than he is.

"He wasn't really involved," I say, pushing my feet free of the cowboy boots I wore for the seven straight hours of recording I did with Gomez—*not* Casey.

"I thought this was sort of his bag? Like…you were his discovery or whatever," she says.

"I guess he's not high up enough yet or something," I say.

"Oh," is her only response.

I listen to my friend recant her day at the office. She was hungover, which I knew she would be. Apparently, Cam was as well, and he opted to stay home with his *girlfriend* instead of coming into the office. Sam met his girlfriend at the end of the night when their party limo dropped him off first and a woman my friend describes as *hot enough to cheer for the NFL* stood in front of a set of steps leading up to a condo with her arms crossed, pissed that she'd been left at home waiting for him. I let her vent, and I fill in the gaps with the best agreeable comments I can muster with little effort.

I'm not really here for her tonight. I'm being a bad friend. But I'm too upset over my day to buck up and put things aside. Besides, she brought a party limo to my gig last night and heckled me with whistles; so, we're kind of even. She's lucky she's getting my staged responses.

Eventually, Sam makes it to her destination and says goodbye. Without her distraction, my stomach sinks, recalling my day. They made me change my song. Not…entirely. And really, I understand their thought process behind it, but it doesn't fill me with confidence necessarily either. My skin's way too thin for criticism from these seasoned pros.

There was no easing in. The comments came about fifteen seconds in to my first cut. Music was paused, Gomez was in my ears, and feedback flew at me fast.

"Try playing one more bar before you come in."

"You're too breathy in that first line. Save it."

And the one that stings most.

"Who the fuck is Casey Coffield? Let's make it Johnnie Walker. Everyone knows Johnnie Walker. It will make it relatable; a better song."

He's right. And really—Casey was never the reason for the song. But he was the feeling. The sentiment—the symbol or trigger for the fire. And the fact that he brought me this far, and the magic that led him to me again in the first place is the first thing others want to change…I don't like it. It makes me sick, when I should be happy.

He's going to find out eventually. But I want to tell him first.

He was gone from the building by the time I exited the studio. They ordered in lunch, and the sun made it from one horizon to the other during the time I was inside.

I thought that he might text to check in, at least a simple *how'd it go?* But my phone's been silent, minus Sam's call minutes ago. I check again, and am just as disappointed to find it blank.

My parents are both at the high school for Lane, waiting to drive him home after a summer league basketball game. My brother manages the team, bringing towels to the players, making sure water cups are ready and chairs are lined up in front of the bleachers for every home game. The school thought it would be a nice way for him to make more friends, to be involved beyond his special education classes. It's turned into something he loves. He does it for any team and season he can, and my parents usually go to watch him work, because seeing that is something *they* love.

I glance at my clock and consider going too, but leap to a sitting position the moment my phone buzzes with a note from *him*.

I heard you put down great stuff today.

I smile. Fucking heart so fast to betray me.

It was alright.

My fingers move to the edge of the case of my guitar that lies next to me, and I pick at the worn spots where the vinyl is peeling. It should have been amazing. It should have been *ours*. He writes back quickly.

You're being modest. I bet you were fucking phenomenal.

I laugh out loud all alone as he complements me with my own words, and suddenly I miss him. I hold a hand over my mouth and shield my grin. This is the first time I've smiled all day. I spent the afternoon trying to please people that I kinda think I maybe don't like very much. None of this is how I thought it would be. But then one small word from Casey makes me think I'm better than them all, and they're the lucky ones. I type before thinking.

I was. We should celebrate.

I send quickly and watch my phone screen with wide eyes as seconds turn to minutes with no response. Minutes turn to five minutes, and then ten, and soon I become the fool again.

Instead of moping, I decide to join my family at the high school gym, making it there in the middle of the third quarter. I eat a stale hotdog and share some questionable nachos with my father while my mother sneaks out her small plastic bag of salted snow peas for a snack. She's a health nut, and after having to endure years of this woman feeding me at home and packing my school lunch for high school, I vow never to eat a snow pea again.

I overplay my enthusiasm when my parents ask how my day went. "It was amazing! I felt like a star!" I say. My mom hugs me to her side, gushing with pride, but my father looks on over his glasses, noting every single tick I make while lying. Our eyes meet just long enough for me to show him how un-amazing my day really was. He keeps the secret and plays the part for my mom, and as we walk out to the parking lot to wait for Lane to finish stacking chairs and putting away the scoring table, my father whispers that he's sorry and pats my back.

"It wasn't that bad," I say, my mom far enough ahead that she can't hear. My dad and I like to keep her in her bubble—the one where nothing sad happens and where her kids are happy. She has enough to worry about with Lane.

184

"Just…not what I was really expecting," I explain.

"Well, you don't have to do anything you don't want to," my father reminds, and I smile with closed lips to keep my mouth shut. I know what I signed. And my father won't like that I didn't show it to him first. I'm locked into doing a few things, whether I want to do them or not.

I wait with my parents until Lane joins us in the parking lot, his Knights jersey on over his yellow T-shirt that hangs longer over his sweatpants on the bottom. The team made him a special jersey with his name on the back, and Lane makes sure to dress out for every game.

"Murphy, you made it!" he beams.

I pull him in for a hug, and we rock while embracing as if my brother hasn't seen me in weeks. It's impossible not to feel healed after moments like this with him. I grin at my parents as my chin rests on my brother's shoulder, and I worry less about the fact that I gave away some of my creative freedom in trade for fame.

"You're a rock star now," Lane says, backing away and looking at me with pride. And for his sake and my mother's, I keep the smile from before in place and simply agree.

"I won't have the song for a while. But I promise, Lane—you'll be the first one I let hear it," I say, cringing inside because Lane will notice every little change from the original, and he'll be disappointed. My brother hums the melody, though a little off, and my mom joins him as they link arms and amble around their car and climb inside.

"We can go home first and drop your car off if you want to join us for sundaes," my dad offers. It's become a tradition after the Knights win a game, and unfortunate for my ass, my brother's school team is on a bit of a streak.

"I think I'm just going to head home and call it a night. I have school tomorrow, and…it's kinda been a day," I say, raising the corner of my lip along with my shoulder.

He squeezes my arm and leans in to kiss my cheek. "All right then," he says, those few words more than just an acknowledgement.

My father winks and offers to bring two scoops with hot fudge home, an offer impossible to refuse. I wait for them to pull away before checking my phone. And when it's blank, I think of how wonderful it would be if ice cream really *did*, in fact, solve all of life's problems.

I don't even bother to turn the radio on as I drive the few blocks back to our house—and when I think about it, I realize I haven't listened to music the entire day. The silence is somehow more comforting. Maybe I'm afraid I'll hear something that sounds like the music we were making today. I tell myself it's because I don't want to feel like I'm not good enough, but really…really I just don't want to know how I could be so much better—if I hadn't compromised.

I'm so lost in my thoughts that I don't notice the rusted Volkswagen parked at the edge of the driveway until I pull around it, into the driveway. When I look in and see the front seat is empty, I snap my attention to the front door—to the small stoop outside, and the rough-looking man sitting with his elbows on his knees and his head in his hands and what I quickly identify as a half-empty bottle of Jim Beam next to him, his thumb poked in the hole at the top.

"Casey?" I ask, stepping up to him cautiously. "You…you go and get your thumb stuck?"

I tease a little, but only because I'm not sure what to expect from him. He looks up at me from under the brim of a dark blue hat, and his eyes are confused. I move downward until I'm close enough to touch him, then I kneel and nod at the bottle he's circling haphazardly on the concrete beneath him.

He reeks. But he doesn't seem incoherent. I'm hopeful that he didn't drive here this way. And I wonder if he was lit when he sent me his texts. His eyes fall to the bottle and he chuckles lightly.

"Want some?" he asks, gripping the dark brown glass with a full hand, but leaving his thumb stuck inside as he quirks an eyebrow at me.

"I try not to drink on my parents' porch on a Monday night, but…thanks," I smile wryly.

186

He smiles back, but it fades quickly. He brings the bottle into both hands and cradles it between his knees, leaning his chin forward and straining toward it for a sip. Not wanting him to make whatever this is any worse, I take it from his hand and slide down so I'm sitting in front of him with my legs folded.

"On second thought, I'd love some," I say, taking a small taste—enough to singe the tip of my tongue and stain my lips with the flavor. I cough, because I'm a lightweight, and even this small amount is enough to choke me. It makes Casey grin, though, so I guess it was worth it.

"I'm sorry I didn't write back," he says, and my heartbeat picks up, because he's talking about us.

"It's okay," I say, moving the bottle to my side, far enough that it's out of his reach. I look down at the label and smirk. "At least this isn't Johnnie Walker."

He laughs, but he doesn't understand what's funny about what I said. He's just drunk.

"Was this...*full* when you started?" I ask, tipping it to my side and noting the liquid splashing behind the middle of the label.

"Just bought it about an hour ago," he says, pressing his palms into his eyes. "I was supposed to go to my parents..."

His head falls to the side in his hands, his hat on the ground between his knees and his eyes land on me, the focus struggling a little, but the light still on behind. "I was going there...to be *the good son.*"

My expression falls at his words. I can't help it.

"Casey," I breathe.

He leans into me until I feel his head against my shoulder. My arm muscles tense automatically, but he doesn't seem to notice, his hand coming up to curl around my bicep while he leans against me with more of his weight, cupping my arm and holding on to me as if I were a pillow.

"I wanted to hear about your day instead," he says, his voice weaker, eyelids heavier. This is not the confident boy who can make people feel anything they want. This is the shell left behind circumstances. "But my sisters kept calling..."

His sleepy eyes grow pained as he lets gravity take over and pull his body to the ground, his head rolling to my lap. I tuck my hands under my legs at first, not sure what to do. Unable to look down into his deep brown sorrow, my eyes instead dart from left to right, waiting for my parents' car to pull up with Lane and ice cream and questions.

"Casey, you can't drive like this…let me take you home," I decide, making mental excuses to tell my family as quickly as my brain will allow for reasons his car is here and I'm gone, driving him half an hour away to his apartment.

"I'm sorry I stole your spot," Casey says. I glance down at him with my brow bunched. The whiskey is hitting him hard and fast—he's not making sense any more. I parked where I always park. He didn't steal anything.

"It's okay," I smile, my hand hovering over his hairline, my fingers twitching, nervous to touch him. I give in and let my hand slide into his silky soft hair, and the feel of it is just as I thought it would be. His eyes soften on my touch and the intensity makes me swallow and have to look away again.

I have to get him up.

"We just need to get to my car. Do you think you can walk?" I ask.

"It's not okay," he says. He's not even hearing me.

"Casey—*my car,*" I say, slowing the words down and speaking more loudly. My hand rests against his face. I look into his eyes, trying to determine how much focus is left in them, when they lock to mine, and his hand comes up to hold my wrist, his touch soft and almost afraid as each finger closes around my skin one at a time and he holds me still.

"It's not okay that I stole your spot, Murphy. I made you wait. It should have been you on that stage. You just needed someone to help you over that hurdle, and instead, I threw more in your way…" he trails off, his head rolling just enough to the side that my hand becomes pinned between his cheek and my leg. His eyes fall shut slowly as he lies in my hold, and he looks broken and overwrought with regret.

188

"Casey, I'm sorry, but I…I have no idea what…" I begin, the words falling away, but finishing in my head—*you're talking about.* I don't finish my sentence because clarity comes. And I can't help but laugh. "Oh my god," I whisper, my gaze coming up to look out at my quiet street, my eyes wide with irony.

Casey Coffield honestly believes that song is about him—that I've harbored some sort of resentment toward him since I was…what…fourteen?

"Casey, look," I start, but he's too lost in his own delusion. I need to let it play out.

"I saw it—your yearbook," he says, his voice coming from my lap. "When I was here the other day. I saw what I wrote, and then it all just came back to me. And I just wanted you to know—I was a prick."

I laugh loud and hard at the way his drunken voice delivers that last word. Shaking my head, I let my eyes close for a moment, and I remember it all. Casey wasn't the only one who laughed when I stuttered on stage. He wasn't even the loudest. He was just the one who always stuck out in my mind—like the leader of everything just out of my reach. But I meant what I said when he first walked into Paul's to ask me about the song and recording—that song isn't about him. Or at least, it wasn't before, but now that the studio made me change it…

"Casey," I sigh, my chin falling to my chest and my hands both falling to either side of his face. He's handsome when he's sorry; I'll give him that.

I chuckle and shake my head, staring into his deep round eyes that are slanted in their begging for forgiveness. I part my lips, ready to tell him the story of how it really went—how I knew I wasn't ready, how my mom promised me fifty bucks for trying out for the talent show, and that was all that really mattered to me— she paid me for just getting on the stage. Then, the memory of Casey's now *infamous* signature comes to mind. I handed my yearbook to Houston to sign on the last day of our senior year, and he passed it down the line of people instead of just handing it back, forcing me to chase it as it was passed along unsigned from popular girl to *it* boy and so on until it landed in Casey's hands. I could read what he wrote upside down, and then he looked up with a smug smirk and told his friend he didn't even know who the chick who owned the book was. It passed through several more hands before someone tossed it on a table and I rescued it. I started to scribble out unwanted messages, and almost took my pen to his, when I decided *fuck him*—and I left it.

Casey didn't ruin me. He didn't set me back. He pushed me out of my nest and is probably partly responsible for the tiny fire I found to dye my hair and climb up on the stage at Paul's a year ago. *Fuck him* was my mantra—*in your dreams, Casey Coffield* just sounds better in a song.

But lying in my lap, drunker by the second, reformed with age and wiser with time, perhaps—or maybe just broken and never whole with a family so cold compared to mine—Casey wants to tell me he's sorry. And since he never broke me in the first place, I let him have this release, because right now it's what he needs, and it isn't a dying father and a house full of women who are probably blaming him for everything that's going wrong.

"You're a good man," I say, and I can see so many things fall away behind his eyes.

A cocktail of forgiveness and redemption, however warranted he may believe, is tucked against my hip. If he weren't drunk. If my father weren't walking up the driveway with a cardboard carrier full of cones and sundaes. If this were another life—I'd lean forward and kiss this sweet boy on the head to show him just how far he's come.

I wish for the perfect time and place, and smile with tight lips as Casey snuggles into me like a lost soul and my father quirks a brow above his glasses.

"He's going through something difficult," I whisper, nodding down toward the chuckling head in my lap. He's amused by something—the kind of thing an hour and the equivalent of six shots makes amusing.

"He can't drive like that," my father says, looking down, his glasses at the tip of his nose.

190

"I agree," I say, moving one hand away, but bringing it back when Casey starts to pout.

"Casey came over—sweet!" Lane shouts, taking long strides up to where my father stands.

"He's not feeling very well," I say, eyes wide and head shaking. My father chuckles, but corroborates my lie, promising Lane he can catch up with his friend in the morning.

My mom furrows her brow and hands me her melting cone as she crouches down next to me. "For god sakes, Casey," she says, sliding one of her arms under his and helping him to stand so I can join them and help her walk him inside. "You're making me regret telling you where to find my daughter in the first place," she scolds.

My mother's brothers are all alcoholics. Grabby ones at that. But that's not what this is. This is the moment when denial comes calling and the heart runs full tilt into acceptance. It's duty and refusal facing off. Either way, Casey is going to lose in the end. What matters now is what scars he wants to live with.

We get him to the hard sofa just inside the door. It's furniture that's only there for decoration—a pointless room my father's been begging to put a pool table in for more than a year. I'm glad the sofa is here now, though. It's the only room that Casey can be left alone in. It's a place for him to sleep it off while he hides.

My mother comes back from the hall closet, her scowl even deeper and her lips pursed. She's about to lay into him when I reach for her arm and whisper in her ear.

"His father's dying—he has cancer," I say.

She freezes, and I see her look at him differently all of a sudden. Casey tries to work himself to a sitting position, but his eyes are so heavy and red I know that it will take little convincing to make him fall asleep. I hush him and take the seat at the end of the sofa, pulling his head back into my lap—the one place that seems to give him peace. My mother throws the blanket over us both, and I meet her gaze and nod that I will be fine.

She leaves the room, turning out the lights and joining my father and brother in the kitchen. I look on from the darkened room, my hand stroking this broken boy's hair until his breathing changes course. I remain there until I dream.

CHAPTER 13

Casey

It takes me exactly six minutes to figure out where I am. I know because I count the soft ticks hitting my ears from a clock sitting on a nearby end table and round the seconds up to minutes.

My eyes hurt, and the blanket I'm weighed down beneath is scratchy, and I think…I think maybe it smells like mothballs. Were it not for harmony being sung by Lane, I would have sworn the humming from the woman making breakfast in the kitchen was coming from Houston's mom. Jeanie and Joyce would be good friends, I think.

I've been thinking about sitting up for the last ten minutes. Everything looks stranger from this horizontal view. Curio cabinets house precious saucers and teacups, and cross-stitch images hang framed on the walls. There is sunlight peeping through the slats in the blinds, and every so often, I catch a glimpse of Murphy, moving plates and bowls from the table to the sink and back again. I let another minute pass, willing my legs to shift so my feet hit the floor, but Murphy beats me to it, and when I see her round the corner, I give in to the embarrassment and press my face into the couch pillow while I remain cocooned in the world's ugliest blanket.

"It's not a very comfy couch, I know," she says, her voice low and soft. Thank god. "But in my defense, you're freaking heavy, and this is as far as you'd let us carry you from the porch."

Us. Her whole family had to deal with me.

"Ugh," I moan into the foam cushion. The harsh fabric scratches my nose. "I'm…" I twist my neck so my face is forward, and I find her kind eyes waiting for me where she sits on the coffee table in front of me. "I'm so sorry I showed up and dropped all this on you. That…that wasn't the plan."

I tug one arm loose and then the other, rolling to my back and kicking the blanket free from my chest and then legs. I came here in the clothes I wore to the studio yesterday—stiff jeans and a vintage baseball shirt that's too tight to sleep in without feeling the collar choke around the neck. I realize my shoes are still on, and it makes me chuckle at my pathetic self. Murphy looks to my feet and nods.

"You sort of used my lap as a pillow, so I couldn't get to your shoes. I didn't think you cared what you slept in, though," she says, raising the left side of her mouth in pity. She's pitying me. This is only getting worse.

I force myself to a sitting position and press my palms against my eyes, feeling the swelling of bad decisions all over my face.

"Your parents must think I'm a massive tool," I say, meeting her gaze again and hoping that thought isn't floating through her mind.

She breathes a gentle laugh and shakes her head *no*, which releases some of the pressure in my chest.

"Lane thinks you have pneumonia, but other than that—no. Nobody thinks anything, Case," she says.

Right on cue, my phone buzzes on the coffee table, and both of our eyes move to it. I can see from the brief preview on my screen that it's lit up with dozens of messages.

"Your sisters, I presume?" she asks. I move my head slowly to signal *yes*, then lean forward and pick up my phone, scrolling through the list of *call me's* that repeat over and over. They're taking turns now—a coordinated effort to pull me into that house.

"I was almost to my parents' house yesterday," I say, thumbing through the never-ending stream of messages that cut off around eleven last night and pick up again about thirty minutes ago. "Then I just got on the freeway instead and came here."

"And Jim Beam came into the picture?" she smirks.

I wince.

"The first time I came to your door, nobody was home, so I went up to the corner, to the convenience store, for some snacks. Then my sisters started calling, asking where I was and why wasn't I there yet? I answered and they put me on speaker, each one taking turns—yelling. They were relentless. I walked to the other end of the store, bought a bottle and drove back here to wait for

194

you. I wasn't going to drink it until I got home, but then I suck on all sorts of levels, and figured I'd just take a swig to chill out," I say, leaning my head to the side and squinting one eye. "My swigs are kinda big."

"You slept like a baby," she says, raising her shoulders and leaning back on her palms. Her eyes linger for a few seconds, and I realize through her words and expression that she stayed with me through the night. I don't acknowledge it, because it's too sweet, and I don't want to ruin it by making it something she did out of obligation or worry. Even if it's pretend, I want to think she *chose* to stay with me. I suck in my top lip and nod.

"My mom made breakfast," she says, twisting and peering over her shoulder. While she looks into the kitchen, I look at the way her loose hair tickles against her neck.

"I should probably just go," I swallow. "I'm sure your dad wants to bury me in a hole in your backyard."

She twists back quickly to face me, and our eyes lock for a second. I feel my heart rush with a dose of adrenaline from her grays, and I move my attention to my feet and body as I stand.

"Don't be embarrassed," she says, standing with me and reaching for my hand. Her fingers connect with a few of mine for a brief second then let go. "Besides, we don't have any holes ready, and dad doesn't like to make boys dig their own graves. That would just be cruel and unusual," she grins.

I chuckle and swallow the hard lump in my dry throat. My head is pounding, and my stomach is somewhere between starving and a storm of old whiskey. My mouth tastes like I've been chewing on newsprint, so I give in with a slight nod and follow my muse into the kitchen.

"I hope you're feeling better," Lane says, moving a few steps away from me. He holds his hands up, then covers his mouth with one. "No offense. I don't want to get sick. I really like summer school, and germs can spread."

I grin because—who likes summer school? And he really does think I have pneumonia. I nod in agreement with him and cover my own mouth, taking a seat on the opposite side of the table.

Jeanie places a plate of what looks like French toast in front of me, and my stomach flips to being completely hungry.

"Thanks," I say, grabbing the fork from the edge of the woven placemat in front of me. I slice into a piece and stuff it in my mouth, immediately going in for more. "This is amazing," I mumble through my bite.

Jeanie's hand comes to my back, and she pats me in a slow circle. I glance to Murphy in question—wondering how much of my messy life her mother now knows. Murphy shrugs with a tight smile. Her mom knows enough.

"Were you able to get a sub, Murph?" her mom asks from somewhere behind me. I work through four more bites, hoping the offer for seconds will come while I listen in on their conversation.

"I did. I can drop Lane off, but…I'm not sure I'll be home in time for his bus," she answers her mom, their conversation happening in plain spoken words that feel like a code.

"Are you recording more?" I ask, wondering if they want to try something else with her or if they ended up needing another day to get it right. I know sometimes Gomez is a perfectionist, and he changes his mind a lot on direction.

I would have let her shine.

I glance up when nobody responds and notice the strange way everyone is looking at one another, talking without words. Lane is the only other person into his breakfast like me, so at least two of us are left out of the secret. I stuff my final bite in and twist in my chair, running a napkin over my mouth while I look up at Murphy. She's rubbing a hand behind her neck and staring at me.

"I'm…I'm taking the day off to come with you," she says. My brow bunches. Come where? Like choreographed thunder, my phone buzzes against my hip, and I swallow as my eyes fall shut.

"You don't have to, Murphy. I'm a big boy. I can handle this," I say.

I'm not sure I want to expose her to that house again. The last time I went there, I was afraid and I just needed reinforcement. I'm not sure what I am this time, though. The messages from my sisters don't explain a very happy environment. My mom is not dealing well, and I guess my dad won't let anyone in the house to help that isn't family. When she sets up assistance, he calls and cancels it. It's become this enormous battle, and my sisters are like adding a peanut gallery to the gladiator ring of a very unfair fight.

I'm pissed off. That's what I am.

"Jim Beam would beg to differ," her father says in a wry tone while crunching on a piece of toast. I glare at him, but he isn't looking at me. He continues to eat, slow bites breaking off and crumbs falling into his beard that he dusts away. My bitterness capitulates to this man quickly, because he's right. And I showed up like that on his doorstep looking for his daughter, so...game, set, match to him.

"Really," Murphy says, bringing a small plate of fruit to the table and sitting next to me. "I don't mind. I...I want to help," she stutters. I catch it now. And suddenly the rest of last night pops into my brain—I apologized for asshole deeds of the past. I don't need to drag her down again.

"You have work; you'll miss the paycheck," I grimace.

She laughs once hard.

"It's sixty-five dollars. Forty-seven after taxes for the day. I think I'll be all right," she giggles, standing and clearing her half-eaten plate.

I stare at my own empty dish in front of me and reflect on how nobody leapt to their feet, up-in-arms that Murphy wasn't doing enough to prepare for her future. Perhaps I could use more of her spirit around today.

"Okay," I nod, glancing up with very weary eyes and a tired body. She bows her head once in return—it's agreed—and she helps clear the rest of the table while nibbling at her fruit plate until it's gone. When breakfast is done, she begins gathering her things for the day. I hope she's packing armor.

I miss floating through life—coasting without a care. I need to get back to that feeling, to card nights with Eli and the boys, to video games, and days spent in my pajamas with nothing to do but jam out in a small club later that night and mix my music—*my* music under *my* direction. Maybe I alter my dream—simplify it to something that hurts less when it doesn't happen like I think it should. Murphy's in good hands, so bailing wouldn't get in her way.

I can't really do much about anything until my mom is no longer locking herself in the bathroom and my sisters quit calling me for solutions I don't have, though, so I'll take this one last thing from Murphy. I'll take her help. And then I'll just be her biggest fan.

Murphy gathers her things, and we make plans to meet outside of my parents' house, giving me enough time to race home and shower and her time to get Lane to his summer classes. Fate gives me a break, and I pull up to my family home before her. I park at the end of the driveway behind Christina's car, which is dead-center, leaving no room for anyone else. I smirk at it, because of course it is. My oldest sister and I aren't so different after all—asshole runs in the family.

The door isn't locked, which is strange, but I'm grateful that I can walk right in. I glance behind me, scanning the street, relieved that Murphy still hasn't arrived. I want to know what we're getting into, because there's still time to save her from it.

The house is quiet. Perfect silence—per the norm. But I can typically find my oldest sister at her usual post—the corner stool at the kitchen counter. But the kitchen is disheveled, grocery bags half-emptied and a pot of boiling water spilling out over the edges. I step close to the stove quickly and recognize what I think was at some point noodles. I shut the burner off and move the pot to the sink, dumping the water and mush of noodle down the drain before running the disposal.

It takes me a few minutes to clean the mess up and finish clearing groceries from bags. When I see the number of pads and adult diapers that were purchased, I shudder and my muscles contract, not wanting to carry me any further into this.

"I'm doing the best I can!" I hear my mom's voice cry out from upstairs. I leave the few cans of broth I was putting away on the counter next to the fridge and dry my hands before rounding the corner and taking cautious steps toward what I quickly recognize as my mom and sister arguing. Their conversation falls to a whisper again, but the kind that's laced with Christina growling and my mother's weeping.

"He doesn't want anyone here but me. I can't have the nurses come. I can't…he doesn't want it," my mother is pleading. Even in this state, my father is bullying her.

"He doesn't know what's best for him, Mom. Do you want me to tell him? I'll tell him—I'll be the bad guy," Christina says. I only halfway understand what this argument is about, but my sister is making sense.

"I'll be the bad guy," I say, stepping into view and startling them both.

"Shit, Casey," my sister says, hand clutched to her chest, a pile of towels at her feet.

"Chrissy, don't swear," my mother chastises her, and I can't help but chuckle.

"Mom, if ever there is a time to swear—this is it. Let the woman slip out a little *shit* here and there, would you?" I say, stepping over what looks to be a week's worth of laundry for a family of eight and making my way to my mom.

As tired as I feel, my mom's look is far more haggard. She holds her hands out hovering over the mess before her, helpless, and finally sighs out a whimper. I pull her into my arms and hug her, feeling the mountain she is carrying shake with every sob.

"I'm sorry, Mom. I'm here now. And I won't let you do this alone," I promise, feeling my lungs shrink and the traps set around my chest with my words. For my father, responsibility has always been financial—making sure there are nest eggs and safety nets. But I kind of think being responsible for someone means stepping in to roll up your sleeves when their world is breaking. This is my world, too. I thought leaving it would be better for everyone, but I see now that it's really only better for me and the man it all revolves around.

Murphy clears her throat, and her meek sound catches all of our attention. I can see the uncertainty written on her face. Stress has the ability to downright cripple her, and yet she signed up as a volunteer to swim neck-deep in it with me. I can't help but look at her with nothing but love.

Her eyes dart around afraid to offend—and I think I love her.

Her hands dive in, picking up towels and folding shirts and sorting colors and whites, pants and socks—and I think I love her.

We've not really done anything but fight through demons and take chances on dreams in one another's presence, but I think I love her.

It's impossible.

It's entirely possible.

My heart is a victim of this stress, and I know that's the cause.

But I also think maybe…maybe it's not. I at least admit to myself that I love the *idea* of loving her.

Together, with my mom and sister, the four of us spend three hours returning the kitchen and other forgotten rooms in my parents' house to normal. My father is heavily medicated, and I haven't seen him yet, but I know that part is coming soon. I also know nothing will prepare me for it. My best friend's warning echoes in my mind: *It's going to be harder than you think.*

Christina has a power of attorney document drafted and a notary friend on call, ready to witness, but my mother is still wavering that it's the right thing to do. Murphy continues to carry out housework, leaving the three of us alone in the kitchen to hash out one last argument, but I catch her eyes over both my sister and mother as she carries a final load of trash through the door. Her gaze is full of empathy, but there's a silent message in it too—I'm doing the right thing.

"Mom, I know you're scared," I say, standing and raising my voice just enough that my sister gives way and lets me have the floor. I square myself with my mom and put my hand on her shoulder, my heart breaking when she leans into it—her fragile face against her baby boy's arm. My father's illness has aged her several years in a matter of weeks.

"He's always made the decisions," I say, and when I see her lips part in argument, I stop her. "I don't mean this in that way. This is not about me and how dad and I cease to get along, this is about the way it's been, the way life has worked, for you. And it's okay, because for you, it *has* worked. But now, Mom? Now…this way is broken. And using Dad's own logic, making the smart choice, even when it's not the one your heart wants, is what you need to do to make sure you are doing what's best for him. He is no longer capable of deciding these things."

"He's afraid things will cost too much," she says through a panicked voice.

"You have insurance," Christina explains, and I sense the conversation starting to spiral along the same path it's been for the last half hour.

"It doesn't matter," I interrupt. My palm to my mother's warm cheek, I move her sightline to me again. "You know he wouldn't have let something fall through the cracks. That man," I say, gesturing toward the stairs, "he would have had everything prepared for something like this just in case. It's all in place. He's just no longer in a state where he can make the call."

My mom's eyes drop and her breath leaves her chest as her shoulders slump.

"I don't know," she says, her fingers pinching at the bridge of her nose. "I don't know; I don't know; I don't know."

"He did," I say, lifting her chin. I bend to meet her gaze until we're tethered—locked so she sees the truth in my expression. "You know he did. He knew. And he wouldn't have let things get this far without being ready."

We stare into each other for almost a minute, and by some miracle, my sister remains silent and still. I hear Murphy step in through the back door quietly, and I feel stronger just knowing she's there.

"He knew," I nod again, this time getting my mom to nod and agree with me.

With my mother finally ready to accept full responsibility, I prepare myself for what I knew would be the hard part about today—I am going to have a conversation with my father, alone, for nobody's ears but ours. And I'm going to have to convince him that he's wrong about something. And I am going to have to lie and capitulate and make promises that I have no intention of keeping, but it won't matter, because it's what's right. If we could travel back in time to a year ago—before there were signs of pancreatic cancer, before my father's appetite waned to almost nothing and his abdominal pain became impossible to ignore—I know it's what he'd tell me to do. None of that is an option, so he's going to have to listen to ones that are real.

With my sister's coaching and the paperwork in my hands, I leave my heart and my family downstairs and step into the dark room at the end of the hall. His frail body is mostly bones, and the sheets are rolled down to his waist, his white T-shirt draping from his shoulders. A month ago, he looked strong enough to punch me. The man before me now is a ghost of the one he was before.

"They all give up on arguing with me? Is that why you're here? Are you the last straw?" he chuckles to himself, his words falling into a coughing fit. He reaches for a tissue and holds it folded over his mouth, coughing into it until eventually he can get his breath.

"Something like that," I say, my eyes meeting his. They're so sunken in.

I sit at the end of the bed, and I think about how all I wanted when I was a little boy was to be able to rush into their bedroom for comfort during a storm. I ran to my sisters' rooms instead, and the older they got, the less often they wanted to take me in, too.

This storm is too big to escape, and my father is no longer able to run.

"You have to sign the power of attorney, Dad. And you know you do," I say.

"Horse shit," he says, coughing again.

I look away, because he's hard to look at.

"I figured you'd say that, but I've been thinking a lot," I say. I draw in a deep breath through my nose and prepare myself for the words I don't believe in one bit. "You were right. I was wrong. I haven't been living a responsible life at all. But I can fix it. I'm finishing my degree, and then I'm going to apply for the apprenticeship."

My father's eyes take me in wide, and he doesn't blink.

I just gave him everything he wanted. I just promised I'd live the life he had laid out for me. I promised it, because I know when the time comes for proof, he'll be long gone. I lied. And it isn't worth not giving him this strange peace of mind just so I can think I won the battle by the time he went to his grave. In death, nobody wins.

"Good," he says. One word. That's all I get.

"Good," I repeat, forcing myself to look him in the eyes. It's as if we're making a deal. Nothing about this feels like a moment shared between a father and his son.

"Mom doesn't think you have plans in place, but I told her that you wouldn't let something like this slip," I begin, knowing my father won't be able to help himself from divulging just how prepared he is.

He scoffs and rolls his eyes, letting his head fall in the other direction, away from me. I get a glimpse at his ribs and his frail body as he turns. My father is wasting away.

"I know, but you know how she worries. I can explain everything to her again if you want. I can show her where everything is, how the files are in order, how the claims work and when the coverage kicks in," I say.

His head rolls back in my direction and his eyes glaze. He's drifting a little. Christina warned me that he might.

"I can do it, Dad," I say, and at the sound of those words, things become suddenly clear and the meaning of that sentence—it changes. My gut twists. This isn't about my father being stubborn at all. This isn't about not believing he needs the care everyone else thinks he needs. This isn't about giving up control. This is about him not wanting to rest that burden on my mother. This is about him carrying out his mission to the grave—about him making sure everyone else is taken care of first. It's the mantra that was literally beaten into his being, and he will die by it.

But me…I'm different. And our relationship is different. It always has been. I'm the man of the house, and giving the burden to me is not against his misguided creed.

"I can do it," I say again, meeting him squarely in the eyes, lucidity there and his understanding perfectly clear. His weak hand rises from under the blanket, moving forward and reaching to grip mine. We connect, and everything about my father feels breakable in my palm, but I don't waver or show how much I'm frightened by the feeble touch of him in my hand.

"I can do it," I repeat. And I know by the flash of relief in his eyes that he accepts.

I nod slowly and back out of the room, grateful to find my sister sitting in the hallway alone. I catch her up on the new plan, and she goes to work immediately in my father's old office, a small room down the hall, until an updated contract is printed that appoints me as the decision-maker for my father's health and wellness.

Christina never questions, and I know it's because she's relieved it isn't her. I've never fit the Coffield mold. I was the child born as a surprise—I wasn't planned, and I never fell into step quietly. But I'm supposed to be here. And today, I've discovered my purpose.

I will do this so my mother and sisters don't have to.

When the notary arrives, my father signs the document quickly and dismisses me accordingly so he can rest. I watch him close his eyes, and as frail as he is, he still manages to smile in his sleep—a certain smugness to it all that his plan in fact did work, and in the end, he got his way.

Christina leaves soon after, and Murphy and I both force my mom to retreat upstairs to what used to be my room, to sleep— something that we've learned she hasn't done in about two days.

With order semi-restored, I fall into the only comfortable chair in the house. It's a padded rocker my mom has had since I was an infant. I have always gravitated to that chair, and I think it's because it's the one she rocked me to sleep in as a child.

"Are you okay?" Murphy asks, sitting on the couch across from me. My eyes hold themselves open and fight against exhaustion as I look at the beautiful girl looking back at me.

"Not even close," I answer honestly.

She smiles, but we both know I'm not joking.

"How was John about you missing today?" she asks.

I shrug and chuckle at the mess I've made of my own dream in the span of a single day.

"I didn't tell him."

Her eyes grow wider, and she swallows.

"It won't matter," I reassure her. "I'm on the hook for six more Fridays at his club. He doesn't want to lose that. I'll show up tomorrow and let his assistant know I had a family emergency."

She nods quietly, but looks down at her twisting hands.

"Don't worry about me, Murphy. I'll be just fine," I lie.

Her eyes come up to mine, and I can tell she knows I am.

We sit in silence for several minutes, and I let my thoughts drown in my present. I have a day, maybe less, left of freedom. And then I know hell will truly begin.

It's harder than you think, Casey. You were right, Houston. And you have no idea.

CHAPTER 14

Murphy

While Casey's dad isn't getting better, for the moment, he's also not getting worse. That's the thing with pancreatic cancer—it can be so rapid, and so slow all at once. It had spread to his liver and kidneys by the time they caught it, the day he left work early for what he thought would be a simple physical exam from his doctor. But he had been ignoring signs long before that.

Casey became guardian of his father's decisions, and while he says he can handle it, I've noticed how it's all changing him. He's gotten nurses involved again, and help for his mom so she's not the only one trying to keep the house in order. But the need to make *real* decisions hasn't come yet. It's always looming.

Casey and I have fallen into a new pattern. He calls me in the morning while I'm on my way into school and he's on his way to his parents' house. I usually check in with him again during my lunch when he's driving into the studio. They let him shift his hours to come in later, which means he's also there well into the evening.

Sometimes, he'll call me while he's logging sound files, and I can hear bits and pieces in the background. He always plays his favorites for me, and our taste is almost always in sync. We talk about little things—like why I always dye my hair purple, and how he wishes I'd try pink. We flirt, but cautiously and sweetly. It's chaste courting, and I love every minute of it. We talk about things like our favorite movies—he likes horror, and I'm more of a jaded rom/com fan—and we share stories from growing up and high school. When he asked what song I was trying to play for the talent show, I told him it would have been Willie Nelson, and he sighed in regret that he never got to hear it all the way through.

I look forward to every call, and I've started watching for his name to appear on my phone minutes before I know it's going to come. That's what I'm doing now, because it's almost seven, and it's Friday. Casey is deejaying at Max's tonight, and he made no promise to call, but somehow I still think he will.

I *know* it.

I've been putting Sam off for days, and my girlfriend guilt has started to get the best of me, so I agreed to meet her downtown for dinner tonight after work. There's a Thunder game, and it took a while to park. The wait for her favorite restaurant is at least an hour and a half, so we've spent the last forty minutes sitting at the bar swapping stories that have nothing to do with anything that's really rolling around in my chest and head.

Eventually, Sam calls me on my bullshit.

"Okay, here's the deal," she says, pulling the spear from her martini and working the olive into her mouth. "You aren't really here. You haven't been with me in days. I can tell when I'm spilling my guts about Cam."

"I'm here, Sam. I just think that guy is a loser and you need to not mess around with people in relationships," I pipe in. While I may have tuned out for some of our conversations this week, I'm always fired up and aware for that one. She's still pining after the cheater, and I'm done pretending the fact that their names rhyme isn't stupid—and that he's not an ass-faced jerk-hole.

"Fine, you're invested *sometimes,*" she says with an eye roll.

I'm regretting coming out tonight even more, and it's almost seven. I could be at home in pajamas listening to Casey get his equipment ready and run sound checks. My friend waves a hand in front of me, and I sigh, leaning forward and drinking my Diet Coke through a straw without the use of my hands. I set my gaze back on her and take the rest of my lashings.

"You're lost in some hazy mystery, and frankly, Murphy, it's starting to hurt my feelings," she says. I shrug, acknowledging my failures with this one small gesture, and then seven o'clock comes and my phone buzzes on the table, bringing my friend to life like never before.

Our gazes lock. She saw Casey's name. She's jumping to conclusions. Her conclusions are probably not far off from the truth, only hers are probably dirtier and contain things, that for me, are only fantasy-level realities right now.

We both reach for my phone.

She's faster.

"Shit," I scrunch my face.

"Miss Murphy Sullivan's phone," she answers, putting on a southern accent as if she's from Georgia.

I lean my head to the side and knit my brow at her as I reach for my phone. She holds up a finger.

"Uh huh…Uh huh…I see," she teases, her fake accent still strong.

"Why are you suddenly from the South?" I whisper with my hands out in question. My best friend moved to Oklahoma from Los Angeles when she was fourteen. South to her is San Diego, and I'm pretty sure it always will be.

She bunches her face at me and sticks out her tongue, and I look to the table of older women next to us and wonder if they act like twelve-year-olds with their friends still.

"We'd love to," she says, bringing my attention back to her conversation with the guy who called *me*. I furrow my forehead and let my face fall to my palm as I spear ice cubes with my straw. "I'm sure she remembers where it's at. We'll be there. Y'all have a good day now."

My brow flies up my hairline.

"We'll be where?" I ask.

She smirks, and sits back in her chair, crossing her legs slowly while her lashes wave at me.

"Sam, what did you do?"

I feel sick. She's going to make fun of my crush. Especially because I made fun of hers, which—come on, hers is stupid. But my ego can't handle teasing, especially since my butterflies are just getting used to this new flight pattern with Casey. This is why I haven't over-shared things about him with Sam. Plus, his situation is private—I wouldn't feel right talking about him and his family without his okay.

"I hope you're comfortable in those shoes," she says, her grin growing more devious as she knocks back the rest of her drink.

My forehead bunches in confusion, and I look down at my feet. I'm wearing my riding boots and my favorite country dress that's shorter in the front, flared in the back. I wanted to look nice, but feel comfortable. It's not pajamas, but I suppose it's pretty easy to move around in, though it would depend on the circumstances, and...fuck. Friday night. Max's.

"Sam!" I yell.

Her smirk grows as she flashes her empty glass to the server who quickly fetches her another one.

"And suddenly it all makes sense," she says, eyes narrowed on me as if she's a sniper. It's friendly fire, but fuck, it still burns. My cheeks flame up and I wish I weren't wearing something so heavy. My body is flushed.

Sam leans in, setting her fresh drink on the table while she folds her arms over her knees, her eyes twinkling in giddiness as she prepares to make me pay.

"That guy from our high school, you remember him, he's working at a record label now," she says, a high, naïve voice that sounds nothing like me. She keeps going with her imitation. "Oh, we're just going to work on some recordings. Someone else handled them, so I'll probably never see him again. Cute? Really? You think he's cute? I don't see it."

And then comes the one where I know she has me.

She has me.

Caught in my lies.

Damn, damn, damn, damn...

"Sure, Sam," she says, amping up her voice so it's *super* flattering, her lips pressed in a self-satisfied grin. "I'll find out if he's single. Oh...yeah...I asked—*he's not.*"

She leans in close for the kill, her eyes twinkle with all of that best-friend-gossip-neediness that I have never been good at. I'm the listener. That's my role. My college boyfriends were boring, my high school ones non-existent. Damn it all to hell if I haven't just shot straight into scintillating territory for her with Casey!

"Fine, I have a little crush," I say, my voice jumping eight octaves, my shoulders shrugging to my ears. Stamp guilty on my forehead.

Her grin spreads slowly. I swear she draws it out just to torture me.

"You don't have a little crush, Murph. You freaking have the hots for Casey Coffield!" she practically cackles. "Oh and girl...mmmmm...he's got it back. I know it!"

"Sam, please, I'm begging," I lean forward and touch her arm. "Stop, please."

Even though I want nothing more than the teasing to end, I giggle. It slips out, from god knows where, and I cover my mouth as if I have the hiccups.

"Oh, girl...we are *definitely* hitting that club now," she teases, raising her hand to get the attention of our waiter. "She's going to need one of these," she adds, lifting her drink, shaking her pinky against the glass and winking.

I grimace. But when it comes, I sip it down fast, because my friend is right—nothing wrong with a little liquid courage.

The first time I came to Max's, I was with Casey—from the very beginning. I was here before the lights were off, which is a lot like getting to see a haunted house before all of the creepy things take over. Things are different in the light. In the dark—things are scary.

Sam and I walk in through a set of elaborate double doors, passing a line of beautiful people who I'm sure assume we're part of the staff, because as beautiful as my friend Sam is tonight, she's still not supermodel hot. The people in line? All supermodel hot. Even the men.

I let Sam take over. She gives our names to security, asks a hostess—who yes, is supermodel hot—where the VIP booths are located, then leads me by the hand through the thick crowd of hot hotness grinding together in one mass sexual motion along the dance floor. I bump into no less than thirty people, and I utter *sorry's* and *excuse me's* the entire distance to the private booth lifted a few feet higher than most of the other rows and nestled next to the best view I've ever seen of downtown Oklahoma City.

I collapse into the leather, crawling on my hands and knees until I'm so deep into the curve that I have an entire six-inch-thick table made of glazed redwood between me and every other person in the club right now.

"You look like the wild woman they find in the forest who has lived her life among the animals and is frightened by the city," Sam laughs, sliding into the booth next to me.

"That's because *that* woman? She's my people," I pant.

A waiter glides by our table and drops off eight water glasses, and I drink through two of them in the time it takes Sam to place an order. She adds a cosmo to the order for me, as well, then slides her water glass my way as the waiter leaves.

"At least you'll get to see what the restrooms look like if you keep that up," she jokes.

"I saw them last time. They're nice. Kind of plain, but," I stop talking to guzzle water. Drinking is sort of like singing—it distracts the millions of synapsis misfiring in my brain and lets me remain calm. The only flaw I've found is that at some point, I have to *stop* drinking, and the panic is usually still there waiting.

"Damnit. You were right, I owe you twenty bucks," a perfect-ten of a blonde says as she slides into the opposite end of our booth. My mouth is agape, and I'm about to bolt from my safety zone when Houston steps up behind her and holds out his hand, which Barbie's twin slides a folded-up twenty into.

"I told you she was real," he chuckles. "Murphy, meet Paige— my girlfriend."

"Nice to meet you," Paige says, reaching to take my hand. Her shake is firm—like a business deal—and her eyes continue to scrutinize me. I was already acutely aware of every square inch of my basic make-up, hair and outfit, but it all suddenly feels tighter under her inspection.

"My friend tricked me into coming here. I have nicer clothes. Not that this dress isn't nice. It's actually really nice. It's Dior. I got it at that little bargain shop in old town, right down the street from the arena, and I was so surprised to see it there because, I mean usually there aren't expensive things mixed in with all of the vintage stuff, but this one was, and when I found it, I was like *score!* And it really only goes with boots, so that's why I'm wearing boots, and…hmmmmm…."

My eyes shut tightly, I let my face fall flat against the table, forehead against the wood and mouth firm so I can try to see if wishes come true and I can zap myself out of this place and time.

I look up slowly and peel one eye open and then the next. Paige is looking at me with the exact horrified expression I sort of expected. Clearing my throat, I smile with tight lips and do my best to start over, sliding my hand her direction again, this time shaking with the same firmness she gives.

"I'm Murphy," I say, meek and demure. "I'm not great with crowds, and stress usually makes me stutter. However, you seem to have the opposite effect on me, and I *deeply* apologize for that assault with words and nonsense I just unleashed."

Her horrified expression melts into something kinder, and her smile is accompanied by a sweet, raspy laugh as she brings her other hand up to cover the top of mine in a gracious shake that somehow calms my chest.

"Murphy," she smiles, looking to Houston as she lets go of our hold and points to me with one waggling finger. "I like her, Houston. If Casey fucks this up, I'll punch him."

Houston pulls my new ally close to his side and kisses the top of her head, and I can tell by the way he dotes over her—the small gestures like his fingertips along her bare shoulder and the gentle casting of his eyes over her face while she speaks—that Paige is someone special. I've been approved by her, and that alone has made the moving sea of people around me feel less threatening.

"Hey, you all made it!"

Casey's familiar voice pulls me to sit straight up in my booth. I'm wedged in the very middle, which means I can't reach him, and I inwardly kick myself for blocking my body in.

"Nice to see you again, Casey," Sam says, a tone to her voice that denotes her eyebrows are wiggling teasingly. I can't see her face, but I know she's doing it by the small chuckle Casey gives before his eyes land on me.

I love seeing him in his element. He's wearing a dark hat with a flat brim, a black long-sleeved tee and black jeans. The only thing that doesn't fit the shadow is the white scarf around his neck tucked under the headphones he has resting there. When I talk to him on the phone tomorrow during his drive to his parents' house, this is how I'm going to imagine him.

"Case, I have to hand it to you, you weren't kidding," Houston says, standing and pulling his friend in for one of those manly handshake-hug combos. "This place is something. These people are here for you, man. For you!" Houston smacks him on the chest once for emphasis, and Casey pushes his hands in his pockets and lowers his head with a bashful smile.

"They're here to drink expensive vodka and hook up, but yeah…maybe I get like one percent of the credit," he says.

"What?" Paige says loudly, her brow bunched. "Are you…was that…did I just hear Casey Coffield be modest?"

"Ha ha, Paige. Yes, I can be modest," he says, his cheek dimpled with his sarcastic smile.

"Can you? Because…and no offense," she says, glancing around the table. Casey shuffles his feet and purses his lips, ready for her. "I've just never seen it. It's usually kind of the *me* show around you."

His mouth a rigid line, Casey looks at her for a beat before he blinks and opens his gaze back on me. My body beads with sweat instantly.

"Yeah, well…new Casey maybe," he says, his eyes square on me, my body literally on fire. "Things aren't always about my needs…I guess."

It's silent for about two seconds, but it feels like hours. In that time, Houston, Sam, and Paige all glance around the table and have silent *WTF* conversations before Casey breaks the awkwardness.

"I've gotta get up to the booth. I have some great stuff planned, though, so I hope you guys like the mix," he says, his eyes

213

catching mine as he turns to leave and his lips curved into that special smile he gets when he's up to something.

Sam introduces herself to Paige, then climbs from the booth to sit on the other side of her so they can scope out each other's shoes and hear better over the thumping taking over the rhythm of the room. I slide to the edge of the booth, but remain behind the table—my protective shield. I watch Casey work, and I wait for the special something he promised with that look until I recognize it.

It's subtle at first—blended with a mix of house music and retro seventies disco. He gives everyone a taste, hooks them like a drug dealer with a dime bag, until their bodies adjust and crave more. My tablemates are lost in their own conversation, and they don't know it's coming. I won't tell them, but I'm sure my voice is going to take over the room in five, four, three…

The heavy beat picks up and bodies jump in unison, their hands high in the air, their fingers free and begging for Casey to give it to them—to let this new melody take over and control everything to come.

My song.

He's debuting it right here, and bodies are obeying his orders. I'm in awe as my voice echoes and beautiful women shake their heads, hair flying and hips moving to an anthem of their time. It's powerful this way—the song so much bigger than it feels when it's just my guitar and voice on a stool in the middle of a bar.

It's fucking beautiful.

"Murphy!" my friend squeals, her palms pressed flat on the table, her body lifted in the air and her eyes on me—glee filling every inch of her face as she points to Casey. "This is you! Oh my god! This is it!"

"Wait, this…you wrote this?" Paige says, her eyes wide. Houston taps her shoulder and cups her ear, whispering confirmation. I grin larger than I have in my entire life.

"Shit, girl!" Paige says with an enormous smile. "You can't sit on your ass to your own song!"

Without hesitation, she wraps her fingers around my arm and pulls me all the way through the booth and out the other side,

214

dragging me into the masses, my body bumped and slammed from all directions, but for the first time—maybe ever—I don't care. I don't care whose hand is touching me; I don't care that a girl I just met is hugging me; I don't care that Houston grabbed my hand and squeezed it and my best friend kissed me on the cheek.

I don't care because "In Your Dreams, Johnnie Walker" is blasting in my ears and my soul feels warm and delicious. It pounds, and Casey lets it play pure and untouched—and I find his eyes waiting for mine through the forest of hands and arms waving and swaying to the beat. I stand still amid my tiny circle of friends and lock eyes with him, his proud smile simply spectacular.

And I cry.

I've heard people describe how bliss feels—the moment when something huge happens to you. Miracles. Reunions. Relief. Happy things so powerful that they induce tears. I could never understand such a phenomenon…until now. I cry hard, and I smile big and my song takes over an entire room filled with discerning ears—people who spend thousands of dollars on food and liquor just for the pleasure of falling in love on a dance floor to Casey's magic. Only right this minute—for four and a half minutes, actually—it's my potion they are getting drunk on.

I…can make…them feel *anything*. I. Want.

The moment my song ends, a new mix takes over, and Casey whispers something in the ear of the guy working with him at the booth. He hands over his headphones and weaves through exhausted bodies until he finds me in the very center of it all.

Steps away, his mouth tugs up to the right and that knowing dimple, dripping with confidence and pride and everything that makes my heart pound, touches his cheek. His left hand reaches up to pull his hat from his head and his right palm slides over my cheek, his fingers run through my hair, and in one swift motion he pulls me to him, his mouth on mine, his lips strong and his kiss potent as he walks me backward slowly, one arm around the small of my back and the other holding me to him—making sure I *feel*.

I feel everything.

The crowd disappears into nothingness as Casey's teeth graze against my top lip before his tongue gently tastes my mouth. Music drowns out everything else, and in my mind we are alone—nobody watching as I give in to something I think maybe I've wanted for longer than I care to admit. My hand slides around his neck, and I grip his soft hair, holding him to me, and we kiss hard and greedily.

When my feet stumble, he holds me tighter, and when our chests crave oxygen, our lips hardly part, and we take our breaths against one another.

I don't know how many songs play, but I know everywhere his hands touch my body—they slide up my back slowly, his thumbs sensuously drawing a line along the bare skin exposed along my spine. His fingers thread through my hair and his chest grows wide, like the lion king claiming his mate. When his hands release their grip they trace along my collarbone, the tips gliding along my neck. Shivers soak my skin and I am drunk. When palms find my cheeks and lips grow raw and breath becomes ragged, Casey holds my head to his and we rock to the music he made.

"Come home with me," he breathes, his lips parted and shaking with need and want.

I cling to him, eyes heavy and heart sure.

"Yes," I say, stopped only by the faint feel of his lips catching one of mine.

"Say it again," he says against me.

"Yes," I obey.

Yes.

Just...*yes.*

Casey

Goddamn she said *yes.*

She said *yes* and I still had four fucking hours of music I no longer gave a shit about to pump out for people—I just wanted to leave so I could be alone with her.

216

Clocks stopped, and life that normally feels like it's rushing toward the meaningless next thing slowed to a crawl. Minutes lasted two. People requested more. Bosses demanded I give. None of it mattered, because I got to touch her.

I held Murphy next to me the entire night. I made her ditch her car so I could feel her thigh brush against mine for the car ride home when we both found ourselves speechless—our bodies teeming with nerves and anticipation. For once in my life, I kept my mouth shut. I wasn't *less* Casey—I was *this* Casey, the better man she makes me.

When I pulled her up to my apartment door, my hand clutched around hers tightly, I growled like a fucking caveman because she is mine. I threw forty bucks at my roommate and told him to "Beat it," and he did.

Hours. Minutes. Seconds. Heartbeats. Sounds. Pauses. Hopes. Dreams.

Fucking dreams.

Never in mine did I think I'd be standing here with Murphy Sullivan, a girl I wished like hell I knew and claimed before anyone else. But I am. And I am weak, and my tongue is tied. Command left somewhere around the exit door of the club, and I stand before her now a slave. But she's so shy and unsure—her hands nervous as they tickle and grab at her dress at her sides, her lip caught between anxious teeth. The pull is strong, but the wait is so much better.

I step toward her in my room, my legs wanting to run and my hands wanting to take, but my selfish needs force things to happen slow and seductive.

"I *really* like this dress," I say, stretching my arm to her and catching the tip of my finger on the lace trim that curves around her breast.

I like the way she takes a short breath the moment my fingertip grazes her skin. She nods, and her eyes widen the smallest bit. Her hands tremble when she raises them and reaches for my hat, lifting it slowly with one hand and running her fingers through my hair with the other. I keep my eyes on her; it's so sexy to watch her watch me.

Her tongue passes over the edge of her top lip and then her teeth. My hat falls, and I let my eyes follow it to the floor, my chin grazing against her arm as I do. When I feel her fingers start to slip away, I grab her arm and hold it to my cheek, my eyes on hers as I open my mouth slightly and press my lips to the softness of the inside of her arm.

She shivers.

"They made me…" she begins, but pauses with parted lips. She bites at her bottom lip again, and I run my thumb over it to free it from her hold, wanting her to do it again so I can touch her mouth once more.

"They made you what, baby?" I ask, stepping closer, not really caring what anyone did or wants or needs if it gets in the way of my hands on her. I kiss at her neck and her head falls to the side at my touch.

"Johnnie Walker," she pants, and I smile against her neck, chuckling and letting my lips tickle against her ear.

"Baby girl, I don't care about Johnnie Walker," I say, my tongue taking a small taste along her jawline until my gaze comes square with hers again. Her lashes fall in long sweeps and her gray truth undoes me as I stare into her. "It's just a song. A fucking…amazing…song," I say, leaning in again and breathing my words against her ear.

"I felt bad," she sighs.

"It was always your song," I say, standing with my feet square to hers, her mouth relaxed finally in a hopeful smile as I run my fingertips up from her wrists to her elbows and shoulders until they once again dance against the lace of her dress.

"I love your song, Murphy," I say, glancing into her eyes before letting my gaze fall along the curve of her neck and jaw until I'm focused on nothing but where my thumbs slide under the edge of her dress. "But right now…" I pause, slipping down the material being held up by her shoulder until her I can see the brown silk and lace edge of her strapless bra. I lean forward to press my lips to the freshly exposed skin, then move my feet on either side of hers so she's completely pinned between my body and the messy sheets behind her. "Right now, I'm going to take this dress off you," I finish, and her lip falls from her teeth as her eyes shut and her head nods slowly.

With one hand on her arm, I tug her tight to me and gather her hair within my other hand, pulling gently until her body submits and she bends her neck as an offering to my mouth. I suck gently, wanting to take more, but stop so I can kiss the next inch and the next as I let go of her hair to turn her body unhurriedly so she's now facing my bed and the sweetness of her perfect back is before me.

My fingers move her purple waves over her shoulder as my right hand trails to her other shoulder, slipping the remaining sleeve to the curve of her arm until the weight of it falls to her elbows. I kiss the very center of her spine as I reach lower in front of me and slide down the small zipper at her hips. I leave my lips against her as I speak.

"You are so beautiful," I whisper, and I feel her quiver against my touch.

My hands curve around her waist and glide up the sides of her body until I reach the top of her dress, now hanging heavily at the ends of her arms, and I push the rest of the fabric until it falls to the floor and her milky skin is cloaked in nothing but the sexiest copper lace I've ever seen.

I breathe in slowly, because I want to take my time, but so much of me is in a hurry. My hands still wrapped around her wrists lightly, I guide her arms behind her back until they rest along the small curve above her ass. Letting go briefly, I bring my fists to my mouth, squeezing them for strength, then flex my fingers as I lean into her. I love how her breath catches when she feels me against her neck.

"I want more of you," I say, kissing against the arc of her shoulder. "I'm going to undress you now. Say *yes*, Murphy. Please say yes, because I want you naked."

Her body shakes again, and her head nods.

"Yes," she says, a soft whisper of a cry.

I grin against her smoothness and scratch her skin with the roughness of my chin before kissing it cool.

My body once again under my control, I squeeze harder around her wrists, her hands still along the base of her spine.

"These," I say, tugging softly so she knows, "stay right here."

She nods again.

My fingers loosen, but I keep my touch on her arms, gliding up her skin, using her own body as my map, following curves and letting it lead. My palms caress around each shoulder as I stand behind her, so close that I can feel her hands and back against my own chest and where my hard-on is aching to be inside of her. Her breath pauses when she feels me against her.

"Do you feel that, baby?" I say. She nods again and I kiss her neck, not able to stop myself this time from taking a small, tender bite. "I want you so bad. Can I have you, baby? Can I taste you? Can I fuck you?"

This time the shaking travels all the way through her, and I hear her lose control with a small cry as she says, "Yes."

Yes.

Her next song needs to be this word.

My hands press against her biceps then slide around her body from her arms to her silky covered breasts, and I can feel how much she wants me, too. Her nipples are hard through the lace, and I run my thumbs over them again and again until she cries out with her ache and need.

"Please," she begs, and I smile against the top of her head, letting my eyes fall to a close as I slip my thumbs inside the top of her bra, sliding it down over the swell of her tits until I feel the pure ecstasy that is her bare skin and the puckered sweetness of each nipple. I cup each peak in my hands and let my thumbs run roughly over her hardness until her head falls back against my chest and her back arches with want.

I let her fight against it, try to will it, for almost a minute while I slowly rub circles around the bright red peaks until I finally give her what I know she's desperate for and squeeze each raw tip between my thumb and index finger. Her knees weaken and her body betrays her, wanting to fall to the bed, but I'm not ready yet. This torture—this *sweet, sweet* song—I've craved it for so long, and it's still at the beginning.

I hold her to me, the pressure hard and her legs trembling as her weight falls into my front. I'm so hard against her I know she can feel me in her hands, so with her breasts under my complete control, I tell her what to do.

"Touch me. Feel it," I say through gritted, sex-hungry teeth. "Grab my cock, baby. Take me in your hands."

Her fingers are fast and her palm is like fire against me as she grabs me through my jeans. I groan at her touch and my hands open and cup her breasts entirely. I want to be free and in her. I need to be in her, but the waiting has never felt so fucking amazing.

"Let go," I demand, and she obeys.

My hands fall away from her breasts at the same time, and she stands still in front of me, her hands resting along her lower back, her breath ragged and her shoulders shaking under the cool air of the room. I lick my lips and hold my right fist to my mouth, wanting to touch her more but forbidding myself until she asks for it. In silence, I stand there looking at her, seeing every curve from behind, where her arms lead to breasts I've touched but have barely seen. Time drags on, and I know she's in this with me, and I begin to chuckle deep within my chest.

"You're going to have to ask me, Murphy. Tell me. What do you want?" I ask, my hands ready to move on her word.

"Touch me," she says.

"Where, baby?" I ask, my hand poised and ready at her neck.

"Everywhere," she breathes, and with her permission, I lay my palm flat on her back and press until she bends forward.

I release her hands from behind her back and drag them slowly above her head as she crawls with one knee at a time to the edge of my bed, her body still facing away from me, and I slide my palm again up the small of her back to the center and coax her gently until she's lying flat against my mattress, her purple hair loose and wild among my blankets and pillows—just like I dreamed every night this week.

"Everywhere," I say, repeating the word she used so she knows what's to come, so she can tell me no—but she doesn't. She only nods as she twists her head to the side and opens her mouth against my bed as her eyes find mine and look at me with equal desire.

I drag both hands down to her hips, my eyes still locked with hers as I grip her firmly and drag her body down until she's bent over the bed, completely submissive. I unclasp the bra, now loose around her waist, and pull it away, throwing it to the floor, before kneeling between her legs and caging her lower body between both of my arms as my chin falls to the small divot at the end of her tailbone.

"So goddamn sexy," I say, my lips brushing against her back as I speak.

My tongue traces along the edge of her waistband as I let my hand drag roughly down the side of her body until I grip the side of her panties and pull the right edge down enough to expose her ass. She makes a noise as she breathes, and I pause to wait for her to stop this—to tell me this is far enough, when she does exactly the opposite and reaches her other hand down to find my left palm, still flat against the bed, and she moves it toward her body, lifting her hip as a guide.

"You want these off, baby?" I ask.

She nods against the bed.

Another "yes" falls from her lips.

I grab both sides and pull slowly, stopping at her thighs to take in the sight of her bare ass and swollen pussy ready for me. Wasting no time, I yank her panties to her knees and around her ankles, then spread her legs apart and run my palms up the back of each until my thumbs tickle along the edge of her. Warmth and softness opens, and I taste it with a slow drag of my tongue to the sound of her moans.

I thought her singing was perfection. I thought no other sound could compare, but when she pants for me and cries with pleasure, I come undone. I kiss her softness hard, sucking until she can no longer handle the pressure and writhes away from me. I grip her hips and force her to stay, to take every bit of my dirty kisses, until I can no longer wait.

Both of my hands work at my zipper as I kiss her pussy while she grips the pillow now covering her head. I stop only to kick away my jeans and boxers and toss my shirt to the floor.

I lean over her, letting her feel me hard and hot against her now soaking self.

"Don't. Move," I say, sliding small strands of hair away from her back while I press a kiss to each shoulder.

I step to my night table, pulling out a condom and sliding it on quickly, returning to her open legs and beautiful body.

"You want me to touch everything, Murphy?" I ask against her, letting her feel the tip of my cock against her swollen entrance, both throbbing and wanting to feel what each other has to give.

"Yes," she says.

"Ask me, Murphy," I grin, knowing she'll say it—she'll say anything I ask. And not because I'm dominating her and pushing her to the edge only to hold back, but because she wants it too. Because she wants to feel me inside of her as badly as I want to be there. Because Murphy Sullivan is that girl for me, my undoing and my discipline. She's what my dreams are made of, and I want to taste her, consume her, and hold her hostage for all of time.

"Say it," I whisper, my bottom lip propped open against the heat of her back as I hold myself at her entry. "Tell me to fuck you."

"Fuck me, Casey. Please," she moans. "I want to be fucked so bad."

My eyes close at my beautiful girl's dirty words, and I give her her wish.

"Yes, baby girl. I'll fuck you," I smile, sliding into her in one slow, exquisitely painful stroke until I can go no further.

She cries out a *yes,* and her fists pound against the bed, tossing my pillow to the side.

"Again," she says, and I obey, pulling out slowly, completely, and waiting at the very edge of her until she pushes back into me, and I enter her again with the same deep, slow penetration of before.

"Yes," she says again, fists grabbing this time, pulling my sheet from my bed and biting at it with her teeth.

"Again, baby?" I ask, wanting to move harder and faster, but knowing if I'm not careful, it will be over.

She nods with a whimper, so I repeat every step, pushing into her hard enough that her body burrows into my bed.

Her back begins to sweat, and the heat starts to take over our actions as I move rougher and more often, letting go of myself so I can rest my body against her back completely, running my hands up her arms and threading my fingers with hers as I push into her over and over.

Still inside her, I stop and pull her against me to the edge of the bed where I lift her with me to a stand so I can feel her breasts with every breath that she takes while I move insider her. Her fingers reach around my neck and grab my hair as I kiss over her shoulder and pull at her nipples while my cock strokes her from behind.

I have never had sex so good in my life, and I know the end is near. My cock is swollen and I'm going to come in any second, but I need to see her—I need to memorize every angle and every face she makes when she takes all of me. I pull out from her and spin her so she's facing me, then push her back against the mattress where I fall on top of her and enter quickly, her legs wrapping around my waist and her center hungry for me, missing me when I'm gone.

"I could watch you take me all night, Murphy. I love the way you look with me inside, so hot, so wet," I say, my hips pushing forward, hers circling with my motion.

"Harder," she says, the word coming out broken and needy. "Please, Casey. Fuck me harder," she says, and I can't believe her dirty mouth—the same lips that kiss so sweet and sing so strong. I lean forward and claim her lips as mine, pushing into her repeatedly, holding on until I feel her release, forbidding my own pleasure until I know she's completely spent.

I feel her clench and her arms and legs wrap around me tightly, her breath held and her head tilted back as far as her neck will allow. I reach with one hand between us, my thumb pressing in firm circles just above where I am entering her, everything slick and warm with our sex, and then suddenly she cries out and her insides clench around me in waves.

"Oh god, Casey. Yes!" she screams, and I press my mouth into the side of her neck and push again and again, draining her of every single moan, cry and whimper until I'm no longer able to hold on and I come hard, my body collapsing into her, my nerves losing control and my muscles giving way to the purest pleasure I've ever felt.

We lay silent for several minutes, our bodies still connected as I hold her to me and dust away long, purple curls now straightened and damp from sex. And when my hands can no longer wait, I trail them lower against her smooth belly, and lower between her legs, pressing against what I want again, what I don't think I can wait for, and to my surprise, her hand covers mine and presses even harder, and she whispers "Again. Fuck me again."

CHAPTER 15

Murphy

My body is sore and my cheeks are red. The only thing keeping me grounded is the warm hand running up and down my back and the pair of dark, round eyes staring back into me. I never slept. I only pretended to sleep. When Casey woke an hour ago, I shut my eyes quickly and faked it for longer, because the woman I was in his room when the sun went down is not the one with stage fright and reservations in the light.

I couldn't *not* look, though, after a while. This sweetness—it's real. He hasn't said a word, other than "good morning." When I bashfully tucked my face into his pillow, he tugged on my chin, lifting me out so he could kiss my nose.

Shame is nonexistent in Casey's world. I must remember that, because the pleasure was more than anything I'd ever had.

"It's Saturday," he says, finally. I think he's smirking, though it's hard to tell with both of our cheeks pressed against his sheets.

"It is," I agree, blushing at the very fresh memories of last night.

"I have to check in at my parents' house, but other than that, my day is completely free. I'm all yours," he says, his lips still askew as if he's up to something.

"Okay," I say, sucking in my bottom lip and looking to the bed and ceiling in an attempt to avoid his stare.

"Is there…maybe…something you have to do? Like…some plans you have or…I don't know," he says, coyly.

I blush hard at his suggestion.

"Again? Already?" I ask.

He holds my stare, but his smile grows as he chuckles.

"I mean, well…sure. I'm definitely up for more of that, but I meant the birthday party your brother keeps texting you about, asking where you've been and what kind of cake you want your mom to make," he laughs, and my breath rushes away.

"Oh, shit!" I yell, covering my mouth. "I completely forgot!"

"You forgot your own birthday?" he laughs, slipping my phone from behind his back. I take it quickly and begin typing a message to my mom, requesting chocolate, and then apologizing for being out late. I delete that last part though because I'm not late—I never came home. But I'm an adult, and this should be normal. I need my own place. And oh my god my brother is wondering where I am. I'm typing feverishly, deleting like mad because my thumbs are massive and I'm the queen of typos, and I just wrote *smurf* for no reason.

"Murphy," Casey whispers. I keep typing, and he says my name again, a little louder with a laugh. His hands cover mine and he makes me put down the phone.

"It's your birthday," he says, his head lifted slightly and his eyes soft. Oh man, he's going to think I'm weird when I explain this.

"Actually," I say, my face bunching with humiliation because I'm a twenty-two-year-old still obsessed with birthday parties. "It's not *really* my birthday. It's my half birthday."

"Your...half birthday," he repeats.

I grab my phone and continue to text my mom, making sure I get the chocolate order in at the very least.

"Yes," I say, now sitting, sheets wrapped around my waist and one of his old T-shirts over my body.

He wraps his hands around mine to force me to pause again, but I shake him loose.

"Just let me send this last one, and I'll explain," I say, my tongue out on the side while I type quickly with my movie request, and a warning that I might be late, and I may bring Casey with me. I hit SEND rapidly, but instantly want to take the message back when I realize that the sequence of my texts pretty much lets them know I spent the night here with *him*, but then I just give in and drop the phone to my lap because fuck it, I'm an adult. My father will want to punch Casey, but he won't *really* do it—he'll just look at him with those threatening eyes that say "I'm not so old I can't whoop your ass."

"Half birthday?" Casey questions, bringing me out of my manic state.

I take in a full breath to reset my nerves and look into his smiling eyes.

"My real birthday is on Christmas Day, and I hated that. I used to complain a lot when I was little, so my parents instituted the half-birthday plan. We've been doing it this way for so long, it's kind of become this tradition. I didn't think we were going to this year, but then the other day, my mom asked me if there was anything I wanted, and I got kind of excited," I admit. I pull my thumbnail to my mouth and scrunch my eyes, ready for how this is going to sound. "I really like presents."

"Awww, baby likes presents," Casey teases, tugging me to his lap and wrapping my legs around his waist. My emotions switch gears at the feel of him against me.

"I do," I say, as he nuzzles his nose against mine.

"Do I get to come to this party?" he asks.

"Uh huh," I breathe, my eyes now closed, because his hands have sunk down to my thighs and are working their way up the curve of my ass, pulling me forward even harder.

"Do you…do you want your present from me?" he teases, but I don't laugh because now, right now, yes. I do want my present. I want *this* present. And I no longer care about the chocolate cake or a party or…

"I am fairly fond of your birthday suit," he jokes as his thumbs lift up the bottom of the T-shirt I'm wearing, dragging it up my body, but stopping when my arms are above my head and my eyes are covered with cotton. His mouth covers one breast, sucking me hard while his hand falls behind my back and pulls me into him.

My phone rings, and Casey flails his hand around the sheets next to us until he finds it, then throws it to the floor. He lifts me up in one single motion to lie flat for him, my arms still tethered and my eyes still covered in his shirt, and for the next hour, I let him do anything he wants.

Casey takes me back to my car near the club, and I make it home around lunch, and I can smell chocolate baking when I enter the house. There's no use in hiding any of this. It was either come home in the dress I wore to the club last night or walk into the house in a pair of borrowed sweatpants and T-shirt from Casey. I was going to get stares either way, so I opted for the soft comfort of wearing him home instead.

When his eyes hit me, my father pauses at the exit from the living room with a small plate and fork from whatever snack he was sneaking in his hand. I step inside the house, and I offer a tight-lipped smile as I hold up one hand for hello, my dress gathered in a pile under my other arm.

"I was…" I start, but then my father holds up his hand, clearly not symbolizing *hello,* but *stop.*

"You were nothing. And the teasing about you and Casey is no longer funny to me, so just…go get ready for your party," he says, not able to look me in the eye.

I nod and look down to my feet, which are still in my boots, Casey's sweats stuffed in the top. I look ridiculous. This is how those magazines get those absurd pictures of famous people doing the walk of shame.

My father moves on to the kitchen, his back to me while he rinses off a plate and dries his hands. I watch for a few seconds, but decide nothing is really going to make the awkwardness of this any better, so I eventually retreat to my room.

"You look good in Casey's clothes," my brother says from behind, following me inside. I grab my chest when he startles me, but chuckle when I look down at my form. Only Lane would think I look good like this, and it's just because he thinks Casey is cool.

"Thank you," I say, tossing my dress to the corner and turning to sit on my bed so I can yank my boots from my feet.

"Mom said you shacked up," Lane says, stealing my breath. My face falls and I fling my boot to the floor as my mouth stumbles for some type of response. "That's like a sleepover, right? I want to shack up with Casey sometime. Is he coming to the party? Maybe I'll ask him."

I shut my mouth and keep my focus on my other boot, which I take off more slowly—buying time. I'm mortified that my brother overheard this and that my mother said this, probably in a conversation with my father.

"You should," I say, looking up at him with a smile. Something funny should come out of my humiliation. "I bet Casey would like that."

"Cool," Lane says, leaving me in my room alone. I close the door and let my head fall flat against the wood.

I'm embarrassed. I should be. This situation…it's super embarrassing. But I'm also…happy. And I'm not nervous, or worried, or feeling like I'm not good enough for something—I'm just happy. Content. And I actually feel kind of beautiful.

I pick at my guitar for an hour before finally showering and drying my hair. I decide on my comfiest pair of jeans and match it up with my vintage Bangles tank top and the necklaces Sam made me with small bottles of pretend potion at the end. My phone dings just as I finish pulling my hair back in a braid, and I skip to it, excited to read that Casey is out front in the driveway.

Then, his next text comes.

Your dad is walking out of the house.

My brow furrows and I glance to the window. I take a few steps forward to glance out, and I only see Casey's form sitting in his car, typing on his phone. I type back.

I don't see him.

And I wait for a breath, watching his head move to look out the window and then back to his lap and phone.

Really? You don't see that man standing on your porch with an ax?

Oh…shit!

I lean completely forward and press my face to the glass of my window, but all I can see under the overhang is the tips of my father's shoes. He's wearing sneakers—perfect for wood-chopping. I shake my head and mumble my way out of my room, past my brother and down the stairs where my father is in fact standing with the door open and a towel in his hand, wiping away the rusted blade for the ax I am pretty sure he hasn't used since I was twelve and we took it up north to chop down a Christmas tree.

230

"Daddy," I sigh.

"Oh, hi, birthday girl," he says, leaning his head back and tilting his chin. I step toward him and kiss him on the cheek.

"So," I hum, nodding. "What's with the ax?"

My father's chest shakes lightly with his laughter, the silent kind that brews in his belly. He runs the towel over the blade a few more times and twists the heavy metal tool by the handle in his giant palm before holding it out in front of him and taking a small test swing.

"I'm just messin' with your boyfriend," he says with a faint laugh.

Boyfriend. I smile at the word.

"He's not going to get out of the car while you're holding that," I say.

"I know, Murph. I know," he says, still chuckling. "I'll let him in after a few minutes. Just let me have my fun."

I twist my mouth and lean to the side for a better view of Casey. He's resting against his steering wheel, hat low on his brow and arms folded, and when our eyes meet, he lifts a hand and gives me a slight wave. I wave back then feel the buzz in my pocket and pull out my phone.

I'm not going in there.

I laugh to myself and put my palm on my father's back.

"Carry on then," I say, turning around and joining my mother at the counter where she is icing my favorite flavor of cake.

"It makes him feel better about you growing up," she says, not raising her eyes to look at me.

"I know," I concede.

After about five minutes, my father walks back through the house and exits through the back sliding door into the backyard. He returns ax-free, just in time for Casey to be standing at the doorway with an opened box of chocolates and a small gift bag. He doesn't cross the threshold until my father meets him there and finally cracks out a laugh, sliding his arm around him and patting him on the back.

"I like to kid," my father says, and Casey responds with a nervous *oh* mixed with his own unnatural laugh.

When Casey makes it to where I'm standing, his hand finds mine at my side quickly, and he squeezes my fingers hard. His palm is sweating, and it amuses me that the boy who isn't really afraid of anything is scared shitless of a man in his late fifties.

My father pulls a soda from the fridge, but turns around quickly, his face bugging in front of Casey's as he yells "Boo!"

"Oh...god," Casey startles, taking a step back, dropping the bag he was still holding in his hand. I hear something break.

My father laughs harder this time, pulling the tab on his Coke— or should I say one of *my* Cokes—and takes a long sip as he passes, shaking his finger at Casey. "You're funny," he says. "I like it." His chuckle grows quieter as he finally leaves the room.

"You okay there?" I ask, not able to hide my grin.

"Oh, ha ha. You thought that was funny?" He bends down and picks up the small bag, sliding it on the counter in front of me. "I'm pretty sure I just busted your gift..."

"And crapped your pants," my mom throws in before licking away the extra frosting on her spatula and tossing it in the soapy water in her sink.

Casey's head falls and his eyes close as he bites his lip.

"All signs of endearment, Casey," my mom says, squeezing his shoulder once as she rounds the counter and begins to bring plates and dishes to the table.

I watch his face for a few seconds, enjoying the smile on it from our teasing. This is sort of the way in the Sullivan house, and while I think my dad was partly also *not* joking with the ax, I know that my parents' behavior does mean that Casey has won them over to some extent.

"Can I?" I ask him, nodding toward the bag he handed me.

"Go on. It's not much, but...it's *really* not much now that I dropped it on the ground," he grimaces. "And I brought chocolates, but I ate four of them in the car because, well...I thought I might be in there for a while—ax and all."

"Four?" I ask, noticing the completely empty top layer exposed in the small box by his hand.

"Maybe six..." he smirks. "Okay, seven. Fine. Eight."

I laugh because he's silly. My eyes remain on him, the sweet dimple when he grins, the way he looks at me—I watch it all as I slide the bag closer and pull out the few layers of tissue on top. There's a card, so I pull that out first and begin to open it, but Casey stops my hands.

"Save that...for later," he says.

Tempted to disobey, I hold his gaze for a few seconds, but finally set the card aside, quirking a brow as I reach into the bright-yellow gift bag. My hand finds something hard, and I grip it, pulling it out to reveal what I think may just be the ugliest coffee mug I've ever seen. The glaze is still sticky, and I leave a fingerprint around the rim just from my touch. The design looks to be like green stick figures, maybe?

"What's...this?" I ask, pointing to a slightly curved line coming out from between one of the green person's legs.

"I know. It totally looks like I drew you a dirty picture, but..." he says, spinning the mug a little in my hand and reaching into the bag for the handle that broke off during its fall.

"Casey, that's *exactly* what it looks like," I giggle.

"But it's not. Look, see? That's you, right there, the green one with purple hair. And that's a guitar, and that's me at the sound board, and...shit," he stops, shaking his head and holding both pieces apart in front of him. "Whatever. Fine...it's a fucking dirty picture."

"It's hideous," I laugh harder, and he rolls his eyes, packing it back in the bag, playing hurt. "But I love it," I say, grabbing for it.

His hands relent, and he gives the bag to me, moving his palms flat against the counter as his tight lips smile and his eyes flick to mine.

"Yeah?" he asks.

"Yeah," I say.

"Leah has a pottery kit, but I didn't have enough time to bake it. She helped with the…" he says, pulling it back out and pointing at the guitar that looks a lot more like a penis.

"Yeah…let's just put this back in the bag," I say, laughing at my ugly stick-figure-porno-mug that was painted by a five-year-old.

"Houston was so pissed when he saw it, and then I told him his daughter drew it, and he was *more* pissed," he laughs. I roll the top of the bag and move it to the cabinet, closing the door.

"You don't have to keep it," he says when I turn around. He doesn't look hurt. He looks…happy. He's happy, too. And that's a far cry from the broken boy who landed on my doorstep two weeks ago.

"I love it. But I don't think my dad will, and since you've already seen the ax…"

"Yeah, cabinet's a good spot," he agrees, kidding along with me, only maybe not as much as I'm kidding.

Lane comes down the stairs and gravitates immediately to Casey, hugging him to the side and punching at his ribs like bros do. Casey compliments my brother's khaki pants, and I catch the way my mother looks over them both fondly. Ax-wielding aside, Casey is all right in her book. I've shared how much Casey has been helping his family with both of my parents, and they're willing and ready to help. I know he would never accept it, though.

"Can we shack up?" Lane asks suddenly, and I watch in shock as Casey is left without words. His mouth falls open then shut before he looks to me, and I try not to burst into laughter. I simply nod with wide eyes, so Casey answers "Sure. Maybe in a few weeks."

I leave Lane and my bother at the counter to talk about their favorite movies and about my song as I help my mother to finish setting the table. She pulls my favorite part of this tradition from the oven—a steaming pan of homemade enchiladas. It's not something that's often done well in the Midwest or South, but Jeannie Sullivan does it right. We all follow the scent to the table, and within seconds, our plates are full and our mouths are busy.

234

"So this half-birthday thing," Casey says between bites, "is this something *I* can get in on?"

"Is your birthday on Christmas?" my father asks from the other end of the table, eyes on his food.

"March sixteenth," Casey answers.

"Then no," my dad says with no reaction at all before taking a bite.

Casey pulls his napkin up and wipes his mouth, and my mother and I both pause our eating, a little nervous. My father looks up, then busts into laughter.

"Ax thing really got you, didn't it," he says, lifting another forkful to his mouth.

"I take axes and daughters really seriously, sir," Casey says, and I keep my hands on the edge of my seat, kind of nervous about what stupid thing he may say next. But those words, however crazy they may sound—they aren't stupid at all. They're lovely.

"If ever you think I haven't done right by her, I hope you'll let me know," Casey says, putting his fork down and placing his napkin next to his plate on the table. His hands fold in his lap and his eyes are directly on my father's. I slide my leg to the right until my foot stops at the weight of Casey's shoe, and my heart thumps wildly. My how far we have come.

My father doesn't respond with words. With a long sip from his soda, he eyes the man who has quickly and not-so-silently stolen my heart, then lifts his brow before raising the can and tilting it in a toast to that very promise before returning to the meal in front of him. I exhale slowly, and pull my plate closer, taking smaller bites because my tummy is too filled with butterflies to eat anything for real. Eventually, Casey's knee moves into mine under the table, and I glance at him, catching his crooked smile on me as I make a mental note that this has now become my most favorite half birthday ever, as in *I'm-pretty-sure-I'll-write-a-song-about-it good.*

Casey

I woke up different today.

I'm not saying a person can mature as much as *I* probably need to in the course of twenty-four hours, but still…I woke up different today. Maybe it's happened slowly, maybe it's been happening for weeks, and I just didn't realize. I'm sure part of it is the responsibility I now carry for my family, forcing me to look at things differently.

But I also kind of think it's the girl.

I would do anything for this girl. And if the time came where I could no longer make her smile, I would want someone else to try. I'm not sure what that is, but I have a feeling.

Her bare feet glide across the carpet as we walk to her bedroom, our bellies sick with rich chocolate cake—the best I've ever had. I was greedy and took a second piece, and when I couldn't finish it, Lane slid it from my plate to his. He said I was like family so germs didn't count. Family.

This is some family. And Murphy is some girl.

I watch her fold up her guitar case, tucking a few loose picks inside along with her familiar notebook.

"Were you playing?" I ask.

"I started to, while I was waiting for my hair to dry," she says. I love the way she's looking at me with sideways glances—bashful, the memory of last night fresh in her mind.

"Something new?" I ask.

She shakes her head *no*, but I bet there are a lot of ideas hidden in there. She'll show them when she's ready.

"Can I open my card now?" she asks, pulling it from her back pocket where she had it tucked during dinner. I shrug, a little embarrassed at how silly my gesture feels now. If I'd had time, I would have done something more—given her a better gift. This was all I could think of at the moment though.

She slides open the envelope and pulls out the thick stack of notebook paper stapled at the seam. Quirking a brow, she moves so she's sitting on her bed, holding the makeshift booklet in her lap, and I sink to my favorite spot on her floor and begin pressing my hand into the carpet just like I did the last time I sat here.

"Senior year," she reads, and I look up, pulling my hat from my head and resting it on the floor next to me. Our eyes meet, and I urge her silently to keep turning pages.

She laughs lightly, folding the paper down and turning it to face me so I can see the round circle with bright red lips and yellowish brown hair.

"You don't have to show me; I drew it," I say, smiling on one side of my mouth.

"Am I going to get more dirty pictures?" she jokes.

I give her a tight smile and our eyes meet and pause for a beat before I shake my head *no*.

I watch her flip each page, and I can tell from her expressions where she's at in the book—her giggle at my sad attempt at drawing the basketball team and the hand she puts over her heart when she gets to the page I drew of my favorite picture of her. I wish I drew better, because Leah's silver crayon could never do those eyes justice. In the margins around each picture, I wrote kind words from made-up people all saying how amazing she is, how beautiful and how they know she's going to be a star.

When she reaches the final page, her fingers turn it slowly, and my heart races so fast that I have to lie down, my hands folded over my chest while I watch silently as her eyes scan back and forth reading. Eventually, I close my eyes and picture the words, having memorized them the moment I wrote them on the page.

Some will adore you.
They will be captivated by your voice and fall for you because of your kindness.
Others will envy you.
They'll yearn for your talent, want your success, and covet your spotlight.
The world will know you. For all of the best and right reasons.
Time will prove me right.
But in the meantime, I will simply wish for you.

I'll wish on stars, on pennies, on candles at half-birthday parties.

I'll wish for you because wanting you isn't enough and having you is too fleeting. And should we find ourselves apart, I'll wish twice as hard, and maybe, just maybe, I'll be lucky enough to run into you in one of our dreams.

~ Casey Coffield

"It's stupid, and corny, I know, but…" I stop, running my hands over my face as I stare up at her ceiling. I roll to the side and watch her finger tracing over the purple crayon-written scribbles I wrote six times, still not satisfied in the end that my words were right or enough.

"I love it," she says, flipping through the pages again from the beginning.

"You can hide it in the cabinet, with the mug," I joke, and she laughs, but it fades quickly as her head lifts and her eyes find mine.

"That's how I *should* have signed your yearbook," I shrug, reaching forward and grabbing her smallest toe between my fingers and tugging gently. "If I weren't such a juvenile prickwad, I would have noticed you a lot sooner."

"No," she says, shaking her head and moving to her knees, to the front of her small bookcase where she slides her new book in place. "I wouldn't have wanted you to. You showed up exactly right."

"Yeah?" I ask.

She rests back on her legs, her palms flat on her thighs, and looks at me, a thick braid of purple over one shoulder and the neck I love to kiss bare on the other side. Her smile is quiet and still, and it lasts for minutes yet seems to constantly change and say something new. She's the Mona Lisa.

"Do you want to go somewhere with me?" she asks, a glimmer in her eye as if she's gone back to that girl she was—the innocent one still in high school—and that girl is giving me a chance to see what would have been.

238

"I'd love to, birthday girl," I say, letting her stand first and hold her hand out for me.

I wait while she slides her bare feet into a pair of black tennis shoes and reaches for her guitar case. I follow her down the stairs and remain quiet and still in her kitchen while she whispers in her father's ear. There's nodding, and a quiet conversation with her mother next, and soon she's holding her keys and is linking her free arm through mine to guide me out the door.

"It isn't far," she smiles.

I don't ask questions.

She loads her guitar into the back of her car, and I notice the scratch that still mars the side. I'll fix it for her next week when she's at school, because I know she can't be without her car long enough to get it done.

She remains secretive during our short drive that winds through her quiet suburb and along a dark country road until I notice a row of flashing lights flanked by two farm fields. When we pull over and she punches in a code on a gate that looks weak enough to just drive through—even with my car—I sit up and roll down my window.

"Is this...a runway?" I ask, tilting my face to the sky. There aren't any planes lining up, but this is definitely some sort of runway.

"My dad has a hangar here. It's where they keep a lot of the crop dusters and the tankers for fire season," she shouts, finishing the code to the countdown of beeps as the gate slowly slides open. She jogs back to the car and slams the door closed, speeding in and racing to a row of metal buildings away from the lights.

"Your dad's a pilot?" I ask.

"No," she smiles, screeching to a stop outside of the last building.

Falling forward, my hands hit the dash and I'm stunned still while she's already out her door and pulling her guitar from the back. I have an odd sense that we're about to visit an alien ship or that I'm about to see the time machine her family's been hiding.

I exit the car and follow her to the door on the side, stepping into the dark space behind her when she gets the door unlocked. She lets it slam closed behind us, and before my eyes adjust, I feel her hand on my cheek and her lips against mine.

"Well, hello there…" I tease, grabbing her ass and squeezing.

She giggles in the dark, and without her touch, I'm lost. I can't find her.

Seconds later, there's a loud clatter and lights begin to buzz on. The glow is dim at first, and it takes my eyes a few minutes to adjust, but soon the plane comes into view. It's red and magnificent, and the propeller at the front looks sharp and well cared for. I'm already afraid of flying, even in seven-forty-sevens, so there's no way I would step aboard something that, at a quick glance, looks like it runs on rubber bands. But I can appreciate its beauty.

"It was my grandpa's; he built it himself," she says, running her hand along a wing as she walks toward me. There isn't even a single speck of dust to be found.

"It's something," I say, taking a small tour around the body of the craft.

"It's just a replica. My grandfather was a history professor, and he was fascinated by flight. It's the same kind of plane they flew in the Czech Army Air Force in the late twenties," she beams. Her hand wraps lovingly around one of the support rods and her head falls against her arm as she looks at me. "My entire family is afraid of flying, so she's never even been airborne," she laughs.

I join her and move to the cockpit, looking to her for approval before I step inside.

"Do you fly?" she asks.

I laugh loud, and it echoes against the metal walls.

"I'm not much better than you. I drink heavily when I fly just so I don't rip the seat arms away with my death grip," I admit, running my fingers over the small switches and levers that have jobs I don't understand.

"Good old Jim Beam, huh?" she chuckles.

"Don't you mean Johnnie Walker," I tease.

240

Her head leaned to the side, she holds on to the rod tightly and swings her body underneath the wing until she's standing next to me.

"If you were a pilot, I'd let you fly me to the moon," she says.

I stare into her eyes and wait for her to laugh at her line, but she doesn't—so I leave it alone, too, and lean my head forward against hers. We rest like this for nearly a minute, her hand running over mine along the edge of the cockpit. She traces every knuckle, and my nerves react by sending signals to my heart. The kick is swift, and constant.

"Thank you for showing me this," I say, finally breaking our silence. "I'm really glad it isn't a spaceship."

She gurgles a laugh, and the sound makes me laugh, too.

"My dad comes to clean it once a week. He was here a couple days ago, and I came along to hang out," she says, holding on to the edge and stretching her body back before finally letting go and urging me to follow.

I climb from the plane, my feet hitting the ground in a loud clap. We both cross back to the other side to a small workbench set up against the wall, and she brings her guitar case up from the ground, unclasping the hinges and pulling her instrument out.

"I would always come here to test out songs, especially when I was still learning," she smiles shyly, holding one of her picks in her teeth while she plucks her strings and twists the bolts for tuning. Taking the pick in her hand, she strums a few times, making minor adjustments until her ears are satisfied. Her eyes come to me and her smile is crooked.

"Even when I sucked…" she starts.

I interrupt.

"You never sucked," I say.

Her head tilts to the left and her lips purse.

"I did. Believe me," she says. "But even then, I sounded good in here."

She strums a few more chords followed by a soft melody that she picks out. It's sweet at the heart, but the echo does something special to her tune. She's right—an old airport hangar off a country back road is the great equalizer.

"Not bad," I nod, sliding up on the metal table and leaning back until my head rests on the corrugated steel wall.

"Fucking phenomenal," she winks.

I could watch her in her element for days and never grow tired. Wondering why we've come here tonight, I begin to ask, but Murphy holds up a finger, urging me to have patience as she reaches back to her case and pulls out the tattered notebook I'd riffled through that day in the mall. She flips a few pages, clearing her throat when she lands on the one I had hoped for. Her eyes flit to mine, and her smile is brief—her nerves alive and evident all over her face. She closes her eyes and begins to work her fingers, letting the melody play out several times while she wills away her demons.

I don't interrupt. I don't become a crutch. I do nothing but wait, watching in wonder as her hands do something I could only dream of having mine do. Nearly a minute passes, and I forget that I was ever waiting to hear her sing at all, my soul too invested in all she's already done, when her lips part and a fucking miracle happens.

Murphy sings her song—the one I like best. It isn't about me. It isn't about guys like me. It's about the girl she was, the one who wanted to break out, but couldn't—the one whose own tongue betrayed her and tangled her messages and held her hostage when she should have been careless and naïve and young and free.

That tongue is a thief, no matter how much I love it. But it's powerless now.

I watch her lips and take in every painful wince and twitch of her eyelids until the very end, when she's completely gone to the other side—fearless and singing in front of only me, singing words so personal they almost look as if they burn on their way out.

I've never been more proud of something in my entire life, and I was only the witness.

When her mouth closes and her hands stop, I sit still and don't make a sound. She brings her guitar flat to her chest, hugging it while her mouth takes on a satisfied form.

I love you, Murphy Sullivan. You are better than me, and I don't care. You will slay dragons.

I never say a word, and Murphy packs her guitar quietly before I hold the tips of her fingers and let her guide me back out through the pitch-black room. I don't speak until I know her heart has finally quit racing, her adrenaline has run out, and her ears are ready to accept the truth.

"You are so special," I say as she starts the car's engine. She lets her head fall to the side against the seat, and I can tell by her expression she thinks I'm just complimenting her. I'm not—I'm warning her. "Do not—under *any* circumstances—give that song to anybody who doesn't deserve it."

Our eyes lock, and several seconds pass with my words the only thing on both of our minds.

"Okay," she says, giving herself back to the road, taking us home.

CHAPTER 16

Murphy

"Oh my god that song is so boring!"

Leave it to a seven-year-old to put me in my place.

It's free-play. Because I said so. Because my heart does not want to be here in this classroom today. It isn't fair to the small group of kids left. They get to sign up by the week, and it seems only the most dedicated eight have stuck around to continue moving into Brahms and Beethoven. Well, seven dedicated students—Sasha is still here, and I am totally convinced it's because her parents have nothing else to do with her.

"You think it's boring, hmm?" I ask Sasha. The rest of the kids are playing on the keyboards with headphones, and she's staring at me with her chin against her table.

"Yeah," she says. "Sorry."

I laugh out a small breath and look down at my fingers. I was plucking out a melody, but I couldn't settle on one I liked. It seems I need to keep looking.

"What kind of music do *you* like?" I ask my worst student ever.

"Rock!" she shouts, her voice loud enough that two or three others hear her and pull their headphones from their ears.

"Rock, yeah?" I nod. She smiles big. "Well, this class is about the classics, but maybe…if you're lucky…I'll surprise you with a little something tomorrow," I wink.

Sasha perks up, unraveling her headphones and pushing them to her ears with a grin on her face that matches the size of the bubble she blows with her gum she isn't supposed to have. I let her get away with it, because there are only a few weeks to go, and if she's chewing, at least she isn't talking.

When class is over, I rush to my car for my favorite part of the day. I wait for Casey to call, because I'm never quite sure what he'll be dealing with. His father suffered a stroke the night after my half birthday, which seems incredibly unfair and cruel, but the doctors told Casey and his mother that it was actually common.

244

Casey was distraught. He rambled through percentages that the doctors gave him, risk factors mixed with medicines that equal likelihoods, talk of another stroke—everything he said seemed entirely *uncommon.* So did he. My cool, calm, nothing-phases-him boy was drowning in what to do.

I pull on my safety belt and lay the phone in my center console so it's easy to see and grab. The *buzz* comes before I leave the lot, so I pull back into a space and rush to answer, pausing when I realize it's Gomez instead of Casey. My heart rushes for an entirely different reason—I haven't heard from John Maxwell since the day we recorded, and I haven't heard a word about my song since Casey played it for me. He's asked around, but didn't get any clear answers.

"Hello, this is Murphy," I answer, squeezing my eyes shut, because I always sound so incredibly unhip with Gomez and John.

"Murph, heyyyyyy," he says, the word sliding out as if it is longer than one syllable. He sounds high—I'm pretty sure he's stoned.

"Hey," I answer back, starting to feel like we might just go round-and-round with this.

"Yeah, hey…so…John wants to get you in. Can you stop by today? We've got some exciting stuff to share, and some new ideas he'd like to run by you," Gomez says.

My pulse is doing triple-time, and I'm suddenly searching around my car for a pen to take notes, even though…I don't really know what I'd need to write. But a pen…I just need a fucking pen!

"Sure, yeah…uhm…" I'm stuttering. I'm sweating. I find a pen and I pull a receipt from my purse and turn it around and begin drawing circles. This is stupid, but it's working. "I can be there in an hour. Does that work?"

"Sounds good," Gomez says, and I hear some laughing behind him along with the clanks of silverware. "Hey…hey, order me one more…" he says to someone in the background, his hand muffling the phone. "You there?"

I don't answer at first, still listening, still full of adrenaline.

"Murphy? You there?" he repeats.

"Oh…yeah. Sorry," I say, pen clenched and drawing triangles now.

"Good, so make it two hours. We're on a business lunch, and John wants to sit in," he says.

"Okay," I answer, my mind searching for what question I need to ask next—there are so many. He hangs up before I get the chance.

My hands are shaking and I'm staring at the 1:37 total minutes stamped on my last call when my phone buzzes again in my palm. I shake my head and try to clear my nerves, to temper my excitement in case Casey's day did not go well.

"Hey," I answer—that same *hey*. I hope I don't sound stoned and disinterested.

"Beautiful girl," he breathes, and I sink into my seat, suddenly grounded.

"How's your dad?" I ask.

There's a deep breath before he responds.

"Good. I guess," he says. "Nothing new, but he's having trouble breathing. They have the oxygen going, and his doctor is coming in this afternoon. I called in to work again. I hate missing so much, but I guess…I mean…whatever, right?"

"I'm sure everyone understands," I say.

"And fuck 'em if they don't," he says, and I frown, because for the first time since I've known him, he sounds so detached from this thing that used to fill him with fire.

"I'm sorry. I didn't mean to bring you down," he says, and I can tell his chest is tight and he's trying just for me.

"You didn't. I'm glad you can talk to me. I'm sorry this has all gotten so…I don't know…hard, I guess," I say.

I hear him sigh long and deep on the other end.

"Me, too," he says. "But hey. I'm okay. Really, Murph. I don't want you to worry about me."

"Okay," I whisper, lying. Not okay. Not at all. And I worry—a lot.

My teeth saw at my bottom lip while I think about how I could possibly mention my news to him. I'm excited, and that doesn't

246

feel right, because I also want to help and I feel bad. Casey is the person who got me here, no matter what he says. And I want to have him with me, at least mentally, when I go into that big board room again in two hours.

"Gomez called," I say. It's not the greatest transition.

"Oh yeah?" he asks. I can hear him working to sound happy…for me.

"They want me to come in to talk about more," I say, my thumbnail resting between my teeth.

"Murph, that's…that's a really good sign," he says, genuine pride in his tone.

"Thanks," I say. "I'm nervous."

"Don't be. You're the one they want. You hold the power. The keeper of the chips. The big kahuna," he chuckles.

"Wow, that's…like…a whole lot of metaphors," I smile.

His laugh is soft and breathy on the other side. He sounds tired, and I know he has to work tonight. I miss him. We've only been voices to one another all week.

"Do you need me to visit your mom while you're at the club," I offer. I know he'll refuse.

"Thanks, but it's okay. My sister's coming in," he says.

"Which one?"

He chuckles. "All of them, actually. I think they're going to watch chick flicks with my mom," he says.

"Sounds nice," I say.

He pauses for a few seconds. "It does, actually," he says, and I don't ask, but I think a part of him likes seeing the women in his life do normal family things that don't involve banking and dinner-table talk about projects and management.

I want to keep him on the phone with me. I want to carry him into my meeting and have him there just in case, whenever I need. But I know he has a lot in front of him today. So I settle with just hoping I'll see him later.

"Can I come tonight?" I ask, knowing I'll show up no matter what.

"You better," he says.

We hang up, and I drive home in silence, because my thoughts are enough to fill my head. I coach myself while changing clothes, and I wait at the table with a sandwich ready for Lane as his bus arrives. My brother has a million stories to tell me, but I'm a selfish sister today—I don't hear them.

What if my song hits number one?

What if John Maxwell offers me a huge deal?

What if they want me to sign on the line right then—without showing contracts to my father?

I need a manager. I should have an agent.

Am I good enough for this?

That last question plays constantly, even though it's the one worry Casey tells me is completely unjustified. I've let my nerves stand between me and so much for so long, but I've always really wanted this. And now that I've had a taste, I'm hungry. I'm starving to be a success.

John Maxwell.

Grammies.

American Music Awards.

Bands I fucking love.

I stop at the coffee shop on my way to the freeway, and order a large. I don't drink caffeine normally—the stimulant sort of works against me and the whole stuttering thing. But I think I need to give some power to the strongest version of my personality, and this is the only way I know how. I'm so ratcheted up with coffee by the time I pull into the Maxwell lot, I run over the parking hump and my bumper scrapes the brick wall between the lot and the road.

"Shit," I mutter to myself when I get out and look at the new texture on what used to be smooth chrome.

I close my mouth and shut my eyes, straightening my posture for a deep breath, then open my sites on the large double doors in front of me. I walk in through the front this time, and the receptionist guides me to the familiar room in the back. I brought my guitar and my book, just to be prepared, but as I amble through the hallway and knock into the walls, I feel more ridiculous than ready. This is not how big girls take meetings.

Gomez is waiting in the room along with the assistant I recognize from last time. I think her name is Cara.

"Murph," Gomez says, walking around the table with open arms. I ready myself for the hug and am instantly grateful for my guitar and heavy purse so it's cut short. "Oh, we're not going to need you to play today," he laughs, and I'm red with embarrassment.

"I know. I have somewhere to go after this," I lie.

"Where you headed?" he asks, and I want to kick him for being nosey. *Nowhere, shit, I was just saving face!*

"My aunt's," I say quickly, my eyes flitting around the room, looking for the most opportune seat. My second lie was worse, so I don't look up again, because I swear if he starts asking me questions about my aunt I'm just going to grab my things and run, probably taking out chunks of drywall on my awkward exit.

John comes in after a few seconds, and as scared as I am, I'm relieved to let him take over the conversation.

"Murphy," he smiles. His hair is a blend of black and gray, and he wears tinted glasses that make me think of gangster movies and Robert de Nero.

"Nice to see you, John," I say, immediately debating if I should call him Mr. Maxwell. Casey's voice echoes in my head: *You're the one they want.* John it is, then.

"Would you like some water?" he asks, holding up a hand and calling Cara to his side.

"I'm okay," I say. Honestly, I would *love* water, but I also have to pee badly as it is from the large coffee jolt. I think adding any more would be self-abuse at this point.

He smiles and whispers his request to Cara, who excuses herself from the room to fetch whatever he asked for. God I hope it's not coffee.

"Do you know why we brought you here?" John asks, leaning back in his seat. His feet fold on top of the table, and I smirk because I remember Casey's imitation of him.

"Not entirely," I say, breathing in through my nose for strength, "but I'm hoping it's for a major record deal."

Might as well come out guns a blazin'.

John's harsh features fall into a smile quickly, but he remains silent. His hands move from behind his head to his lap, and I watch as he folds his fingers together and cracks his knuckles, almost for his own amusement.

"We'd like to pair you with one of our new artists," he says, and my head starts to spin instantly. I'm sure I don't mask my expression well. I think I'm still smiling, but I can tell by the way his lips purse and Gomez fidgets that I probably look forlorn. I'm just glad I don't look pissed, because that's also brewing in my belly.

"Pair me," I reiterate.

"Yeah, like what we did with Johnnie Walker," he says.

I pull in my brow and look to Gomez.

"Yo, I don't think she's heard it yet," he says.

I part my lips, about to protest, but I think better of it and wait for them to call Cara back from wherever she went so she can fetch Gomez's laptop. Coffee comes, and I give in and pour a glass, the taste bitter and my bladder almost as pissed as I am. Cara's back again in minutes with the laptop, and soon Gomez is turning it toward me, a sound file beginning to play.

The start is familiar—the same as it was in the club more than a week ago. But then suddenly it isn't my song any more. It's nothing of what I heard, heavy beats taking over the melody completely and some rap artist who I am now picturing as Porky the fucking Pig tossing out lyrics that are anti-feminine and just plain abrasive.

I point, unable to speak, because I'm not sure if I can come up with a word strong enough to accurately portray how deeply I hate what Gomez is playing for me. Vile—I think that's the best I've got. It's what I say…like a question.

"Vile?"

Gomez's eyes snap to John's and he taps the keys, the music, if it can be called that, stopping abruptly.

"His name's Shaw Chris. He's going to be huge. His YouTube numbers are sick, and that whole soft with hard vibe is so in right now," John says, and I picture myself poking my fingers through the orange tint of his gangster glasses.

"He's shit," I say, and my belly thumps wildly with my heartbeat. I'm not scared. I'm not intimidated. I might cry, but only because I'm that angry. I'm so angry, I don't even know whether or not to sit or stand. I begin to rise, but fall back to my seat and cover my mouth, slowly letting my eyes look to them both.

"I assure you he's not…*shit,*" John says, clearing his throat. His eyes move to Gomez.

"Quit looking at him. It's not his song!" I yell.

"It's not yours either," John says, and I fall back, sure that I'm not hiding the shock I feel. My skin is tingling with it.

John sits forward, and I let my eyes zero in on the gold of his very expensive watch. I observe his fingers twist it around his wrist while in the periphery I can tell he's preparing what I'm sure will be a very lovely, very staged speech.

"This releases Tuesday, Murphy. It's coming out as Shaw Chris featuring Murphy Sullivan, but we don't have to bill you at all," he says.

"Good. Don't!" I yell, my eyes still on his watch—his watch that I'm imagining running over, back and forth, and back and forth…

"I know you're upset…" he begins, and my gaze snaps to his. I swear he flinches. Maybe I imagine it. "This is the new model, and I'm really sorry if Casey didn't explain it to you very well. But the days of the quiet singer-songwriter…they're over. You need to hook into something different, something gritty—and with a song like this, people will listen, and they'll sing along with your chorus, and when you come out at performances as his guest, everyone is going to want to know who you are—the mystery voice in that hit song they can't quit singing."

It takes minutes for all of his words to sink in. Mystery girl. Gritty. Performances. No way in fucking hell am I *ever* going to stroll up on a stage with some guy who sounds like his first and last names are reversed. *Shaw Chris* is stupider than *Sam and Cam*. In fact, I owe my girl an apology. I stand at the table slowly, and my eyes notice the copy of the contract I signed sitting in front of Cara, who isn't even listening to us. She's busy on her phone, probably Snapchatting about the sad girl getting taken to school by her boss right now.

I gave him my song. I signed it away that day—blinded by my own fucking dreams. I gave it to him, and even relented as his minion pecked away at my favorite parts. I lived with it and found renewed love for it when I heard what Casey played in the club. This is nothing like what I heard. I don't know why I heard something so different, but I do know that I don't want to be any part of this.

Without a word, I pull my bag up to my arm and wrap my fingers around the handle for my guitar. I step around the table to the door John Maxwell hasn't even bothered to close, and I stretch it open wide, my movements slow and methodical. I turn so I fill the space between this room and my way out, and I stand incredibly still, my eyes settling on Gomez's first until he looks down at his computer. And then I turn to John, and I pull my mouth up ever so slightly, because he's not even masking how smarmy his is now that I really look at him.

"All you do is ride the hype," I say. He doesn't flinch, but the smoke-stained lips above his overly-manicured goatee curve enough that I get his response. He's saying "yes I do."

I look to the wall, crowded with awards—gaudy and unearned. I point to it, chuckling, then return my gaze to him as I shake my head.

"You're not collecting me on that wall of yours," I say, my breathing coming easier somehow. "And something tells me that means that shitty-ass rapper you just signed won't be up there either. You see..." I narrow my gaze, lowering my brow, as if this is a secret for his ears only. But he's left the door open. And people have paused in the hallway behind me. And Cara...she's not typing on her phone anymore. "I know that I'm the best part of that song. And you know it too. So good luck finding someone else to make your bad talent look good. It won't be me."

"We'll see, sweetheart," he says. "Sometimes all it takes is one. Good. Record. And I own part of you right here."

He pulls my contract into his hands and rolls it up in his palm. He's right. That song, it could get good play. But I've also heard it, and as much as I believe my part is good, I also believe that Shaw's part sucks major fucking balls.

"You hold onto that real tight, John. Maybe it will keep you warm at night when you realize what a lonely prick of a human you really are," I say, turning and managing to stride my way back through the cluttered hallway without hitting my shit into a wall once.

I walk right to my car, I throw my things inside and I pull out smoothly, getting lucky with traffic and exiting in one motion without even scraping my undercarriage on the dip from the lot to the road. I drive for thirty seconds, until I reach the corner where two teenagers are buying pot from some man in a black Chrysler 300. They run away when I pull in, but the drug dealer stays put because he sees my face and the tears falling down my cheeks. I'm not here to bust anyone. I'm here to hide. He probably hopes I'll become a customer.

And for the next hour, I sit in my parked car next to the north side's king of pot as I cry my fucking eyes out because I just threw away my dream.

Casey

I knew the minute she walked in. Murphy wears her emotions. Her eyes were puffy and her mouth was a hard line, her jaw working and her nostrils flaring. She got to the club when I was setting up—no text for a warning. I heard her arguing with security at the front, and I ran over to rescue her. She flew at me with fists and beat my chest for about five full minutes. I'm pretty sure I'm bruised because I didn't stop her.

"Did you know?"

She asked that a thousand times. She hit me and cried, and I watched her fall apart. She only stopped a minute ago, and I've managed to calm her and convince her to sit here by my gear, away from ears I know should not hear my girl right now.

"Did you know?" she asks again.

I hold my tongue in my teeth, no honest way to answer this without her hating me.

"Not for sure," I say. That's a pussy answer. Deep down, I knew. I only hoped I was wrong.

I can access everything. It's probably not a good idea, especially given how close I'm sure they've come to realize I am with Murphy. But dumb-asses will be what they are, and I got curious about the progress a couple weeks ago and started poking around the edit files. I found the cut I played for her that night at the club, and I was blown away. I'm willing to admit it's better than mine. That cut, it was all Gomez and his years of finely-honed skills. It was the right ear making the right choices, and the result was magic.

But I also saw the short clips with the sound cut out in the background. I'd heard other projects they've been working on lately, mash-ups with rap and quieter artists they label not-so-kindly as background. Those edits I found of hers—they were in that pile.

"I found different versions, and the one I brought to the club—it was the best one," I say, keeping my eyes locked to hers, breaking under the scrutiny of her grays. "I just thought…"

I sigh and let my head fall to the side. She's so beautiful. I'm so mad that they broke her. Fucking fools.

"You thought what," she chokes out, still holding on to some of her anger. I understand.

"I just thought…how could *this* not be the one they go with," I say.

She sucks in her top lip, and I see the tears coming miles before they reach the well of her eyes. I lean forward and cup her quivering face in my hands, wiping them away one at a time as they fall.

"But you played it," she pleads. I know she's hoping for a loophole, something I can say that will make that moment—the one where a roomful of people heard and loved her song as it was meant to be—the only one that counts.

"I stole it," I say through a small guilty laugh, shaking my head. "I knew I had to be right, but just in case...I wanted you to hear it."

Her chest fills slowly, so full that her shoulders lift and her neck strains for air. It's the panic attack, the ones she fights when her mouth quits working. There are a million things I've learned about what I would do differently if I had my own studio. Top of the list is not make beautiful girls cry.

Hands fisted in her hair, her eyes fall to my knees and she takes long draws of air to calm her demons and fight against her body's instincts.

"I called him a prick," she says through a chuckle. She looks up at me, her eyebrows high on her head and her mouth flies into a manic smile. "Ha! He's a fucking billionaire, and I called him a *prick*!"

"He is a prick," I laugh with her. "And I'm pretty sure he's only worth millions, so joke's on him!"

We laugh like crazy people for thirty seconds straight, until the distraction leaves her system and she falls limp again, her head in her hands in front of me. I pull her close, and eventually to my lap where I hug her and lock my fingers with hers to kiss them.

"I still have the song with me," I say in her ear. "The one I played last time. I have it here. I could play it again."

She shakes her head and closes her eyes, leaning into me, her face nestled into my neck and shoulder.

"I don't ever want to hear it again," she breathes, and I die, because her voice in that song is about as close to heaven as I think I'll ever get.

"Okay," I say.

I sit with Murphy on my lap for the rest of the hour, and I let her pick songs for the night that fit her mood—her tastes run from borderline death-metal to James Brown. I mix it all, and the drones on the dance floor don't notice. I work in beats like a chef with spare ingredients he needs to get rid of, and they eat it up—grinding and pulsating until it's two in the morning and Murphy is fast asleep on the line of chairs I set up for her behind me.

I carry her to my car, and I wait for her to wake up so I can ask her if she wants to go with me or let me take her home. When her hand grips mine tightly, I don't even bother to ask. I drive her to my apartment, show the middle finger to Eli when he opens his bedroom door and I hold her until Saturday's highest sun is in the center of the sky.

"Your father is going to pull out the ax again," I say, my nose on hers. She runs hers back and forth.

"Eskimo kisses," she giggles.

"Whatever those are," I shrug.

"You don't know Eskimo kisses?" she says, her voice raspy from her sleep and emotions. I shake my head *no*.

"We weren't a very touchy-feely family," I say, and her eyes grow sad, so I lean in and nuzzle my nose to her again. "But I love doing them with you. I'm an Eskimo-kiss virgin."

"Awe, I popped your cherry," she teases. I laugh with her, but it's faint and tired on both ends.

I run my fingers through her messy purple curls, and wonder how anyone could not bet the entire bank on this amazing creature.

"You really are amazing. Don't let him get in your head. I'm *way* smarter than that guy, and remember…I said you're special," I say.

She nuzzles against me, but only to hide her frown. I tug her cheek up with my finger, but it's no use.

"I signed up for Paul's tonight," she says, rolling to her back and stretching her long arms over her head. I run my finger along one and down the other. "I think I'm going to call and cancel. They have a ton of people on the waiting list."

"Don't," I say, faster than I really have a reason. Her head falls to the side and she blinks at me slowly. "Just…I think you should play. For you. Your way. I think it will help you feel better."

She holds my gaze for a few seconds before pulling her mouth up on one side in a half grin. "Yeah, well I think you're nuts," she says.

"Says the woman whose dad is an ax murderer," I say, rolling over and caging her between my arms.

"He hasn't killed anyone...yet," she says.

My forehead falls to hers and my lips dust hers gently. Every time I open my mouth to speak, I'm left with nothing. I don't know how to fix this for her. I feel like I fed her to the wolves. I know she doesn't blame me, but I can't help but feel like my father's right—this, none of this, was very responsible.

"I'm sorry," I say, finally, and her hands touch both sides of my face tenderly.

"Don't be," she says, kissing me again, harder. "Zero regrets," she says, her nose running along my neck and her lips finding my chest.

I hold her to me tightly, and as much as I feel her trying to use *us* to forget about all of the reasons her heart hurts right now, I don't give in. My body wants her. My fingers ache to touch and feel, but I've been the user before. Murphy and I are different, though...we can't be distractions to one another. We can't be. Because distractions are disposable, and I don't know how to think about anything else but her.

When I left Murphy with her car, she promised she'd stay on the list for Paul's. I made her cross her heart—literally—and I promised to come and sit in the front row. With every ring on my phone, I say a prayer, to a god who has never heard from me, that Murphy keeps her promise. Then again, she's not the one known for breaking them really.

"Hello?"

His voice is nothing like John Maxwell's, but it's intimidating all the same. I hardly know him, save for his card left at one of my gigs over a year ago, telling me to "call him." Noah Jacobs is John

Maxwell…only completely not. He's quiet and thoughtful. When he dangled the carrot for me last summer, he was still off the map. I saw him as nothing more than a slightly-more-together version of me—some chump with a dream of opening up a label.

Only Noah comes from money. And it turns out he's more than just a *little* more together than I am. He's got his shit figured out completely. I dug his card out of the pile I had in my glove box when I read about him in Rolling Stone a few months ago. I recognized the name—and the list of people dying to work with him. He isn't big like John, but he will be. And soon.

"Hi, Noah. I don't know if you remember me. My name's Casey Coffield; I deejayed the OSU Alumni party before the bowl game last year…" I don't even have to finish. He either remembers, or he's faking it, because I dropped the right event name. Either way, he's working me so I feel important, and he's doing it well.

"Oh yeah, I remember…" he starts. There's a pause, and I think for a minute I might have him stumped, but he fills it quickly. "You never called."

I never did.

"I've been trying to get my own thing going, and…I don't know…you're Nashville, I'm OKC…" I fumble through excuses. They're weak because I leapt at John Maxwell. I wish I could remember that saying about hindsight, because it's spot on.

"I do love the Smokies," he says, his chuckle low and deep. "So tell me, Casey Coffield from the OSU Alumni party…to what do I owe the pleasure of your call now?"

He knows I'm working for John. And there's a smugness to his tone that tells me he probably also has an idea exactly what kind of style John uses to run his business. He thinks I want to jump ship, and he's right. But I'm not jumping anywhere with anyone else ever again. I'm jumping on my own. This call…it's for her.

"Respect?" I ask.

There's a pause, because he's not sure I deserve his. I probably don't—I'm the punk asshole ten years younger than him who thought I knew more. Creatively, I kick everyone's ass. But

Murphy needs good business sense, and she needs someone who believes in her. Noah's quickly building a brand that doesn't do bullshit. He's either in, or he's out.

"Respect," he says, finally. I sense that it's probably provisional.

"Any chance you're in town for the dedication?" I hold my breath and close my eyes.

They just added about twenty million in skyboxes and luxury shit to the stadium, and I know Noah's dad is part of that circle who ponied up the cash. My father's alumni—I check his mail. The flyer could have easily been tossed away in the trash were it not for the fact that my mother saw it and saved it to show my dad, who hates football and will only think it's a tremendous waste of money. But the date flashed in front of my goddamned photographic eyes—it's Monday.

"I am," Noah says.

"I have someone in mind that I think you need to see…and I've got nothing to gain," I say. When he tells me to *go on*, I breathe deeply and give Murphy my best sell, and I promise to forward him the demo—the *really* hot one Gomez made that technically isn't my property, because fuck him and fuck John Maxwell.

And when we're done, there's about a fifty-fifty shot I'm going to see Noah somewhere at Paul's tonight, until that stat falls quickly to zero with my phone call from my sister Christina.

"Dad's in a coma," she says. "He's been having several small strokes for weeks, it seems. They think this is probably it. He has a DNR, Case. Mom's…you need to be here."

I need to be there.

I can do this.

I can't…do…this.

CHAPTER 17

Murphy

I should have called Sam. She would have come. But I haven't
told her about my day yet, how everything fell apart in the matter
of eleven minutes. She was so proud of me; I'm just not ready to
watch her have to backtrack on all of that and pretend that
everything is right and for the best. None of this is for the best.
Today—walking out on John Maxwell, signing away so much
power to him—that was all for the worst.

The motherfucking worst.

Casey was going to be here. But he's not. And I've thought
about leaving at least a dozen times. Everyone here tonight is so
good. They're always good, and I'm starting to think maybe I'm a
delusional hack. John Maxwell could roll out my friend Steph,
who's playing now, and wind up with the exact same record he
played for me. Of course, it would still suck, because that Shaw
guy is shit awful.

"You about ready, Murph?" Eddie asks, tapping his fingers
against my upper shoulder as if I'm a piano. I jump in surprise but
deflate quickly.

"Yeah, I'm ready whenever, Eddie," I say.

He pauses in front of my dangling legs along the back table
while he pushes his tie closer to his neck and straightens his lapel.

"Half of anything we do in this world is show, Murph. I'm not
sure what's chewing at your insides right now, but how about for
the next ten minutes, you get up there and show 'em your best
smile, huh?" He bends his head down to catch my eyes.

I chuckle and take a deep breath, pushing off from the table and
tugging my guitar strap over my body.

"That's good advice, sir. You got a deal," I wink and force my
cheeks to dimple.

"Ah that's my girl," he smiles back, taking a few steps toward
the stage to help Steph off and announce me next. "And it's better
advice than you think."

There are a lot of things that are better advice than I think. There are a lot of things that are worse advice, too. The trouble is telling them apart. Smiles are harmless, though, so I keep it plastered on my face, and when Eddie calls my name, I give my familiar crowd at Paul's a very friendly wave. These are my people. Baskets of food, retired couples dancing, a few stray college kids who prefer light crowds to sweaty clubs—all my beautiful, wonderfully introverted people.

"Good evening," I say, adjusting the level of my mic so I can stand rather than sit on the stool I usually hide on. Maybe I'm still angry, or maybe I just want a little change—perhaps I'm finally so comfortable playing at Paul's that I no longer need the four-legged barstool crutch. Whatever it is, I carry it to the side and Eddie runs up to take it from me.

"Sorry, I just…I kind of felt like standin' tonight," I say through light laughter. Nobody's really listening yet, minus the older couples at the tables near the front.

"I've got a few new things I'd like to try for you, if that's okay," I say, tuning and adjusting to my sound on the stage. "It's called 'Boxes.'"

My fingers find their newly familiar place, and I close my eyes and imagine I'm in my dad's hangar, with Casey cheering me on. I only play the intro through once before I'm ready—the way it's meant to go—and I sing with the force of everything that's still lit up in my chest and belly. I open my eyes and look people in theirs. I make people feel, and I pull them in and take them with me, until they begin to clap with my rhythm and I can't help but pick up speed and play harder.

It's not exactly how the song is supposed to go, or maybe it is. Maybe this is what was missing—connection. I play the final verse through one extra time, improvising, because I'm having such a good time and I don't want the feeling to end. I roll my vibe right into another new song, then two or three covers, going a good ten minutes over the time I'm given. Nobody stops me.

The cheering at Paul's is usually polite. When I play the Casey song, I get the clapping and whistles, but that's because people recognize that song now. I didn't touch it tonight, because it's officially retired, and yet they whistled all the same. They stood, and two people shook my hand as I stepped from the stage. Steph hugged me, and I let her. I hugged back.

That felt…that all felt amazing.

Only Casey…he missed it all.

I put my guitar away half paying attention to how I put it in the case. My eyes are busy running over the crowd, searching in dark corners—anticipating. He isn't here. And there's no message on my phone. I'm worried.

"Murphy Sullivan?" a man asks, his accent the thick kind that belongs to someone from a family who has lived in Stillwater their entire lives. I recognize it because my father has that accent, too.

"That's me," I say, looking over his shoulder, still expecting.

"That was pretty impressive stuff. Those originals—those all yours?" he asks, his hands moving into the pockets of his gray suit jacket. It seems expensive. I narrow my eyes on him, suspicious, and scan down his body—a Harley Davidson T-shirt on under his jacket, Wranglers on his legs and cowboy boots on his feet.

"They sure are," I say, flitting my eyes to his, hand on my hip. "And they're not for sale."

His head cocks to the side a tick and his left eye squints as a slow smirk takes over his lips. He reaches out a hand, and I stare at it for a few long seconds before I shake. When our palms meet, I shake with a tight grasp, like that girl Paige did. When he looks down at our grip, I smile with tight lips and he nods at my nonverbal sign that this girl—she's not going to be taken advantage of.

"I'm Noah Jacobs," he says, reaching into his jacket front and hauling out a wallet stamped with the OSU Cowboy mascot.

I'm about to say "I bet you are," just to keep my guard up and my gates drawn, when he adds one more little piece of information.

"Casey Coffield told me I should stop in here tonight…I see why," he says, stepping back and leaning to sit on the table.

Casey. Who isn't here. I must appear confused, because Noah chuckles silently and folds his arms over his chest and looks at the tips of his boots.

"You didn't know I was here," he says.

I shake my head. "I don't even know who you are," I say, drawing my lips in tight. My chest squeezes as stress begins to chip away at my temporary bravado. Shit, I bet he's important. I'm two-for-two today.

He reaches into his coat again and pulls out a well-worn pack of gum, slipping out a stick and then stretching his hand forward in an offer to me.

"No thanks," I say, truly baffled.

"I'm quitting smoking. I'm on four days now, and bars..." he raises his brow and looks around. The man is enormous, at least six-foot-four. "Bars are hard," he grins, unwrapping his slice of spearmint and popping it in between his teeth.

"I'm sorry. Is Casey...is he coming?" I say, awkwardly resting back on the table behind me and knocking my guitar case to the ground. "Damn," I mutter under my breath, pulling it back upright and catching Noah's amused expression.

"I guess he's not," he says, his mouth working at his gum like an addict. I'd say he has a long road ahead of him in the whole quitting smoking thing.

"Oh," I say, still confused. I look down at his card in my hand. It's simple, but the paper is nice and the print is classic. Noah Jacobs and a phone number.

"I can call him. If you were supposed to meet him here? He has some family things going on, but I'm sure he would have been here if he could have..." I start to defend my guy.

I stop when I notice him laughing silently and scratching at his stubbled chin.

"I'm sorry," I apologize. I'm not quite sure what for, but it feels warranted.

"Murphy Sullivan," he says my name again, pushing from the table to a complete, towering stand. He nods through a smile as he squares with me, and I struggle to make myself taller. "Casey didn't come, and you have no idea who I am…do I have that correct?"

My lungs are empty, but I manage to utter a "Yes."

"Good," he says, pointing to the card in my hand. "That's…well…that's *real* good, Murphy."

"Okay," I say, not completely on board with his assertion of the last few minutes of our talk. Not sure how anything over the last twelve hours is really good, let alone everything that's happened since he said my name. "How?" I say, surprised to hear my thoughts out loud. Too late now.

He chuckles. I'm glad I amuse him.

"That means Casey is a man of his word—he's got no juice in this," he says, waving a hand up to the stage and then at my guitar. "And…it means you were that good without even trying."

I take in a quick, sharp breath, then freeze.

"How do you feel about Nashville?" he asks.

I don't feel about anything right now, but I manage to utter a decent response.

"I like it. My cousin lives there. The weather's sketchy, but…" Okay, less than decent, but a response.

He smiles, pulling out his pack of gum and adding to the distraction in his mouth with one more piece.

"That's where I work, Murphy. And I'm bold and aggressive. And I don't compromise on people," he pauses, eyes closing in and his mouth curving fondly. He isn't a sexy man, but damn can he play the part. "Call me…soon. I'd like you to come to Nashville."

He pats his hand along the top of the chair nearby, then takes a few steps backward, his eyes still on me as I try to piece together his card and Nashville and then…oh my god…

"Let's make a record. Me and you. And let's make it sound…just…like…that," he points to the stage, where I was, where I had the most fun I've ever had playing my songs.

His back is to me a blink later, and within two more, he's out the door. I don't move from the place my feet are glued for at least ten minutes, only half listening to Steph talk about what she'd like to play next week and ask if I'm signing up again for Saturday. I

264

tell her I will. Only, when I pull my guitar to my body and gather my things, I walk in the opposite direction of the comfortable and easy yellow notebook. I don't write my name, because I'm not so sure I'll be here next week.

"Bet you're glad I made you smile up there, aren't you Murphy girl," Eddie says, coughing mid laugh as I pass him at the door. Our eyes meet and I question him with my look. Eddie knows who Noah Jacobs is, and I'm going to find out soon.

As soon as I can figure out where the hell Casey is.

Casey

Ending a life is complicated.

That sounds so flippant. As if I'm not really here for any of this. I'm making it analytical. That's what my sisters are saying, at least. Of course it's complicated. It's souls and debates and choosing sides and respecting wishes and…I volunteered to be the judge. I was the only name on the ballot.

He knew this needed to be me. As pragmatic as the rest of them are, they come at things with arguments for their own personal theories. As unloving as our relationship may have been, I still come at my father's death with feelings—*his* feelings, my sisters' feelings, my mother's. I choose what is right based on his wishes, and then I work like hell to make it okay with everybody else.

It's exhausting, and it's killing me…and it isn't even really time for the hard choices yet. That time is coming. It looms around the corner, death rearing its ugly head, crooked fingers begging me forward and asking permission to take.

Take, take, take!

I sent everyone away. My sisters weren't helping, and my mother wasn't coping. My parents' room has become an ICU in a matter of hours, and there are people coming and going on a constant basis. I simply sign forms. I think that's my only role in life now—to sign forms on behalf of my father.

Don't listen to Annalisa. She's not mature enough to handle this.

That was the last text I got from my middle sister, Myra. Their bickering and opinions keep coming even though I sent them away. The noise is nonstop—they're like hyenas. None of them *wanted* this job, though. They want it by proxy—like a fucking senate that will spin its way out of responsibility if I make the wrong move in the end. This will become my legacy—the choice I live with.

Only it's not. My father was very specific. I've read everything, and there is a very precise moment that is going to come when my father is going to want everyone to just stop.

Going to want. Even having that thought guts me, because he doesn't want anything. His brain activity is the great barometer for everything that comes next, and as with all other things in this nightmare journey, those results are in the long list of things I'm waiting for—even though I already know that my father is gone.

My mother took two Xanax and is fast asleep now in my old room. I haven't been to my apartment for actual sleep in so long, I forget what my bed and sheets feel like. And thinking of them only makes me crave Murphy, because the few hours I *have* been there have been with her. She was probably looking all over for me tonight. I wasn't there, and that kills me. I haven't even had a second to breathe, and I knew she'd be on stage at some point over the last two hours. On the off chance that my plan worked, I didn't want to interrupt. This had to be about her, and only her. In fact, it's probably best that I wasn't there at all.

I hope she sees it that way.

Weary and alone in a house that has done nothing but ever make me feel lonely, I step out to the front lawn that is not so perfect any more. The summer night air is warm, and my limbs are worn from holding my body up and my mind together for the last eight hours, but this grass—it needs to be cut. All the planning in the world, but this one detail was something my father let go by. He probably figured nobody else would mow and edge to his satisfaction.

With sleep begging my eyes, I walk to the side of the house to my parents' garage where I punch in the code that I only recently realized is my birthday—0316. The door lifts slowly, and my

266

father's car rests still clean from its last wash, not driven for weeks, only a thin layer of dust covering it. I think about how this will be something my sister will deal with—the lawyer in the family will settle who takes what. I don't want anything. My father wanted to make sure my mom was taken care of, so I figure everything should go to her.

The red sheen of the lawnmower amuses me, how it matches the shine of his car. Everything always so well cared for—if only he'd given half of the attention he gave material possessions to me. I let the wave of bitterness pass as I roll the mower out to the edge of the driveway, and I unwind the cord to plug it into the socket by the front porch. My father liked the idea of being green. This translates to yard work taking four times as long as it should, though—as I worry about mowing over cords and electrocuting myself.

I flip the switch and the motor begins to hum. I wait for a full minute, listening to and watching for a sign from neighbors on either side or across the street to tell me to stop. It isn't very loud, so I step forward, pushing the blades over the grass slowly until I look behind me to check for the evidence that my mowing job is doing any good at all. The grass is noticeably shorter, so I turn around and push the other way, winding the cord around my shoulder and elbow as I come close to the house and unwinding as I move away.

I'm halfway through my manic project when I feel the slack of the cord lift from my shoulder and I let go of the handle, letting the mower engine idle off.

She's beautiful in the moonlight.

"You missed Paul's tonight," she says, winding the dirty cord on her own arm.

"You don't have to do that. It's going to get your dress dirty," I say, the weight of my last few hours starting to push down harder.

She keeps rolling the cord, so I let go of my end and give into her. I look out over the half-mown lawn. It looks like a comical mess, zigzagged and burnt in a few spots. I bring my hands up to my forehead and jut my elbows out as I take in the work left to be done.

"Gahhh, I'm really bad at this stuff," I say, turning in a slow half circle until I feel my girl's hand on my back. My eyes close, and my cheeks quiver as my mouth falls into a frown.

"I went by your place first. Eli told me. Casey," she breathes, dropping the cord at my feet by the mower and running her hands around the front of my body, pressing her face to my back from behind. She holds me, and I hold onto her hands for dear life.

"This is so hard, Murphy. It's so hard," I say, feeling the wet streaks start to take over my face.

"I know, Case," she says. "I'm so sorry."

The neighbor's door opens, and I hear someone's voice. Murphy rubs my back and squeezes my shoulders, and as I turn, I watch her walk to meet my parents' neighbor at the hedge that divides their properties. I bend down and tug the plug for the mower from the wall socket, giving up for the night, and begin to wind the cord to put my failed project away until sunlight.

After a few minutes, Murphy shakes hands with the older woman she was speaking with, and she comes back to me.

"Your parents' neighbor is really nice," she smiles.

"Oh," I say, watching the woman step up on her own front stoop and hold up a hand to wave. I do the same as she opens her door and goes back inside. "I've never met her. I think she moved in last year some time. When I was a kid, it was this old man who didn't like me because I kicked my ball in his lawn once. She's nice though, huh?"

"Her husband said he'd mow the grass for you in the morning," she says.

I nod.

"I think, maybe, they also thought yard work at midnight was a little…"

"Crazy?" I cut in, wincing.

"A touch," she says, holding two fingers up to form an inch.

"My dad always kept things so…perfect out here, ya know? I just wanted to see if I could keep that up," I say, realizing now how impossible that is. This lawn will never again look like it did when my father cared for it.

I walk to the front steps as that realization smacks me hard in the chest, and I sit down quickly, my head dizzy and my stomach sick. Murphy sits next to me and her hand finds mine fast—like magnets. We look out on the quiet street, and my mind plays through the jumbled mess of my day on fast forward—decisions, medications, pain, forms, likelihoods, arguments, sisters, my mom, my father, and me.

Perfection and chaos at war.

"How was Paul's?" I ask, deciding I'd rather hear about her night than remember mine.

"Good," she says, her face plain and her expression satisfied enough. I feel that pang of disappointment, because it doesn't sound like Noah made it after all.

"Was it airplane-hangar good?" I ask, and when her eyes meet mine, they smile even though her lips don't. She had fun on stage, and that feels good, because it means she doesn't want to quit.

"I was fucking phenomenal," she says in a tired raspy voice that sounds as worn out as my own, but still finds the strength to laugh and make me do the same.

"I bet you were," I say.

I fall away in her grays for as long as she can keep them open out here under the stars. When her breathing begins to change, I lift her in my arms as I stand, and carry her inside to the small pallet of blankets I've piled in my father's den. I stroke her hair and stare at the sheen on each strand from the dim light of the hallway until I don't remember seeing anything else.

When morning comes, I wake her before madness begins and my father's in-home nurse wakes to start what will be the beginning of loss for everyone else in this house. My father will officially be pronounced dead today. I lost him years ago.

I never really had him at all.

CHAPTER 18

Casey

It was harder than I thought it would be. Houston was right.

Everything was so formal—slow and clinical. I signed papers that freed everyone from legal ramifications for following through with my father's wishes. I stayed in the room while my sisters couldn't bare to witness and held my mother's hand while slow beeps turned to long tones and jagged lines became straight and flat.

It's been almost a week since my father's spirit left this earth, and I have yet to cry. I'm not sure I believe in spirits anyway. I didn't think my old man did, but for all of his practicality, the man insisted on a grave. The service was basic—the plan the least expensive I'm sure, but he wanted there to be a place where my mother and sisters could go. Somehow, he knew they would need it. Whether his spirit is there or not doesn't matter, I guess—it's about what they believe and need.

He's been in the ground for twenty-four hours, and I've been under this tree—yards away from the fresh dirt and simple marking stone—without sleep for twenty. I left only to take Murphy home. She has been by my side through it all, running errands, making calls, placing announcements in the newspaper, graciously accepting food and help from neighbors I don't know. I could see the worry in her eyes when I took her back to her home this morning—*I haven't cried.* I told her I'm just being strong for my family, that I would let myself feel whatever I needed to when I knew they would be okay.

That time has come.

It's harder than you think.

My emotions are so mixed when it comes to this man who gave me life. Everything more confused now that I'm starting to understand his twisted logic, and the fact that his ideas are starting to make sense scares me. I still don't entirely believe he was right, but I'm beginning to see that his way wasn't meant to be cruel.

I talked about the man a lot with my mom and Houston while he was with us during the week—he'd seen me on the other side of many of my memories, the rebellious and jilted teen who didn't think his father gave a damn. My mom's perspective, though—it was a little eye-opening. My father lived a life of selfless decisions, and they weren't the flashy kind like when wealthy families donate money to institutions or fund scholarships or build a house for the homeless. They were understated—cloaked in a hard exterior easily mistaken for self-righteousness. He gave up everything to make sure she had it all—family, a home, security. He sat up worrying that we were all going to be okay…that *I* was going to be okay. That revelation, that he worried about me at all, is something I'm still trying to swallow.

My grandfather scarred the man who would become my father with the worst kind of mental poison. He led him to believe that following his heart would kill everything else that was good in his life, that he could only have one dream—a career he loved or a family that was cared for and safe. My father chose the latter—all the way to this very spot on the outskirts of town near a beautiful garden and the Oklahoma state route, a place my mom could easily drive to when she needed to talk.

She's been sitting there next to his grave ever since he went in. And seeing that—the way she runs her hands along the cold concrete carving of his name, breaks me slowly. The tear is a surprise. I don't touch it. I don't pretend it isn't there, and I let it fall to my lips where I taste its saltiness.

"It isn't fair," I whisper, my eyes frozen open on my mother's form, my lips parted with breath that comes with great labor. The bricks on my chest are invisible, but they are heavy. I want to scream those words—that none of this is fair, what was stolen from him, the relationship I missed out on, the role I was forced to have to take in the end—but my mom can't handle hearing them. She has her own words in her own head.

My phone *buzzes*, and I slip it to my leg, expecting to see Houston or one of my sister's names. When I see the familiar area code from Nashville, I pull in my brow and let the phone ring again. I'm not sure why Noah Jacobs is calling me today, and I'm not sure if I'm in the mood to talk to him. I glance up and watch my mom hold her fingertips to her mouth then press them to the ground, and my eyes sting again. He was her life—even if it wasn't the kind of life I wished it was. He lived for her.

I answer and think of Murphy.

"Let me guess…you want a second chance to see if my tip was right?" I say, not bothering with hellos. I'm too tired for them. I smile, though, thinking of how good and amazing she is, and the unnatural movement hurts my mouth.

"Your girl never called, Coffield. I was starting to think you were toying with me after all," he says. I sit up, pulling my legs in and covering my ear from the faint sound of the highway traffic.

"You went to Paul's," I say.

"I did," he confirms.

Why hasn't she told me? That was a week ago, and she hasn't said a word.

"I left it in her court, just so you know. You were right about that one; she has it. And the fact that you're just giving her to me means you know it too and believe in her. That's why I'm calling, because I thought you should know—I'm in, if she's willing…in case you want to nudge," he says.

"She does have it," I agree, a real smile casts lightly over my face for the first time in days. It hurts a little less, and I think it's because of her. Why hasn't she told me though? Why is she pretending? What is she afraid of? My mind races to put puzzle pieces together, to understand why my girl would give up on her dream. I know she wants it—I saw it in her eyes that night on my parents' porch after she played at Paul's. She loves this life, this *potential* life. She's meant for it.

"Things didn't work out with John I'm guessing," Noah leads. I figured he would do his research.

"That was my fault…all of it," I say.

I should have protected her, made John give her time to think the deal through. Noah's only response to me is a knowing chuckle. John's ruthless, and I thought that was just his pathway to success, and it would be fine to travel on it. I never wanted it to derail Murphy though. Or maybe I just didn't care at first, too blinded by what signing her would mean for me.

"If I had a nickel for every artist he's screwed over that has come my way," Noah says.

"Yeah, well…I hear he's trying to put out a few rap artists, so be ready for those calls soon," I joke, not completely.

The laughter on the other end comes hard and fast. My guess is Noah's opinion is the same as mine—John Maxwell should stay in his lane, the one that made him famous. R&B is going to burn him, and if what Murphy told me about the butchered mashup they tried with her song is any indication, he's not going to survive the fire.

"There's only one artist that's fallen through his fingers that I'm interested in, but I don't deal with people who aren't serious, Casey. I work hard, and I need my partners to be one hundred percent committed. And I don't beg. I've got too many people waiting in line. If your girl isn't ready, I don't want to waste my time. If I don't hear from her in the next week or so, I'm going to have to pass," Noah says, the laughter dead. He's serious about Murphy, and I can't let her mess this chance up. It could make everything right.

"I'll see what I can do about that," I say, and my eyes scan the quiet lawn, my mother and I the only two left here as the sun begins to fall.

"You do that, and maybe we sit down and talk about you again sometime, huh?" he adds. I'm sure it's only to sweeten the pot, and for a brief moment, the hook is enticing. I'm flattered, and there's that familiar pull—that selfish one that thinks this could be a ticket. Then I catch my mother's gaze, her gentle smile sending me a sign she doesn't realize.

"Thanks for the offer, Noah. It means a lot, but like you said…you don't want to waste your time, and I think my next move is going to be completely on my own," I say, and for once, I think I mean it—and the leap? It doesn't scare me at all. Nothing can be as hard as everything I've survived.

My seed money isn't much, and I need every penny I can get. That's the only reason I'm sticking around for three more weeks of making John Maxwell's club look like *the shit*. This is all I am to him now—the link to his club's long-term success. I've made it the buzz. I've created the ambience. I've given him enough hype. I'm done working for him. Leather booths and city lights out the windows are all well and good, but I'm the one who has been making people feel good when they were here.

I haven't been in to the main studios for a week because of my family, and I know at this point, turning in my badge is really just a formality. They don't care if I'm there. When Murphy didn't work out, they wrote me off too, because she was my pet project—an indicator of what I could bring to the table.

John sums her up as trouble, and that's what he thinks I'm good for.

Fine by me.

I love trouble. Maybe I should have made more of it. I amuse myself with thoughts of causing a little mayhem at his club tonight, but I also know that the amount he's on tap to pay me for the rest of my gigs is money I can't laugh away, so I'll play nice. Besides, when he moves on to someone else hosting his big Friday evenings at the end of the summer, people aren't going to be talking about this place as much as they're going to be looking for the next one to find me at. I'm going to make sure of that. For the next three weeks, I'm going to make the people in that club feel like they've had orgasms just by standing on my dance floor. I will be the brand they remember. And when I'm no longer there, they're going to miss me. I sell heroine for the ears of the twenty-something masses. They will all be addicted if they aren't already.

I need more gigs of this caliber, and that's just a simple fact. If I want to move my goals from things on paper stored in a box—to reality—it's going to take a lot of money. I'm a bit of a jumbled mess, and there are a lot of stars that need to align, but I'm beginning to believe in them. Time is a constant, and I'm willing to wait through it.

274

Murphy's career, on the other hand, needs to begin now. I feel it in my gut. I owe her. I can't let the bad experience she had derail something so perfect. The world would resent me for it if they ever knew what they missed hearing. But I know that means I'm going to have to let her go. And while I may talk a big game in my head, I'm not so sure I can do it when faced with losing the one thing that has felt like future and home.

When she walks in to Max's, she stands tall, ready to support me and hold me up after what was easily the worst week of my life. One look at her grays, and I vow to do whatever it takes to be fine on my own. I catch glimpses of her smile as she approaches, and my feet itch to go to her and pick her up in my arms. If I do, though, I won't let go, and I won't tell her to take this chance. I'll be selfish.

"Why didn't you call Noah?" I ask, stopping her mid-step on her way into my booth. Her mouth is hard set and her eyes are on the floor. I had to ask first, before her lips said hello and before I got lost in that feeling I get when she's near. I had to broach the subject, because Noah has a deadline.

Her brow furrowed, thoughts sorting behind her eyes, she shakes her head, dismissing me. "The timing was bad," she answers, barely looking up.

My chest collapses with the sinking of my heart because I know she didn't bring it up because my life was imploding.

"I'm all right, Murphy. You should call Noah," I say.

Her eyes flit up to me briefly as she moves to the small chair behind my board where she likes to hide. She scratches nervously at her head, then folds her arm across her body, her eyes not quite making it back to mine. "He's in Nashville, and I'm not so sure I want to relocate on another whim," she admits.

"Noah isn't John," I clarify quickly. Whatever her apprehension, I'll find a remedy.

There's a worry line in her forehead, and I know it's because I've taken steps away from her. I've created distance, and she can tell I'm doing it on purpose. If I touch her, I'll beg her to stay, because I will miss her. Weak and selfish is in my nature, and I

275

need to fight against it. She can't make a decision based on *us*—I'll fuck that up, and then she'll be left with nothing. She needs to make a decision based on her heart, and I know she wants *this*. I read it in that notebook. You don't write songs like Murphy Sullivan's without hope that they'll touch someone who hears them.

"I'll think about it," she says, a faint smile on her lips as her eyes will me to drop it. It's a lie to get me to quit asking, to get me to come close again.

I hold her stare until she has to look away. But I watch longer, taking in every single nervous tick and habit she has until she has no choice but to give in and she locks on me again.

"Why didn't you tell me about his offer?" I ask, my fingers tight around the cords in my hand, hoping that she says she kept it from me because she's afraid of taking a risk. I can work with that; I can fill her with confidence again. But if she's staying for another reason—because of me—

"You sent him to see me," she says.

"I did," I say.

"Why?" she asks.

Because you deserve it. Because I believe in you. Because I didn't get it right for you the first time, and I have a history of messing up your life.

Because I love you.

I think it all, but I don't say it. I'm afraid if I do it will only make her want to stay here more. She'll think I'm only trying to make amends, and she'll dismiss it all as a kind gesture, something sweet for us to build our love on. She'll stay because of me, but she can't give up that much. So I shrug and look down again.

The silence drags on. She fills it with my worst fears.

"Maybe in a few months, when things aren't so…crazy," she says, suddenly on the other side of the table, close enough that her hands reach forward and cover mine. I want to let her soothe me, to just say "okay," but I glance up and know—if I let her now, it will never stop. I will take and take.

276

"He won't wait forever," I say, my eyes on her hands. I work hard to keep my tone even, taking a step back to break our touch. I pull my headphones on and turn the other way, because I know if she looks into my eyes she'll see the truth—that I'm just as afraid of her leaving. Time is her enemy though—my girl needs to be backed into a corner, otherwise she'll always choose limbo and stay here with me, playing at Paul's and teaching for pennies while I fill in the role my father vacated and peck away at my own dreams slowly on the side. We'll both stall, and she'll never get the spotlight she deserves—the one that is literally waiting for her to stand in it.

I ready my playlists and ignore her while noticing every single breath she takes. It kills me, but I decidedly act, as Houston would say, *more Casey* than normal. The club begins to fill, and I say hello to people I barely know. I talk to anyone who passes by that I recognize, showering them with my time and attention, giving them what Murphy desperately wants so that it will eat away at those feelings that are tying her to me. At one point, I see her look to the side and run her palm under her eye, and I feel sick, but I keep putting her last so that way I can put her first.

When the lighting switches, I go to work, and Murphy excuses herself to the restroom. I nod. I don't say a word. I watch her walk away and hate every pair of eyes that falls on her body in the crowd, but I give up the right to be jealous. I surrender it all—and by the time she comes back to my booth, the reason why she escaped in the first place clear with the remnants of red puffiness in her eyes—I'm resolved.

Welcome to the asshole, Murphy. The one who loves you. He's sorry, but it's for the best.

"Hey," I nod in her direction, urging her to step closer to the board. She bounds up next to me, anxious and full of hope. I crush it in a breath as soon as her eyes ask me "what?"

"You're not putting off Noah because of *us,* are you?" I ask.

Her expression switches to puzzled and afraid. Her eyes dart to my work, to the lights and screens and people beginning to crowd around us, the space we're losing.

"I'm just not…I'm not…not ready," she says, her stutter stronger than I've ever heard. She grinds her back teeth and flexes her jaw in frustration. "It's not a good time."

"Bullshit," I say, making the word harsh and disgusted, as if I'm tired of her excuses. She winces. I die a little more.

She inhales, the deepness of the breath lifting her shoulders high as her head falls to the side and her hair tumbles off her shoulder. I think about reaching up with one finger and brushing the rest away. I think about touching her.

I don't. I can't. I shouldn't.

"Your father just died, Casey. It hasn't even been a week. We can talk about this later. It doesn't have to be now. It can wait," she says.

"My father died, Murphy. *Mine.* Not yours," I say sternly. My brashness makes her cringe.

"Fine. Okay, fine!" she says, her hands fisted and shaking at her sides. I can see she's growing angrier, her eyes tearing a little in mixed emotions. Good. Get angry. Don't pick me, Murphy. Do not feel loyal. Be greedy.

"You should go to Nashville," I say, praying she's mad enough that she'll just say *yes* and leave. Wounds are better when they're fast. But nothing is that easy.

"I don't know," she shakes her head, looking down, more tears replacing the ones she just dried.

"Don't stay here because of us. Noah Jacobs is not going to wait forever. And I'm not worth it, Murphy," I say. She takes a step into me and her lip quivers.

I take a step back, but it only makes her completely fall apart.

"I don't want to leave you!" she admits, her hand cupping her mouth fast. Hearing her say it out loud is both beautiful and tragic all at once. Her eyes come up to meet mine, and she shakes her head, begging me to ask her to stay, and god…I want to. I can't bare it any more, and I touch her, grabbing her wrists, placing her fists on my body and running my hands to her shoulders, up her neck, under her eyes. I swipe away fast-falling tears, and she shakes her head, afraid.

"This is your shot. A real shot. Take it," I say.

She shakes her head *no.* I nod mine *yes.* She collapses to my chest, and I hold her to me, rocking her slowly as my lips whisper "go" in her ear over and over. We remain like this for long minutes, and she never gives in; neither do I.

When I have to play through another mix, Murphy retreats to the corner again. She's wearing her anxieties, their colors showing up all over her body—the grays deeper, her cheeks redder, her lips paler.

I fill my chest with the club's dirty air and change the mood, letting sex and music meld into one, the thump deep and hard and felt in my bones. I set everything just right, and make sure I have time before smirking at my girl and luring her to me with the call of my finger. She leaves her things under her chair and comes to me quickly. The control I have over her isn't good, and it's the problem.

It ends now.

I lead her willing body down from my platform and into the crowd, and pull her to me close enough that I feel the curve of her ass against my body. I lower my head into her neck and taste her one last time, breathing deep to remember her perfect scent. If I do this right, I'll need this memory in order to sleep again.

My hand starts at her thigh and runs up her leg, fingertips snagging the bunched silkiness of her dress on the way up. Her arms rise above her head automatically, and I follow the line, fingertips grazing the insides of her arms, and my mouth humming just behind her ear. I am temptation—Eve's apple here for her to eat. I am nothing but a trap.

"Go to Nashville," I say, and she shakes her head again.

"It's too long. We'd never make it," she says, her eyes on mine as she turns into me, and I circle my arms around her bare shoulders and tiny frame.

Thing is, if it were only going to be a few months, I would bet on us and convince her she's wrong. But I know better. When Murphy leaves, she's not coming back. She might not believe in herself, but I do. She's going to be huge, and our run ends here in this club. Now. Because my life—at least for the foreseeable future—is here, with my mom, keeping that promise I made and seeing it through. Then keeping the one I made to myself and finally taking one of those leaps I talk so much about to other people.

Closing my eyes, I feel her one last time. I guide her hands into the air and move my body against her hips, my hands finding her waist when I know she's lost to the dance, the sway taking over. We move together as one song shifts into another on my playlist, and from one heartbeat to the next, I step back, leaving nothing but our fingertips connected.

Her mouth parts as her head falls forward and her eyes land on mine. In a blink, what was moments ago a look of hunger, turns to lament.

"Go," I say.

"I won't," she says.

I grimace and look down at my feet, searching for a better way to do this, but there just isn't one. The more I beg the firmer she is about staying. Stubborn meets stubborn.

"I'll make you," I nod, not bringing my gaze up to hers completely.

"You can't," she says, and I laugh sadness. I'm sad because I can. I could walk up to the brunette grinding against her friend two feet away, high on ecstasy, and kiss her until Murphy hated me to the core. But I'm too selfish for her to hate me so much and for so long. I only want her to hate me a little.

"I just want what's best for you, Murphy. You'll regret not trying," I say, one last attempt.

Her head shake comes fast and her smile seems so sure.

"I'm happy where I am," she says, falling back into me. I take her because I'm weak. I hold her for the rest of the night and let her believe she's won. I kiss her and memorize every curve and scent, and I don't ask her to go again. She'll only say *no*.

But I will make her go. And she'll hate me a little…at first.

I can live with that.

280

Murphy

Not a single call.

No visits.

When I go to his apartment, he's never there, and I can't bring myself to drive to his mother's house. They're mourning; he's mourning. That's what I've told myself for days. I pictured it finally hitting him, the weight of everything, and then I only wanted to find him more. I started calling, and those calls were unanswered. They were unreturned.

They were unwanted.

Those terrible thoughts continue to mix in with the good ones and battle for dominance. One minute I believe he hates me, the next…I hate him.

I don't leave messages. He can see it's me. I have nothing to say, really, other than "Stop!" He's shutting me out. He said he would make me leave, and I didn't believe him, but I'm at a crossroads, and for the first time since falling in love with Casey Coffield, I'm considering choosing something else.

I let the week play out. I drove to the club, knowing he'd be there. But when my name wasn't on the list of guests to enter early, I knew. I think I knew the last time his lips were on mine days ago that he was saying goodbye. But I just kept saying "No."

I'm not sure when *no* changed to *yes,* but it did.

The only thing I've gotten from him is a single text.

Go. We won't survive it if you don't.

I texted back the opposite—over and over. He never replied again.

The phone rings twice before someone answers, and I'm shell-shocked and afraid sitting in the parking lot of my school—the one I just put in my notice at. Somehow, I speak anyway, and I don't stutter—not once.

"Hi, it's Murphy Sullivan, and I'd like to take you up on your offer. I can be in Nashville in two weeks."

His response is warm and melts like butter. "I can't wait for our future, Miss Sullivan. I suggest you bring your lawyer along to make sure we do this right."

My eyes fall closed and my chest deflates; I'm not scared, but I'm also not happy. This feels nothing like it did the first time. I only wish I could talk to Casey about it.

But then I wouldn't be doing this if he were here.

CHAPTER 19

One Year Later

Casey

"Your sisters are going to be the death of me. Really…truly. I can't take them. And I can take anything. But they're constant. They never go away. And oh my god, their opinions—which, *hello!* Are like, maybe the worst opinions in the history of perspectives ever…"

I chuckle to myself as I carry the last box to the back room of what is now officially my business office. Paige has been a godsend, which I will never say out loud. More than her design skills—and ability to bargain with the property owner to get me something I could afford—she has been a defense against my siblings.

Like my father, they all have opinions on this risk I'm taking. They disagree with the location, with the structural integrity of the building, with the proximity to the railroad tracks. Christina didn't like the contract for the building, but I shook her advice off. Really, this shithole in the warehouse district is the only thing I can afford, and it's going to be the only thing I can buy for a long time. I was tired of waiting, and if I'd held out for the ten years it would take for me to save for the type of property my sister found acceptable, I would no longer be relevant to the music industry.

Relevant.

I shake my head and clear that word. John Maxwell called me relevant, but last I read, he was being sued for plagiarism by at least twenty-seven artists from other labels. Murphy's name wasn't one of them, but only because the law turns a blind eye to what he did to her song—crooked and unethical, but legal on the dotted line.

"I sent them home. I did. I just told them to get out," Paige says, leaning against the arched doorway to my office space and holding one shoe while she stretches the arch of her foot on the floor.

There's a smudge of cream paint on her cheek, and I motion my hand to it.

"You've got a little something," I say, and she wipes her hand on her face, only making it bigger. I laugh and scratch at my neck, shaking my head. She scowls and marches to the file cabinet drawer where her purse is stored, pulling out a small makeup mirror to see for herself.

"Shit, Casey. That's paint," she says.

"I told you…"

"You told me I had *a little something.* A little something is like an eyelash or a crumb, not fucking latex," she says, licking her thumb and rubbing the drying smudge on her skin.

She exhales and lets her hand fall to the side, dried paint and a red cheek now left behind. "Are we done here for today?" she sighs.

I chuckle and nod. "Yeah, I think I'm going to spend some time getting files set up. The sound guys are coming tomorrow for the equipment installs, and I want to have everything ready so they can bust that out in a day…" I say, realizing she's now standing at the door with her purse pulled tightly over her arm, staring at me.

"So we're done. I can go," she confirms, clearly not interested in my evening plans.

"Yeah, you can go," I smile.

She spins before I'm even done speaking and holds her hand up over her head.

"Bye," she throws in.

I hear her heels click down the hallway and the door opens and closes with the sound of a small set of bells tied to the handle. This is the first time I've been here alone. It's not the old gas station, but it also doesn't cost a million dollars and come with underground oil wells that would need some serious time, money, and attention. I looked at fifteen, maybe twenty different properties, and this one was dead last. I almost crossed it off the list. But then the address caught my eye.

Murphy Lane.

284

I've never been big on reading into symbolism, or maybe I've never slowed down long enough to pay attention. This street, though—it was too obvious to ignore. I drove up with my realtor and something settled in my chest.

The street is ordinary, and, according to the Coffield sisters, it's "horribly unsafe." But I disagree. My mother did, too. There isn't a lot of traffic, sure, but there's a certain peacefulness here. There's a distillery next door to me and the two large warehouses across the street are up for sale. There's been some talk about converting them into music venues, and I've even reached out to one of the owners about lending my time there if he decides to go the club route.

When I saw this space, I saw a neighborhood on the verge. My sisters pointed out that neighborhoods have people, but my mom was quick to defend, saying this one has ghosts. My sisters pounced on that, but I got what she meant. There's a spirit about this place. I'm here at just the right time.

I pull a few files from the last box I carried in and set them on my desk. I don't have much yet, only some prospective contracts to work with a few people on demos and some editing work to remaster for some small labels who learned about me from Noah, but it's a start. I have to work out my advertising plan, and it's going to need to be thin on dollars and fat on creativity. But so far, the grassroots word of mouth has been paying the bills along with a few weekend gigs every month.

My mother brought my father's painting by this morning. I kept it turned around against the wall in the corner of my office, not wanting it to become a conversation piece for the rest of my family just yet. My sisters won't know what it is, though I'm sure they'll recognize it's of our mother. The symbolism is deeper for me, though, and that's why she gave it to me. It's like righting my father's path and making amends for the passions he missed out on, though I've come to terms with the fact that in his own way, he was very happy and satisfied. I just wish he could have been proud. My mom says that somewhere he is, but I doubt that. And it's okay.

I lift the painting from the ground and test a few places along the wall where I think it would look best, deciding on the space by the doorway, across from my desk. I'll see it daily, and it will renew me with determination.

I make a small mark on the wall with a pencil, then tuck my writing tool between my teeth and hold the painting with one hand and a hammer in the other as I step from my office in search of a nail. I don't expect to run into an angel, but when I do, I halt and take every bit of her in.

"It was unlocked," Murphy says, her voice the same as the last time we spoke, when she told me she was happy where she was and I knew she wasn't really.

I spit the pencil out on the floor to free my lips. She laughs. My chest fills up.

Home.

"I'm glad it's you and not one of the vagrants my sisters swear are going to come in here and loot the joint," I say, my eyes not blinking, not leaving her face. I'm taking a thousand pictures in my mind.

She laughs again at my words, and it's that familiar laugh, the one that comes from knowing the truth behind the little things. She knows my sisters.

"I'm pretty sure I was the only person out on the street a minute ago. This place," she says, looking around at my humble headquarters. Half-painted and torn-up floors, it isn't much to look at yet, but the vision is starting to come together. She grins when her gaze lands back on me. "It's hard to find, but wow…Casey."

Hearing her say my name is like a dream. Maybe she's a ghost.

"I know…it's rough. Paige is helping, and she's got plans for just about every wall in this place, and I've got a few clients lined up. Business will come," I shrug.

"I know it will. I saw the article in the paper. Mom sent it to me," she says. "And this building…I see it. It's good it's hidden. Only the right people will find it."

"Exactly," I say.

There's a pause—a beautiful one—after she compliments me. I live in it and revel in her beautiful face and the silence and her smile. Looking to the side, I search for a place to set down the painting and hammer, deciding on a box filled with plastic sheeting and paint supplies.

"I heard your single," I say, and her eyes brighten. She's nervous, afraid I won't approve. How could I not. "They're playing it on heavy rotation on the country station here. Your brother…" I start, falling away into an "ahh" at my slip.

"You've been talking to Lane," she says, her smile falling a hint as suspicion and questions come into her eyes. I'm a little surprised he's kept it a secret, but then again, he promised he would.

I breathe in deeply.

"I have," I say.

I missed her. And I missed her family. I let two months go without a word, but I knew she had gone. I kept in touch with Noah, just enough to make sure this time, things went as they should for her. I knew they would though. He's class. I stopped by her parents' house one afternoon on my way to a club opening in St. Louis. Lane answered the door, and before I knew it I was at the dinner table being fed and listening to stories about crazy renters and how the football team has decided Lane is lucky, so they insist he leads them out on the field. My cheeks hurt from smiling that night. It had been so long since I had a reason to, I was afraid I didn't remember how. I didn't care that I was five hours behind schedule in hitting the road. I skipped sleep in return for time with them. Lane's been texting and calling ever since. Hell, at this point, I think he calls me more than Houston does.

"We're kind of like…bros," I say, taking a fist to my chest, my mouth twisted in a smirk.

She laughs lightly because I'm ridiculous. Her eyes fall to where my hand touched my heart, and I wonder if she can see how fast it's beating?

"Lane loves your song," I say, clearing my throat and rolling my shoulders to get feeling in my fingers again. I scratch at the side of my face and try to hide the fact that I'm looking at her. I'm studying her, looking for changes—the effects of fame. She's only on the brink, but that fame is here. She's still the same girl though—nails polished, but chipped, hair fading, but purple, clothes lost somewhere between country and rock.

"It's his birthday, you know," she says.

"Real? Or half?" I tease.

She bites her lip, leaning her head as she walks a few steps into the front room, running her finger along the dusty windowsill. "Are you saying half birthdays aren't real, Casey Coffield?" she accuses. It's flirty, the way she talks, and my heart pounds harder. God, I miss this girl.

"I wouldn't dare say such a thing," I say, shaking my head for a slow *no*. She can have any birthday she wants—a million birthdays. A year's worth. I would shower her with gifts. "And no, I didn't know it was his birthday. I'm surprised he hasn't told me—Lane's a talker."

She giggles, nodding in agreement.

"You can come to the party…if you want. It's tomorrow. You know the drill—cake and Ghostbusters," she says.

"My favorite combo," I chuckle. I rest my weight on the wall opposite of her, and it's quiet again.

I breathe. She breathes. Our eyes dance, but we hold our tongues. I didn't know seeing her again would be so hard, but then, there hasn't been anyone since she's been gone. I've been driven, and nobody else has what she had. The focus has been good for me, but now, all I want is her to distract me every day.

"You look good, Casey."

She says my name again, and I feel it in my chest.

"You…" I begin, stopping and letting my mouth curve into a slow smile as I stare at her long enough to watch her neck and face blush from my attention. I look down to my feet, my chin tucked to my chest as my hands find my pockets to hide how nervous I am. I look up at her with a sideways glance, and smile like a fool. "Well you're as beautiful as you've always been. But a little more so. You look…you look happy."

Her eyes crinkle, and eventually she breathes out a laugh.

288

"I am happy," she says.

"I'm glad," I answer, feeling the waves of adrenaline roll through my insides. I knew I'd see her again, but I also knew I would never be prepared. I was right. I'm not.

"I should go," she says, her words hesitant, her feet still here despite them. She doesn't want to leave, but she should—she's on her way. Or maybe she's already there. Perhaps she *is* the destination now. I'm still in the beginning, trying to figure out how to fly.

I swallow my nerves.

"I'll walk you out," I say.

I lead her to the door, pushing it all the way open, noticing the bells on the ground outside that must have fallen when Paige left. I chuckle to myself and pick them up, looping them over the doorknob. This is how my muse snuck up on me.

She's paused a step or two away from me, and I wonder if I look as afraid and unsure as she does. She glances over her shoulder to her car parked a few yards away along the side of the road, then turns back to me.

"I think I can find my way. But maybe I'll see you? For Lane?"

I hear her, but I don't answer right away. I'm too busy counting the freckles that stretch from one side of her smile to the other. When I meet her grays, I fall all over again.

"You will," I say, "for Lane."

For you.

Always for you.

She smiles and nods, and her timid fingers form a delicate wave before she finds the courage to step into me and touch my face with her small but gifted hands, pressing her lips to my cheek as old friends do when it's been a while.

But we aren't friends. And with every step she takes further from me, the more my chest breaks open and reason and logic fly from our picture. I'm here. She's seven hundred miles away. None of that matters though, because it only takes me a dozen steps and a single heartbeat to catch her before her hands reach for her car door. My fingers wrap around familiar shoulders as Murphy stops everything, dropping her keys from her hands while her body trembles.

"Casey," she whimpers, and my lips fall to the back of her head as I breathe her in with closed eyes. I've missed her so much. I can't do this. I can't, because I'm selfish. I need her.

"Don't go," I say before I know any better, and I squeeze my eyes closed hard, hating that I will have to take this all back. And I will, because that's what's right, but I still have to say it. I have to, because I mean it. It's the only real truth there is, and I can't not let her hear how much I struggle when we're apart.

"Why," she says, turning slowly in my arms. Her hands find the center of my chest, and her eyes square on the small diamond shape on my shirt as if it's a shield for my heart. Her fingers grasp at the fabric as she slowly looks up at me, honest eyes that have missed me too. "Why did you make me go?"

I shake my head in tiny movements, because at this very moment, I have no idea. If I had this task to do all over again, I'm certain I'd fail.

"Why, Casey? You said you would make me go, and you did. You shut me out. You ignored my calls. You disappeared so I had no choice. You broke my heart," she says as the cry that's been building for a year escapes her throat. It's harsh and ugly, and the tears come fast, and they cut me open. "Why did you make me go?"

"Because I love you," I say. It comes out so simple and fast, but it makes everything so complicated. Telling her is greedy, and it's why I never could. But I can't lie to those eyes, and a year has only made the hole left behind larger. It's impossible to fill with anything but her; I only hope the truth might make not having her bearable.

"I did it because I love you. Because I'm *in* love with you. And I want more for you, even if it means that I die a little inside giving you up," I say to eyes that blink away tears. Her lips quiver and her body shakes, so I move my hands up her arms to her face, cupping cheeks that tremble in my touch.

290

"Because. I. Love you," I exhale, my forehead falling against hers as our lips barely touch.

I hold her here like this, swimming in my confession, while her own mouth struggles to find courage to respond. I'm prepared for whatever it is. I'm ready for rejection, for the "it's too late" and the "I've met someone else." I've had those nightmares ever since the day I promised myself I'd let her go. I can survive them knowing I get to hear her voice where it belongs—on albums and in soundtracks—in the ears of girls who need someone like her to look up to. I can handle it all, because for once in my goddamned life, I did the right thing by someone. I have no regrets. Only wishes.

"I'm coming home," she says.

I don't react at all, because I'm not sure I heard her right.

"For you. For us," she says, and I lean back to put distance between us so I can read her face and make sure I'm not dreaming.

"I lied," she says, her eyes locked on mine. My stomach sinks before she lifts me up again. "About Lane's birthday. There is no birthday. I made it up. I…" she twists to the side, revealing more of her car. I follow her gaze and see everything she owns piled in the back. My eyes are wide as they return to her. "I lied, Casey. I'm coming home, because I love you, too. I spent a year figuring it out, and I knew, deep down I always knew…I just needed to hear you say it. You made me take the leap, and I love you for it. But now that I have, I want more. I want you. And I can go to Nashville when I need to go to Nashville. I don't have to live there. It isn't where my heart is. It's not where *home* is. Home," she says, pressing both palms flat against my chest, her head falling to rest on them next. "Home is here with you." "Your record," I ask in a half question.

"It's done," she says.

"And Noah…"

"Is fine with me being here. When he needs me there, when it's time to work on something new, I'll go back," she says, peering up into me.

"And you...*love* me?" I ask, baiting her, just wanting to hear her say it again. I'm still in disbelief.

She smirks on one side and grants my wish.

"I love you. And I thought maybe...this new studio in town would be up for a few side projects, or maybe just jam sessions where we play nothing but Van Halen songs," she says with a shake of her head. She smells so sweet and her hair is still like rows of silk between my fingers. I move as close as I can without completely folding into her and look down on her angel face, so happy and so bright in my messy world.

"I will celebrate half birthdays, plaster on those weird-ass nose strips, and rock out to hair bands with you every night if that's what you'd like to do," I say as she moves to the tips of her toes until her nose tickles against mine.

"I'd like that very much, Casey Coffield. I may even write a song about it," she says against my lips, and my impatient mouth takes over, kissing her and pressing her body into the still-scratched car door that marks the first time she stole my heart more than a year ago. She's never gotten it fixed, and I've never been the same.

Beautifully broken, but whole together, I take her hand in mine and walk her back into my bare-to-the-bones building of my dreams. It isn't the one I thought I'd be in, but then again, I'm not the man I thought I'd be, either. And thank god for that, because that Casey wouldn't have deserved Murphy Sullivan's kisses. He just deserved her lyrics, and the journey she took him on to get here.

THE END

292

ACKNOWLEDGMENTS

This book is for the dreamers—the real-life Casey Coffields and Murphy Sullivans out there. Dreams come in many shapes and sizes, and the things in our way are just as varied. More than anything, that's what drove me to write this story.

I get to live my dream. And that is something I owe to you. Thank you for reading my stories, for sharing your reviews and passing along recommendations to "try me out" to your friends. I'm nothing without your generous and vocal support, and I don't want you to think for a minute that I take that for granted.

This book is for you.

I owe you many more.

I'm working on them now—I promise.

I have a few people that I need to give tremendous shouts out to in making this book come to life. First, and always first, Tim and Carter—my dudes. You put up with my late nights, laptops at baseball practice, and I won't say lack of dinner on the table because we all know I don't cook, but you feed me, and that does not go unnoticed! I love you two to the moon.

As always, Shelley, Ashley, Bianca and Jen—you are the Jedi Knights of beta reading. You let me leave you hanging, and say those things I so desperately need someone to say. Thank you so much for spending your nights and weekends with my sweet, selfish, *smackable* but adorable Casey. He's better for it—and I know it!

Tina Scott and Billi Joy Carson—you are mega-warriors of words, and your editing and proofing is my foundation. Seriously—my entire building would collapse without you. You're so vital and important.

Wordsmith Publicity—you ladies simply rock! Thank you for making my words echo, my promos live on, and my reach stretch for miles. I'm so grateful for what you do. And to every blogger, reviewer, podcaster and Goodreader out there—thank you for the spotlight. I know you have lots of writers you could spend your time on, so I'm incredibly humbled that you give it to me.

Now, about that cover. Smokin', right? This one's my favorite, and for lots of reasons—I love the vibe and I love the message. But more than anything, I love the team that helped me put it together. Michael Patrick Gleason—you are the hunk of hunky chins and smirks, and you embodied Casey Coffield in every sense of my imagination. Thank you, sir, for becoming *The Chin*. But you and I know the real master here: Frank Rodriguez of DLRfoto. I've known you since skateboards and pegged pants, and your talent has matured into a real art, my friend. This cover is special, and you're the reason. Can't wait to do this again. #TeamNeat

Also, because he was so unbelievably cool to me—Matt from Lids, you're the man for letting me hang out and design Leap hats in your store. I think the final product was pretty tight, yo;-)

I hope you loved Casey and Murphy's journey. I hope, as with all of the Falling books, you enjoyed the fall. If you did, please consider leaving a review, sharing your thoughts on this book with a friend, or any of the other little ways you can give us indie authors a boost. We notice, and we're so grateful.

Until next time…

XO

Ginger

BOOKS BY GINGER SCOTT

The Falling Series
This Is Falling
You And Everything After
The Girl I Was Before
In Your Dreams

The Waiting Series
Waiting on the Sidelines
Going Long

The Harper Boys
Wild Reckless
Wicked Restless

Standalones
Blindness
How We Deal With Gravity

Ginger Scott is an Amazon-bestselling and Goodreads Choice Award-nominated author of 10 young and new adult romances, including Waiting on the Sidelines, Going Long, Blindness, How We Deal With Gravity, This Is Falling, You and Everything After, The Girl I Was Before, In Your Dreams, Wild Reckless and Wicked Restless.

A sucker for a good romance, Ginger's other passion is sports, and she often blends the two in her stories. Ginger has been writing and editing for newspapers, magazines and blogs for more than 15 years. She has told the stories of Olympians, politicians, actors, scientists, cowboys, criminals and towns. For more on her and her work, visit her website at http://www.littlemisswrite.com.

When she's not writing, the odds are high that she's somewhere near a baseball diamond, either watching her son field pop flies like Bryce Harper or cheering on her favorite baseball team, the Arizona Diamondbacks. Ginger lives in Arizona and is married to her college sweetheart whom she met at ASU (fork 'em, Devils).

GINGER ONLINE

@TheGingerScott
www.facebook.com/GingerScottAuthor
www.littlemisswrite.com

Made in the USA
Coppell, TX
01 June 2021